TAKE THIS HEART

THE WINDY HARBOR SERIES
BOOK 1

WILLOW ASTER

All rights reserved.
No part of this book may be reproduced in any form or by any electronic or mechanical means, including information storage and retrieval systems, without written permission from the author, except for the use of brief quotations in a book review.

Willow Aster
www.willowaster.com

Copyright © 2025 by Willow Aster
ISBN-13: 978-1-964527-08-6

Cover by Kira Sabin
Photo by Wander Aguiar Photography
Map by Kira Sabin
Edited by Christine Estevez
Formatted by Natalie Burtner

Windy Harbor

- The Loon
- Windhaven
- The Rusty Trunk
- Elm & Echo
- Cox Trading Post
- What The Book?
- Windy Fit
- Kitty-Corner Cafe
- The Cozy Palette
- Juju's House
- The Hungry Walleye

Lake Superior

NOTE TO READERS

A list of content warnings are on the next page, so skip that page if you'd rather not see them.

CONTENT WARNINGS

The content warnings for *Take This Heart* are sexual content, profanity, cancer diagnosis, loss of parent in the past (off page).

CHAPTER ONE

BEAUTIFUL DEVIL

GOLDIE

Minnesota is in my bones.

Apparently, the *cold hands, warm heart* myth was debunked by scientists, who said that how toasty your body is has a direct correlation to how nice you are to others.

I beg to differ.

On some winter days in Minnesota, it doesn't matter how nice you are—you, your hands, and the rest of your body parts are going to be cold.

But the cold is familiar, like a cantankerous grandma who pinches your cheeks too hard but knits you colorful half-finger gloves because she knows you love them…Grandma Donna. The kind who always smells like Vicks VapoRub and who, no matter how much you eat, thinks you don't like her food because you didn't have three helpings…Grandma Nancy.

I've missed that. The mercurial seasons. The lakes—there

are more than 10,000, no matter what the license plates say. The fact that (some) people say "doncha know" without irony...both Grandma Donna and Grandma Nancy.

It's not always cold; in fact, in the sweet days of summer and fall, you can almost forget that winter is around the corner. But the consistent 70-degree sunshine in California was delightful, as were the palm trees and delicious food and people whose whole personality was yoga pants. Traffic, I didn't enjoy so much, and after I had a horrible car accident on the 405, something inside me shifted. Eternal sunshine didn't seem so important anymore. I wanted roots. Comfort. The kind of sky that makes you wonder what craziness is rolling in next.

So I came home.

I'm an interior designer by day—farmhouse kitchens, cozy cabins, the occasional baby nursery—and I paint by night. Oils, mostly. I've worked nonstop for the past four months getting ready for my art installation at MIA—the Minneapolis Institute of Art—a place I never imagined showing my artwork. I've thrown everything into it. Late nights. Early mornings. Meals scarfed in front of half-finished canvases. I love creating, that feeling of bringing an idea to life. I get some of that creativity out through interior design, but that's breathing life into someone else's ideas. It's the most rewarding feeling when I paint a piece that's all me and watch it transform with each layer of paint.

For a long time, any form of creating energized me, but the exhaustion is catching up.

The last thing I feel like doing right now is attending a gala at the Walker Art Center. I love the place, but a room full of intimidating people on a night when I just want to be painting at home? No, thank you. But I've heard I need to put myself out there and get acquainted with the art community if I want to be part of it.

I miss Addy like crazy. We met in California. She was my roommate in college and remains my best friend, the one person who always knows what I need. FaceTime calls are never enough. She lives in Silver Hills, Colorado, with the love of her life, Penn Hudson—who happens to be a pro football player and is *the* running back of all time—their kids, Sam and Winnie, and a baby on the way. Oh, and she also houses a family of Sphynx cats whom I get daily pictures of…insert full-body shudders here. They're super sweet. And so ugly they're almost cute. Almost.

I've made a few friends at work, but I don't see any of them here yet. So I'm clutching a glass of champagne like a security blanket and sipping more than I should on an empty stomach.

I smile at people I don't know and compliment a woman's earrings, wondering how long I have to stay.

"There you are." Luna puts her arm around me. "Come on, I'll introduce you to a few people."

I sag into her. "I'm so glad to see you. I needed to see a friendly face."

Luna has taken me under her wing. She's the one who got me into MIA, and she thinks I will need to quit my job and paint full-time after my show. That's the dream. We'll see.

She flits around confidently and introduces me to so many people, I don't retain the names, and then she's called away to talk to someone else. I'm near an exhibit that's caught my eye, so I tell her I'll catch up with her.

The exhibit is intriguing—it's an architectural model of a park with sculptures integrated with nature. I study it for a while, but when I realize that it's actually a proposal to rehaul the sculpture garden I love across the street, I frown.

"You don't like it?"

The voice is low and husky, and when I look up, I struggle not to gasp. The beauty of the man in front of me is…wow. Holy buckets. I swallow and try not to appear as shaken as I feel. His black hair falls over his forehead, firelight eyes cool and assessing beneath thick curly lashes. Perfect lips. He's also *tall*. I'd put him at 6'5" like my youngest brother Dylan.

He blinks and tilts his head, like he's waiting for my response.

"Oh. Well, it's an interesting concept, but is it really meant to replace Spoonbridge and Cherry? That sculpture is iconic! It's been part of the landscape of Minneapolis since before I was born. Why would anyone want to bulldoze it or anything else in the sculpture garden?"

He's smirking until I say *bulldoze*, and then his eyes narrow.

"I'm sure it wouldn't be bulldozed, more like moved to another location," he says.

I turn to face him and shake my head. "Part of the beauty of it is the skyline in the background. It would be a travesty to move it." I nod toward the model and make a sweeping gesture with my hand. "*This* is a travesty."

He snorts derisively, and now, I'm really annoyed. I cross my arms over my chest and stare back at him. He's *snorting* at me now?

"Art is evolving," he says. "We preserve it, yes, but we also make room for the new."

"And you think *that*," I point at the sculpture replicas in the model that are admittedly very cool, even though I will never admit that now, "is worthy of booting out the old, I take it?"

He steps closer and leans in, his breath skittering over my skin. "Yes, I do."

When I look up at him, we're about an inch apart.

I poke his chest. "*You* are what's wrong in America."

Poke, poke, poke.

He arches an offensively perfect brow, and if it's possible, moves even closer. "Is that right? And how does wanting to move a few sculptures make me so wrong?"

It's hard to think straight when he's this close and smells so good. Like cedar and honey.

Those eyes make me want to cuddle up to him and enjoy the fire.

Focus, Goldie.

"We don't appreciate history here," I say—somewhat breathlessly, but I soldier on. "We build things and tear them down when we're tired of them. Massive structures that cost millions to build become rubble if someone gets tired of them and wants to put something else there. It doesn't even have to be better, just new. Different. Why can't we appreciate our rich history and preserve it? At least the beautiful things?"

"Like Spoonbridge and Cherry," he says dryly, his lips lifting as he mocks me.

"Like Spoonbridge and Cherry," I say emphatically.

"Why not let someone else enjoy it for a while?"

"Why mess with perfection?" I volley back.

I had no idea I felt this passionately about Spoonbridge and Cherry, but it *is* really cute.

"Perfection?" he scoffs. Scoffs!

"It's the principle of the thing!" I say, louder than I intended.

He rolls his eyes and takes a step back, crossing his arms over his chest.

"Wonderful! You've met Milo," Luna says, appearing at my side.

Milo? Ugh. Even his name is cool.

Luna beams up at him. "The man of the hour."

"Man of the hour?" I say under my breath. *Man of the hour, my big, fat toe*, my brain shouts.

"Yes! He's the architect who designed this model. What do you think of it? Isn't it incredible?" Luna says, grinning between Milo and me.

I feel unsteady and then hot all over. My eyes narrow again, and I look around Milo to find the museum label next to the park model.

Milo Lombardi.

Oh my God. *The* Milo Lombardi? I can't believe it. World-renowned architect. Ridiculously talented.

Ridiculously *hot*.

Hmm. They say Satan was pretty too.

"She thinks it's a travesty," Milo tells Luna, while still staring me down.

I tilt my head as if to say, *you're not wrong.*

Luna gasps and turns to gawk at me. "What are you—"

"There's someone over there I need to see," I say, pointing behind them.

Milo nods—smug and with the kind of confidence that suggests he invented air. And maybe also a little smug because he sees right through me and knows I want to get away from him as fast as I can.

I walk away and grab another glass of champagne, downing it.

A few minutes later, my phone dings and I look at it, happy for something to distract me.

TAKE THIS HEART 7

DAD

It's pretty quiet. Everyone okay? Take a pic of what you're doing right now, so there's proof of life.

TULLY

<photo of his hockey jersey crumpled up in his locker> Pretty sure I saw you in the stands, so you know I'm alive. Lol Love you, Dad.

CAMDEN

<photo of a Food Network-worthy meal> Love you, Dad.

> ^ I don't recognize anything but the mashed potatoes. <Photo of me in front of a nude sculpture of a woman> The closest you'll get to a naked woman tonight. Love you, Dad.

TULLY

That's what you think.

> That's what I KNOW because I don't want to think of my brothers around naked women, thank you very much.

DYLAN

<photo of him holding a surfboard and standing next to a woman who looks like a model> The picture speaks for itself, Golds. 😎 Love you, Dad.

NOAH

<photo of him and Grayson eating Taco Bell> Love you, Dad!

> What about me? Does anyone love me?

TULLY

Can't you feel the telepathic waves of twin love?

> If I had, I wouldn't have asked.

NOAH

Grayson wants his Aunt Goldie to hurry up and visit. You are loved.

CAMDEN

I just texted that I loved you an hour ago in another thread. But I'll say it again.

> ...waiting.

CAMDEN

OMG, the kitchen is backed up and I am texting my sister how much I love her.

DYLAN

You're needier than me, Golds. 😉

> And you know you're all here for it. Love you guys. I'm at the Walker tonight and would much rather be with you.

DAD

<photo of the sun going down over Lake Superior> I love you all so much. Hanging at the lake. Homesick for all of you.

CHAPTER TWO

CURATED

MILO

She called my work a travesty.

I've heard worse. Hell, I've read worse in published reviews. But not from someone who looked at my work with what I thought was such admiration. And then the way she looked up at me. There was a spark that crackled back and forth between us.

I'd noticed her before she said a word. There'd been a moment, before anything was said, when I thought she understood what I'd built. That she caught the vision of it all.

But that spark turned into acid when she spoke.

Now, she's halfway across the gallery, standing beneath a sculptural light installation and looking like she owns the place.

She's in a deep emerald green dress, the fabric off one shoulder and clinging to all the right places. Her long blonde hair falls in waves down her back. Even the way she holds her glass of champagne looks proper. She has the aura of someone important. She never introduced herself. Just dropped her opinion like a bomb and then walked away without an apology.

Wait a minute.

She just took a step, and instead of heels to match her fancy gown, she's wearing black Dr. Martens.

That makes me smile.

Who is this woman?

I lean against a marble pillar, bourbon in hand, trying not to let my eyes drift back to her.

Futile.

I look.

God, help me. She's gorgeous. And infuriating. She's laughing now, her head tilted back just enough to let the man at her side believe he said something clever. He didn't. I know because I've met him before. Seth Patterson. He's a lightweight in design. Paper-thin ideas. No substance.

He leans closer to her and she steps back half an inch, graceful, practiced. She's good at this.

It's only after she takes another step back that I see her hand shaking just a bit. Maybe she's not as calm and collected as she seems.

I want to step in and save her from the lackluster and uncomfortable conversation I know she's having with Seth, but she called my work a travesty.

The gala is louder this year. Or maybe I'm just noticing more. The clinking glasses and carefully curated laughter—it's sitting wrong on my skin, like a cat who's petted in the wrong direction.

My model sits in the center of it all. This was actually a passion project. I've put all my efforts into designing a beautiful library in Duluth for what feels like forever and needed something else to focus on during the weekends or the nights I couldn't sleep. What was just passing the time became something I now love and believe in.

Elevated on a white platform beneath spotlights, the installation looks pristine. Every detail precisely constructed.

But her voice echoes over it all. *Travesty. You are what's wrong in America.*

Hell, I'm sure there are more scandalous things I've done than this park model of exquisite artwork and skill. I could dip her over the model and show her a thing or two that would truly be outrageous.

In fact, it'd almost be a travesty *not* to dip her back on the installation and show her just how wrong I can be. So wrong that it'd feel so right. The way she stared up at me, her big brown eyes with the gold specks gazing up at me with desire, her tongue sneaking out to wet those cushiony red lips, made me certain she wished I would.

I almost respect her honesty. Because she didn't critique the materials or the execution. She critiqued the lack of soul, specifically my very own dark and twisted one.

And I have to admit that what bothers me most is that she struck a nerve. I've loved Spoonbridge and Cherry for as long as I can remember. She's also right that it's a part of the Minneapolis landscape that will be missed, but isn't it worth it if more people around the country are allowed to enjoy it for themselves?

I circle the gallery, greeting board members and donors and answering questions from junior curators and well-dressed influencers. My practiced smile is in place—it's second nature by now.

But my eyes keep tracking back to her.

We run into each other again near the back wall, where one of the smaller installations is failing to impress anyone. She turns as I approach, almost as if she felt me coming.

"Milo Lombardi," she says, sipping her champagne. "Still brooding?"

I arch a brow. "Still spewing venom?"

Her eyes flash. "I thought you'd be off collecting compliments from the press."

"Thought I'd take a break. Let someone else enjoy the sound of their own voice."

She lifts her glass in salute. "How generous of you."

There's a weighted moment of silence that hangs.

She tilts her head, looking past me to my model.

"They love it," she says bitterly. "You're going to get everything you want, aren't you?"

I follow her gaze and then stare at the long curve of her neck as she spits daggers at my work. "Not everything."

She turns back and meets my eyes, her cheeks flushing. "Meaning?"

"No one gets everything they want, do they?"

Her eyes narrow. "I'm sure you're not lacking."

"You don't seem to be either."

"True. I can't complain."

"You make it a habit of wearing Doc Martens with your evening gowns?" I smirk.

A strange expression crosses her face, but she recovers quickly. "I do now."

I want to ask what she means by that, but instead, I say, "Well, it says something that you've stayed all evening… for me."

Her eyes flash. "I didn't stay for you."

"Didn't you?" I point at the banner that has my name on it and she rolls her eyes.

"You're impossible," she says.

"You're worse. You make a lot of assumptions."

"And you think you don't? Trust me, I didn't even notice your name. But I *have* worked with a lot of men like you." Her eyes flicker over my face with accusation.

"Men like me?"

She turns now, fully facing me. "Talented. Celebrated. Used to being the one who gets the last word."

"You think I don't listen?"

"I think you don't like being wrong."

She's not wrong there.

I take a step closer. "You hovered over the installation like you were falling in love, right until you gutted it in one sentence."

She lifts her shoulder. "I never said it wasn't beautiful. I'm just not willing to sacrifice history for it."

"You really think you're the only one in this room who understands intention? Don't you want to be part of progress?"

"When it matters, yes."

The silence between us sharpens.

I can't decide whether I want to kiss her or walk away forever. Both, I think.

Before I can say anything else, I hear my name, and from the way everyone's turned to stare at me, I think maybe it's not the first time I've been called. I'm too busy watching this obnoxious woman, watching me.

Luna clears her throat at the mic and smiles at me.

"Friends, thank you for joining us tonight to celebrate the intersection of community, art, and innovation," she says.

I tune in and out, too keyed up while standing next to this woman.

"…transforming the way we think about public spaces…"

"...a visionary who's brought something truly unique to our city..."

I hear the woman groan next to me and turn to glare at her. She looks at me with innocent eyes. Little minx.

"What is your problem?" I say under my breath.

Just as Luna says, "And now, please welcome Milo Lombardi."

Applause circles through the room.

I step forward, moving to the low stage near the model and blinking beneath the lights.

I give the speech I prepared. It's smooth, a nice mix of humble and polished. I wonder what the beautiful woman is thinking the entire time. I need to get her name before the night is over. When I finish, the applause is louder. A few of the board members shake my hand, pausing me mid-step. When I look back at the corner where we were standing together, she's gone.

I find her on the rooftop terrace. I tell myself that I came up here to get space, not that I was hoping to catch a glimpse of her again. She's there, overlooking the sculpture garden, Spoonbridge and Cherry a touch of whimsy for the towering Basilica of Saint Mary in the background. She's not overshadowed by the splendor behind her, not in the slightest. I've never seen a woman more beautiful than her, and for a second, I allow myself to enjoy the view.

She turns and meets my eyes.

"You again," she says, but her words have no bite this time. "I didn't come up here for company."

"I didn't come up here for you," I lie.

She looks away. "But you're staying."

"Maybe I like the view."

She looks at me over her shoulder, the corner of her mouth twitching when she sees my eyes on her. "Are you always so insufferable?"

"Maybe," I say, stepping closer. "But you haven't walked away."

Her breath catches and then her jaw tightens like she's angry with herself for not moving.

And then we're not talking anymore. Her mouth is on mine. I'm not sure if I started it or she did.

The kiss is sharp-edged and heady, a rush to all my senses. Her hands fist in the lapels of my jacket, and mine slide to her waist, pulling her against me like I've wanted to since the moment she insulted me in the gallery.

She tastes like champagne and defiance, and I'm half drunk on the combination.

She pulls back slightly, breath ragged. "This is such a bad idea."

"Probably the worst," I whisper, and kiss her again.

It's reckless. Irresponsible. A dare to wreck my world. Yet I keep going. I'd do just about anything she asked right now.

She pulls away long enough to mutter, "I don't know what to do with you."

I brush a strand of hair from her cheek. "You don't have to do anything. Just stop hating me for five seconds."

She stares at me for a beat and then her lips are on mine again, soft and urgent. Nothing else exists. Her body melts against mine, her fingers fisting my hair.

When she pulls away again, I want to chase her mouth, but instead, I grin. "You kiss like you have something to prove."

She freezes. "Excuse me?"

I frown. "I meant—intense. Fiery."

"Something to *prove*?" she echoes, voice rising. "That's what you got out of that?"

I close my eyes, sighing. "That came out wrong."

She laughs, but it's hollow. "Let's just go back to admitting this was a *bad* idea."

"It didn't *feel* like a bad idea."

She moves past me.

"Come on. Don't walk away. Stay, please—"

But she doesn't stop.

I stay rooted to the rooftop, watching long after she's out of sight.

CHAPTER THREE

THE LAKE IS CALLING

GOLDIE

TULLY

Dad, you don't have to send me an Uber Eats gift card for texting you a picture. Thank you though. I'll use it. 😊

DYLAN

Dang. I could've used that.

DAD

Early bird gets the worm.

I can hardly sit still on the drive to Windy Harbor. Four hours from the Twin Cities, the ride gets prettier and prettier the farther north I go. When I catch the first glimmer of Lake Superior through the trees, I feel my shoulders relax, the tension in my chest easing like a slow exhale. I hadn't realized how tightly wound I've been lately, juggling work deadlines and the looming exhibit at the Minneapolis Institute of Art.

My move back to Minnesota from California is fairly recent. I bought a little house that I love near Lake Nokomis. Like that maddening man who shall not be named, I'm not lacking in resources. At all. In fact, it's been a point of unease many times, just how privileged I am. It isn't that I'm not proud of our family, I'm extremely proud, but it's been important to me to pave my own way as much as possible and not rely on the wealth I've grown up with. Even saying that, I know the Whitman name is a door opener and one I'm grateful for, but I try to step outside of it when it comes to my career. My artist name is G. Waters, honoring my mom's maiden name.

But there's plenty to love about my upbringing. One of them being our family home on Summit Avenue, my favorite street in St. Paul. My dad has lived there since before I was born and even after my mom died and my brothers and I eventually left home. He would've been near the house I'm in now if he'd stayed at the Summit house, but lately, he's been spending a ton of time at our lake house in Windy Harbor.

He asked that we all come up this weekend for an impromptu family weekend.

It's hard to get my brothers and me together at the same time these days, and the fact that Dad made it happen is huge. My twin Tully lives near me in Minneapolis, but the rest of our siblings are spread out. Camden lives in Denver, Dylan in California, and Noah and his little boy Grayson, who's three, live in Duluth.

I cannot wait to see everyone.

Windy Harbor is one of my favorite places on Earth. I can't believe it's been so long since I've been there. I know the drive like the back of my hand. I turn toward Betty's Pies in Two Harbors without thinking about it, practically tasting the toffee cream pie before I even step inside. I eat it in the car with the windows down, listening to the sound of passing cars and enjoying every sticky, sweet bite.

By the time I drive into Windy Harbor, my voice is hoarse from singing my lungs out with the radio. God, I missed this place. Even the uneven road feels like home, bumping underneath my tires. My stomach growls when I see The Hungry Walleye on the corner, its faded wooden sign swinging slightly in the wind. I can smell their beer-battered fish and fries from blocks away.

Across the street is the Kitty-Corner Cafe, tucked into the cutest blue building with white shutters. One of my childhood besties runs the shop, Juliana Fair, also known as Juju. I could go for her coffee and cinnamon rolls right about now too. Dang, that pie didn't tide me over long enough. Out front, the chalkboard sign reads: *Today's Special: Tomato Basil Soup & Grilled Cheese!*

That sure sounds good.

Next to the Kitty-Corner Cafe is What the Book?, the town's cozy, slightly chaotic bookstore. Its hand-painted colorful window is faded but still charming. That place is dangerous. I could get lost in there for hours.

A few storefronts down, Miss Idella is sweeping in front of The Rusty Trunk. The best antique store ever. Miss Idella and her daughter Emmy refurbish furniture too, and I'm a sucker for all their pieces.

My eyes widen when I see Windy Fit. That's new. I wonder if Erin had anything to do with that. She's wanted a gym in town for a long time. Erin and her family run Cox Trading Post, the general store that looms ahead. It's crammed with every possible thing you could ever need—groceries, fleece jackets, knickknacks with loons and canoes and pine trees on them. I really want to stop in and see her. From the day we met, we were best friends. She was what I looked forward to the very most about coming to Windy Harbor. I miss her. But this weekend is already crammed tight, and I don't know if I'll have time.

Finally, The Loon stands proudly at the edge of the small downtown, a neon loon flickering over the door like she's beckoning me in. Same wooden steps, same red stools lined up inside. Best greasy burger and coldest beer in town for ten bucks. It makes me smile. Windy Harbor doesn't change much. Thank goodness.

I coast forward, heart squeezing at the sight of Lake Superior stretching out forever. *I'm home.*

When I pull into the long drive leading to the lake house, the sun is low over the water, casting gold and orange streaks across the rippling surface of Lake Superior. The house stands proud and beautiful at the end of the drive. It takes my breath away every time I see it. French provincial charm blended with countryside cottage, the design of this home was the last labor of love my mom did before she died. I'm glad she was able to see it completed. This house is what inspired me to become an interior designer. I knew I wanted to be an artist before that, but I came by my love of house design and interiors honestly. My mom was an architect and my dad is a real estate mogul. The two of them were a powerful team. They owned many houses and made each one spectacular, but the Summit home and this lake home are the two that they chose to raise their family in.

Growing up, I couldn't wait to come to Windy Harbor. We went every summer and as many weekends as possible throughout the year, and I lived for those times. There's something about the water; it's so vast it's like the ocean, with the sound of the waves beating against the rocks and sand lulling me into contentment. It calls to me. Even now, living in Minneapolis, I need to be by the water, but though Lake Nokomis and the other lakes around the Twin Cities are beautiful, they're not the same as Lake Superior.

A few cars are already parked out front. I'm the last one here. Not surprising. I had to stay late at the house I'm working on. Lately, I've barely slept, painting into the night, trying to be ready for the installation next month. I should've kept working this weekend, but my dad rarely asks anything of us, so I didn't hesitate to say yes to this.

I've missed my dad and brothers so much. Spending time with them is exactly what I need.

I barely have the car in park before I jump out. The front door swings open, and I'm swallowed up by my giant brothers.

"Goldie!" Tully pulls me into a hug first, then looks at me like he didn't just see me at lunch yesterday. "You made it."

Minnesotans are known for their hardy stock. It doesn't always mean tall, but for the Whitmans, it does. Dylan's the baby of the family—twenty-three, three years younger than Tull and me—but he's the tallest at 6'5". He wraps me up from behind and then tickles my side, making me yelp. My older brothers, Camden, twenty-eight, and Noah, thirty-one, swarm in, tousling my hair like we're kids. They're both 6'4" and even though they're older, they look the same age as Tully and me. And last but not least, Tully blames me for taking some of his height in the womb, but he's not suffering at 6'3". I think it's more accurate to say he's the one who stole my height, but I'm okay with being 5'8".

Now.

As a kid, not so much.

I'm the shortest, the only blonde, and the only girl. Severely outnumbered.

"It took you forever!" Dylan says. "We thought you got lost."

"She stopped for pie," Tully says knowingly.

"Don't tell all my secrets," I say, breathless from the crush of bodies.

Noah steps back and Grayson barrels into me. His cheeks are pink, his dark brown eyes bright.

"Auntie Goldie!" he yells.

"There's my favorite nephew." I bend down, holding my arms out, and he wraps his arms around my neck, squeezing me as hard as he can.

"Crusher!" we both yell. And then we pull back and look at each other, and at the same time, we say, "Hi, I love ya."

It's something my brothers and I have done since we were little, and of course, we had to do it with Grayson, too. His little voice is raspy and adorable.

We all dote on our sweet boy. Noah's girlfriend, Margo, died a few days after she had Grayson. It was a nightmare, and too much grief for any of us to deal with fully, but we had to, for Grayson's sake. He has been the light of our lives.

A hand touches my back and I turn to see Grandma Donna, and next to her is Grandma Nancy.

"*What?* I didn't know you'd both be here too! This is the best surprise!"

I hug them both and Grandma Nancy pulls back, still holding onto my cheeks. "Yep. We need to get some meat on ya. Gotta have some padding come winter, doncha know."

I laugh, lifting my hand over hers. "Good thing we're heading into summer."

"It wouldn't be unheard of to snow in April or May. We're not in the clear yet," Grandma Donna tuts, putting her arm around my shoulder. Grandma Nancy takes the other side, her Vicks VapoRub wafting in the breeze.

My grandmas are the best of friends. I think their friendship began because, like most grandmas, they could agree that their wisdom was needed to fill in our gaps, and it grew even more after my mom passed. Grandpa Augustus passed away two years ago, and Grandpa Otis just six months ago, and I wouldn't be surprised if Grandma Donna and Grandma Nancy moved in together.

"Where's Dad?" I ask when I straighten and walk toward the house.

"He's inside with our surprise guest," Camden says, lifting his eyebrows.

"What? Who else is here?" I frown, not wanting to share my dad with anyone besides my brothers after not seeing him in so long.

Dad comes rushing out the front door and hugs me before I can step inside. "Okay, now we're all here," he says, hugging me tight.

I sigh, soaking in the love. "Hi, Dad."

"Hey, buttercup. Sure have been missing you."

"I've been missing you too."

"Come inside. There's someone I want you to meet."

I step inside and then I see him.

No. No, no, *no*.

He's standing by the fireplace, hands in the pockets of his dark jeans. He's still slap-me-silly gorgeous, and his simmering intensity is more unsettling than ever.

I wish I didn't know how his lips feel on mine. I've relived that kiss countless times since it happened, and my cheeks heat thinking about it now.

I'm glad I didn't show up in paint-splattered clothes, but I wish I'd worn something cuter than my green velour flare pants and matching top. I get compliments from strangers when I wear this, which gives me hope that it's not all bad.

The color makes my hazel eyes look greener. Maybe he'll notice that instead of how messy my hair must be after a long day at work and then driving for hours.

"Goldie," Dad says, his voice cutting through the noise of the room. He's smiling, his eyes soft with affection. "This is Milo Lombardi."

Milo's eyes meet mine, and for a second, the room goes silent.

"Milo," I say curtly.

"Goldie," he volleys.

"What are you doing here?" I say, sounding a little winded.

"Oh, you've already met? I had no idea." Dad sounds excited.

"We have." Milo nods slightly. His voice is low and steady. "Although I never caught your name." His eyebrow lifts.

I refrain from rolling my eyes. "We met at the Walker gala the other night, Dad."

"Excellent!" Dad says.

Milo and I continue to stare at each other.

Noah clears his throat. "I've, uh, been hearing about Milo for weeks," he says, looking at me with a puzzled expression. "Architect. Apparently, he's a genius."

"I wouldn't go that far," Milo says smoothly. There's a trace of a smile, and confidence oozes out of him.

Dad claps him on the back. "Don't be modest. This guy designed that new library in Duluth. Beautiful work."

"Thank you," he says simply. And then he turns toward the window, as if something more important caught his attention.

Cocky much?

"Such a handsome fella too," Grandma Donna says, looking him over and then winking at me.

I try to give her the zip-it stare, but of course, she keeps going, ensuring that Milo's ego explodes.

"Oh fer crying out loud, you know it's true," she whispers. Too loudly.

"The stature on you. Good gravy." Grandma Nancy shakes her head and gives Milo a wide smile. "I've always thought a tall man was like a tree—sturdy and strong…and able to look out for whatever's ahead. Good for climbing. Isn't that right, Marigold?" She laughs and bumps my elbow.

I'm not sure if the art of subtlety is gone when you get older or if you just don't mind throwing your granddaughter under the bus for the sake of gaining a man. Whatever the case, I'm ready to send these two Betty Whites back to St. Paul until Milo leaves.

Milo chuckles, his eyes flitting over me. "Yes, would you agree, Marigold?"

"It's Goldie to you," I say between clenched teeth.

Grandma Nancy moves closer to Milo and his nose twitches. When he sneezes, I have to bite back my laugh.

"I know it's late, but your grandmothers and I went ahead and prepared dinner, just in case any of you didn't eat enough on the way here," Dad says. "And I know you're not eating enough these days, buttercup, working nonstop." Dad levels me with a look.

"I'm starving!" I lean into him and he grins happily.

We pile around the long table in the dining room. Grayson is perched on Noah's lap. Everyone passes around plates of roasted chicken, mashed potatoes, and salad. Conversation flows easily. It's more common for everyone to be talking at once than for it to be quiet, and Milo sits at the far end of the table, listening and watching us. I wonder what he's thinking. His eyes give very little away.

"So, you've known Dad for a while?" I ask, finally giving in to my curiosity.

He blinks. "We met a few months ago."

"And how did you meet?"

Dad answers for him. "He worked on the Lake Minnetonka project. I needed the best that there is for that one." He smiles at Milo, and Milo's smile back is the warmest I've seen him doling out. "A friend introduced us, thought we'd get along."

After dinner, we drift into the living room. Noah and Grayson build a Jenga tower on the floor, while Dylan, Camden, and Tully discuss the cold front supposedly coming through tonight. It's April, so the weather is still finicky. I curl into one of the armchairs and pull the throw over my legs, feeling the day catch up with me. Milo sits near the window, staring out at the moon over the water.

Dad clears his throat. "Hey, guys. I'd like to say something to all of you. Thank you for coming. I know taking a break from your busy schedules wasn't easy, but I'm so glad to see you."

We all chime in with how glad we are to see him, and when he clears his throat, we all stop to listen again.

"I don't want you giving up your responsibilities. You've all got busy lives and successful careers. But I'm not gonna complain about a weekend visit here and there," Dad says, grinning.

My eyes meet Milo's. I wonder why he's here. Why my dad trusts him so much.

"Anyway, I've got news," Dad says, holding out his hands and grinning. "The Windy Harbor Lodge and cabins… all that land I've coveted for as long as I can remember—

guess who put in a bid for that property?" He points at himself and then all of us. "We did!"

We all stare at him in shock. That property must span almost a thousand acres.

"What?" I gasp. "Did I hear that right?"

His grin grows as he pulls out a portfolio and sets it on the table. "You heard right. The details are all right here. If we play our cards right, that land will be ours."

CHAPTER FOUR

IT'S PERSONAL

MILO

How the fuck is this my luck?

I like Everett Whitman a lot. We've become friends in a short amount of time, and I love what a visionary he is. And this stretch of waterfront property is stunning, no question. Sweeping lake views, pine-scented air, and enough light to make any architect go old school and pull out their sketchbook and scaled ruler.

But I had no idea she was his daughter.

Goldie Whitman.

This is going to be a problem.

The woman whose voice has been in my head for days—sharp, clever, and a little reckless. The woman whose mouth I regret chasing away with *my* stupid mouth because I couldn't just keep it shut. It was the best kiss of my life. And now she's across the room in a sweatshirt that falls off one shoulder, looking six ways to Sunday beautiful, while her dad outlines the plans for a sprawling resort that I'd normally be dying to work on.

I've heard Everett talk about Goldie a lot. She's the shiny apple of her dad's eye.

"I've wanted this land for years," Everett says, practically glowing. "A thousand acres of pristine lakefront. I want you all to be a part of it as much as you can. We could put a wellness retreat in the existing lodge, update the cabins, build a gorgeous hotel up on the ridge. Can you imagine?"

My chest tightens. I *can* imagine.

"You mean the ridge where we used to sled every winter?" Goldie asks. "Where the treehouse collapsed and you swore we wouldn't go near it again?"

"And you won't." He grins. "Because we're going to bring new life to the place. Aren't we, Milo?"

Everyone turns toward me.

I nod, but slowly. "If you get the land, there is endless potential."

"Is someone else bidding on the property?" Noah asks.

Everett's eyes narrow. "Bruce Granger."

What? Fuck me. This is the first I've heard about Bruce wanting this property. What the hell. It just gets worse.

The name sends a ripple of anger through the family, and I wonder what Bruce did to get on their bad side. They've seemed like such a calm bunch until now—well, except for the sassy blonde whose kisses have haunted my dreams every night since we met. Last time I heard from Bruce, he was talking about building a hotel near the Boundary Waters.

Everett is still holding court behind me, talking about the property like it's folklore. "It borders the ridge line all the way down to Clearwater Point. I've wanted that land since I was a teenager. Never thought the opportunity would come, but here we are. And there's no way in hell I'm letting the

Grangers walk away with it. They've spent a lifetime trying to ruin me, and I wish they'd give up already."

"Why does that man always show up at the worst times, trying to ruin everything?" Goldie had looked like she might nap earlier, curled up in that cozy chair, but now restless energy bounces off of her.

She stands off to the side, arms crossed, mouth tight, eyes flicking between me and her dad like we've both betrayed her.

She doesn't know the half of it.

The way they're talking about Bruce and the Grangers sounds like they're the only thing standing in the way of Everett getting the land he's always wanted. Everett is a stand-up guy. What did the Grangers do to get on his bad side?

I'm digging myself into a deeper hole. The more the name Granger is mentioned, the more I'm certain I wouldn't be allowed in this house if they knew the truth. I should mention it now, but I don't. I'm still too shaken that Goldie is here, that she's Everett's daughter. That, potentially, I might be seeing a helluva lot more of her than I realized.

"Tell us what you're thinking," Everett says, turning to me with a hopeful gleam in his eye. "You've got some ideas, I know. Don't be shy."

I glance at Goldie and then at her brothers around her. Their faces are a lot friendlier.

I clear my throat. "Honestly? The land's incredible. We can do a ton with it. Smarter structures. Integrated water systems. Minimalist builds with full-window lake views. Elevated walkways for accessibility. Modern materials—glass, steel, stone."

Goldie scoffs. "We grew up on that land," she says, voice softer now. "Hanging out with the guests who stayed in the cabins. There's a clearing where my brothers used to camp out every summer. My mom would bring lemonade and tell us stories about the lake spirits. You build a steel structure there, and I swear I'll chain myself to a pine tree."

"That might complicate permitting," I say dryly.

She glares at me. "This isn't just about you and your sleek ideas. It's about roots and memory. My mom's gone, and this place is what's left of her. I'm not going to stand by while it turns into another metal-and-concrete tribute to capitalism. You want to glass over everything that makes this place *real*."

The room is still as everyone's gaze ping-pongs between Goldie and me. Tully and Camden have eased next to Goldie protectively, Tully crossing his arms as he stares at me.

A loon cries out in the distance. The sound never fails to make my chest ache.

"I didn't come here to erase anything. I want to honor the land while making it sustainable, desirable, and usable year-round," I say.

Her voice drops an octave. "You want to make it a luxury destination with infinity pools and helicopter landing pads."

"Oh, you've seen inside my mind and know what I want?"

"Someone has to. You clearly haven't looked at the soil erosion data or the wildlife survey." Her chest is rising and falling, pink dusting each cheek.

"Okay, okay, let's not get hostile," Everett says, clearing his throat.

"We're not hostile. We just have incompatible visions," she says.

I let out a long whoosh of breath. "I apologize," I say, looking at Everett. "I'm here to bring your ideas to life, should you get this land."

Goldie's head falls back and she groans. "He wants to tear down Spoonbridge and Cherry, for God's sake."

Damn, she's something when she's mad. Her cheeks flush, and her hands gesture like she's trying to lasso the right words. Her sweatshirt is slipping off her shoulder again, and the distraction is criminal.

"That thing is iconic," Tully says.

"Right?" Goldie says, flinging her arm out.

"I don't want to tear it down. I simply want to move it so someone else can enjoy it."

Tully looks between Goldie and me and I can see his wheels turning.

"Sounds fair," he finally says.

Goldie groans again.

Everett puts his arm around his daughter and squeezes her shoulder. "Hey, don't run Milo off before he's even gotten started." He laughs.

"I'm sensing we missed another important conversation somewhere along the way," Camden says, barely containing his laughter.

"Yeah, what did you do to get Goldie all worked up?" Noah says, laughing. "Our little free spirit here rarely gets wound so tight."

Goldie folds her arms again, like she's holding herself together. "Shush, all of you."

Dylan comes over and kisses her cheek. "I didn't say anything."

She turns to him and puts her hand on his cheek, smiling up at him. "Another reason you're my favorite," she says sweetly.

"*Hey,*" her brothers all protest.

It's hard not to laugh at that.

"You really believe you can design something that matters here, Milo Lombardi?" she asks.

I meet her eyes. "If you'll let me."

"Don't forget we don't own the land yet," Noah says.

"We will," Everett says. "Anyone need dessert? I sure do. I've got Dutch apple pie with that hard sauce from the Pioneer Woman's website. Except I did rum instead of whiskey."

"Hanging out with the Pioneer Woman again, huh, Dad?" Camden teases.

"She was your mom's favorite," Everett says, smiling fondly. "Besides your fancy ass cooking, of course." He winks. "She got a kick out of that woman's humor."

"Good for us…because she introduced a lot more butter into our diet," Goldie says, rolling her eyes.

Everett pokes her in the side and she jumps, laughing and yelping. They go into the kitchen, chatting happily.

And I stand, once again watching her walk away, and wondering what the hell I've gotten myself into.

CHAPTER FIVE

MORNING STROLL

GOLDIE

Milo isn't at breakfast the next morning and I tell myself I'm happy about it. Certainly more relaxed. Last night, his presence was like a rock in my shoe that I couldn't shake loose.

"How 'bout we go for a walk?" Dad asks.

Milo walks into the room and all the air is sucked out, at least for me.

"We were just talking about a walk," Dad says. "But you're probably hungry."

"I got up earlier and had coffee and toast," Milo says, smiling at Dad. "I'm up for a walk."

I sigh and Tully shoots me a questioning look.

Everyone agrees to a walk, and we set off. The wind carries the scent of damp earth and pine as we walk the bluff trail that edges our family property, high above Lake Superior. The lake stretches out beneath us, cold and gray-blue under the April sky, waves lapping against the shoreline like a heartbeat.

As we walk, I trail my fingers along a mossy birch tree, listening to the chatter between my brothers. Camden's talking animatedly to Dylan and Noah about a celebrity couple that showed up at Whitman's, his restaurant in Colorado. Noah grunts his approval as he scans the worn path, probably making mental notes about trail maintenance. Tully throws a pine cone at Camden and laughs when it smacks him in the back. I'm finding rocks with Grayson when Tully moves next to me. As Grayson runs ahead to pick up a rock I point out, Tully leans in.

"Hey, what's your deal with Milo?" he asks.

I groan. "We didn't get off to a very good start at the Walker gala the other night," I whisper.

"He seems decent," he says.

I frown as I look at Milo and shake my head. "He's annoying."

Tully laughs and gives my shoulder a little shake. "This is so not like you, little miss sunshine. You find something to like about everyone, even old Bosco, who no one can stand."

I smile. "Aw, I haven't seen Bosco in so long. I wonder if he's still at Kitty-Corner Cafe all the time. Bosco's sweet. You just have to get him talking about his cat Francine and then he's not as prickly."

Tully gives me a doubtful look.

Dad strides past us. When he reaches a clearing, he motions for us to come closer.

"Right there," he says, pointing down at the sloping ridge below. "That's where I want to put the new lodge. I'm thinking something along the lines of Rivendell, you know… where the elves lived in *The Lord of the Rings*? With those views? Just imagine—you kids could help make it happen."

"Legolas…" I sigh.

Camden whistles. "It'll be gorgeous. You're right, Dad. But I'm not sure we've all got the time it'll take to put into it."

"It'd be an experience we'd never forget," Dad says, his eyes bright. "And the legacy would live on forever."

Camden rubs the back of his neck. "Yes, it would, but I've got the restaurant. It's going really well, and it's all hands on deck."

Dylan nods. "I'm probably the most flexible of any of us, but my surfing and board repair shop is doing well too. I'd lose momentum if I left it in anyone else's hands right now."

Noah puts his arm around Dad's shoulder. "I could help consult, but moving up here full-time would be a challenge."

Dad turns to me. I already know the look in his eyes before he speaks—hope, bordering on pleading. "Goldie? You bought a place in Lake Nokomis. You're the closest. I figured—"

"If I'd known you were thinking about this," I cut in, "I wouldn't have bought that house." I feel bad as soon as I've said it. "It's amazing, Dad. I want this for you. Once the installation is behind me, I can put more thought into this with you."

He smiles and silence falls over the bluff.

"I didn't mean to blindside you," Dad says, softer now. "But this opportunity…it's everything I've worked toward. And I'd rather build something with my family than just about anything."

I want to let him pull me into his vision. But I glance again at the dilapidated cabins barely visible through the trees. Their shutters hang loose. The paint is peeling. Roofs sag. It's not just a fixer-upper—it needs a resurrection.

"Milo said we've got the bones of something good here.

You should see the mood boards and plans we discussed before you got here yesterday."

Tully raises his brows, looking at Milo. "You have mood boards?"

"Your dad brought them," Milo says quietly.

Dad grins, looking around at all of us. "Yes, I did. Because it's happening, kids. I'm not giving up on this. If you can't be here full-time, maybe part-time? Summers. Holidays. Weekends..."

Noah shakes his head. "My time's not as flexible as it used to be. Grayson's in preschool."

Camden sighs. "We all want this place to thrive for you, Dad, but we've got careers…commitments."

"I know," Dad says, the brightness in his eyes dimming just a little. "I know. It's just…I look at this land, and I see all of you. I see bonfires and late-night swims. I see your mom's wind chimes on the porch. I see the life we had here, and I want that back. Not the past—just…something new that still feels like home. Working on this project together would be a huge expansion of what we've already had here, and it'd also be something new. New memories, new history being made."

Something cracks in my chest at that.

We walk a little more. Nobody talks, each of us in our own thoughts. The old trail loops down toward the lake, where the remnants of the old dock jut out. Tully crouches to pick up a smooth stone, flipping it in his hand like he used to when we were kids. He used to claim he could tell fortunes with lake rocks.

"This one says we're all doomed," he jokes, tossing it into the water.

It skips once, twice, then sinks.

Thoughts about Milo filter in, without my permission. I watch him talking to my brothers, laughing even. But there's something about him—something restrained, elusive. Like he's constantly measuring what he says. Holding something back. I haven't figured him out yet, and that unsettles me. Sometimes though, especially when he's laughing like he is right now, I forget how much I dislike him. Just for a second.

Instead, I think about the beautiful structures he's masterminded and wonder how his mind works. What inspires him?

It's a lightbulb moment.

"We could do it differently," I say, whirling around to face everyone. "Not just the wellness retreat Dad mentioned. Studio spaces. An artist's retreat. Nature conservation internships. If we want to keep the integrity of the place, that's one way to do it. Blend the old with the new. Have a place that inspires people whose wells are empty…or a getaway for anyone needing that extra spark and space for creativity."

Everyone blinks at me. Milo's eyes narrow on me. Because it's not a bad idea and he knows it.

Dad crosses his arms. "Hmm. I'll think about it. Seems like that would leave out the family vibes I'm thinking about. But a board of investors would eat it up."

"Families could still vacation here. There's room for everyone," I say, lifting my shoulder.

"A thousand acres is something to work with, all right." Noah whistles.

"Lots to think about, right?" Dad says. "At least let me believe you're *thinking* about helping me." He laughs. "Come on, let's head back. I've got some meat in the smoker."

We start the trek back, teasing Dad about all the cooking he's doing now. It's a relatively new thing for him to be cooking and he's surprisingly good at it. The clouds shift and sunlight breaks through, warming our backs. For a moment, I just soak in the contentment of having all of us in one place. It'd be amazing to work on something like this together, but it also seems impossible that we'd all give up our careers to focus on this.

I don't know what I want. I love this place. I love my dad. But I also love my work and my life in Minneapolis. I'm not ready to give that up.

And if Milo Lombardi were a part of it? We'd clash nonstop.

I don't want to share anything with him, thoughts, or work…or kisses.

He catches up with me while we're walking back.

"Smart idea back there," he says.

"You think you're the only one with good ideas?"

His laugh is low and rough. "You know I'm not the villain here, right?"

"You sure?"

He gets a weird expression on his face and then shakes his head. "You're stubborn, aren't you?"

"So I've been told. I get it honestly. Grandma Donna and Grandma Nancy gave it to me in double doses." I glance at him and his amber eyes are dancing in the sunshine. "And you're arrogant."

He smirks. "Your grandmothers don't seem to mind, yet you're insistent on finding something wrong with me."

"Guess you'll have to prove me wrong."

"Guess I will."

He walks ahead, leaving me to stare at his perfect backside.

Definitely nothing wrong with him there.

By the time we get back to the house, everyone's dragging a little. The porch creaks under our boots, the screen door groaning from the lack of use. Every time I come here, I ache for my mother, but that also goes for the Summit house. I see her everywhere, but I miss her physical presence with every bone in my body.

I rub my hands together to shake off the chill and sink onto the edge of the couch.

Tully leaves the room, muttering that he needs paper to sketch some things out. He's a professional hockey player, but he might be the most artistic of all of us. My grandmas busy themselves in the kitchen, while Dad flops into his chair, and Dylan lays back on the couch next to me. Camden scrolls on his phone, kicking his boots off.

"Is it warmer than usual in here?" Noah asks, moving toward the thermostat.

There's a thud from farther back in the house. We all look at Dad and he frowns.

"I found this in your office, Dad. What the hell is this?" Tully's voice slices through the air.

I jerk upright. My heart pounds before he even storms into the living room, a thick folder clutched in one hand.

Dad stiffens across the room, his whole body going rigid.

"It's nothing," he says, too fast. "Please keep it down. I don't want them overhearing this." He tilts his head toward the kitchen where my grandmothers and Grayson are laughing.

Tully flips open the folder. His jaw tightens as he reads, his hand shaking slightly.

"No, it's not nothing," he says, his voice low and shaky. "It's hospital paperwork. Tests. A biopsy. Surgery consults." He lifts his head, eyes locking on Dad. "You have cancer?"

The room sways a little around me. I push off the couch and step closer to Dad, my legs stiff.

"What is he talking about?" I whisper, looking at Dad.

His face is pale, drawn tight like a seams-about-to-burst suitcase. His hand scrapes over his jaw, a telltale sign that he's stalling for time.

"It's early," he says gruffly. "They caught it early. It's a tumor on my pancreas. Operable. Treatable."

"But it's cancer." Tully's voice is flat.

Dad nods. "Yes."

Dylan swears under his breath, a sharp sound in the silence.

Noah crosses his arms over his chest, his face working through a dozen emotions at once.

Even Milo looks shaken.

And I just stand there, staring at Dad like he might break before my very eyes.

"When were you going to tell us?" I croak out.

Dad's eyes, so much like Noah's and Camden's, flick to me. I see it then—the weight he's been carrying alone.

"I didn't want to ruin the weekend. I wanted to talk to you about the land. About dreams, not..." His voice breaks and he clears his throat. "Not about hospitals and treatment plans."

"But we want to know what's going on with you, Dad," Camden says. His voice cracks halfway through. "We *need* to know."

"I know," Dad says, closing his eyes for a second. "I just...I needed to hold onto normal for a little while longer. And your grandmothers have been through too much the past couple of years. I'll tell them eventually. Just give me some time."

The clock ticks too loudly on the mantel. Someone's breathing raggedly. I think it's me. I step into Dad's space and wrap my arms around him. His hands come up slowly, pulling me in tight.

One by one, my brothers close in. We crush Dad between us, Whitman hearts banding together without a word.

I'm *terrified*. Already lost just *imagining* a world without my dad.

No, don't go there. Do *not* go there.

"I'll do whatever you want, Dad," Camden says, voice broken. "It may take a few months, but I'll visit…and I'll work on handing things over to my manager so I can get here as soon as possible."

"Same," Dylan says.

Noah nods. "I'm not sure how long it'll take me, but I'll come every chance I get."

"Me too," I say, wiping my face.

Tully takes a deep breath and his fingers grip my shoulder and Noah's as he stares at Dad. "I'll hold off on signing any new contracts. May as well go out on a high note."

"Absolutely not," Dad says to Tully. "You're not quitting hockey. I can't ask any of you to do this," Dad says, his face streaming with tears. "It was different when I was trying to get you here to work on this project. That would've been your choice because you wanted this opportunity and were excited about the possibilities, not because you feel obligated to be with me."

"We're not leaving you to go through this alone," Noah says. "And the project will be a bonus. Something to get our minds off of what's going on with you."

My dad still looks distraught.

"Ultimately, it could be a huge addition to each of our careers, if we all put our skills toward this one endeavor," Camden says. "You'll need a Michelin-star level restaurant with this new resort, right?"

Dad snorts out a laugh, wiping his cheeks. "Right."

"We'll get through this, Dad," I tell him. "Together."

CHAPTER SIX

FAMILY TIES

MILO

Fuck. I can't believe Everett has cancer. Why does it always happen to the good ones?

I'm out on the deck, looking at the lake and trying to give Everett and his family privacy, when my phone buzzes in my hand. It's my uncle.

Of course it is.

I glance back through the big windows where the Whitmans sit inside. Goldie's silhouette stands out the most, perched on the arm of the couch, one knee pulled up, a wine glass dangling from her fingers. She's laughing at something her brother said, her head tipping back, and my gut twists.

I'm glad she's laughing. It hurt to see the tears falling down her cheeks earlier.

I ignore the call, but it just rings again a few seconds later.

I answer.

"Milo!"

"Hey, Bruce," I mutter, already regretting answering.

"What, I'm not Uncle Bruce anymore?"

"I think I stopped calling you that the first time I did a job with you."

He chuckles. "Fair enough. I miss it though. Any updates? You had your meeting yet? What's the scoop?"

I stare at the stars reflected in the black water below. I rub the back of my neck, feeling like I might be sick.

"You said the land you were interested in was farther north," I say. "Not Windy Harbor."

"Same difference," he says breezily. "Just nudge the guy. Tell him it'll be too expensive, too much work to restore."

"You didn't say it was this land," I say again, my voice rough. My heart hammers against my ribs. I hear the echo of Everett's voice earlier today, talking about how much this place means to him. How he wants to leave it better than he found it. "Why didn't you tell me it was the *Whitmans* you were bidding against?"

Bruce's laugh grates in my ear. "Didn't know it mattered."

"I get the impression that there's a lot of tension between you and Everett and I find it suspicious that you didn't tell me any of this."

He barks out a laugh and my skin crawls. "Where have you been, Milo? Can you seriously say you know nothing about the Whitman/Granger divide?"

I frown and start pacing. "What are you talking about?"

He sighs. "Goddamn it, Milo. This goes way back. And if you want to be part of this family, you'll help me put the Whitmans in their place once and for all."

"No, I don't want any part of whatever this is."

"Too late. You were part of this before you were ever born."

"This is ridiculous. Everett's a good man. And business is business. I'm not going to ruin my reputation over some silly family feud."

"This goes deeper than that."

He hangs up and I stare at my phone in confusion.

The stars blur, and for a second, the ground feels like it's tipping. I sit heavily on one of the deck chairs, dropping my head into my hands.

This is a goddamn disaster.

Everett Whitman has cancer.

It's awful. On the outside, the man seems to be the epitome of good health. And he's certainly loved. Through the window, his family still looks like they're on the brink of tears. Goldie's face went white when she heard, like someone punched her.

No one but Everett knew until today.

I shouldn't be here. The asshole who's been working against them without even realizing it. The enemy.

I rake my hands through my hair, tugging hard, like pain might help this make sense.

I was so damn eager for the project. Speaking to Everett yesterday before the family arrived, he'd gotten me fully invested. Now that I've seen the property, I feel even more so.

Bruce is my mom's brother. He's a complicated man and we rarely see eye to eye, but when he mentioned an exciting opportunity to revitalize underused lakefront land up north, I didn't see any reason to not pursue it. I had no idea he wanted this land.

And what the fuck is the Whitman/Granger divide?

The door creaks open behind me.

Light footsteps and a soft, familiar scent drifts on the breeze.

Goldie.

"Hey," she says, voice cautious.

I force myself to turn and meet her gaze. Her eyes search mine.

"You okay?" she asks. "You don't have to stay out here."

"I know. I just…didn't want to intrude. I'm really sorry about your dad."

Her face softens, her eyes filling with tears. She wraps her arms around herself. "It's serious, but there's treatment. Hopefully they caught it in time."

I stare out at the dark water, guilt tightening around my ribs until it's hard to breathe.

I hope there's time for Everett to do all he dreams of doing.

If no one rips it out from under him.

"I'm sorry," I say again, running a hand through my hair. "I just…need some air."

"You're already outside," she says gently.

But she doesn't stop me when I go.

I pace down the steps, gravel crunching under my boots, the air slamming into my overheated skin.

I fish out my phone again, thumb hovering over Bruce's name.

Calling him won't fix it.

I turn in a slow circle, heading back to the house. I don't know what to do. I need to find out more about our families and what Bruce plans to do. Maybe I can encourage him to look elsewhere for land. Bruce is an ass, but he's powerful. He's got lawyers on standby. I need to think this through.

The door creaks as I step inside. The conversation has

quieted, everyone scattered around the room, tired and heavy from the news.

Goldie's standing at the fireplace, staring at an old photo on the mantel. It's of her as a little girl, hair in pigtails, sitting on her dad's shoulders.

God, the way she looks at him. Like he's her hero.

I swallow hard.

Everett's sitting in his recliner, a blanket draped over his lap. I don't know if it's the heaviness of what he's shared with his family or if it's the sickness, but all too quickly, he looks exhausted and pale.

I make my way over, heart hammering.

"Everett?" I say quietly.

He looks up, eyes sharp despite the weariness dragging his face down.

"Count me in. For all of it. Whatever you need. With the property. With your plans. I want to help as much as you want."

His face breaks out into a huge smile. "Thank you, Milo. It's great to have you officially onboard."

I have no idea how I'm going to clear this up with Bruce, but I meet Everett's gaze and say the one thing I know is true.

"You believe in this place and I believe in you."

He claps his hand on my shoulder. "All right then. I believe in you too. Have from day one."

Later, after the house is quiet, I can't sleep. I sit on the deck with my laptop open, light from the screen making me squint. I go back through all the emails from Bruce. There's nothing in there about this particular piece of property, so that must be a relatively new development. I just hope and pray that Everett gets this land, not Bruce. If Goldie thought I was an opportunist out to squash history with the new and flashy, she'll really despise my uncle's vision. He'll have gold statues leading to the golden brick path to a massive resort if he gets his hands on it.

A crack of light shines across the deck, and I hear the door shut.

Goldie pads out, barefoot in leggings and a hoodie. Her hair's loose, haloed by the moonlight. She curls into the chair next to me without speaking.

We sit in silence for a long time, the waves lapping against the rocks.

Finally, she says, "Thank you."

I look at her, startled. "For what?"

Her smile is small and sad. "For being here. I know my dad must really like you for him to invite you here this weekend while the rest of us are here. It says a lot that he wants you around. He doesn't allow just anyone in…"

I swallow hard, feeling like there's a stone in my chest.

"He's a good man," I say.

"The best."

"The best," I echo.

I ache to reach out and touch her, reassure her, but I fight it. We sit there for a long time, watching the stars burn holes in the sky.

"Couldn't sleep?" I finally ask.

She startles slightly. "Too much on my mind."

"You don't have to carry it all alone, you know," I say.

She turns to look at me, her eyes shining in the moonlight. "Maybe you're not so bad. Dare I hope that you're going to stop this foolishness about Spoonbridge and Cherry?"

"Oh, my plans haven't changed, but we don't need to worry about that tonight."

"What a disappointment." Her eyes flash and she gets up and walks away.

Dammit, why does this woman get to me?

CHAPTER SEVEN

IT'S BEEN A WEEK

GOLDIE

When I wake up the next morning, Milo is gone. *Good riddance.* I'm happy to not see that arrogant, history-destroying man.

On the drive home Sunday night, my eyes won't stop leaking. They haven't all weekend. Cancer. And I know it's the least of things to be worried about, but my dad's beautiful, thick, white hair is one of his most striking features.

"Your mom always said I had a head for hats." He'd laughed when we brought up his hair.

I can't breathe. My heart is pounding out of my chest. My ears are ringing.

"Dad," I whisper.

He apologized before we all left.

"I didn't want to tell you until I knew what we were dealing with. I've got a good doctor, and the odds are pretty

good. I was going to tell you. I wanted all of you to hear it from me. I just wanted a little more time."

"But—"

"I'm fine," Dad insisted. His smile was steady, but his eyes were too bright. "And I'm glad you're all here. There are probably a few things we should discuss."

I'd burst into tears. Again.

Dad crossed the room and took me in his arms. "Goldie. I'll be okay."

I squeezed my eyes shut and shook my head against his chest. "You don't know that."

"I will be," he said. His hand cupped the back of my head. "Being by the water has been really good for me."

"How long have you known?" Dylan asked, his eyes shining with tears.

"Just a month."

"A month?" I whispered, crying harder.

The thought of him carrying that without us was crushing.

I pulled back just enough to see Noah, Tully, and Camden looking stunned.

Dad's hand rested on my cheek and I focused on him. "It's not a big deal, buttercup."

But it is. It's such a big deal. I've already lost one parent. I don't think I can handle losing another.

As soon as I'm home, I check on my dad and then open the text thread that's just my brothers and me.

> It was so hard leaving him. What are we going to do? He got upset with me for trying to stay, so I finally left! But I feel awful about it.

NOAH

Same. I'm still going over there every other day despite his grumbling about it. He's going to be okay. We have to stay positive—for him and for each other.

> I'm not feeling very positive right now.

TULLY

I'm not either.

CAMDEN

It seemed to really help boost his spirits that we were there. I've never hated being so far more than I do right now.

DYLAN

I know. Going back to California tomorrow feels impossible, but he's insisting that I don't hand the business over just yet. I'm going to as soon as I can though.

> I love you guys. Once I have this week behind me, I'll be with him as much as I can.

NOAH

Sorry to make you carry that alone for a while, Golds. Grayson and I will come often too, until I can wrap up all my projects and be there more.

CAMDEN

I hate doing that to you too, Goldie.

> It's okay. None of us saw this coming, but we'll get through it together.

I stand in the middle of my tiny studio, hands on my hips, a paintbrush clamped between my teeth. My heart hammers against my ribs, a wild, uneven rhythm that mirrors the chaos around me. Canvas scraps, wood frames, jars of paint, and too many half-drunk mugs of coffee scatter the room.

"You have to be done," I mumble around the brush.

The installation is called "Fractured Light" and is a tribute to survival, to piecing yourself together when life shatters you. I didn't realize I'd be shattered more before it was even completed. Hidden faces are woven through the artwork—some clearer than others—representing the trauma I endured after my car accident and the concussion that left me feeling so unlike myself.

I don't even like to think about the accident. I was in the hospital for a couple of weeks and my dad and brothers didn't leave my side during that time. For months after I went home, I still didn't feel like myself. Honestly, I still don't, but I'm getting better all the time. Working on these pieces helped.

The paintings are delicate. Heartbreaking and beautiful.

And they're due at MIA in *six days*.

Six days to pull this off. Six days to outrun impostor syndrome.

Each day blurs into the next.

Monday, I wake up on the studio couch with paint streaked across my face and my back aching.

Tuesday, Tully stops by, juggling coffees and yelling, "You need sunlight, Golds! You're starting to look like one of those pasty art school kids!"

Wednesday, Camden calls from Denver to remind me,

"No matter what happens, we're proud of you." I cry in the middle of shading a hidden face into a panel.

Thursday, Dylan FaceTimes me from his surf shop in California. He's wearing a wet suit and holding a mini Dachshund.

"How are you holding up?" he asks.

"I'm not. How about you?"

"Nope. I'm not either. You look a little loopy. Are you keeping your windows open so the air can circulate?"

"You're the loopy one. Whose dog is that?"

He shrugs. "I don't know. He turned up at my shop and hasn't left."

On Friday, I haul the finished pieces into the back of my dad's truck. We swapped vehicles over the weekend so I could take everything in one trip. I drive to the museum for the setup process, heart in my throat.

Saturday morning, I'm still tweaking. Adjusting lighting angles. Swapping paintings to other spots. My hands shake when I finally step back and survey it all.

It's done.

Hidden faces glint in the light, half-seen, half-felt, like memories that refuse to stay buried.

That night I stare at myself in the mirror, surprised that I look human. For all the tears I've cried this week, all the junk I've eaten, all the sleep I've lost, it's a shock that I look good. My black dress hugs my waist and flows out like a waterfall toward my feet. My hair is down so I can hide behind it. My makeup is covering the splotches and looks flawless. I look ethereal and somewhat haunted, like one of the faces in my paintings.

"You ready?" Tully asks, poking his head in.

I turn, swallowing hard. "Ready."

The Minneapolis Institute of Art is all lit up. Fairy lights thread the trees outside. Everything has an extra shine, and inside, voices and laughter spill across the space. It's unbelievable to think that my work, my heart, is tucked inside these walls tonight.

I stick close to my family. I was certain that Camden and Dylan wouldn't be able to make it. We're all floundering, trying to figure out how to get to Windy Harbor as soon as we can, and this night is not on the list of priorities. But they're here with Noah, Grayson, Tully, my dad, Grandma Nancy, and Grandma Donna. I'm so overwhelmed, I burst into tears.

"I can't believe you're all here," I say, hugging each one of them.

"You think we'd miss this?" Camden asks, coming in for another hug.

"We're so proud of you, buttercup," Dad says.

I try to balance a flute of sparkling rosé in one hand and the tangle of emotions in the other when I hear it.

A whistle. Loud. Familiar. Followed by: "Ohhh, *hell yes*. Look at this moody masterpiece! Goldie Whitman, you little legend."

I whirl around.

"ERIN?!"

She barrels toward me in her signature black combat boots, cuffed jeans, and a blazer over a T-shirt that says *Queer and Cozy*. Her wing-tipped eyeliner and red lipstick are perfect, as always. Her arms open like she's about to tackle me. I set my glass down and fling myself into her. There's a small gasp from a woman behind us—I might have almost taken out a pedestal—but I don't care. Erin is here.

"You're really here," I breathe, clinging to her like a life raft.

"Of course I'm here," she says, her voice thick. "You think I'd miss your big artsy debut? Please. I cleared my whole calendar. Even rescheduled a shipment of tourist hoodies. That's love, babe."

I laugh, even as my throat tightens with emotion. I haven't seen her in months. Too many phone calls and not enough hugs.

"You look incredible," she says.

"*You* do," I say, pulling back. I grin and wipe at the corners of my eyes.

Her expression softens. "Hey. I'm really sorry, Golds. About your dad. He came to the trading post and told me and my parents. I know you're trying to handle everything like the stoic, Midwestern martyr you are, but knock it the hell off."

I make a face.

She squeezes my hand. "Whatever you need. I mean it. I'm so damn glad you're gonna be in Windy Harbor more. That place needs you. *I* need you. Even if it means you'll put me to shame in Thursday night trivia."

"You should be worried. My reign is far from over."

Erin is still laughing at me when we hear a voice.

"Oh my gosh. Am I late?"

I freeze.

No way.

I turn and see her, weaving through the crowd with the biggest smile on her face.

"ADDY?!" I burst into tears again, covering my mouth as she rushes toward me.

"Hey, my girl," she says, throwing her arms around me.

"I can't believe you came all the way from Silver Hills! How are Penn and the kids?"

"You think I'd miss this? Penn and the kids are great. They send their love."

I'm shaking. Laughing. Crying. "I can't believe you're both here."

Addy pulls back slightly, still holding my arms. "This is much more fun than when we hung out while she was recovering," she tells Erin.

They hug like long-lost cousins, and I blink at them.

"Oh, I forgot you'd already met."

"You were a little busy recovering from that awful accident," Erin says. "Are you still driving?"

"Yeah, I'm back at it. Took a minute," I admit. "I'm gonna start sobbing again," I say, voice wobbling. "Thank you so much for coming."

"Everything looks beautiful," Erin says. "You should be so proud."

Addy smiles at me and then looks at my work. "I'm blown away, Goldie. And I'm ecstatic for you." She squeezes my hand.

I lose it all over again, loving my people so much.

And then it's all happening at once. Strangers swarm—smiling, praising, asking questions. I answer as best I can, while part of me floats above it all, barely believing it's real.

Then I see him.

Milo Lombardi.

He's leaning against a marble column and looks like *he's* an art installation in this museum. Dark suit, no tie, shirt collar open. His hair is a little messy, like he raked a hand through it moments ago. His gorgeous, infuriating eyes are locked on me.

The breath whooshes from my lungs.

What is he doing here?

I didn't bite his head off the last night in Windy Harbor, and I didn't let myself admit that I was disappointed when I woke up the next morning to find he'd already left.

The way he's looking at me sends a chill down my arms and spine and I square my shoulders, nodding slightly at him. He just nods back and stands there, looking too sexy for his own good.

I force myself to turn back to my conversation with an older woman raving about the "emotional resonance of the hidden faces." I nod and smile, but my body is humming, hyperaware of the weight of Milo's eyes on me.

Minutes later, I feel him before I see him.

"Congratulations," he murmurs, close to my ear.

I stiffen. Turn slowly.

He smiles, not a full smile, just a tilt at the corner of his mouth.

Ugh. Why is he so annoyingly charming?

"You're full of surprises," I say coolly.

"Thought I'd see if the rumors are true." His eyes finally drift off of me and to my paintings. Somehow that makes me feel even more naked.

"And?"

His gaze roams over me, lingering in ways that make my skin feel too tight. "You're better than the rumors."

Heat rises up my neck. I loathe how easily he gets under my skin.

"You crash a lot of events you weren't invited to, or just mine?"

His laugh is low and lazy, like he has all day to mess with me. "Last I checked, anyone was invited. And maybe I like seeing you all dressed up…"

I arch a brow. "It's the only way you've seen me so far… all that's missing this time is the rage."

"I liked that version too," he says, voice dropping lower.

A shiver slips down my spine.

Something flickers in those stormy eyes. "I wanted to see you shine."

My chest constricts and then a million butterflies take flight.

We're interrupted by a wave of people who want to talk about the artwork and get their picture taken with me. Some just want to talk about how much they know about art, but that comes with the territory. I meet a lot of great people who say such nice things about my work—it feels surreal to know other people care this much about something I created. My face aches from smiling.

And then it's just a few lingering people. My eyes widen when Milo walks up to me.

"You're still here," I whisper.

He closes the few inches between us, handing me a stunning bouquet of roses, peonies, and anemones.

I'm speechless as I take the flowers from him.

"You terrify me, Goldie Whitman," he whispers. "Good night."

He walks away and I'm dizzy as I watch him go.

"You terrify me too," I whisper.

CHAPTER EIGHT

SHUT DOWN

MILO

I can't get her out of my head.

Goldie Whitman.

Her artwork was vivid and aching and alive. Like her. Standing in front of her pieces, she looked like she was stitched into every canvas. It was as if I could see her pulse beneath the paint.

I've also thought about Everett a lot. I'm still in shock that he's sick…and that my uncle wants the same property. I shouldn't be surprised. Both are successful businessmen, and it's not like we're as large as New York or Chicago; our pool of business moguls is a lot smaller. And Bruce is specifically relentless about Everett. This will eventually bite me in the ass.

I've put off seeing Bruce, but I can't any longer.

I rake a hand through my hair and stalk across my penthouse, the skyline of the Twin Cities standing proudly beyond the windows. I like my place. It's sleek and minimal, but lately, it feels hollow.

I grab my jacket and head to Bruce's office.

Once I'm inside his building, I slide my cell into my pocket. The elevator dings, and I step into the vast atrium of my uncle's building, the polished floor echoing my footsteps. Anna, the receptionist, a young brunette like all of Bruce's receptionists have been, lights up when she sees me, her red fingernails pausing their clacking across the keyboard.

"Is Bruce free?" I ask, casting a glance at the enormous clock on the wall.

"He always has time for you," Anna says, her smile wide. She picks up the phone and lets Bruce know I'm here. "You can head on back."

"Thanks, Anna."

Bruce's office is at the end of a long corridor, the carpet thick, muffling my resolve with each step. I knock lightly and push open the door.

"Hello, Milo." He rises from behind his desk and rounds it to greet me, his handshake firm. We're not one of those families who hugs or exchanges long pleasantries. Bruce is tall and imposing, his square jaw showing a hint of stubble, his hair graying and cut short. He's wearing a three-piece suit, a timeless cut that reeks of money and power. The same could be said for me. I can appreciate a nice suit and am wearing one myself, albeit somewhat more casual. I'll save the three-piece suits for winter.

"What brings you here this afternoon?" he asks, motioning for me to sit. "Can I get you a Scotch?"

It's always Scotch with him. He pours a glass, lifting it, and I shake my head.

"No, thank you."

"Suit yourself." He grins and brings his glass over to his desk, sitting across from me.

"When were you planning on telling me you were bidding against Everett Whitman?"

Bruce's lips twitch into something that's not quite a smile. "That's important to you?"

"Yes, it is. I've worked with Everett in the past. He's a good man."

He snorts. "Well, working with him was your first mistake. And believing he's a good man is your second. I've been waiting for you to apologize to me about that project, by the way. You say you didn't know how I feel about the Whitmans, but now you do. It's outrageous that you're so blatantly siding with him on anything." He gives me a pointed look.

"I have no intention of carrying out this ridiculous vendetta you have against the man. Whatever you have against him is not my business."

"Your grandpa would be devastated to hear this."

"What does Grandpa have to do with it? *What happened?*"

He slams his fist on his desk. "I don't have time for this. It should be enough that I'm asking you, as family, to back *me* and not my enemy. I'm appalled by your lack of loyalty. Family sticks together. Haven't your parents taught you anything?"

"They've taught me to be fair and to look for the best in others."

He scoffs. "I can't believe how naive you are. I thought..." He shakes his head. "Well, I just thought you were more of a man than this spineless, weak-kneed—" He waves his hand toward me like he can't even find the word for how pathetic I am.

It's quiet for a minute as we stare at each other. I have no interest in defending myself. My uncle is incapable of hearing reason when he's like this, and I'm self-assured enough to know he's fucking wrong about me.

He clears his throat. "I want this property, Milo, and I want you to help me with the perfect plans."

"I can't do that, Bruce. I'm sorry, but I was under the impression the property you wanted was hours away from this parcel of land. I believe in what Everett's doing. I think he deserves this. I'll be happy to work with you on another property, but not on this one."

He frowns. "Do you hear yourself? He's a fucking Whitman! What do you mean, Everett deserves it? What does he want to put there that's so deserving?"

I shake my head. "I'm not going to betray his trust to tell you that."

"You'd really pick that man over your family?" His eyes narrow. "You've always been soft, to the point of stupidity."

I give him a cool look. "Then why did you want me in on this?"

"Because I thought you'd finally learned to play the game." He leans back, disappointment etched into his features. "You're more like your dad than I realized."

My jaw tightens.

His words hang between us, heavy and bitter.

I stand and straighten my jacket. "Thank God for that—my dad is a great man. I have no room in my heart for hate. I'm sorry that you do, Bruce. I really am."

He doesn't reply, just watches me as I turn and leave, the door clicking shut behind me. Anna's eyes flicker with curiosity when I walk past her and nod briskly.

When the elevator doors close, I let out a breath I hadn't realized I was holding. My uncle can be intimidating, but I meant what I said. If he just wants family that mimics his behavior, he shouldn't have bothered with me. I'd been more than willing to help him with another project, but not this one.

A few days later, Everett's number flashes on my phone.

"Hello?"

"Hey, Milo!" Everett's voice booms through the line. "We got it! We got the property!"

A breath punches out of me. "That's incredible, Everett."

"I put in a high bid. Higher than I probably should've." He chuckles. "But dammit, I wasn't letting that old goat Bruce Granger outbid me. Not this time."

Relief swells through me. I wasn't sure Bruce would let the matter go without more of a fight.

"I'm so happy for you."

It's on the tip of my tongue to tell him everything, but something holds me back. I'll tell him in person.

"Now comes the real work." Everett laughs. "How soon can you get your butt up to Windy Harbor? We need to start talking plans."

I grin, leaning back in my office chair. "How soon do you want me?"

"Yesterday."

Windy Harbor hits me like a sucker punch the second I roll in the following Saturday.

The air is crisper here. Boats bob lazily in the harbor. Shops line the main street, the lake glittering in the background. A perfect backdrop.

It feels different than the last time I was here.

Maybe because now, in my mind, this town is tied to Goldie.

To her fire. Her stubbornness. Her family.

I drive down Wildbriar Lane, the main street, eyeing the colorful buildings tucked close together. A couple of them look like they may have apartments above the shops. I've always loved this town. It has more of a coastal vibe than the usual North Woods vibe—nothing wrong with that, but I appreciate the color and the quirkiness of this place more.

I pull in front of the Kitty-Corner Cafe. Inside, the place smells rich of coffee and baked goods. My stomach growls.

A young woman behind the counter looks up and gives me a friendly smile. "Can I help you?"

I glance around. "I'll take a cup of coffee…and what smells so good?"

She grins wider. "My cinnamon rolls. Take a look at that top shelf." She points to the glass cabinet and my eyes go big.

"Hell, yeah, I'll have one of those."

She laughs. "Coming right up."

"Actually…I'm looking for a place to stay. Are there any hotels or rooms available for a few weeks at a time?"

"The nicer places are about half an hour up the lake. Our lodge closed, and now Windy Harbor just has a few places over our shops. They're usually occupied, but we've got one open right above us. Cozy little studio. Nothing fancy, but the view's not bad."

I nod. "Can I see it? I'm not sure when I'll need it exactly, but I'd like to know my options."

She opens a drawer and pulls out a key. "Go on up. I'll work on your coffee and heat up your cinnamon roll."

"Thanks." I look to see if she's wearing a name tag, but she's not.

"I'm Juliana, but everyone calls me Juju."

"I'm Milo. Nice to meet you."

"You too!"

"Juju, you didn't tell me you'd put in a new oven!" Goldie comes out of the kitchen and comes to a dead stop when she sees me. Her hair's twisted up in some messy knot that still somehow looks like it belongs on a magazine cover, a few strands falling over her cheek. Her mouth parts and I can't help but grin.

Her eyes narrow.

I chuckle. Everything I do seems to rub this woman the wrong way.

She sighs. "This is *my* coffee shop."

"Didn't realize it," I say, leaning an elbow casually on the counter. "Maybe you should put up a sign. 'Beware: Goldie Whitman. Death by rudeness.'"

"Very funny. I guess I'm gonna have to get used to seeing you in my town, huh," she says, folding her arms.

"*Is* it your town? Are you claiming Minneapolis too?" I lift my shoulder. "You can't just take over the whole state."

She growls. "If you're looking for a fight, Lombardi, you're going to lose."

I grin. "Define 'lose.' Because sparring with you sounds like my kind of morning workout."

Juju covers her mouth as she laughs, looking between the two of us with interest.

"Don't scare off a potential renter, Golds!" she says.

Goldie's hands go to her hips and she shakes her head. "*No.* You're not letting him stay here, are you?" She scowls at Juliana. "So I'll have to see you every time I want coffee?" Her head falls back and she groans.

"Wow," I say. "Dramatic much?"

"Oh, you have no idea," Juju whispers, giggling. "We've

been best friends since we were little and she's always had a flair for the dramatic."

"I heard that!" Goldie groans.

Juju points to a door in the back corner. "The apartment is that way."

The apartment is small but clean, with windows that overlook the lake. Hardwood floors. A little kitchen tucked into the corner. A nice couch and a bed. Not exactly the luxury of my penthouse, but it'll do.

Everett expects me to stay at the house, but with his family coming in and out, I don't want to be in the way.

I'm sure Goldie will be happy about this decision.

I go back down and collect my coffee and cinnamon roll. And holy hell, my eyes sink back into my head when I taste the cinnamon roll. I'll have to up my running if I live above this place.

"These are criminal," I tell Juju. "Instantly addicted."

She laughs. "Glad to know you'll be back. What did you think of the place?"

"It'll be great. I'll find out my schedule and stop back in once I know."

"Sounds good." She smiles.

"I don't know—it's no penthouse apartment," Goldie says.

I smirk. "You gathering intel on me, G. Waters?"

Her cheeks flush. "No. Just took a wild guess."

"Mm-hmm." I knock on the counter. "Thanks, again, Juliana." I look at Goldie again. "Guess I'll see you at the house."

"Don't hold your breath."

I smirk once again. "Wouldn't dream of it."

CHAPTER NINE

KICK IN THE SHINS

GOLDIE

I drive over to the lake house, annoyed that Milo will be all up in my space this weekend. And he's already frequenting Kitty-Corner Cafe? Ugh. To be fair, we don't have many choices here, but I was hoping he'd stay out of all my favorite places.

True confession: I was already annoyed before I even saw him. I got a little relief when I drove into Windy Harbor, the tension gradually peeling off of me. But that was short-lived when I saw Milo's cocky face in my coffee shop. The frustration and self-doubt came rushing back, but that's not all on him.

People have been raving about my installation. Even the tough critics. One reviewer called it *achingly beautiful*, and another said it *captures the resilience of the human spirit with breathtaking subtlety*.

Those two reviews alone should have me dancing on my tabletop. And there are dozens more that are just as amazing.

I should be elated.

But instead, I'm fixated on this one stupid review by someone named Ava Piper, who apparently thinks my work is *trite, predictable, and self-indulgent*.

When I read that last night, I paced my kitchen, muttering what I wished I could say to Ms. Ava Piper and her bitter little mind. I don't even know this woman, but I have lots of thoughts about *her* now. Is she a professional critic, or a bored woman who just likes to rain on anyone's parade? Is she right? *Is* my work trite, predictable, and self-indulgent? I mean, isn't all art somewhat self-indulgent? And trite, for that matter, when the bigger scope of what's going on in our world is taken into consideration. Definitely trite when I think of what's going on with my dad.

But even in the worst of times, art is what helps people survive.

It's certainly helped me in my darkest times.

Ugh. See? She's gotten in my head. I'm spiraling. Whoever she is, she's sitting behind a computer screen wreaking havoc with my thoughts. I wish I'd never read her review. She can go suck an egg.

I groan when I see the black Range Rover in the driveway. Sleek. I swear, even his SUV reeks of smugness. Parked like it owns the damn place.

I slam my door harder than necessary as I haul my bag out of the trunk.

The front door swings open, and there he is.

Looking far too pleased with himself.

"Well, well, well," he drawls, leaning against the doorframe like he's posing for a photoshoot for an outrageously expensive car or a watch that costs more than most people make in a year. "If it isn't Minnesota's sweetheart."

I grind my teeth. "This is going to be torture, isn't it, Lombardi?"

He shrugs. "Doesn't have to be."

My heart flutters like he said something charming and I want to kick my own shin for being such a traitor. *We don't like this man, remember?*

"There's my girl," Dad says from inside, carrying a plate of cookies like this is a casual family picnic and not the beginning of my personal hell. "Time to celebrate our good news! The land is ours!"

We make it about an hour into discussing preliminary plans before I want to throw something.

"You can't just slap a bunch of modern monstrosities on the lakeshore," I say, jabbing a finger at Milo's sketchpad. "This is a small, *charming* town. Updating and building something new doesn't mean steamrolling over the character of the place."

"No," he agrees easily. "It means not living like it's 1954." He flips a page dramatically. "This is an opportunity to build something that actually attracts visitors. Younger people. Families."

I lean forward, fuming. "Younger people want authenticity. Not concrete and glass boxes with sad little rooftop gardens."

I actually adore rooftop gardens, so I don't know why I said that.

Milo taps his pencil against the table. "You seem pretty confident about what *younger people* want, considering you sound like a ninety-year-old shouting at the neighborhood kids to get off your lawn."

"You are *such* an ass."

"Goldie!" my dad gasps.

"And you," Milo says, flashing a grin that could melt glaciers—not mine, of course— "are tragically naive."

"I'd rather be naive than a sellout."

That wipes the grin off his face.

We stare at each other across the kitchen table, the tension so thick it could be sliced into angry little ice cubes.

Dad clears his throat. "Maybe we take a break?"

"Great idea," I say, standing so fast my chair screeches. "I'm going to take a walk before I commit a felony."

Milo smirks and leans back in his chair. "Take a long walk, Whitman. Maybe it'll knock that chip off your shoulder."

"Hey now, you guys," my dad starts. "Go easy on each other!"

I flip Milo off over said shoulder as I storm outside.

The lake air is cooler than I dressed for, biting at my skin as I pace along the shoreline.

Thinking about Milo's patronizing face. His maddening voice. The way he seems to get under my skin in record time.

And of course, because the universe clearly hates me, when I turn back toward the house and round the corner by the old boat launch, he's there.

Hands in pockets. Staring at the water like he's the tragic hero of a movie that I did not ask to be made, thank you very much.

If I wanted to see perfection in movie and hero form, I'd

watch either of the *Pride and Prejudice* movies and get my fix.

"Don't worry," I say, crossing my arms. "I'm not here to disturb your brooding session."

"Good," he says without looking at me. "Because I'm not going to save you when you trip over your own outrage and fall into the lake."

"Nice." I clap slowly. "I wish I had my phone. I'd play "True Colors" by Cyndi Lauper right now."

"Sounds about right. A song our parents played in the eighties to fit with the vibe you envision for this place."

"Ugh!" I growl, stepping past him. And carefully, so he *doesn't* have to pull me out of the water.

He reaches out and gently touches my arm, and there's something in his eyes that stops me cold.

The mockery and arrogance are gone.

"Why do you hate me so much?" he asks, voice low.

The question throws me off balance. I open my mouth, but nothing comes out.

"You don't even know me, Goldie. You've created this version of me in your head."

I swallow hard. "Maybe because every time you open your mouth, you confirm exactly who I thought you were."

"And who is that?" He steps closer, and despite myself, my heart rate kicks up.

I lift my shoulder, unable to put my thoughts into words when he's so close.

"Or maybe," he says softly, "you're just scared that if you gave me a real chance, you might actually like me."

I snort. "Highly unlikely."

His mouth twitches. "Your lips sure liked me."

I roll my eyes and he lets go of my arm. He brushes past me, heading back toward the house, leaving me rooted in place, the wind tearing at my hair, and an ache blooming in my chest.

After dinner that night, I find Dad out on the back deck, sitting in one of the old Adirondack chairs and nursing a hot tea. The lake stretches out in front of us, dark and endless.

I grab a sweatshirt and slip outside, plopping down in the chair beside him.

"How you feelin'?" I ask, nudging his shoulder with mine.

He shrugs. "Good enough."

"You're a terrible liar."

Dad chuckles. "Maybe. Your mom always saw right through me too. I had a hard time telling her I didn't like one of her plans, but she'd know it by the look on my face." He shakes his head. "You're so much like her." He looks at me and smiles.

I swallow the lump in my throat and pick at the frayed edge of my sleeve. "You have that appointment next week...I want to go with you."

He shakes his head immediately. "No way, Goldie."

"Dad, please—"

"I appreciate it, buttercup. But I need you to keep living your life. Not hovering over mine. Besides, you've got a job to keep up with."

"Wanting to make sure you're okay isn't hovering."

"It is if it makes you stop doing what you love."

I blink back tears and take his hand. "I'm almost done with the project at work. I'm going to give my two weeks' notice on Monday. I love interior design and now I can put all my focus into designing something *we* want. I'm really looking forward to it actually. I've spent a lot of time fulfilling my customers' wishes and now I'd like to make your dreams come true!"

"Goldie...I know I really talked up this property and the dreams I had for *all* of us, but I've had time to think about it, and it isn't fair for any of you to put your lives on hold for this. Follow the course of what *you* want to do."

I sigh. "God, you're stubborn," I mutter.

He grins. "Look who's talking."

"I want to be here, Dad. I want to be here for all of it."

"Less so before you knew I was sick."

I pause because, of course, he's right. "I've had time to think about things too, and I'm excited about everything. I think the potential here is huge and I promise, I want in. Like Noah said—the bonus is the time I'll get to spend with you."

There's a beat of silence, filled only by the sound of the water lapping against the shore.

"So," he says casually, "what is your deal with Milo?"

I nearly choke on my sip of beer. "There's no deal. He's...infuriating."

Dad laughs. "With you, he certainly seems to be. You're not quite yourself with him either, though, I've noticed. Felt like swords were about to be drawn earlier."

"He's arrogant and bossy and he wants to change the history of things that shouldn't be changed!"

"Mm-hmm."

"He thinks he knows everything."

"Ahh."

"And he's smug."

"Mm-hmm."

I glare at him. "You're enjoying this way too much."

"Maybe." He shrugs again, looking far too pleased with

himself. "Or maybe I think you two are more alike than you realize."

"Watch your mouth," I say, horrified.

He just laughs harder, and somehow, despite everything swirling around us—the tension, the fear, the uncertainty—I find myself laughing too.

The next morning dawns crisp and clear, with the kind of bright, golden sunlight that should make me feel hopeful. And I am hopeful as I take in glimpses of the water on my drive toward Wildbriar Lane.

Kitty-Corner Cafe is bustling with the chaos that fills me up. Bosco grumbles at everyone who walks in, a staple at the cafe.

"How's Francine, Bosco?" I ask.

His eyes brighten slightly. "Fatter'n a tick. She caught a mouse last night and laid it at my feet."

My nose wrinkles up before I can stop it. "Good…for her."

Juju yells, "If anyone touches that last lemon scone before Goldie gets her hands on it, I swear I'll start flinging biscotti."

"Listen to you," I say, grinning at Juju. "I approve."

"You know I love you," she says.

"I love you! And your lemon scones," I add.

I shrug off my sweatshirt and look at my corner. It's the perfect spot by the front window, sunlit in the morning and tucked just far enough from the door to be warm in the winter and breezy in the spring. When I'm in town, everyone leaves my spot open or moves when they see me coming. It's sweet and makes me feel loved around here.

But no. No, no, no.

Not today, Lucifer.

Milo is sitting at *my* table with his mug of coffee, his dumb, perfect profile looking maddeningly relaxed.

Once I have my coffee and scone, I go and stand over him, glaring and judging his basic coffee. I don't see even a hint of cream in it.

He's drawing and it takes a moment for him to look up. When he does, his eyebrows lift slightly.

"Excuse me. You seem to be in my seat."

"Morning, Whitman. I wasn't aware it was assigned seating."

"It is, Lombardi."

"Fascinating. I just sat down." He makes a show of inspecting the table and chair. "Nope. Don't see your name scratched into the wood or embroidered on the cushion."

"I'll scratch into the wood all right."

His lips twitch like he's fighting back a smile. "Tempting."

I lean on the edge of the table, trying to get a better look at what he's been drawing. A magnificent sketch of the antique chairs near the door. Why is that so annoying?

Annoyingly endearing.

Excuse me while I dry-heave.

We stare at each other. The café hums around us, but we're locked in a stand-off.

"Fine," he says finally, closing his sketchbook with an obnoxiously patient air.

I blink, momentarily disarmed.

He stands, but instead of picking up his things, he pulls out the chair across from where he'd been sitting—*my* chair—and gestures to it like he's a freaking gentleman. As if.

"Sit," he says. "We can share."

"Share?"

"It's a table, not a toothbrush." He leans in and whispers so only I can hear, "But we've kissed, so why would it matter?"

I give him a disgusted look.

Juju snorts behind the counter. "You two are gonna combust. Do it quietly."

I glance at her, betrayed. "You're taking *his* side?"

"I'm taking the side of my entertainment."

I sigh, drop into my usual seat, and scowl across the table at him. "Don't talk to me."

"Wouldn't dream of it." He takes a sip of his coffee, his shoulders relaxing like he's just won something.

"And stop bringing up that lapse in judgment," I hiss.

He doesn't say anything, just gives me wide, innocent eyes.

I growl and he laughs.

Back at the house, my dad is set up in the living room, plans and sketches sprawled across the coffee table. Dad tells Milo and me about a meeting he just had with Meredith Strong, Windy Harbor's mayor. He's keeping her in the loop with our plans and she's excited about this project, which is great news.

Things go smoother than yesterday. Until Milo brings up a floating staircase in the lodge.

"A floating staircase?" I cut in. "Are we building a villain lair? Is Batman going to make an appearance? *How is that charming?*"

"It can be done with elements that fit the look you want," he says, ignoring me. He slaps another sketch down dramatically. "Imagine this...separate from the resort, but nearby... closer to the water. A lakeside glass pavilion. Glass on three sides, floor-to-ceiling. Double-paned, well-insulated. In the winter, it'll be warm inside, with a full lake view. In the summer, we open the sliding panels along the south side and let the breeze roll through."

I narrow my eyes. "That's...actually not a terrible idea."

Dad perks up. "You're keeping the view."

Milo nods, hands in his pockets like he knows he's nailing this. "I'm framing the view. Always. We don't compete with Lake Superior. We collaborate."

I tilt my head. "Wow. How many times did you practice that line in the mirror?"

He doesn't miss a beat. "It's a good one, right? I might use it again sometime."

I shake my head. "Arrogance for days."

"Only when it's deserved." He pulls out another drawing. "Inside, we're going with clean lines and reclaimed timber beams from that old barn you mentioned tearing down, Everett. Radiant floors. Modular seating for gallery exhibits, lectures, small concerts, or meditation if someone is so inclined." He grins at my dad.

I make a face. "Always kissing ass."

He smirks. "You'd like that, wouldn't you?" he says under his breath.

I shoot him the deadliest glare I can muster.

"I'm just saying there are possibilities." His smile is ingratiating and it makes my teeth clench.

This man.

Deep breaths.

"What's all this?" I point to a drawing of flowers and stone.

That's what I really care about. How all we're doing lives with the land.

He motions to the area around the pavilion. "That's where the stone courtyard goes. Hand-laid limestone, sourced locally. Raised beds around the perimeter with native plants and herbs—some for scent, some for texture, some for pollinators. I want it to feel alive. Not ornamental."

I blink. I wasn't expecting him to have given so much thought to this already. He's already laid out a fabulous plan for the resort and cabins, a restaurant, day spa…the full gamut. But this is next level.

"There could be kinetic sculptures in the corners," he goes on. "Pieces that move with the wind. Wind chimes, maybe. Perhaps weather vanes designed by local artists. Something unexpected that plays with sound."

Dad leans over the sketches, nodding slowly. "I like that." He looks up at me. "Does this inspire you at all, buttercup?"

I hate to admit it, but it does. It *really* does.

Milo points to another page. "And here—three gas fire features, low and wide, built into rounded stone pits. Not too modern. More organic. They'll be spaced out to create heat and encourage conversation." He glances at me. "I imagine string lights overhead and fleece blankets available in winter. It's meant to be year-round. Cozy, even when the lake's frozen over."

He says it like that's easy to do.

But it's not. Designing something that works with the environment instead of against it is hard.

I keep my voice neutral. "You're heating a mostly glass structure. That's not exactly green."

He nods. "Passive solar homes work well here. We'll capture the sunshine here." He points at the southern wall. "And it'll retain heat and reduce energy use."

I look back at the view. The lake stretches out in every direction. I can picture this gorgeous glass structure out here where it'd feel like we're almost walking on water. The bones of this idea are solid.

"Wow," Dad says beside me. "I love it."

I sigh and Dad elbows me.

"Come on. Admit it. He's winning you over."

I glance at Milo. He's watching me carefully. Hopeful.

I don't give him the satisfaction of a full smile. But I do say, "It could be…magical."

The smile that breaks out on his face dazzles.

I feel weak in the knees and I'm sitting down.

This is not good.

His eyes catch mine, and something flickers. Something hot and dangerous.

I look away fast and pretend I didn't feel it.

CHAPTER TEN

DOMESTICATED

MILO

I'm beginning to think Goldie Whitman is personally trying to kill me. Not with poison or a shove off the deck, but with nitpicking every single thing I do. She shows up to every design meeting like she's emerged from a Pinterest board—perfect hair, biting commentary, and an uncanny ability to find the one architectural detail that might *not* be structurally feasible—and then she makes it my problem.

"You're going to put the steps *there*?" she says one morning, eyes narrowed. She'd be clutching her pearls if she were wearing any. "Why not just beg people to fall?"

"Great idea," I mutter, pretending to write it down on my sketchpad.

She hums. "You'd like that, wouldn't you?"

She's frustrating beyond belief. And brilliant. And unfairly gorgeous in her puffer vest and boots and that ridiculous hair that's so beautiful I want to touch it.

We've been working on the Windy Harbor project for a few weeks now, and somehow Goldie's managed to wedge herself into every aspect of it—even the parts that don't concern her. My planner? Annotated. My blueprints? Covered with sticky notes in every color with her many, many thoughts.

Yet, her ideas are really solid.

I just thought it was a lot before she quit her job, but now that she's here most weekdays too, she is a control freak to the nth degree. She hasn't moved here yet. Small mercies. But she'll be moving here full-time soon. Her house is on the market, and she brings boxes whenever she comes to Windy Harbor. I'm staying at the apartment over Kitty-Corner Cafe, which helps since Goldie is invading every other part of my life, including my dreams.

Fortunately, Everett still loves me.

And unfortunately, I still haven't talked to him about my uncle. He either doesn't know I'm related to his archrival or he doesn't care, and since I don't care that he's a Whitman, I'm going with the latter. Now, the longer it's gone unsaid, the more nervous I am to find out.

Bruce said I was spineless, and I would've never believed him until now. It eats away at me, but I've been so busy and so preoccupied with Goldie. And Everett gets weaker and weaker. I'm ashamed to say I still haven't made it right.

Goldie's twin, Tully, shows up the next weekend and I'd expected him to give me the same shit she does, but he surprises me.

"You still driving my sister nuts?" Tully grins as he offers me a handshake that nearly dislocates my shoulder. "Respect."

Goldie glares at him. "Don't encourage him."

"Too late," I say. "We're already planning our fantasy

hockey league." I point at him. "You're my number one, by the way."

"Oh, I am absolutely not letting you two bond over this," she mutters.

But we do. Within minutes, Tully and I are shoulder-to-shoulder on the back deck, trash-talking teams like we've known each other for years.

My eyes flick to where Goldie is pacing the yard with a clipboard and what appears to be an extensive collection of paint swatches.

"I take it you're a glutton for punishment," Tully says when he catches me watching his sister.

"I must be. Every conversation feels like I'm failing a test."

He laughs, but then his voice softens. "Honestly, I've never seen her like this. I expected you to be a real asswipe."

"Glad to know I failed expectations," I say dryly.

The next weekend, it's Noah who shows up carrying a toolbox and Grayson with the dimples. Grayson is three and loves worms, pine cones, and throwing rocks into the lake. He also decides he loves me, which is both heartwarming and inconvenient, because he wants me to go on worm hunts with him when I should be finalizing elevations.

"Can we keep Milo?" Grayson asks his dad as I hoist him over a puddle.

"I don't think he's the domesticated type," Noah replies with a grin.

"No, he's not," Goldie says firmly, arms crossed as she watches from the deck.

I can tell she's annoyed that her family likes me. Tully's already texted to invite me to a game. Noah asked for my opinion on renovating a client's lake house. And Everett? He handed me a bourbon last night and called me *son*.

Goldie's eye twitched when she heard that one.

It's become a game. A slow-burn game of chicken. She pushes. I push back. And in between, there are these tiny, electric moments—when her eyes catch mine and hold a beat too long, when her laughter is so genuine it knocks the breath out of me, when I forget to be annoyed because she's said something brilliant and I want to tell her she's brilliant, but I make fun of her instead.

The truth is, I like the chaos she brings. I like her sassy mouth, the way she stares into space when she stirs her coffee or tea, and the way she draws trees like they're living things with secrets. I like how she knows the name of every plant on the property and how she can tell when her dad's having a rough day just by the way he sets his coffee mug down. I like how fiercely she defends this place, even when she's being completely unreasonable. I like the way she looks at me when her guard is down, and the way her eyes fire up when she's annoyed by something I've said.

I like her. A lot more than I should.

Everett's first chemo treatment leaves him pale and weak. The man who usually stands with such quiet authority now slumps slightly in the oversized leather chair, his skin a shade too gray, his movements a beat too slow.

And Goldie?

She's the perfect combination of attentive and calm.

Her brothers have made frequent visits. They're all trying to figure out how to navigate this transition with their careers. I don't envy them. But Everett made Goldie swear she wouldn't tell them the date of his chemo treatments, and she hated that, argued until she cried, but then agreed to do what he wanted.

I hover awkwardly by the doorway at first, unsure if I should even be here, but I've grown to really care about Everett and want to make sure he's okay. Goldie doesn't miss a beat. One glance and she waves me in, her expression wiped clean of the usual fire. Then she turns back to her dad, adjusting the blanket on his lap.

"Want ginger tea or ginger ale?" she asks him gently, already walking to the kitchen before he fully gets the words out.

"She doesn't give you time to argue," I murmur, stepping closer.

"She never did," Everett chuckles, hoarse but smiling. "She used to boss her brothers around when she was a tiny thing. She could convince them to play tea party with her." He laughs again. "Now she bosses me around with ginger and electrolytes."

Goldie returns with both drinks, ignoring our smirks, focused only on getting her dad comfortable. She fluffs the pillow behind him and gently rubs his back when he coughs. She tucks an eye mask next to him and kisses the top of his head.

The way she loves him undoes me.

It shows in every breath she takes.

I don't say much. I don't trust my voice not to crack. But when her dad drifts off and she comes to sit next to me on the couch, I reach for her hand. She lets me take it, lets me thread my fingers through hers. Her other hand still holds the ginger tea, growing cold.

"You're kind of incredible," I whisper.

She looks at me, surprised. "I'm just being a daughter."

"Exactly."

She exhales a long, weary breath.

I feel a gut-punch of—I don't even know what—for her.

Warmth? Longing?

Not because she's beautiful, or smart, or stubborn enough to drive me up the wall. But because she shows up. When it's hard. When it's messy.

When most people would run, Goldie Whitman stays.

I have no idea what to do with all these…feelings.

"I'm fascinated with large families. I always wished I had siblings," I blurt out.

She turns to look at me. "Really? It's just you?"

I nod. "My parents wanted more kids but weren't able to have them…"

She winces. "That's really hard. Are you close to your parents?"

"Very."

"I don't know what I'd do without my brothers. We might all be a little too co-dependent, but it works for us." She shrugs. "I think when you lose a parent, the family either scatters with the loss or they grow even closer. We've definitely grown closer."

Seeing the way she loves her brothers makes me long for what I never had.

I call my parents after dinner. I'm pacing the shoreline behind the lake house, enjoying the longer days with more sunshine. The second Mom answers, I regret how long it's been since I checked in.

"Milo!" she says, voice bright. "You're alive. I miss your face. Lake Minnetonka is not that far, you know."

I smile. "I know. I miss yours too. And I'm sorry. Let's do dinner next week. How's Dad?"

"We would love that. Dad's here. Being nosy. Say hi, Anthony."

"Mio figliolo!" my dad booms in the background. "Come stai? You still working too much?"

"Always."

"When are you ever going to find a woman, working all the time?"

"Okay," I cut in, laughing. "We're not doing that tonight."

Mom laughs too. "Are you doing all right, honey? You sound a little...tense."

I sigh and sink onto one of the big rocks. "I'm fine. Just dealing with some stuff up here. I've been working on a project out by Lake Superior...Windy Harbor."

"That's a beautiful area. Bruce mentioned you'd been working with Everett Whitman."

"Yeah, I have," I say slowly.

Silence.

"Hello?" I look at the phone to make sure the call hasn't dropped.

"We're here," Dad says.

Another pause.

Then Mom says, "Are you sure that's a good idea? It's not something we talk about often. It's old. Silly, really. But the feud between our family and the Whitmans goes back decades. I've always tried to stay out of all of it, but I'd also be careful of getting too close to them."

"I never knew anything about it until Bruce mentioned it. And then I assumed, since you hadn't ever said anything about the Whitmans, that you wouldn't care if I continued a working relationship with Everett. Honestly, he's become a friend. I've wanted to ask—what's the story there?"

"Your grandfather and Everett's father—Augustus—were friends once. Best friends, actually."

"What happened?"

She sighs. "I haven't talked about it because I *hated* what all of this brought out in my dad and brother. Everett's father and mine went into business together," Mom says more gently. "They were starting a business together in St. Paul, but there was a falling out. Your grandfather believed Augustus went behind his back and tried to steal his idea. Augustus claimed it had always been his baby and that he was just bringing Dad along for the ride. It got ugly fast."

"Ugly how?"

"Court battles. Public accusations. Families dragged through the mud. And Bruce was always a little too eager to carry the torch. He's the one who escalated everything after Dad passed. He's been trying to outmaneuver the Whitmans ever since. Bruce and Everett went to school together and never got along."

"And now you're getting closer and closer to him," Dad says, whistling under his breath.

I run a hand down my face. "I didn't know you'd be against this too. And since we rarely talk about business relationships—even the people I get close to—I've never talked about Everett with you." I sigh. "So you're saying I'm deeper in a long-standing war than I realized."

"Yes," Mom says. "And Bruce isn't taking it lightly."

"Well, I don't like being on his bad side, but I like Everett…I respect him. And it didn't feel right, what Bruce was trying to do."

"It's okay, honey. We don't always agree with my brother either."

"But you're not thrilled I'm working with Everett."

"Not especially," Mom says.

"Everett's not his father," I say.

"Maybe not," Dad admits. "Just be careful, Milo. These things have a way of repeating themselves."

I sigh and stare out at the water, the sky exploding into shades of pink above it.

"We love you," they say together, because they're weirdly in sync like that.

"I love you too. I'll call again soon."

"Soon better mean *this week*," Mom warns. "And dinner next week, don't forget."

"All right." I laugh. "Promise."

I hang up and sit there, letting the sound of waves roll over me.

I know that it's critical that I have a conversation about all of this with Everett, but he's got more important things to be worried about right now.

I work in Minneapolis for a few days and when I drive back to Windy Harbor, I realize how much I've missed it. I've especially missed arguing with Goldie.

When I rap on the door and she answers, her face brightens before she schools it back into nonchalance, and my life is made.

"How are things going?" I ask.

"He's sick of me hovering," she whispers, leaning forward. "He's not feeling bad anymore and now he's just cranky."

"I heard that," Everett says, shuffling to the door. "Hey, Milo. Have you come to mother me too?" He grins to soften his words.

"I think that's already covered." I walk in when Goldie opens the door wider.

"Is it ever," Everett groans. "Do me a favor and get her out of the house for a while."

"Dad!" Goldie gasps. "I'm not leaving you."

"Please." He leans over and kisses her cheek. "Please leave me. Go do something fun. It will make me feel better." His eyebrows lift and he points at her. "It's Thursday! Trivia night at The Loon…that sounds like just the thing. Huh? Huh?" He elbows her and she scowls at him before sighing.

"Okay. But only if you promise you're feeling fine."

He holds his hand up. "I swear. I'm feeling fine." He points at me. "You should go with her. We can get back to work tomorrow."

I open my mouth to protest and he shakes his head.

"I think the only place you've been is Kitty-Corner Cafe. You gotta see more of this place than that!"

My eyes narrow and I bite the inside of my mouth. "Okay. You'll message us if you need anything?"

He holds his hand up again. "I swear. I'll message if I need anything."

I glance at Goldie. "I see now where you got your sass."

She rolls her eyes and starts reciting a list of rules for her dad to follow while she's gone. He shoos us out the door.

"How's your week been?" I ask on the brief drive to The Loon. I feel strangely nervous with her in my SUV.

"Well, you saw that man at the house. Impossible." She grins fondly. "The highlight of the week was the chocolate-covered strawberries I made last night." She sighs. "I can never resist a strawberry. Put chocolate on it and I'm gone." Her hand flies up in the air and I laugh.

Trivia night at The Loon is already loud when we walk in. There are lights strung haphazardly above the booths and the floor is sticky with beer. Someone yells, "Oh, fer the love of Pete!" across the room, only to be met with, "I s'pose you thought you could schlep that attitude in here!"

Goldie beams. "Man, I've missed this," she says, practically bouncing as she spots someone.

A woman who looks like she could be the *We Can Do It!* lady walks over from the corner booth. Except her bandana is blue with white polka dots and her tank top says *Trivia Slut*.

"That's Erin," Goldie tells me. "Brace yourself."

Erin thrusts a laminated sheet at me and waves a dry-erase marker. "You must be the architect. Very sexy, very proper. You look like you alphabetize your porn collection and silently judge people who don't."

"Doesn't everyone?" I say, raising an eyebrow.

"Ah, he's quick, Goldie." She winks at me. "And you're hot. I get it now."

"Erin," Goldie groans, but she's laughing as she motions for me to sit down. I do, and she slides into the booth beside me, her knee brushing mine. "Hands off. He's on my team."

"Baby, you know I swing for the other team," Erin says, giving Goldie a mischievous smile. She points at me. "My last name's Cox and I've had enough Cox in my life…that's why I turned to women."

With that gem, she winks and walks away.

Goldie groans. "That is not what I meant, and you know it," she yells over the racket.

"Team name?" the host calls, looking at us.

Goldie grabs the marker from me and scrawls: Whitman Genius + Architect Who Thinks He's Right About Everything.

"Menace," I mutter.

She beams. "*Thank you*." Her head tilts. "Or would you

rather do a celebrity couple moniker?" She crosses out the long title. "Mildie? Golo?"

My eyes narrow and I grin. "Couple, huh? Damn, Goldie, I knew you were into me, but I didn't know you were ready to commit."

She lets out an aggravated sigh and her cheeks flush bright pink. "You and Erin are determined to misunderstand me tonight. I see how it is."

But she doesn't cross out Mildie/Golo, which pleases me more than it should.

Round one begins. I answer the first three questions before she even uncaps the marker. She snatches it from me by question four.

"Excuse me," she says under her breath. "Let a *real* nerd shine."

"Oh, it's on," I whisper back.

We start tallying points between rounds. It's neck and neck with a team called Smarty Pints, and Goldie is vibrating with competitive energy.

"I will *die* before I lose to that tourist in the Green Bay jersey," she hisses, pointing two tables over.

"He's a cheesehead," I say flatly. "We cannot lose to that."

Round five is a disaster. One of the questions is a *Star Trek* reference and Goldie writes down an answer with such confidence that I hesitate—then erase it and write mine.

When they announce the answer…it's hers.

She looks at me, completely insulted. "You didn't *trust* me?"

"I panicked!"

"You're sleeping on the deck tonight."

"I don't live with you."

"You're moving in *just* so I can throw you out," she snaps.

That gets me. I laugh and she straightens, trying to hold back her laugh too, but then it bursts out of her and we can't stop. We barely get it together enough to keep playing the game.

But we manage and we win by two points. Goldie jumps out of her seat, arms raised victoriously. I stand too, caught up in her joy, and we both yell something unintelligible while Erin films the whole thing on her phone.

"You're buying me a drink," Goldie says, breathless, her face flushed from adrenaline.

I step closer. "Only if you admit I carried us through the literature round."

"I will *never* admit that," she says, poking me in the chest.

And then it's like she realizes she's touching me and she drops her hand, taking a step back.

She turns on her heels and walks off, and I sigh.

I guess the brief truce was a fluke.

CHAPTER ELEVEN

ESCAPADES

GOLDIE

I open up the family thread.

> <photo of the WINNERS> $100 to the first to congratulate us on WINNING

As we're weaving through the crowd toward the door, I bump into someone hard enough that her drink sloshes a little.

"Oh gosh, I'm so sorry," I say, instinctively reaching out even though it's too late to help. "Get one drink in me and I'm like a newborn fawn."

The girl—no, not a girl, definitely a woman, and one who has the most perfect cheekbones—glares at me.

"Watch where you're going," she snaps, brushing past me.

I turn to watch her walk away.

"Okay, excuse me," I mumble.

Erin leans in, eyes wide. "Who is that? You know what?" She grabs my arm. "She came into the store the other day and asked a bunch of questions. She asked about you."

"She did? What did she want to know?"

"Well, she asked about all of you…if you were usually in town full-time or not."

I frown. "I wonder why."

I look around the bar, but now she's nowhere to be found.

"Hmm. Well, she didn't seem very happy to see me." I snort and grab my jacket, trying to shake off that little dark cloud. "It's been so fun."

I hug Erin and she groans when I hug too tight. "Okay, okay. *I'm* glad to see you, but you're cutting off my circulation."

I let her go, grinning at her, and she grabs her stuff.

"I'll walk out with you guys," she says.

I try, but I can't quite get my arm in the sleeve of my jacket. Milo takes it from my hands and helps me out.

"Tipsy trivia queen," he murmurs.

"I have a tiara in my purse," I whisper back. "Don't test me."

My knees are a little wobbly as we walk out of The Loon. Milo takes one look at me as I try to open the passenger side door of someone else's car and gently steers me away.

"Not ours," he says patiently, unlocking his SUV. "Come on, Mildie. You're with me."

Erin blows me a kiss and yells, "Don't make out too hard!"

"ERIN," I hiss, not too tipsy to set her straight.

"Bye, babe! Bye, hottie!" she sings, disappearing into the night.

She lives close enough to walk, lucky her.

Inside the SUV, it's warm and quiet. Milo's hand brushes

my leg when he hands me a bottle of water, and suddenly I am *very* aware of him. And this tension that's been building for *weeks*.

"You make an okay partner," I say, leaning my head back against the seat.

He glances over at me. "Yeah, you too."

We're quiet as he drives. And then, all too soon, we're home. When I glance at Milo, he's staring at me.

"That was fun," he says.

I nod, my eyes dropping to his mouth.

He lets out a quiet laugh.

"What?" I ask.

"You should probably not look at me like that."

"Like what?" I whisper.

"Like you want me to ruin you."

The breath leaves my lungs and my skin prickles with heat. Suddenly, I'm leaning in before I even decided to.

"Milo—"

He's already there.

My insides light up when I feel his lips on mine. His mouth. It's the mouth of *champions*. The lips that dreams are made of. He kisses me like today is our last day on Earth and the only thing he cares about is worshipping my mouth. He savors me, slowly at first. His hand comes up to cradle my jaw, thumb sliding just under my ear as his lips part mine. I gasp—he takes it. And then all carefulness is gone. I lean into him, my hand fisting his shirt, and he tugs me closer. Pretty soon, I'm halfway over the console.

It's hot and clumsy and crazed. I don't even know who moans first. Might've been me. Might've been him.

He pulls me closer, his hands on my waist, and guides me into his lap. He groans when I'm flush against him and I let out a little whimper. He's *so* hard. I want my hands all over him, my mouth, every part of me touching him.

We don't stop.

And it just gets better.

Better than the art gala. Better than a minute ago.

His fingers tangle in my hair, tugging just enough to tilt my head back as he moves to my neck. I'm making sounds I didn't know I could make—soft, needy, wrecked.

He's ruining me all right.

"You're so beautiful, Goldie…"

His lips find mine again and we kiss until the windows fog. My hands are under his shirt, and his breath stutters when I rake my nails down his chest. My thighs are shaking with how much I want him.

Milo pulls back, resting his forehead against mine. Our breaths are fast and shallow, and his hands stay firmly on my waist.

"Have I just complicated everything?" he asks.

"Yes," I whisper.

It sobers me right up and I start to move off of him. His fingers lift my chin and his eyes meet mine.

"I've wanted to do that since the last time we kissed." His voice is husky. His expression is raw.

So have I, but I don't dare tell him that. I don't trust myself not to complicate things even further because I want to repeat everything that just happened, and then some.

This time when I move off of him, he doesn't stop me. I open the car door and he opens his.

"Oh, you don't have to get out," I tell him.

"I'll make sure you get to your door okay," he says.

I fumble with unlocking the door, feeling all thumbs. Dad surprises us by opening the door.

"Need help? Looks like someone had a drink," he teases.

"Hi, Dad," I say, kissing him on the cheek. "You okay? I'm surprised to see you up."

"I was just having a cup of tea. But Milo, do you mind if I show you something? I have an idea and it won't take long."

"Sure," Milo says.

"Good night." I lift my hand in a small wave.

Milo's eyes slide over my face, pausing on my mouth. I swallow hard.

I stop by the kitchen, putting away a few of the dishes I'd left in the dishwasher, and when I go to my room, Milo has already been there. A glass of water sits on my nightstand. Two ibuprofen. And a little square of white paper, torn from what looks like his sketchpad.

Sleep well. You need your rest so you can hurl more insults at me tomorrow.
~M

I put my hands on my heated cheeks and try not to smile.

I wake up feeling like I didn't sleep at all. My hair is a nest on top of my head, and my shirt is doing this off-the-shoulder thing that makes me feel like an eighties chick. I smile, thinking of what Milo would say if he knew I'd made an eighties reference. I'd never hear the end of it. I'm in my underwear, but one glimpse down the hall shows my dad snoring, so there's time to go make a quick cup of coffee and toast. I'm too tired to brave Kitty-Corner Cafe today, and frankly too nervous about seeing Milo. I shuffle down the stairs toward the kitchen and then stop dead in my tracks.

Milo is on my couch. It looks like he's just waking up, his long body stretching like a glorious panther.

And before I can slowly back away, his eyes find mine.

His dark lashes blink once. Then again.

And then he smirks.

"You slept over?" I ask.

Okay, it seems to be stating the obvious, but I'm not operating on all cylinders here.

He moves his arms behind his head. His voice is all morning gravel and cock-itude as his eyes travel down my body.

Oh shit. The only time I've ever regretted not wearing pants.

"Your dad fell asleep over there." He points at the chair. "And the door wasn't locked. I didn't want to leave like that."

I snort despite my mortification. "It's Windy Harbor. No one locks their doors."

His brow crinkles. "Oh. Right."

"Okay, good then," I mumble, turning around and marching back toward the stairs.

"Hey, Goldie?"

I pause at the bottom step, slowly turning my head.

He's sitting up now, his hair mussed, T-shirt wrinkled, and smile warm.

"You're cute when you're flustered."

I stare at him. "You're infuriating when you open your mouth."

He shrugs. "Didn't seem to mind last night."

My mouth drops and he chuckles.

"You kissed me first, you know," he says.

I gasp. "I most certainly did not!"

"But you *wanted* to. Same difference."

I bolt up the stairs, his laugh following me all the way.

He is *so irritating.*

My teeth grind together.

And he's *impossible* to ignore.

I'm sure he's used to having hookups wherever he goes. Everything about him screams *I can get whoever I want, whenever I want.*

Well, I refuse to be another notch on his belt.

Those (very impressive) balls will just have to get bluer because I won't be his convenient little summer fling.

Later, my phone startles me with all the vibrating from our family texts.

> **DAD**
>
> I was going to ask you all to send photos to cheer Goldie up. She's turned into quite the grump with Milo around. But after seeing the picture from her that came through at some point in the middle of the night, I think she must be turning it around.

> Grrrrr. Wait—what picture?

> **NOAH**
>
> Geez. Believe me. We've noticed the grumpiness. <Photo of Grayson's smiling face> Guess we have Lombardi to thank for turning that frown upside down.

TULLY

<photo of a family of geese crossing a busy street> I'm going to text Milo right now to thank him.

Scrolling up as fast as I can. Oh *my* God. Apparently last night I sent a photo of me cuddled up to Milo, smiling as wide as I can smile, and looking like a loopy, lovesick fool.

I groan into my hand.

CAMDEN

<photo of a strawberry smiley face on pancakes> I didn't get much sleep last night, but Goldie's picture is making it worth it to be awake.

DYLAN

<photo of the Dachshund cuddled up to him> Bill says howdy! And that he thinks you and Milo look cute together.

TULLY

Bill? You named him Bill? What the hell?

> I am NOT a grump. But Grayson and Bill are the only ones I want to see right now. Seriously, Bill? Okay, pictures of the geese will do as well. And as you can see, I'd had a drink. Otherwise, I never would've been smiling next to Milo Lombardi.

DYLAN

Sure sounds like you're a grump. You're the sunshine of the family! That is your role in the Whitman family. No changing the lineup now. What is going on? He seems like a great guy!

> Someone else can handle the sunshine for a while. And you would think that Milo's a great guy, Dylan.

DYLAN

> What does that mean?

I sigh. I've got nothing. Milo's kiss has robbed me of my snappy comebacks.

TULLY

> I've had to take the sunshine role in this twindom. For some reason, everything Milo does makes Goldie irrationally irate. However, this picture proves otherwise. You look PRETTY happy in this picture, Golds.

> It's highly unnecessary and a stretch to say irrationally irate. <Photo of my hand, giving them the bird>

DAD

> Ahem. See what I mean? Maybe I should leave you and Milo alone today too, and see if he can work his magic again.

> Ugh.

CHAPTER TWELVE

LOST

MILO

Noah and his crew started working on the renovation this week. He was able to bring his crew and find others who had worked with Everett in the past to come on board, so the project will get done faster. The quality of Noah's work is some of the best I've seen, bar none. And they're just getting started.

They're starting with the lodge, which will transform what was formerly a quaint North Woods hotel into a sprawling Rivendell-esque resort. It's going to be unbelievable. Grand, yet exuding coziness and charm. I'm freaking obsessed with the plans, if I do say so myself. I can't take full credit for them—Everett and Goldie have contributed greatly—but playing on such a large scale has been the job of a lifetime.

At least it's felt like play…even though Goldie keeps me on my toes at all times.

That woman…

She's avoided me all week and *it is driving me crazy*.

When we have to interact, we're back to our banter with bite.

If I can't kiss her, I may as well keep her riled up.

The woman is maddening, to say the least.

Camden is coming soon to contribute his ideas on the restaurant, and then we'll work on the condos and smaller cabins. I've been toying with a surprise for Goldie, but I've got to think about the logistics a bit more.

I walk along the path toward the resort and see Goldie with Josh, one of the guys on Noah's crew. He's an annoyingly good-looking guy and nice enough…but he can't take his eyes off of Goldie long enough to do his fucking job.

Her head falls back as she laughs at something he says, and I see red.

I stalk over there and when she turns to see me coming, her smile drops.

"We need to review material samples," I say.

Her eyes narrow and she folds her arms. "Okay, let's review them."

I mimic her stance and wait. When she doesn't budge, I sigh. "They're at the house, not here."

"Why didn't you bring them out here?"

Because I didn't come up with this excuse until just now.

"It's hot out here," I say instead. "And your dad is inside."

That softens her and I feel the slightest pang of guilt for using her dad as an excuse, even though it's the truth. He is inside. He just doesn't know we're looking at material samples.

"Okay," she says.

She looks at Josh and smiles again. What is her deal?

Why has she given me all forms of hell since the moment we met and yet looks at him with melty eyes?

"I'll talk to you later, Josh," she says.

"Sounds good, Goldilocks," he says.

I snort. *Goldilocks? Talk about unoriginal.*

His eyes meet mine and he gives me a knowing look.

I give him a look of my own. One that says *I'm watching you*.

She doesn't speak to me all the way to the house, and when we get there, she looks around.

"Was my dad waiting on us?" she asks.

"I thought so," I lie, looking around the room.

She heads to his bedroom and I put my fingers on my throbbing temples, frustrated that I'm succumbing to this childish behavior.

Fortunately, he comes out with her and is happy to look at the samples. We're done all too soon and go our separate ways.

It was a mistake to kiss her again.

"It's so good to see you," Mom says.

I kiss both her cheeks and then hug her tight. My dad is next and he kisses both my cheeks, laughing as he hugs me.

"Mio figliolo." He leans back, both hands on my arms, and studies me. "You look good. There's something different about you."

"I've been spending a lot of time outside…"

His lips pucker. "Maybe that's it. You look happy. There's a little light in your eyes that I haven't seen in a long time."

I shift, unsure of what to say. I do feel happier lately.

"I guess it's been nice to get out of the city more. I didn't realize how tired I was from working so much…and I'm still working a ton, but it feels different in Windy Harbor. The pace is slower, being by the water is invigorating in a way I didn't know I needed."

"And what are Everett and his family like?" Mom asks.

"Everett is great. Easy to work with and I can see why he's been so successful. He's a true visionary. And his family is equally talented. Goldie is a lot to handle, but her ideas are excellent."

"Who is Goldie?" Mom's head tilts.

"Everett's daughter."

"Ahh. And how old is she?"

"I don't know. 25? 26 maybe?" I frown.

I guess I've never really thought about how old she is. She feels like my equal in every way, but I suppose she's probably a little younger than me.

"Is she pretty?" Mom asks, shooting me a look that says she sees right through me.

My mouth parts and I shake my head, starting to laugh. "I'm not even in the door yet and the questions are already endless."

"Well, get in the door and we can ask more," Dad teases.

I put my arm around his shoulders as we walk to the dining room. My parents live right on the water in Lake Minnetonka and the sun is dancing across the water. Their view is beautiful. I'd always thought one day I'd have my own home on this lake, but now that I've been staying by Lake Superior, it's in my blood. I guess I could always have a home in both places…

We catch up over dinner, and then the conversation turns back to Goldie. I should've never brought her up.

"So, this Goldie girl *is* pretty, huh?" Mom asks.

"She is," I say reluctantly. "And she's opinionated, and

feisty. Colorful. Absolutely infuriating. She wants to have her hand in *everything*, and she doesn't let me get away with shit."

Mom's head tilts and then she starts laughing. "You *like* her!" She clasps her hands together like this is the happiest news.

"She's all right," I grumble. "She's a lot of work, is what she is."

And it takes a lot of work to not think about her every minute of the day, I almost add, but that would just lead to more questions that I don't want to answer.

Mom's eyes are amused as she says, "Well, I hope to meet her. You should bring her over sometime. She sounds like my kind of woman."

"Sounds like she's his kind of woman too," Dad teases.

They both laugh when I roll my eyes.

My mom's shoulders stiffen. "What am I saying? She's a Whitman!" She shakes her head. "I'm so excited about you finally being interested in someone, I momentarily forgot the woman is a Whitman. Maybe you ought to distance yourself a bit, go out on a date with someone else. It's probably just that you're spending so much time together."

And I miss her when I'm not.

"She's really gotten under your skin, hasn't she, son?" Dad asks.

"That's one way to put it." I sigh. "Now, can we please talk about something else? I finally have a break from her. The last thing I want to do is think about her right now."

I've wondered obsessively about what she's doing tonight. If she went out at all, or if she's home with Everett. Is she wearing that green shirt that makes her eyes look the same shade? Or maybe those tiny red shorts that make it so hard to concentrate…

I hope she ate enough. Lately, she's been so focused on Everett eating something that she forgets to feed herself.

My heartbeat skips a beat as another thought comes to mind. That Josh guy better keep to his fucking self. The last thing she needs to worry about is some needy ass guy who thinks books are good fire starters. So help me, if he interrupts her night of rest, I'll need to have a word with Noah and tell him to keep his crew in line.

What am I thinking? I'm from the enemy camp. She'll find more reasons than ever to hate me when she figures it out.

My dad snaps in front of my face and I blink groggily, like I'm coming out of hypnosis.

"Ah, there you are. I thought we'd lost you to the Whitman girl." Dad laughs at his own joke.

"Ha. Very funny," I volley back, but it packs no heat.

We all know he's right.

I *am* lost to the Whitman girl.

There are messages from Everett the next morning.

"Can you give me a call? We've hit a roadblock."

I try to reach him, but it goes to voicemail.

On my way back to Windy Harbor, I get a call from an unrecognized number. I accidentally push the button to accept the call and there's a long pause before the person's voice fills my SUV.

"Hello? Is this Milo Lombardi?"

Dammit.

"Yes, it is."

"This is Helen from the Star Tribune. Can you confirm

that you are working on the new resort project in Windy Harbor?"

"Yes," I say.

"Can you comment on what the locals are saying?"

I'm quiet and she keeps talking.

"Our source tells us that the locals are protesting the project. Can you comment on that?"

"No."

"Are any of your sculpture ideas incorporated into this new build, or is that just for the Minneapolis Sculpture Garden?"

"No comment."

I hang up. Should've done it sooner, but then they'd be writing that I was rude and uncooperative. It's probably what they'll be saying anyway.

When I pull up to Everett's, reporters are lined up outside. Why are they making such a big deal about this?

Everett likes to call it a mini Rivendell, but the scope of his plans isn't anything outrageous. Yes, it'll be beautiful and special, and no comparison to what was here before, but he's not doing anything drastic to take away from the land.

I'm happy to drive past the reporters, but I don't have a good feeling about this.

According to Everett, the locals have been happy about the boom this will bring to their small town. The lodge that was here before used to provide a lot of jobs and it's been a huge loss for it to go downhill. Maybe the people who voiced their approval have changed their minds.

CHAPTER THIRTEEN

FEELING REAL

GOLDIE

The past twenty-four hours have been unreal. I stand at the front window of the lake house, chugging coffee like that will help mellow me out. Outside, two vans are parked at the end of our long driveway, one with a news logo on the side, the other unmarked. A guy paces back and forth, talking on his phone, while another talks to a camera. There's a girl with long wavy hair who has such a big camera in front of her, I can't even see her face as she snaps pictures.

"Are we in the middle of a scandal right now?" I mutter.

"If so, it's a boring one," Dad says, coming up behind me. "Oh, there's a girl out there now. You think Camden will have any trouble getting through?"

"I'm sure he can handle it. I warned him there were reporters out there."

The phone has rung off the hook since first thing this morning. Dad's cell. My cell. Even the landline we keep because Dad's too weirded out by getting rid of it altogether. Most of them want a quote about how the people in town are upset by what we're doing. They want drama and I have no idea how they even found out about us.

"Oh good, Milo's here." Dad hurries to the door to open it when Milo's close, and I take the moment to glance in the mirror and check my hair before he comes inside.

In theory, the past few days have been a nice break from Milo.

Except I thought about him ten bajillion times, so it didn't *really* feel like a break.

My heart vaults into the ground and does a sweeping up and down motion when I see him. He looks good this morning. He's toned down the formal wear considerably since we started working together and while I appreciate him in a button-down shirt or a suit, the sight of him in a T-shirt stretching over his *stellar* body is…better than I'd like to admit.

It's mouthwatering, okay?

I will never admit this out loud, not in a thousand years.

But it's true. My brain is chanting it like a mantra.

"Hey," he says when he walks inside. "What's going on?"

His eyes meet mine and do that slide down my body that makes me forget all about the reporters outside.

Which is why I say, "Not much."

Dad and Milo do a double take at me and then Dad laughs, thinking I'm joking.

"Hey, Milo. It's been nonstop this morning. *Someone* is fanning the flames and I didn't even know a match had been struck." He looks bewildered. "I'm not sure where all of this is coming from."

I shake my head slowly. "Me either. You said you talked to everyone, right?" I move next to Dad and close the curtains tighter so we won't be tempted to stand here all day. "Ope, look at that nasty curtain, chasing our stalkers away."

He chuckles and sighs, moving to his chair and sitting down. "Yes, I did. I spoke to all the business owners first and then at the town meeting, where everyone and their brother seemed to show up. But the calls we've gotten today have been another story."

"Have you talked to anyone yet?" Milo asks.

"Nah." Dad waves his hand. "I'm not worried about it. This one is." He motions toward me. "But Camden and Tully should be arriving any time and I'm too excited to see them to think about that mess out there."

"Has it slowed anything down at the lodge today?" Milo asks.

"The only thing that's slowed down is us getting over there," Dad admits. "Noah said everything is running there as planned."

"Good." He nods.

"Sorry if my call worried you," Dad tells Milo. "I've settled down since I left that message this morning."

"Well, the reporters have thinned out too," I add, "so that helps."

A sound at the door grabs our attention and then Camden and Tully are walking inside.

"The hell is going on out there?" Tully asks.

I give Camden a huge hug and then Tully, while Dad fills them in on everything. A little while later, Camden asks to see the progress, and we go out the back way, avoiding the reporters.

We show him the plans once we're out there, and then take a look at the resort.

"I can't believe how much has been done already,"

Camden keeps saying. "Wow. *Wow.* This is feeling real, guys."

"You like what you see so far?" I ask.

"I'm blown away," he says, glancing at us. "It's going to be incredible." His gaze goes back to where dozens of men are at work, and he shakes his head. "Okay. I feel bad that I wasn't fully invested before. I wanted to be, and I was still going to do it either way, but…now…this…I am *in*."

He's grinning when my dad pounds him on the back.

"You just needed us to do the hard part before you got all in?" I tease.

He pokes my side and I yelp, laughing. "Exactly. No, seriously. I did have a hard time getting the old lodge out of my head. The dark walls and the floral carpeting." He makes a face. "Don't get me wrong, we loved our time over here, but it was more about exploring outside than all that." He points to the lodge. "Now, the inside will match the splendor of Lake Superior."

"Watch out, he's getting poetic now," Tully says, squeezing Camden's shoulders.

Camden pretends to be annoyed for a second but laughs with everyone else.

Noah comes out to say hi to Camden and Tully, and one of the workers calls me to another room with a question about outlets. When I come back out, it's just Dad and Noah.

"Where are the guys?" I ask.

Dad's brow furrows. "I believe they were just going to lunch. I told them to bring us back something."

"Nice of them to invite us," I say under my breath.

"I also asked your grandmothers to come. I'd hate it if they heard about my health from anyone besides me, and with all that's going on outside, I don't trust that they won't."

"That's probably a good call. When will they be here?"

He checks his phone. "I expect them sometime within the hour."

"Okay, good."

I tap away on my phone to my brothers, getting more annoyed with them by the second.

> I like eating too, you know. Where's the loyalty?

No answer.

Grandma Nancy and Grandma Donna are punctual, arriving forty-five minutes later. My dad goes out to meet them, despite the reporters jumping to attention when he walks out, and I do my best to block them from getting a shot of him. It requires quick footwork because these people are not messing around—they're the only ones who stuck around, so they're serious about finding out what's going on. It's sad if it's such a slow news day that they'd consider this newsworthy.

I reach the car first and get hugs from Grandma Nancy before rushing around to Grandma Donna.

"You said there'd possibly be activity out front, but I didn't believe they'd still be here nearly an hour later," Grandma Nancy fusses.

She hugs Dad and then studies him, a crease forming between her brows. "You look tired, honey. Are you not sleeping?" She loops her arm through his, holding onto him even while Grandma Donna hugs him. "You can take a nap while I make some soup and popovers…"

"You don't have to—" he starts.

"I most certainly do. It's been too long since I've seen ya

and it shows!" She smooths down his shirt and smiles up at him.

"I should've brought that sweater I've been knitting for ya," Grandma Donna adds. She looks at me and grins. "I *did* bring that knitted toaster cover I've been telling you about."

"Great," I say, with all the enthusiasm I can muster.

We get inside and Dad asks them to sit down with him before rushing off to make food. He has to swear that he's not hungry right now before Grandma Nancy will let it go. They reluctantly sit down and I look at my dad, silently asking if he wants me to stay. He nods slightly and I sit on the couch next to Grandma Donna. Grandma Nancy is in the chair closest to Dad.

"I need to talk to you about something," he says. "I haven't wanted you to worry and I still don't, but I want you to hear this from me." He reaches out and takes his mom's hand and she goes still, as if she already knows she needs steadying.

I take Grandma Donna's hand and she pats the top of it. The energy in the room intensifies and I press my nails in the palm of my free hand, trying to hold back tears.

"I have a very positive prognosis and I feel really good about my chances of recovery, but I have cancer," he says, and they both gasp. "I've started chemo, and it's not been too bad so far."

Grandma Nancy's face crumbles immediately and he reaches out for both of her hands, holding them on her knees.

I put my arm around Grandma Donna when her shoulders begin to shake with her tears.

My dad's eyes are glassy as he looks over at me and Grandma Donna.

"I'm so sorry for this news," he says. "But please...we

have to trust that I'm going to be okay. And if not…then it was my time to go, right?"

"I can't lose you," Grandma Nancy cries. *"I cannot lose you."*

He gets up and hugs her and we're all sobbing by now. We all gather around him, hugging hard.

Finally, he clears his throat and wipes his face. "Okay, enough of that. Goldie has been a godsend. She's taken care of me…more care than I need." He gives me a pointed look, and I giggle and hiccup. "We have to be positive."

Grandma Donna pulls one of the many tissues out of her pocket and blows her nose. "Okay, we can do that. Right, honey?" She goes to Grandma Nancy and they look at each other for a long moment before Grandma Nancy finally nods.

"Yes," she says softly and then a little stronger, "*Yes*." She turns to look at my dad and points her finger at him. "I'll be positive, but you are not getting rid of me. I hate to tell ya, but I am gonna be a *pain in your wazoo*. You think our girl here has been too motherly?" She reaches out and squeezes my hand then taps her chest, all while staring Dad down. "Your mother here will not back down. I am going to make sure you are fed and looked after and I won't hear another word about it."

"She's not the only one," Grandma Donna says. "When you married my girl, you became my son too," her voice cracks, "and you need all the family you can get right now."

Dad exhales and his lip trembles as he nods. "Okay. You know there's room for you here. I don't think it's necessary, but you're welcome to stay." He looks at me and sighs.

"It'll be like a party," I tell him.

He rolls his eyes. "Yeah, where I can't get away with *anything.*"

"Darn tootin'," Grandma Nancy says.

I get some work done and while Dad's napping, I go into town for a little bit. The grandmothers shooed me out the door, telling me I needed to get some fresh air. The reporters gave up and hopefully that's the last we'll see of them. I push into Cox Trading Post, and the little bell jingles. I'm still stewing over the Milo-Camden-Tully lunch and instead of baking my feelings, I decided to come see Erin.

"Look who's here," Erin calls. "You look like you could use a hug or a wooden moose lamp. Maybe both."

"I'm not opposed to either, although moose lamps are not typically my aesthetic."

Erin taps her chin. "We just got a box of hand-painted mugs with raccoons wearing sweaters and sneakers."

I give her a look.

"I know." She lifts her hands. "Mom had to have 'em. I tried to talk her out of the whole thing. But take a look. They're weirdly cute."

I go where she's pointing and nod. "Huh." I pick one up. "You're right. They *are* cute."

Next to the mugs are a line of T-shirts I haven't seen yet. I pick one that says "Don't Moose With Me" to be my new sleep shirt. At the counter, I put a bag of Cherry Sours on top.

"You doin' all right?" Erin asks. "You're awfully quiet."

She rings me up but keeps studying me.

"I'm fine. Annoyed with my brothers at the moment, but fine. What's up with you? You're looking at me funny."

"Nothing," she says, a little too innocently. "You know what's cute? The Havanese puppies the Alexanders have right now. They're ready to adopt in a week. Carrie says they're already potty-trained. I think I'm gonna get one and you should too. We'd have siblings and they could play with each other when we get together."

"It doesn't feel like a good time for a puppy. I've been crazy busy."

"It's never a good time for a puppy, but it's always a *good time*."

"Is that going on your next T-shirt?"

"Maybe." She smirks. "It could apply to a few things." She points at me. "I'm not done with this topic. You need a puppy in your life. Your dad too. It'd bring him lots of joy."

I tilt my head, eyes narrowing. "You might be onto something there. Dad would love having a dog again. It took him forever to get over Meggie, but this might really cheer him up."

"I knew it. Yes. Meant to be. Here, this is Carrie's number." She jots down a number. "She asked me to help spread the word, so she'll be excited to hear from you."

"Thanks. I'll keep thinking about it. Did you hear about all the reporters outside our house?" I ask.

She frowns. "No. What's up with that?"

"I don't know. Seems like some people in Windy Harbor might not be as glad that we're updating the resort as we thought."

"I haven't heard anyone say anything negative," she says. "And you know I'd hear it if it were being said."

"It's so weird. We've gotten calls all morning and then there were reporters out there—two stayed for hours."

"That's creepy. I don't like that. I'll mention it to my brother and I bet he'll do regular drive-bys. You know Justin loves him some Whitmans."

I grin and hug her. "Thanks. I already feel better."

"That's what I'm here for." She leans in. "And don't be too hard on your brothers. They love you."

"Okay." I sigh. "I'll try."

But then I get a text with a photo of them cheersing with their beer at lunch and am over all of them.

I guess Ava Piper was right—I am trite…and possibly predictable and self-indulgent too.

When I get home, I walk in with my things and everyone is standing there, looking sheepish, even Dad…like they're up to no good.

"What's going on here?" I ask, setting my things down. "You're making me nervous."

The door opens and Noah jogs in. "Did I miss anything?"

Tully shifts to the side and there's something big behind them. It's covered with a big blanket and Camden lifts the blanket to the side slightly, so I can see a large wooden crate with my name written on it.

"Is Dylan in there?" I ask, hopefully.

That cracks them up.

Noah lifts his phone and Dylan waves.

"I wish," he says. "I'll be home soon, but not quite yet."

"We had something shipped to Cox and weren't sure how we'd hide it from you, so we figured we may as well give it to you now," Camden says, smiling at me.

"What is it?" I ask, excitement building. "You know I'll never turn down a present."

They all laugh.

"Dad has told us how much you've been doing, how helpful you've been, and—"

"She rarely leaves my sight," Dad interrupts Camden.

"Try to sound a little less irritated by that, Dad," I say, which makes him cackle.

"I love you, buttercup. Only you could make these days fun. I've loved this time with you."

My eyes fill with tears. "I've loved it too," I tell him.

"Okay, enough or we'll all be crying," Tully says.

"I've already started," Grandma Nancy says, dabbing her eyes with tissue.

I squeeze her hand.

"Dad said you're the reason his spirits have been so high, and the whole reason this project has gotten underway so fast is because of all the work you've put into it, and we just wanted to let you know that we've noticed and we're grateful." Camden tugs the blanket off the rest of the way.

I walk over and Milo hands me a crowbar. When I pull off the lid, I gasp. It's a huge, *gorgeous* easel made of walnut. And on the front is a small engraved plaque that says G. Waters.

My hand flies to my mouth. "You guys…" I look at all of them, standing there looking so sweet and vulnerable. Even Milo looks like he's set his cockiness down for the moment.

"I love it. I love you. Thank you," I say, my voice breaking.

They swarm around me, hugging me until I'm swallowed up. When we finally break apart, my eyes meet Milo's. He's standing a couple feet away from all of us, looking on with a soft expression. His lips lift.

"Thank you," I say again.

Sometimes feeling seen is all it takes to be okay.

CHAPTER FOURTEEN

TO MY KNEES

MILO

Something isn't sitting right with me about all the reporters suddenly camped out on the Whitman property. When I have a free moment, I step outside and pull out my phone. I'm surprised when my uncle answers on the first ring.

"You change your mind about joining the right side?" Bruce says.

"No. But talk to me straight—did you have something to do with the animosity toward the Whitmans in Windy Harbor that popped up overnight?"

There's a low chuckle and I have my answer. "You wound me, Milo. It's not too late. You can turn this around and make everything up to me."

"What are you up to?"

"What am I *up to*? You make it sound so salacious. The citizens of Windy Harbor deserve to know that the new build going up in their town will destroy their way of life. Not only will this disturb the waterfront and cause an eyesore to that pristine land, but it will bring more traffic into town than they know what to do with. People live in Windy Harbor to get away from the hustle, not to invite more of it into their backyard."

"So, what—you're whispering in their ear about going against Everett Whitman so you can get your hands on that property? You think your plans for that land are any better?"

He makes a sound of derision. "Milo, Milo, Milo," he sighs. "I had such high hopes for you when you were the youngest person to ever receive the Pritzker Award. What a fucking waste." Another exaggerated sigh. "I don't need the land. I know when to move on. My plans are simply this: Keep Everett Whitman from getting what he wants."

It's quiet for a second as he lets me digest those words.

"You're really that petty?" I finally ask.

He chuckles. "Petty? I'm saving the community of Windy Harbor, Milo. And you should know…Whitman is no saint." He pauses for a second and I look at the phone to make sure the call hasn't dropped. "Come to dinner tonight. There's someone I'd like you to meet."

It's on the tip of my tongue to say no, but his next words are different…earnest.

"It's important, Milo. Please."

I'm the one sighing now. "I can't tonight…I'm in Windy Harbor this week."

"Even better," he says. "So am I."

What is going on here?

"It doesn't feel right, Bruce. I'm working with Everett. I *like* the man. I consider him a friend."

"We're family, Milo. Doesn't that mean anything to you? I'm asking you to meet me for dinner. You're really going to turn down a meal with your flesh and blood?"

I pinch the bridge of my nose and stare up at the clouds that almost look fake, they're so perfect. "All right. What time?"

"Excellent. Let's meet at The Hungry Walleye at six."

"Okay. And Bruce? As far as business goes, Everett Whitman could be a snake, but I've signed a contract with him. I'm not going anywhere."

"I hear ya. I'll go easy on you tonight. Like I said, there's someone I want you to meet."

"Got it. I'll see you tonight."

I hang up and stare at the water in frustration. I don't have a good feeling about all of this.

I turn to walk toward the house and Goldie is standing there with a strange expression.

Shit. What did she hear?

She smiles and my smile back is reluctant. Maybe she didn't hear anything.

"I hope I didn't interrupt," she says.

"What? No." I shake my head. "I was done. What's up?"

"The guys said you told them where to find the easel." She leans forward conspiratorially. "They're not usually quite *that* good with gifts. I mean, they're not terrible, but—" She wrinkles her nose and I relax even more.

She couldn't have heard my conversation with Bruce. There's no way she'd be talking to me like this if she had. And why the hell have I kept it quiet anyway? It's not like I can help who I'm related to. But I'm on such tentative ground with her as it is…

"I need to stop while I'm ahead, don't I?" She laughs. "Anyway. I just wanted to thank you."

"It was their idea," I say, shrugging. "I just suggested the easel."

"That had to be weeks ago…when things weren't very… when we weren't—" She wrinkles her nose again.

"Semi-peaceful?" I suggest, grinning.

She fights a smile. "Is that what we are?"

"I thought we were getting there. Until you started avoiding me."

"What? Don't be silly," she says, biting the inside of her cheek.

This woman. She's relentless. Determined to bring me to my knees.

"I'm never silly, Mildie."

She snorts and rolls her eyes. "Okay, Golo."

I grin and we stare at each other until she starts blinking fast.

"Dad's got a craving, so I'm trying to make sure he gets what he wants. You in for dinner with all of us tonight?"

"I—" Shit.

Why do I feel like I'm betraying her?

Because in a way, you fucking are.

Fuck me.

"I wish I could. I have plans for tonight. Maybe tomorrow?"

She stares at me for a beat and then nods. "No problem."

When I walk into The Hungry Walleye, a young girl moves into action without making eye contact. She grabs a menu and only looks up when I say, "I'm meeting someone."

Her mouth drops and she freezes mid-step. I turn around to see what's wrong, but there's no one behind me.

"He might already be here." I look around and see Bruce at the table in the back. "Spotted him." I point to the back table and the girl continues to stare at me. "Should I take that back with me?" I ask, pointing at the menu.

Her mouth moves slightly, but no words come out. Finally, she blinks and motions for me to follow her. She must be painfully shy. I suffered that affliction, especially when I was younger, and it's no fun. Bruce and I say hello to each other and the girl hands me the menu once I've sat down, but she doesn't leave.

"Cat." Bruce snaps his fingers and she jumps. "Bring my nephew a Wild Brunette." He shakes his head, chuckling when she gulps and nods. He shoots me a look when she scurries away, and I glare at him.

"That was rude," I say.

"You've got those Granger good looks. You should use it to your advantage— it comes in handy when you need it."

I sigh, already wishing I hadn't come. One of the first things that ever put the nick in my uncle Bruce's armor was the way I saw him treat servers. I was young, but it bothered me so much, that someone I loved could be so demanding and rude to others.

I open the menu and hear a throat clearing. I look up and see an older woman grinning at me. She smacks her gum and puts her hand on her hip, jutting it out to the side.

"What'll you be havin'?" she asks.

"What's good?"

"Our walleye is the best in the state. Bob caught it this mornin', and my batter is better'n sex."

My eyes widen and Bruce laughs.

"You know what, Helen? You're right about that," Bruce says. "Give us a few of your baskets."

"I'll give you my basket all right," she says, still grinning at me. She blows a bubble and it makes a loud pop. "Fries or Tater Tots?"

I swallow, feeling like she'd batter me up if she could. "Fries."

"Tater Tots are always the way to go," Bruce says, shaking his head.

"Gotta agree with ya there." Helen nods and winks at Bruce.

"Okay, Tater Tots," I agree.

"You still on that health kick?" Bruce asks when Helen walks away.

"I wouldn't say a health kick necessarily, but I guess I stay away from junk most of the time."

I haven't eaten anything fried in five years, but this feels like the wrong place to bring that up. Helen's affection feels like it could turn on a dime.

"So what's this dinner about, Bruce? You said there's someone you want me to meet?"

He leans forward, about to say something, when his face brightens. "Oh, there she is now. Ava! Over here."

I turn, expecting to see a new girlfriend or at least someone close to his age, but she's closer to my age—late twenties or early thirties, sharp green eyes, sleek dark hair, and a command to her walk that has everyone in The Hungry Walleye sitting up straighter and taking notice. Bruce likes them young and he's older than my mother, but this woman feels a bit young, even for him.

Shit, this better not be a setup.

"Hi, sweetheart," Bruce says, standing to kiss her cheek. "Thank you for joining us. Ava, I'd like you to meet your cousin, Milo. Milo, say hello to my daughter, Ava Piper."

I blink. "Your *daughter*?"

"Hello," Ava says. "I'm not sure what we do…shake hands? Hug? High-five?" She laughs and I do too, shaking my head.

"Wow. Hello. It's nice to meet you." I stand up and shake her hand. "This is crazy."

Bruce's chest puffs with pride. "Isn't it amazing? She found me recently. All these new-fangled tests that people can do now…"

"23andMe," Ava fills in, sitting down across from me.

"I don't have many cousins my age…and definitely not many who live close. You've probably met Dahlia though," I say, tilting my head toward Bruce.

Dahlia is his daughter with his ex-wife and she's about eight years younger than me.

"No, I haven't yet." Her eyes move to Bruce and he shifts uncomfortably.

"Do you live in Minnesota?" I ask.

"I do now." She lifts her hand and when Helen looks over, she points at my drink. "One of those, please. And your walleye basket."

Helen nods. "Coming right up."

Now that I look at Ava more, I see similarities to my uncle and my mom. "My mom will be so excited to meet you. Or have you met her already?"

She shakes her head. "Besides Bruce, you're the only family member I've met."

"Oh…have you told anyone else about her?" I ask Bruce.

He shakes his head. "You're the first."

"Well, I think I'm in shock." I shake my head and laugh. "And Mom is going to kill you for not telling her immediately."

"I hope it's a happy shock," Ava says, smiling.

"A very happy shock."

She asks a lot of questions about my work and my life. She's easy to talk to and I quickly lose track of time. Ava has recently moved to Minneapolis and is a freelance journalist. She's smart and funny, self-deprecating in a light-hearted way. I almost forget Bruce is even sitting across from us, despite him being the reason I've been so stressed lately.

He excuses himself to use the restroom while our food comes. I take a few bites and then lean back in my chair, still digesting this news, when I hear the unmistakable sound of Goldie's laugh.

I look toward the entrance, and there she is, walking in with her family. She's changed into a short summer dress and her long, blonde hair spills over her shoulders. I want to tug on that hair and kiss some of that sass out of her. And then when that sassy mouth inevitably returns, I want to do it all again.

But then her eyes land on me and brighten for a second... until they flit to Ava.

Her expression freezes and then shifts, her jaw tightening. She stops walking and Tully bumps into her from behind. She brushes it off and forces a smile for her dad, and then looks everywhere *but* at me.

I start to rise, maybe to wave her over and explain who Ava is, but before I can move, Bruce returns.

Goldie's eyes narrow like she's seen a snake.

She pivots hard and says something to Tully. He directs them to the only table that doesn't go past ours.

"Oh look," Bruce says. "It's the family that everyone has thought was perfect...until now."

My eyes narrow on him and I stand, excusing myself, and walk over to the Whitmans' table. Before I can get there, Goldie pushes her chair back and walks toward me.

"Hi," I say carefully.

"Well, this explains *so* much."

"Let me explain—"

"No. You're here. With her. *And* him." Her tone slices through me, saccharine sweet, but venomous.

"She's not…it's not…what you think."

"Really? Because what I think is that we were finally—finally—starting to be civil, and then I walk in and see you on a date with some rude woman who's been asking about my family, and with *Bruce Granger,* our sworn enemy."

"Wait, first…what do you mean *some rude woman*? You know Ava Piper?"

Her eyes get huge and she looks over my shoulder like she's willing Ava to burst into flames. "*That's* Ava Piper? You have got to be kidding me." She crosses her arms and turns that glare back on me.

My balls shrivel a little, but then my dick raises its head belligerently, never one to back down on a sparring session with Goldie Whitman.

"What is going on here? What game are you playing? I want the truth. *Now.*"

I scrub my hand over my head. "There's no game, I swear."

But I sound guilty as fuck.

"Oh, come on. Ava Piper wrote the only negative review of my art installation. Then she acted like I was a pariah at The Loon the other night. Erin says she's been asking a lot of questions about my family. And then Bruce? Well, you know about the family rivalry between our family and the Grangers. You've heard us talking about him and said nothing!"

I wince. "I just met Ava tonight. She's my cousin. Bruce just found out she's his daughter."

Surprise crosses her face.

"And I know I should have told you sooner that I was related to Bruce, I just didn't know how. I haven't seen eye to eye with my uncle for a very long time."

"Wait, am I hearing this right?" she sputters. "You're related to Bruce? How did you fail to mention this?"

I wince again, like I've been struck. "I'm so sorry. I should have said something sooner, I wanted to…but it's not an issue for me. I swear it isn't. My mom is a Granger. She's Bruce's sister, but my mom has stayed out of it. As soon as I knew Bruce was trying to purchase the property, I let him know I wouldn't do anything to jeopardize my relationship with Everett."

Her eyes glitter with tears and anger, flicking over my face like she's not sure whether to believe me or punch me.

"I can't believe I let my guard down for a second with you," she says, and I feel the blow.

CHAPTER FIFTEEN

COTTON BALLS AND BUSYBODIES

GOLDIE

"Goldie, please." He steps closer, lowering his voice. "Whatever horrible thing you're imagining here, don't. I am one hundred percent behind you and your family. Beyond being a relative of Bruce, I have no interest in carrying on any bad blood between our families. Believe me when I say that."

"I don't know what to believe. If there was no agenda here, you would've been upfront about Bruce. My dad is sitting over there wondering what the hell is going on. This is the last thing he needs right now. He trusted you." I shake my head, stunned.

I can't believe *I'd* started to trust him.

My hands tremble and I need to sit down. Fast.

He runs his hand through his hair. "I'll talk to him."

He turns and heads to my table and I follow him, not wanting to leave my dad to deal with him alone. By the time I get there, he's already apologizing and saying the same things to my dad as he said to me.

My dad looks tired.

"The truth of it is, I didn't tell you I was a Granger because it never mattered to me that you are a Whitman," he tells my dad. "I only recently heard about the feud for the first time. It was something my mom never spoke about. She didn't agree with the way my uncle and grandpa handled things and didn't instill that bitterness in me. And when I realized Bruce was still intent on giving you trouble, I let him know I was standing with you. It's no excuse, but I had good intentions. I didn't want to bring more stress while you were going through chemo. I think so highly of you, Everett...you and your whole family."

He takes a deep breath and looks miserable, but he's obviously an excellent liar.

The difference between my dad and me is that my dad seems to believe him.

"If you say that's the way it is, I believe you, son," my dad says.

My mouth falls open. He's really going to let him off that easily?

My dad's head tilts as he smiles fondly at Milo. "I always thought your mom seemed different than the rest of her family. I can see why you turned out to be such a good egg. Your dad must have a good head on his shoulders too." He nods as if that settles it.

"Dad, don't you think it's suspicious that all this drama started...and it turns out that Bruce is in town? He's got the perfect mole right here." I wave my hand toward Milo, who starts shaking his head.

"I assure you, I have kept everything we've discussed private. I signed a contract with you, Everett, and I take that very seriously. I plan to see this job through to the end and to do so with integrity," Milo says.

"That's good enough for me," Dad says. He glances at me and smiles. "Don't worry, buttercup. I've been dealing with Bruce for a long time. I've got my family beside me and I don't intend on letting him ruin my night. If I've learned anything from having cancer, it's that life is short and grudges and hatred are not the way I want to live my life." He smiles at Milo. "I'd ask you to join us, but I'll let you get back to Bruce and that young lady. I'll see you tomorrow."

Milo nods. "Thank you, sir. Have a good night." He raps on the table with his knuckles and turns to look at me once more before walking back to his table.

"That woman looks familiar," Tully says, glancing at Ava.

"I thought so too." Noah nods.

I'm about to tell them my thoughts on Ava Piper when Helen walks up to take our order. And then I decide to put Milo and Bruce and Ava out of my mind for the rest of the night and enjoy the time with my dad and brothers. As my dad has been saying so much lately, time is short. We need to enjoy it with the people we love.

And whatever was beginning to crack open between Milo and me?

It just slammed shut again.

Hard.

I'm not dealing with Milo today.

Nope.

Every time the image of him laughing with Ava freaking Piper, Bruce's art-critic daughter from hell, comes to mind, I get angry at him all over again.

My dad might trust him, but I don't.

More than ever, I don't.

I manage to avoid him all day, once turning around and walking the other way when I spot him across the property. By the end of the day, I'm exhausted. Noah has a few questions for me about the plans and I deal with those and then call Erin.

"Puppies," I say when she answers. "I'm ready."

"Meet at Carrie's in ten?" she says, no questions asked.

"See you there."

Carrie's house smells like cinnamon and the Garden Phlox flowers that are blooming by her front door. She ushers us in, giddy. "The puppies just woke up from a nap. Come on back."

The moment we step into the room, we're rushed by a flurry of floof. Five marshmallows with wagging tails tumble over our feet.

"Oh my God," I breathe. "I wasn't prepared for their cuteness."

Erin already has a silky black puppy in her arms. She holds it up and kisses its nose. "Look at this face. This is therapy right here."

A smaller white one bounds over to me and belly-flops right on my foot. When it looks up at me, I melt even more. I swear it's saying, *Hi, I've chosen you.*

"Okay," I whisper. "I choose you too."

I scoop up the puppy and it nuzzles my chin before nestling against my chest. I don't stand a chance. We never had a dog growing up because my parents always said we were too busy, and they were always doing different house projects where a puppy would be in the way. I didn't even know if I was a pet person.

But oh my goodness, this is love.

Carrie beams. "Looks like you've been won over. They're ready to go today if you want them!"

Erin and I exchange a look and nod. We're done for.

On the drive back, my new furry sidekick sits in a little nest of blankets on the passenger seat. Every time I glance over, he's looking up at me adoringly. I pull into the driveway, feeling lighter than I did earlier. Maybe it's reckless to adopt a puppy in the middle of a family project during a stressful time, but I feel pretty good about it.

Dad's in the living room looking like he might've just woken up from a snooze when I walk inside. He's covered with the blanket Grandma Donna made. After they found out about Dad, they made a trip home to get their things the next day and were back that night. They haven't stopped fluttering over him since. I'm surprised they aren't now.

"Where are the grandmas?"

"Making more food than any of us will ever eat." He points at the bundle in my arms. "What's that?" he asks.

I hold up the puppy and his head pops out of the blankets. "This is the new love of my life. Also known as a puppy."

He squints. "Is it alive?"

"Well, actually I stopped at Build-A-Bear on the way home," I tease.

I walk past him and set the little guy next to Dad on the couch. He scrambles out of the blankets and toddles over to Dad.

Dad looks at him and then at me, shaking his head. "Oh my, buttercup. You've always added more to your plate than any one person should. I mean, it's not like we don't have a million other things going on right now."

"I know, but hear me out. I thought we could use some joy around here. Erin got his sister, and just look at him." I pick him up and hold his face next to mine. "Look at this face."

Dad tries not to smile. "He looks like a cotton ball."

"Yeah, but cotton balls don't cuddle." I set the puppy back on the couch and he moves to Dad's side and curls up.

Dad glances down and his face softens, like he's not totally immune to this little guy either.

"Well, I guess we're stuck with him," he says.

"Yep."

"Have you named him yet?"

"No," I say, curling up in the chair across from him. "I thought we could name him together."

Dad's quiet for a beat. "What about…Crouton?"

I snort. "Crouton?"

"Yeah. Small…but a vital addition to any salad."

I pretend to be concerned. "Are you feeling okay?"

He chuckles. "Yes. Admit it, it fits him."

I look down at the puppy, who's now flopped dramatically on his back. "Okay, I'll consider it an option. Any other ideas?"

"Kevin."

I stare. "Kevin," I repeat. "That's as bad as Dylan naming that cute little guy Bill!"

He shrugs. "Kevin." Like it's only natural that he'd think of Kevin. "He looks like a Kevin, doesn't he? He's got that mischievous twinkle in his eyes like Kevin Bacon did in *Footloose.* That guy could dance the daylights out of a warehouse and also sings a little bit and likes to hang out with his wife after umpteen years. Seems like a solid name for a solid guy."

I cackle at this. "Okay," I say, cracking up again. "Kevin, it is."

The puppy lifts his head and lets out a tiny sigh like it's confirmation.

Dad nods, satisfied. "Kevin Whitman, the first of the Whitman puppy line."

"I like it." I giggle.

I pick Kevin up and take him back to my chair, where he turns around and around until he finds the perfect spot on my lap before plopping down and falling asleep.

And just like that, Kevin is part of the family.

Grandma Donna walks in. "Oh fer cute!" she says, coming over to pet the puppy. "Whose dog is this?"

"Ours," Dad says. "His name is Kevin."

Her smile drops. "Oh fer cryin' out loud, a dog is the last thing we need around here."

"But look how happy it makes Dad," I say, pointing at the dopey grin on my dad's face.

She looks at Dad and softens. "Well, I s'pose it won't hurt. Just don't let him get underfoot—we don't need any falls 'round here."

"Okay, Grandma." I smile at her and then lift Kevin's head. He keeps sleeping. "Just look at that face," I say in a goofy voice.

The doorbell rings a few minutes later. Or at least it feels like it—I've been too caught up staring at this adorable little creature.

"Were you expecting someone?" I ask Dad.

He shakes his head.

I set Kevin on the chair and get up to look through the peephole. "Oh, it's Val and Sandy. Should I answer it?"

The doorbell rings again and Kevin's head pops up. He starts barking and it's shocking, the volume that can come out of the little fella.

"Sure, why not," Dad says.

Because they're nosy little busybodies who find something negative to say about everyone, I want to say but refrain. Instead, I open the door and say, "Hi!" with a wide smile because…Minnesota Nice.

"Goldie Whitman," Sandy says, already halfway through the door before I've invited her in. "Oh my gosh, you look just like your mother. That hair! That smile!"

Val follows behind her with a little wave, eyes scanning the house like she's doing inventory. She jumps when she sees my dad sitting there quietly. She laughs, clutching her chest. "Ope, you startled me, Everett. We didn't wake you, did we?"

"No, just chatting a little before bed." I scoop Kevin up and cuddle him to my chest.

"Well, we won't stay long," Sandy says. Her voice lowers. "We were just wondering…about the renovation next door on the Snodgrass lodge." She leans closer and whispers, "I heard they took the money and retired in California."

Dad nods. "I hope so. They put in a lot of time and care into that place, and we hope to do the same."

"So you're still going through with it? I heard," Sandy pauses and looks at Val, and it seems to bolster her resolve. "I heard there was a lot of controversy with it and that it might not be happening anymore."

"There's no controversy," I say.

Val waves a hand. "People in town are just curious. You know how rumors spread. We just wanted to see for ourselves what's going on. We were surprised we didn't hear the details about all the updates you're doing on the lodge and condos sooner."

"Funny," I say sweetly. "Dad talked to everyone in town before he bought the land, both of you included, and you were all in support of what a thriving business like this could potentially bring to Windy Harbor. Didn't get a single negative response, did you, Dad?"

"Nope."

"My guess is someone…maybe you could tell us who…is trying to stir up dissent."

Grandma Donna crosses her arms over her chest and huffs in support.

"I…don't know anything about that," Sandy says, adjusting her purse strap. "We'll let you get back to your evening. We just wanted to say hi and, you know, check in." Sandy's brow furrows. "Oh, and are you feeling okay?" She looks at Dad and takes a step closer. "I'm so sorry to hear you've been sick. Val and I can put together a meal train for ya. You'll have more hotdish than you know what to do with." She laughs and Dad gives her a pained smile.

There's good hotdish and then there's Sandy's.

"I think we're good there, but thank you, Sandy," Dad says. "That's nice of you."

"If you change your mind, let us know," Val says, smiling at him.

Val has had a thing for him for years, but my dad pretends to not notice.

"We appreciate the thought," I say, walking them to the door. "Thanks for stopping by."

Kevin lets out a single bark that makes both women jump and I laugh.

"Kevin! I didn't know you had it in you!" I tell him. "Good night." I wave to the women and shut the door behind them.

My brothers walk in.

"What is that?" Tully says, staring at Kevin.

"This is our puppy." I hold him up high. "Guys, meet Kevin."

"Kevin?" Camden laughs. He pets his ears and Kevin leans into his hand. "He's really cute."

Tully and Camden take turns petting him.

"Did Noah go home?" I ask.

"Yeah, he needed to get back to pick Grayson up from day care," Tully says.

"You just missed Sandy Parker and Val Mitchell," Dad says.

Tully wrinkles his nose. "What did they want?"

"They wanted to know if we're really going through with all the renovations and such...acted surprised that it's still on." I groan. "Basically itching for gossip and stirring the pot."

"Maybe with different steps into the renovation, we could have little events going on. Like when the pavilion's done, we could have a concert and a food tasting to give them a view of what the restaurant and general vibe will be like," Camden says.

"I love that idea! Maybe something fun for fall. There'd still be a little time to plan that." I sigh and stare up at the ceiling. "I should've pushed harder for them to say who's got them all rumbling about this."

"There's no question it's Bruce," Dad says. "I'm just surprised he hasn't caused more trouble by now."

"He's probably distracted from finding out he has a daughter," I say.

"What?" Dad sounds floored.

I glance at him. "That woman that was with them tonight. *Ava Piper.*" I roll my eyes.

"*That's* Ava Piper?" Tully asks.

They've all heard me griping about Ava Piper and her stinking review.

"I didn't know it until last night, but yes. Can you believe it?" I reluctantly hand Kevin over to Camden's grabby hands.

"Well, that explains why she had all those nasty things to say about you," Tully says. "She's Bruce's daughter. That should make you feel better about everything."

I glance at Dad and pause. "Dad, are you okay?"

He swallows and nods slowly like he's coming out of a stupor. "Yeah, I'm…I'm fine."

We all look at him and then at each other. He doesn't look fine. He looks pale and shaky. I walk over and grab the blanket near him, putting it over him.

"Are you cold? You should probably go to bed," I tell him, bending over to kiss his forehead. His skin is clammy.

"Yeah, I think I will go to bed." He looks at each of us and smiles, but it's weak. "I love you all. It sure is nice to have you boys and my buttercup under one roof."

We're quiet when he leaves, concerned about what the future might hold.

CHAPTER SIXTEEN

BALLOTS

MILO

I knock on the Whitmans' door and wait. Everett's told me to just walk on in, but with Goldie doing everything in her power to avoid me after seeing me with Bruce and Ava the other night, it doesn't feel right to do that.

I hear high-pitched barking and frown, looking around for the dog. Nothing.

Goldie opens the door, trying to grab a tiny white ball of fluff.

"Shh. It's Milo freaking Lombardi. He's not worth the energy," Goldie croons to the pup.

She's in leggings and a paint-smeared sweatshirt. Loose hair is falling from her messy bun and her cheeks are rosy. She looks beautiful.

The dog stands next to her and keeps barking with his whole body. She scoops him up and he stares at me smugly.

I grin. "You got a dog?"

"I did," she says coolly, stepping aside so I can come in. "His name is Kevin and as you can see, he has excellent instincts."

"Kevin." I chuckle. "Is he trained to attack all men who talk to you, or is it just me?"

"I haven't trained him yet. He just sensed your," she waves her hand all around me, "atmosphere."

"My atmosphere," I snort.

"Your lying, betraying atmosphere."

I cringe, reaching out to pet Kevin and he growls, the tiniest teeth bared.

I hold out a hand and say, "Hey, little guy. I come in peace."

He sniffs my hand and nestles into Goldie's arms. My eyes meet Goldie's.

"I don't think he likes you," she says.

I lift an eyebrow. "He takes after you, huh?"

She shrugs.

"Goldie." I sigh. "I'm just trying to figure out where we stand."

"We don't stand," she says.

We stare at each other for a few long seconds.

"How's Everett?"

"He's a little better now."

He had chemo two days ago and I haven't seen him much since then.

"I'm glad." I watch her pet the adorable dog with the ridiculous name and my heart swells with something I don't want to name. "Can you please stop avoiding me? It's making it really hard to do my job when everything we say has to go through your dad or Noah."

"I don't mind it."

"Well, I do. We had a good thing going."

"Speak for yourself."

"I am speaking for myself!"

Kevin growls again when I raise my voice and I sigh, this time speaking softly.

"Can't we just talk about it? You really think I'd work with Bruce to sabotage you?"

"I don't know what to think. But what I *know* is you lied. And I don't have room for liars in my life."

"I believe you do know, but then you latch onto every possible reason to think the worst of me. I feel terrible that I didn't tell you the truth from the beginning, but your distrust of me was there before this. What are you so afraid of? Who did you *so wrong* that you don't trust *anyone*?"

A look crosses her face and she takes a step back, swallowing hard.

"Shit. Goldie, I shouldn't have said that. I'm sorry." I take a step back too.

"I've learned my lesson the hard way. I was engaged once," she says softly. "Wes Chandler. I thought I'd hit the jackpot. He adored me, I adored him. Everyone did. My family, my friends, his professors at school. He was the perfect guy who did everything right." She shakes her head and her eyes are glassy. "He liked that I was creative, wasn't threatened by my big dreams, didn't mind that I'm a lot…" Her eyes shoot to me like she's daring me to argue with her.

Finally, I take the bait and tease her. "You *are* a lot, but in a good way."

"Mmm. Yeah, no. You don't get to sweet-talk me." Her eyes soften and I feel hopeful that maybe she doesn't really hate me after all.

But then they get defiant and I'm not hopeful at all.

"He had everyone fooled," she says. "Me, most of all."

"What happened?"

"I found out that the entire two years we'd dated at school, he'd had a girlfriend he was also engaged to back home. He went by his middle name at school and wasn't on any social media, and was a little funny about taking pictures, but I thought it was just because he wanted to *live in the moment*. That was his line and I thought that was so charming and unique." She rolls her eyes. "I had my wedding dress, invitations, flowers, *everything,* planned and paid for. His college roommate was the one to finally tell me the truth, and I think that was only because he knew Wes was really going to marry the other girl...which he did, the week before *we* were supposed to get married."

"*Fuck*." I've moved closer to her again and she's softly petting Kevin's ears. I want to find Wes Chandler and destroy everything he's ever worked for.

She glances down at the little puppy and blinks, a tear falling down her cheek. She swipes it away.

"I hate talking about it. I *don't* usually talk about it. Ever. I avoid even thinking about it. It's the most humiliating part of my life." She shakes her head when more tears fall. "I'm not crying because I still love him. I haven't loved him in years. I'm crying because I was such a fool."

Her eyes are devastating when she stares up at me. I put my fingers on her chin and lift it up, so she won't look away.

"You could never be a fool," I tell her. "You're the smartest person I know."

She lets out a shaky laugh. "I'm a lot smarter now." She takes a deep breath, a big step back, and resolve washes over her face. "And I will *never* be a fool again."

Fuck. Me.

"Have you been in love?" she asks.

"I thought I was."

"When?"

"It was six or seven years ago."

"What happened?"

I make a face. "If anyone's been a fool, it's me. Roshana. We weren't living together, but occasionally she'd stay at my place when I was out of town. I think she was pushing for that, but I wasn't ready for that. Anyway, I flew in earlier than she was expecting and I caught her on my desktop, transferring a large sum of money to her bank account. Sort of broke my trust." I lift a shoulder. "I would've gladly given it to her if she'd asked, but once she did that, I saw it wasn't the first time she'd taken something from me. A watch of my grandfather's…"

The door bursts open and Camden walks in. Goldie and I jump apart like we're doing something wrong. Camden smiles and then it falters when he sees Goldie's face.

"Hey, you guys. You okay?" he asks her.

"Yes, totally. I'm fine," she says.

"Okay." He looks uncertain, but when she doesn't offer anything else, he puts his hands in his pockets. "You're just the two I wanted to see," he says.

"What's up?" I ask, while Goldie turns and tries to subtly wipe away any stray tears from her face.

"I hoped we could brainstorm a little about the restaurant."

"Oh, yes, I really hoped we could solidify the plans before you head back to Colorado," Goldie says, perking up.

"That's what I was thinking too," he says. "You know how the property has that open meadow just north of the cabins? I was thinking we could turn part of that into a working garden."

Goldie brightens. "And do farm-to-table?"

"Exactly. I've been talking to Dad about it. Real produce grown right here. Tomatoes, squash, herbs, berries, you name it. We could have a small greenhouse too, for year-round fruits and vegetables. Whatever we don't grow, we still get locally. McMann's cheese and milk. Apples from the Snyders."

"I love this idea." Goldie grins.

"I'm thinking a little more rustic than my restaurant in Colorado. A big wood-fired oven, open kitchen, that kind of vibe."

"I bet Dad loved this idea too."

"He did," Camden says, grinning. "I'm excited about it too. I just need to hire a few more people to make things run smoothly without me in Colorado. I've had one excellent hire since I was here the last time, but I need a few more. Then I can sell my house and be here full-time. I'm ready. I don't want to miss out on any of this."

Goldie hugs him. "When Dad first started talking about it, I couldn't imagine it really happening—that we'd all be here, building something amazing together—but now that I've been here a while, I'm seeing it, and I can't wait."

He pulls away and looks down at her, still holding onto her arms. "I know what you mean. I hate the reason we're all making our way back home, but I love what's coming out of it. I think this place is going to be really special."

Goldie glances over at me and sighs, like she's just remembered I'm here and isn't happy about it. She looks exhausted. It's a heavy load she's been carrying, with her dad being sick, this massive project, and the baggage that her asshole ex has left her with.

And the bomb I've dropped on her, right as her walls were coming down with me.

I want to make her load a little lighter from here on out. I don't know how to do that exactly, but I'm going to try.

"You know what?" Goldie says. "It's time we come up

with a name soon. Nearly everything else is coming together, but we're still missing that. I think we should do a FaceTime tonight and have everyone throw in their suggestions."

The intensity in the Whitman household is higher than some design meetings I've had with billion-dollar stakeholders. Camden is standing in front of a whiteboard. Tully's sprawled on the floor with a bowl of pretzels, throwing them in the air and catching them in his mouth. Goldie is bouncing on the couch next to Kevin, who's curled up on top of a throw pillow. Everett is in his chair sipping tea, calmly watching his kids yell over one another.

Dylan and Noah are propped in the middle of the coffee table via FaceTime, both squinting into their screens.

Grayson pops his head into Noah's shot, all nostrils. "Hi!" he yells.

"Hi, buddy," Goldie says, laughing and waving. "Looking good."

"Hi, auntie!" He holds up a rock and Goldie hums.

"Ooo, you found a good one," she says.

"Can everyone hear me?" Dylan shouts.

"Loud and disturbingly clear," Goldie mutters. "Okay, focus, everyone. We're naming the resort tonight."

"I submit The House of Kevin," Tully says, without looking up.

Kevin stretches his little paws out like he agrees to that.

"No," Goldie says. She reaches over and pets Kevin apologetically. "I love you, but no."

"North of North?" Everett says.

"That's a show on Netflix," Goldie says.

"Really? Gosh darn. I thought I was being really creative," he says.

"I've got it," Tully says. "Moose N Us."

Grandma Nancy cackles at that and Tully looks around proudly.

"No," Camden and Goldie say at the same time.

Tully's eyes narrow. "You're supposed to always agree with me," he tells Goldie. "I'm your twin, not him."

"Well then, act like it," she sasses back. She holds up her hand. "Oh...I thought of one. The Windy Shore."

Everyone's quiet and then Everett nods. "I like it. A nod to the town and the water that we all live for around here."

"All right," Camden says, writing it down. "So far we have..."

He starts writing on the whiteboard and talking at the same time.

"Number one, North of North, which we can't use because it's a TV show...

Number two, Moose N Us, which we can't use because it's dumb..."

"Hey!" Tully protests, laughing.

"Number three, The Windy Shore...which we kinda like...And number four, Wild Haven—that's my addition..."

"What about Windhaven?" Goldie asks.

"Ooo, that's a nice one," Grandma Donna says.

She and Grandma Nancy have been pretty quiet, just enjoying watching their family. It's sweet. Reminds me of my grandmothers.

"I like that," Camden says, adding it to the list. "I like that a lot."

"Me too," Everett says.

"What about Elm & Echo?" Noah asks.

"That's actually really nice too," Goldie says.

I nod. I like that and Windhaven, but I don't want to sway the votes. It should be their decision.

"Okay, let's add that one," Camden says. "Final contenders…"

He erases the other list and makes a new one.

1. The Windy Shore
2. Windhaven
3. Elm & Echo

"Anything else?" he asks.

No one says anything.

"Okay, let's vote." Goldie passes out papers. She looks at the screen. "Do you have paper there to write your answers?"

"Yep," Dylan says.

Noah nods.

We all write our answers, fold them up, and then toss them into a big bowl. Camden shakes them up and reads them off, tallying on the whiteboard as he goes. Then Dylan and Noah read their votes.

"All right. Two for The Windy Shore, six for Windhaven, and two for Elm & Echo," Camden says. "We have a clear winner."

"Wait, who voted twice?" Goldie asks.

"I really like Windhaven," Everett says, chuckling.

Everyone laughs.

"Windhaven, it is." Camden circles it on the whiteboard. "And I think Elm & Echo could be a high contender for the restaurant."

"Woohoo! I love it," Goldie says.

"Good job, guys." Everett grins at everyone.

"Feels big, naming the place." Goldie reaches out and takes his hand.

"It is big." Everett gets a distant look and then shakes his head slightly. "It's not just about the buildings or the land, you guys. It's about a legacy. For all of you."

Both grandmas pull out tissues and blow.

"You want to leave something behind," Goldie says softly.

He doesn't deny it.

"Are you scared, Dad?" Goldie goes over and sits at his feet, her head leaning on his knees.

He puts his hand over her hair and nods. "I am, buttercup. But I'm not going anywhere just yet. I've got things to see. Buildings to finish. A son-in-law and daughters-in law to meet…" He looks at everyone over his readers and grins. "Grandbabies to enjoy…a puppy to win over."

For the second time today, I see Goldie cry, but this time she's smiling through her tears.

"You already won the puppy over." Goldie smiles up at him.

And God help me, if I'm not careful, this woman could win me over so thoroughly, I wouldn't even recognize myself —I already don't.

If I'm not frustrated with her, I'm ready to bend her over the closest surface and show her how good we could be.

Who am I kidding? I want to show her how good we could be all the fucking time.

Before I leave for the night, I touch Goldie's arm and she pauses in mid-step.

"I'd like to think that we're becoming friends, Goldie." I make a face. "Or something…hell, I don't know what we are. But I don't want to lose it. I don't want to lose *you*." My laugh is gravelly, and I clear my throat. "I'll prove to you that I'm different," I tell her. "You can trust me."

She doesn't say anything, but I feel better for saying it

anyway. They're not just empty words. I intend to show her that I mean what I say.

CHAPTER SEVENTEEN

TOO MANY STRIKES

GOLDIE

I've felt like an open wound since finding out Milo is Bruce's nephew. Because he *lied*. For months he kept it from us, knowing that there was every reason to distrust him.

I shouldn't have told him about Wes.

There's a reason I've kept that history squashed down somewhere that I try not to revisit. I don't like thinking about those months after I found out, how small and broken and foolish I felt. I promised I'd never let myself feel that way about anyone again, and I haven't come anywhere close to that.

Until now.

And it makes no sense because Milo and I aren't even together.

But my heart seems to get more attached to him each day, whether I even see him or not.

My brain says *no, do not let him in*, and my heart says

yes, please—there's room for him right here. Trust is a precious commodity as far as I'm concerned, something that I'm not sure I'll ever be able to fully give someone else. At least not anyone outside my circle of trust.

I can't believe I was starting to let Milo in that circle.

He says I can trust him, but how is that possible? He already has a strike against him because he's a man I'm attracted to.

I can't believe he's a Granger. That would be a big enough strike in itself. Not to mention, Ava Piper is also his cousin?

But the lies.

It's just *too* many strikes against him.

I know better than to get invested in anyone with red flags, so why is he all I can think about?

I go to Kitty-Corner Cafe in desperate need of distraction…and Juju's lemon scones and coffee won't hurt. I see all the regulars—Bosco is even at the front—but it goes quiet when I step inside. Juju looks worried when she sees me and waves me back. I follow her into the kitchen where she's been piping cream into a row of eclairs.

"I was going to call you," she says, picking up a piece of yellow paper and handing it to me. "Have you seen these?"

I frown and flatten the page on the countertop.

Protect Windy Harbor. Say no to overdevelopment. Say no to the Whitman Project.

I stare at the bold font, feeling sick to my stomach. There's a grainy, unflattering photo of the project that's underway. The flyer warns of traffic congestion, corporate greed, and environmental destruction, like we're planning to build a shopping mall.

I flip it over. There's no name or group listed.

"Where did you get this?" I ask.

"They've been popping up all over. One was taped to the light pole outside and someone set this on the front counter. I asked Bosco if he saw who left it and he didn't know but said he'd seen one at Cox earlier this morning. I have no idea who's behind it."

I don't have proof, but I have a pretty good idea of who it could be.

Bruce Granger has always played dirty, and if his nephew wasn't cooperating with him to bring us down, maybe he convinced his newfound daughter to do it for him. I'd like to think this is all circumstantial, but there are just too many coincidences that involve Ava Piper.

If I'm right about her, she has played dirty from day one. And now she's going after my family? I don't think so.

The bell rings on the door and Juju lifts her thumb behind her.

"Sorry, I better get out there. I just wanted to make sure you were aware of these."

"Thank you."

I follow her out to the restaurant and she works on my coffee. I look around to see who came in and Ava Piper is setting her things down at my table. Of course she goes for my table too—she's Milo's freaking cousin.

When she walks to the counter, my blood runs hot. She pauses only for a second when she sees me. Her hair is in a sleek ponytail and with her heels, we almost see eye to eye. I hold up the flyer and watch for her reaction. Her eyes drop to the paper and then back to me.

"Is there something you're trying to say?" she asks. "I'll have my usual, Juju. Thanks."

I scoff. "You've been in town two seconds and you already have a usual?"

Juju shoots me an apologetic look as she sets my scone

and coffee out for me and gets to work on what I assume is Ava's order.

"I'm sorry, were you under the impression this town belongs to you?" Ava asks coolly.

I ignore her attitude and wave the paper. "Did you have anything to do with these showing up around town?"

Her expression is bored and I have to say, she's maintaining her cool. I'd at least have the decency to be nervous if I was confronted like this.

"I think the people here have a right to be concerned." She folds her hands. "Something your family should've considered before bulldozing a piece of Windy Harbor's history."

"We're restoring it. Reviving it. And no one had any objections until you showed up. I'm not sure they do now. What I do know is that you and your dad are stirring up trouble."

Her eyebrow lifts slightly. "Maybe the locals didn't realize what was really at stake."

"Oh, give me a break," I snap. "You don't care about Windy Harbor. You're not from here. You don't know the people or the history. Why don't you admit what this is really about?"

I think something flickers in her eyes, just for a second, but then it's gone.

"I'm just offering people information," she says.

When Juju sets the coffee on the counter, Ava picks it up and puts cash on the counter, thanking Juju.

"What the people do with the information is their decision," she says, turning to go.

"What's in it for you?"

She steps closer, voice low and icy. "Maybe I enjoy seeing the Whitmans get a taste of discomfort. Everything's gone pretty sunny for you, hasn't it, Goldie Whitman?" Her lips curl as she steps back. "Enjoy the fall. I know I will."

When she walks away, I stare after her, everything inside me shaking.

"What was *that* about?" Juju asks. "She's always seemed so nice when she comes in here!"

"She's been in here often?"

"Not super often, but maybe four or five times in the past few months?"

"I think she was threatening me," I say slowly. I look incredulously at Juju. "From what Milo said, she just found out she's Bruce Granger's daughter. Would she really take on the rivalry that seriously as a new member of the family?"

"No way. I didn't know Bruce had another daughter!"

Juliana's family lived near us in St. Paul. Our families were close, and they got a lake house here around the same time as us. It wasn't until she got her associate's degree from college that Juju decided to move to Windy Harbor full-time. She was my best friend growing up, and her brother Jackson and Camden were best friends. Still are. One of the Fairs was always at our house, or we were at theirs. So Juju knows all about the Grangers.

"My dad has told us about the Granger rivalry for years, and we always knew to steer clear of them, but I've never seen any blatant hatred firsthand until now. Dad always kept us kids out of it, but it seems like Bruce isn't doing the same thing with his kids."

Juju shakes her head. "It's such a waste. I hate it." She leans closer and whispers, "And I'm sad that I was ever nice to Ava."

I wave her off. "Don't be. I don't expect you to carry this grudge on my behalf." My eyes narrow. "But if she tries to be your best friend, I'm gonna bitch-slap her."

Juju snorts. "I'd like to see you try."

I laugh. "I'd probably bump into something first and end up hitting myself. Seriously though, I *really* dislike her."

"As much as you dislike Milo?" She smirks and puts *dislike* in quotes.

I roll my eyes. "I feel a whole different kind of dislike for him."

"Is it the kind of dislike that makes you want to ravage his body and have his babies?" Erin's voice comes in low from behind me and I startle and then smack her in the arm.

Erin and Juju cackle and I groan, shaking my head. I lift my coffee and take a big bite of my scone.

"Better go. Coffee's getting cold," I say with my mouth full and hightail it to the door.

"That's right. Leave like a scaredy cat," Erin says loudly.

"I've gotta get home to Kevin."

"I can't believe you named that little angel Kevin," Erin groans.

"What did you name his sister?" I ask.

"Sabrina…which is a perfectly fitting and beautiful name for a dog. *Unlike Kevin.*" She pouts.

I point my scone at her and open the door to leave. "Take it up with my dad."

"Fine, you win!" I hear her yelling as I walk out.

Back at the property, Milo is crouched in the gravel going over drainage for the courtyard. He looks up when I stomp toward him, and his brows draw together.

"What's wrong?" he asks, straightening.

I hold the crumpled flyer up and wave it. "Your cousin is stirring up a smear campaign against my family and this project. How great do you think she is now?"

His expression darkens and he curses. "This is…" He

shakes his head. "I'm sorry, Goldie. I'll have a talk with my cousin and see if there's anything I can do."

"So you didn't know about it?"

Hurt crosses his features, but he just shakes his head. "No," he says finally. "I didn't."

I stalk off to the house and my dad and I hang out with Tully and Camden until they have to leave for Camden's flight. We go over the new plans for the restaurant Milo had already drawn up this morning and Camden is excited about them.

Dad says his goodbyes and goes to lie down as I walk them out. I pull out the flyer and show them and it infuriates them like it did me.

"I want to believe Milo, but I just don't know," I admit.

"I think I trust him," Tully says. "He's done nothing but help us. It's not like he's bringing the project down. If anything, he's gone above and beyond, don't you think?"

I nod. "It seems like it, yes. I don't know…I hate that he's related to them! And why did he lie?" I pace a few steps and turn back to look at them. "*For so long*," I add. "I don't want to upset Dad with this. I don't think he needs to know, do you?"

"No. He's been off since seeing Bruce at the restaurant. I think we keep it to ourselves," Tully says.

"I agree. He's been really quiet," Camden adds. "And the bottom line is, we have the permits in place. Unless someone brings up any serious objections that they can legally back up, there's nothing anyone can really do about it now."

"Yeah, I just don't like to think that anyone in town hates us." I make a face. "It was important to Dad to have their support and if they're not giving it now, I'm not sure he'll be as happy about moving forward."

"Keep telling people about what we're really planning to

do and I think they'll get excited about it," Camden says. He looks at his phone. "We better go."

We hug again and I have a lump in my throat as my brothers drive away.

Later, I'm sitting out on the deck with a glass of wine, Kevin snoozing in my lap. Dad went to bed an hour ago, and it's quiet out here except for the sounds of Lake Superior lapping against the shore.

"Got room for me?"

I look up and Milo is standing there. Ugh. There's no avoiding the man. I hold up the bottle of wine and he laughs.

"You want me to chug it?" he asks.

I shrug. "I have a glass here, but chugging it sounds more fun."

"You're right."

He holds the bottle to his mouth and takes a drink. He sits down next to me and smiles, handing me the bottle. I take a long pull and he stares at me, swallowing hard.

"Feels like we should be playing Truth or Dare or something," he says, chuckling.

The wine warms my chest. My body is relaxed for the first time all day and that's probably the only reason I find myself saying, "Okay. I haven't played that since high school. Right over there." I point to the firepit closer to the water.

"I bet you always chose truth," he says, taking another swig.

"And I bet you always tried to charm your way out of answering. That's the way liars work."

He flinches but then lifts his shoulders, eyes smiling. "The charm, maybe."

"Truth or dare," he says. "Ladies first."

"Okay, fine." I narrow my eyes. "Truth or dare, Lombardi."

"Dare." He doesn't hesitate.

"I dare you to hold Kevin and pretend you're a dog person."

He reaches for Kevin and I hand him over. The puppy groggily opens his eyes and settles quickly into Milo's lap.

"That's easy," he says. "I *am* a dog person."

I harrumph. It figures.

"Truth or dare?" he says.

"Truth."

His grin widens. "Okay. Admit that I'm not that bad after all."

"You're not bad, you're awful!"

"Come on, tell the truth." He laughs. "I'd started to win you over."

"If you are what you seem…you might not be quite as bad as I thought you were. But are you?"

He smirks. "How do I seem?"

"Cocky and arrogant."

He laughs. "You were sure ready to go with those *lovely* attributes. Hmm. I'd say yes to cocky, not as much to arrogant. Arrogance is more about looking down on someone else, isn't it? And I don't do that." He makes a face. "So, really, I'm not so bad, right?"

I roll my eyes and bite the inside of my mouth, trying not to grin. How could he possibly be getting to me? "It's my turn. Truth or dare?"

"Dare."

"Mmhmm. Thought so. Okay, I dare you to tell me what you thought about me the first time you met me."

"That's just another way to get the truth out of me!"

I snort and hand the bottle back to him. "Deal with it."

"I knew you wouldn't play fair," he grumbles. He turns to look at me and I shift under his gaze. "I thought you were beautiful and mouthy and probably going to ruin my life."

My throat tightens and I laugh because I don't know how else to respond. "Two out of three isn't bad."

"I'm still waiting for you to do the third," he says. "Truth or dare?"

"Truth."

He points at me. "You scared of what I'd dare you to do?"

I shake my head. "Shush."

"Okay…tell me something you hate about me."

"Ugh. Let me count the ways." I take another long pull of wine. It must be the alcohol and his honesty that make me say, "I hate that you lied. I hate that you're impossible to stop thinking about. I hate that I want to yell at you and kiss you and set your smirk on fire. Even your hair smirks and it's *so* hot and *so* annoying."

He stares at me for a long moment, his mouth twitching, before he leans closer and *smirks*, dammit!

I groan and it just makes him laugh.

"Come here," he says, leaning closer yet. "Come here and set my smirk on fire."

CHAPTER EIGHTEEN

OH, TO BE A DOG

MILO

"Uh-uh-uh," she tsks. "That wasn't a truth or a dare, so I'm afraid I can't."

"Okay, I dare you to come here and set my smirk on fire."

She pretends to contemplate it and shakes her head. "I'm pretty sure it's the alcohol talking, and besides, I don't want to disturb Kevin."

"Not the alcohol talking," I say, despite feeling a little intoxicated just by being near her.

I stand up with Kevin and take two long strides inside. Goldie's stare heats me even through the window. I place Kevin carefully in his little bed by the couch, and when his eyes open, I tuck the blanket Goldie bought around him. His eyes drift closed again, and I walk outside and stand in front of Goldie. I hold out my hand and she takes it, standing up when I give her the slightest tug. Her look is shy and compliant and my body aches for her. I'm not thinking beyond this moment and my nearly constant desire to kiss her.

Why do we need to have anything else figured out?

She surprises me by leaning up and kissing me, and it's *so good*.

She pulls away, looking dazed, and I protest. "Please don't stop."

"I can't be thinking clearly because I don't want to stop," she whispers.

"Come here." I pull her face toward me, both hands on her soft cheeks, and we inhale each other.

She tastes like everything I want. Sweet and wild and just right. Her fingers curl in the front of my shirt and I lift her slightly, moving us until her back is against the house, and we kiss like we were created for this one thing.

The wind picks up and whips her hair around us and we never stop kissing. I want to do this all night long.

She pulls me even closer, her hands greedy, and I chase her whimpers. When I hike her leg over my thigh, she grinds against me, hot and reckless. My body shudders, my stomach bottoming out—this *woman*…she has an effect on every part of me. I want her like I want air and water and *life*. I need her. I thrust into her and she gasps, arching back. It's heaven and torment—I can't get close enough to her, and the sound she makes is so filthy, I nearly lose it.

"Goldie," I breathe, catching my breath, my forehead against hers. "I need to touch you."

Her eyes are heavy, her lips puffy. Her breath is warm against my jaw when she whispers, "Please."

I set her down and drop to my knees like I've wanted to do since the night I met her. I don't know how she managed to own me from night one, but she has.

I look up at her and she gasps when I hook my fingers

into her waistband and tug. The look on her face is pure wonder and I'd love nothing more than to have her look at me this way all the time.

Good God, the thoughts I have about this woman are unhinged. I don't let myself dwell on them very long. I press a kiss to the inside of her thigh, slow and reverent, and enjoy the way she trembles under my touch. When I shift her panties to the side and finally put my mouth on her, her fingers tangle in my hair like she's holding on for dear life. I swipe my tongue over her, and the moan she makes is long and so sexy, it hits me right in the chest.

I want to be the one to make her unravel.

I lick and suck and tease, every move deliberate. Her sounds will be embedded forever in my memory. She whispers my name over and over, like a prayer, and it's how I will hear it from now on.

I drag my tongue across her and then dip inside with precision, my flicks going faster as she shudders against me. Her sounds and the way she bucks against my mouth spur me on. My finger dips inside of her and she arches into me. I'm desperate to make her feel so good that she never looks at anyone else again.

Am I wrong to want that? Probably. But you think I care about being right?

She fists my hair, panting, a mess above me and strung so tight that she's about to break. And God help me, so am I. She looks so beautiful I can't think straight.

She tastes like *mine*.

Mine, mine, mine.

"Milo—oh my God, Milo, don't stop—*please*—" she groans.

My lips drag against her as I add another finger, and another, deeper, faster, giving her everything she'll take.

She's close. I can feel it. My body is as taut as hers, my dick begging to reach out and touch her. Every plea she makes drives me harder. I clutch her ass with my other hand, holding her steady—I could spend days worshipping that ass—and when I suck just right, her entire body arches into me.

Her cries split the air, raw and perfect.

I hold her through it, feeling her fall apart against me. My fingers slow and my mouth softens when she collapses against the house. I press a kiss on each of her thighs, then rest my forehead there, catching my breath.

When I finally look up, her eyes are wide, lips parted, her hair wild around her face.

"You're so goddamn beautiful," I tell her.

She leans down and kisses me, and I push myself up slowly, our kiss never breaking. She kisses me with a hunger that tells me she's not done with me yet, and I couldn't be happier about that. I never want this to end.

Somewhere along the way though, sense takes over and I know I should put the brakes on. I don't want her to wake up in the morning regretting this, regretting *me*, and I'm afraid if we go any further, she will.

"You okay?" I ask, brushing my fingers down her side.

"Yes," she says.

Her hands reach behind my neck and she stands on her tiptoes, kissing me again.

Then she brushes against my ear.

"But I want to make you feel good too," she whispers.

"Trust me, you do," I say, taking a step back.

She pouts and I grin.

"How about I see you to your room?" I say, wanting to prolong this night.

I'm afraid that when we wake up in the morning, we'll be back to sparring again.

She nods, her smile seductive as she tugs me into the house. When we walk inside, Kevin's still asleep in his little bed, and Goldie whispers, "'Night, Kevin."

That name never fails to make me smile and now is no different.

When we reach her room, she turns and pulls me by the collar, tugging me inside. This side of Goldie is almost more than I can take. She kisses me and I kiss her back, but I stop when she tries to pull off my shirt.

"You drive me crazy," I murmur against her collarbone.

"Good," she says, arching into me.

I close my eyes tight, my restraint hanging by a thread.

"Goldie, I want nothing more than to sink inside you and never leave, but I want you to be fully sober when I do."

"I'm fully sober," she argues.

I smile against her skin. "Maybe I'm not because I've clearly lost my mind, stopping here."

I bend slightly and pick her up, and her faint smile makes my chest ache. I lay her carefully on the bed and pull the covers up to her neck.

"Are you a gentleman in disguise?" She yawns and stretches. "You've been keeping this under wraps, Lombardi."

"I won't tell anyone if you won't." My voice is gruff and she gives me a wide smile.

I stare at her, feeling the bottom of my stomach dropping out again. *Fuck me.* When have I *ever* gotten butterflies or felt weak in the knees over a woman? Or anything else for that matter. Never goddamn ever.

Kevin pops in the doorway, saving me from doing something foolish, and when he runs toward me, I pick him up, setting him next to her. She turns on her side and he twirls around a few times before nestling against her chest. He lets out a huge, contented sigh.

"I know, little guy. You're in the perfect spot, aren't you?"

I'd give anything to be that fucking dog right now.

"Night, Goldie Whitman."

I lean down and kiss her forehead and then brush my lips lightly over hers. Her eyes flutter closed and she smiles against my mouth.

"Night, Milo Lombardi," she whispers.

CHAPTER NINETEEN

COMPARISON IS THE ENEMY OF JOY

GOLDIE

My dreams are a jumble of Ava Piper and Bruce Granger yelling at me in Kitty-Corner, people from town giving me dirty looks, and then they shift to Milo's mouth between my legs. I wake with a start, wet and pulsing around nothing, and my cheeks flame when I remember the night before. I'd be certain last night was a dream too, if it weren't for the way my chin and inner thighs tingle from his stubble. My nipples pebble as I relive him staring up at me while his tongue and fingers made me see stars. I press my fingers against my lips, feeling their puffiness from our kisses, and smile. I've never felt the way I do when he kisses me, and the memory of the magic he inflicted with his touch makes me hot all over. It's crazy to say that it was the hottest experience of my life.

I was so serious with Wes. I thought I'd marry him one day, but he never made me feel anything close to the way Milo does. He also didn't drive me crazy like Milo...*every-*

thing about Wes feels bland and dull when I think about him now. I hate comparing the two, but it's hard not to since I opened up about him to Milo.

But then I remember Milo stopping us from going any further last night, and it's like cold water being sloshed in my face. What man doesn't want to have sex when he has a willing body? All my words about not trusting him, yet I practically threw myself at him.

He must've regretted going as far as we did. I know he liked kissing me—I could feel how much he liked that. That was impossible to ignore.

I cover my face with my hands.

Oh God, oh God, oh God, maybe he didn't like how eager I was, how I tasted…how I tried to lure him into my bed.

Maybe he's still hung up on Roshana.

I jump up and stare at my reflection in the mirror. Horror stares back.

How am I going to face him today?

I shower and get dressed, gradually numbing myself in preparation for the day. I don't like being this way. I want to be an evolved human and deal with emotions and feelings head-on, but I think that ended with Wes and when I lost my mom in a car accident. Don't even get me started on my own car accident. I press my lips together after I apply lip gloss and force a smile.

"You're doing good to still be standing. Don't be so hard on yourself," I say to myself in the mirror.

But then I walk into the kitchen and Milo and Dad are sitting at the table, laughing and having coffee, and I nearly turn around and go back to my room.

Milo looks over, a wide smile on his face. It falters when he sees me.

Probably has something to do with the blank look on my face.

I'm not proud of it, okay?

But he's the one who put a halt to things, and if there's one thing I've learned about myself, it's that I need to protect this heart.

"Hey, buttercup," Dad says.

"Morning, Dad. Milo."

Dad chuckles. "Milo was just telling me this funny story about the guys out there—"

"He's a good storyteller," I say, moving to the coffee and filling my fattest mug.

"Well, you should have him tell you this one," Dad says. "I'm having Second Breakfast with Jason today." He smiles and gets up, stopping to kiss my forehead.

"You're such a hobbit. What's next? Elevensies?" I grin. "Tell Jason hello for me."

Jason is Erin's dad and one of my dad's good friends.

"I will." He points between the two of us. "I'll probably be gone a while. Stay out of trouble today, would ya?"

My face flames. "Of course. Don't overdo it, okay?" I smile at him and he squeezes my shoulder before walking out.

I move to the fridge to get the half and half. I'm pouring it into my mug when I feel Milo behind me.

"So, we're doing this, huh?" he says.

I glance over my shoulder and he's closer than I thought. I swallow hard and turn back to my coffee.

"Doing what?"

"Acting like last night didn't happen."

"I'm not acting like it didn't happen." I lift my shoulder and turn, leaning against the counter as I take a sip of coffee.

"Why are you being distant?" His brows furrow in the center and I want to reach out and smooth it.

"I'm not." My voice comes out sharper than I mean, so I soften it. "What's on the agenda for today? I thought we had a clear day."

He lets out a short laugh, and it's not the easy one he had with my dad. "Tell me we're not just rewinding to the beginning, please."

"What do you mean?" I frown and straighten, which brings me closer to him.

I move around him to the other side of the kitchen and set my mug down, lifting myself onto the countertop. He leans back, his eyes drilling into mine, and then he stalks toward me. I gasp when his hands widen my legs as he steps between them.

"Are you really gonna go back to being frosty Goldie?" he whispers and I shiver when his warm, sweet breath hits my face.

"What? No." I scowl and he scowls back.

He steps back and runs his hand through his hair before dropping it to his hip. "Last night was—" He shakes his head. "I thought we were past pretending we don't care."

"I'm not pretending anything." I gesture between us. "So there's chemistry between us sometimes. You're able to shut it on and off just like that." I snap my fingers. "And I'm still not even sure whether or not I should trust you, so it's just as well that you run hot and cold."

His mouth drops. "*I* run hot and cold?" His jaw tightens and then he lets out a sardonic laugh. "Right. I knew you'd be like this today." He shakes his head. "It's why I didn't have sex with you last night," he hisses, low enough that only I can hear. "I was afraid you'd use it as ammunition today, and I was right…without us even actually having sex."

I leap off of the counter and get in his face. "How nice that you were calling all the shots. You had it all figured out, didn't you? It's a good thing we didn't have sex, isn't it? Big, bad Goldie would've eaten you alive this morning."

He leans forward until he's an inch from my face. "You're welcome for me eating *you* alive last night."

I gasp, my head rearing back. "I didn't realize I had to thank you for the orgasm." I step back and take a bow. "Thank you. I'm glad we've cleared this all up."

"Crystal clear, Whitman." His voice is clipped, my name sounding like a curse.

"Excellent," I mutter, but there's no victory in it.

He turns and storms outside, the screen door banging behind him.

I stand there, my heart pounding like I just ran a sprint. Dad walks in and clears his throat, and when I glance over, he lifts his eyebrows.

"Everything okay?" he asks.

"Oh, you know…it's me and Milo."

"I thought you had worked things out. The two of you have seemed more peaceful lately."

"I thought we were getting there too, but—" I scrunch my face and try not to cry. "How can you just trust him so easily?"

"Come here, honey." Dad reaches out and hugs me. A tear drips down my cheek. "That man cares about you. I've seen the way you look at each other. It's okay to let someone else in. He's not his uncle. And he's definitely not Wes."

"How can I be sure?" My voice cracks.

He pulls back and wipes my tears with his thumbs. "He's too selfless to be like either one of them. Listen, buttercup, we can never fully be sure when we give our hearts away. But if we didn't take the risk, imagine how cold and empty our lives would be." He sighs wistfully. "Your mom was shut off when I met her. We didn't get along at first."

I stare back at him in surprise. "Really? I never knew that. Why was she shut off?"

Pain flits across his face. "It's a long story…and one I should tell you soon." He sighs again and looks tired. "But for now, I better go. Unless you need me here?"

I shake my head and squeeze his shoulder. "No, Dad. Go…have fun."

He smiles weakly. "I probably won't last as long as I think, so I might see you sooner than you think."

I smile. "I'll be here."

"Love you, buttercup."

"I love you too, Dad."

I take Kevin for a walk and the fresh air helps clear my head. I'm pushing Milo away, but I think it's necessary. If I let him in, I'm the one left heartbroken when he decides it was all a mistake. Or when he returns to Minneapolis, and I'm more entrenched in my life in Windy Harbor. Or when the truth comes out and we find out he's more of a Granger than he's pretended to be.

Or when he lies again about something else…I think that's what scares me most.

There are no scenarios with a happy ending for me, so as I told him, it's a good thing we didn't have sex last night.

CHAPTER TWENTY

SHARPEN THAT BLADE

MILO

It's a hard day. A struggle to concentrate, a battle to get out of my head…I'm still pissed at Goldie, but I'm just as pissed with myself.

Her words—"I'm still not sure whether or not I can trust you"—rattle in my head like a loose screw. Hell, I can be the first to admit that she makes *me* a loose screw. But out of everything she said, her lack of trust where I'm concerned is the blade that sharpens more every minute I'm away from her.

Because I get it.

After what happened between her and that scum of an ex, Wes, she deserves to be treated with so much care. And even though I don't think it's exactly fair that she holds the fact that I'm a Granger against me, I understand it. Where I messed up was in not being honest with her.

That's all on me.

Then there's the awful reality that her dad is struggling with cancer, she's already lost her mom, and even though she seems happy with what she's doing in Windy Harbor, she gave up a good life in Minneapolis to help fulfill her dad's dreams.

If I was dealing with half of what she is, I wouldn't handle it as gracefully as she has.

After stomping over the property and staring way too long at the lake, getting some work done and staring more at the lake, I'm not as angry anymore. I'm just…restless. She's burrowed under my skin, and every time I tell myself to back off, my heart ignores me.

If I want her—and fuck all, I think I have to admit to myself that I really do—then why am I stalling? My career has always come first and I've avoided complicated relationships for a long time, but it's too late for all the normal excuses.

Goldie cannot be denied. Even when she's not saying a word, her presence demands to be heard. When she's trying to hide behind her bluster, her vulnerability and strength demand to be seen.

God help me, I don't know what to do with all these fucking feelings.

That night, when I'm back at the apartment over Kitty-Corner Cafe, I call my mom. She answers on the first ring.

"Hey, son. How are you?"

"I'm…okay." I let out a long sigh.

"That answer didn't convince me! What's going on?"

"I care about Goldie Whitman. More than I saw coming." I run my hand through my hair, tugging it as I groan. "I think I'm falling for her, Mom."

Her laugh is shaky. "Wow, Milo. This is…" Her voice

cracks and sounds teary when she says her next words. "I'm so happy for you, son. But why do you sound so troubled?"

"Because I keep messing it up. She's been hurt before. She doesn't trust me because I wasn't honest about being a Granger. And we are like a match being struck around dry hay—if there's a way to spark, we do. Sometimes it's a dumpster fire and sometimes it's…" The vision of her head falling back as she chanted my name last night comes back and I have to sit down and take a deep breath before I continue. "Sometimes it's like that time we went to Disneyland when I was five and I saw fireworks for the first time. It's magical and explosive and wonderful."

"Oh, Milo," she whispers. "Then you have to win her heart. Feelings like this don't come around very often. I know you've never talked about someone like this. You can't just ignore these feelings."

"I don't want to anymore, but…I'm not sure she's ready. I don't know…I just don't know."

"What can I do to help, honey?"

"What if…could I bring her over for dinner? Show her that we're not the villains here. If I can even convince her to talk to me again. She's kind of…really mad at me right now."

"Of course! I'd love to meet her. If she's won my Milo over, she must be so special."

"She is. She really is."

"I'm so happy for you." She's for sure crying now and I smile despite feeling like a train wreck.

"Well, I haven't exactly won her over. We can't make it a solid week without being at each other's throats."

Mom laughs. "Acceptance is half the battle. Sounds like you're just now admitting to yourself how you feel and she's still fighting it. I bet if she knew how you felt, it'd go a long way in her admitting it too."

"If she feels the same way. That's a big if."

"Oh, stop. You're Milo Lombardi. You and your father are the best-looking men in the whole wide world. I know—I've traveled a lot."

I laugh. "Yeah, you're not biased in the slightest."

"I'm not. All my friends agree with me. Most of them wouldn't hesitate to go all cougar on you, and their daughters would fight to take their place."

I shudder. "I didn't need that mental picture. Esther and Desiree better keep their distance."

She laughs. "I had to give them a detailed report on your whereabouts just the other day."

"No," I groan, laughing.

"It's true. So, when are we doing this dinner? How about this weekend? Friday night? Weren't you planning to come into town then anyway?"

"Yeah. I'll see if I can talk her into it and keep you posted."

"I'm so excited." She sounds giddy. "But…do you think she'll like us? Me, specifically?"

I stand up and start pacing again. "I think she won't be able to help but like you."

"I hope so."

"Love you, Mom. Tell Dad I love him too."

"Okay. He loves you too. He's right here and saying it."

I laugh. "See you both soon."

When we hang up, my fingers hesitate, but then I don't overthink it…I call Goldie.

She answers on the fourth ring, her voice guarded. "Hello?"

I swallow, shifting on my feet. "Hey. I don't like the way we left things earlier."

She exhales. "I don't either."

"Would you have dinner with me on Friday night?"

There's a long pause. "Dinner?" she says slowly.

"With my parents," I add, the words rushing out. "I want you to meet them. I want them to meet you."

There's another pause—longer this time. I can almost hear her processing, chewing on her bottom lip.

"Milo…"

"I know it's a big ask," I cut in. "But I'd love to take you to their place."

"They're in Lake Minnetonka, aren't they?"

"Yeah…it'd be more like a weekend trip. Leave Friday after lunch and come back on Saturday."

"What makes you think we can get along for that long?"

I laugh. "I'm not sure we can, but I'd like to try. I know we're capable of having great moments together. Unforgettable moments."

I hear her quick intake of breath and wish I was standing in front of her.

"You're sure they want to meet me?" she asks softly. "Your mom's a Granger…Bruce's sister…"

"Yeah."

"So she probably doesn't love my family too much."

I wince even though she can't see me. "She thinks the feud is stupid, if that helps. And honestly, she's more worried about whether you'll like *her*."

Goldie is silent again, and just when I think she's about to tell me no, she says, "Okay. I'll go with you."

"Good." I exhale with relief and grin like an idiot. "How about I pick you up at one on Friday?"

"That works," she says, still cautious.

"Thank you," I tell her. "I promise we'll have fun. My parents are warm and welcoming, and we can either stay at their house or go back to my penthouse. I, uh…there's a guest suite at both places, so you'll have plenty of…space."

I run my hand over my face, silently cursing this awkwardness. It's foreign to me and I fucking hate it. I prefer control by far, but that went out the window the day Goldie came into my life.

CHAPTER TWENTY-ONE

OFF WEEK

GOLDIE

> Any chance we could meet at The Loon tonight?

JUJU

Ooo, I'm in...as long as it's on the early side. You know me—I'll be drowsy by 8:30 due to my middle-of-the-night wake-up time.

ERIN

I don't know how you do it, Juju. And I am so in. I need Tater Tot Hotdish like I need a redhead. And I hope Lorraine still has seven-layer bars by the time we get there. We should probably aim for 5:15 to make sure that happens.

> Should I be offended that you care more about hotdish than seeing me?

> **ERIN**
>
> Babes, you, hotdish, and seven-layer bars are my favorite kind of night…besides the one in my dreams with a redhead.
>
> **JUJU**
>
> LOL. It does sound delish…hotdish and bars, not the redhead.
>
> **ERIN**
>
> Don't rain on my fetish parade.
>
> **JUJU**
>
> 😬 Never!
>
> > You have both made me very happy. Not as happy as Erin with a redhead…but happy. See you at 5:15.

The Loon is busy when I walk in. Lorraine waves from the bar.

"Erin called ahead and asked that I save the window table for you," she says, pointing to our favorite table overlooking the lake.

"Thanks, Lorraine!"

I stare out the window, endlessly amazed that the lake goes as far as the eye can see. I hear Erin and Juju before I see them, already laughing about something as they walk in together. We hug and order hotdish and bars right away to ensure we don't miss out, and we catch up for about twenty minutes before Erin bumps my elbow.

"Okay, lay it on us. What has you so pensive tonight?"

"What? I don't think I'm pensive." I shake my head.

Juju points at me. "That's the perfect word for it. I was trying to figure out what was up."

"Uh…not much is up. *Except…*"

"Here we go." Erin waves her hand for me to continue.

"Well…Milo asked me to go to his parents' house for dinner in the Cities this weekend and I said yes."

Juju gasps, delighted. "Oh my gosh! This is so exciting!"

"I hope you've packed your Scarlett Landmark lingerie," Erin says, winking at me. "And you need to binge on Zoey Archer's books to get you prepared for sexy time."

"No, not necessary. There will be no sexy time," I say emphatically. "We've had an…off week."

"Define off," Erin says, eyes narrowing.

"Mm-hmm. This just got even more interesting," Juju says.

I sigh. These two can always see right through me, dangit.

"We had a little too much to drink and made out the other night and then had a fight the next day and then we didn't speak and then he invited me to his family home and I don't know what to do and—" The words rush out of me and when they're out, I sit back, winded and flushed.

"Breathe." Erin puts her hand on my shoulder and I take a ragged breath.

"So…was the makeout sesh awesome?" Juju whispers.

I wrinkle my nose and nod reluctantly. "So, so awesome."

"And the fight?" Erin's eyes widen. "Super sexy?"

I laugh. "No, it was not sexy. It was infuriating, just like him."

"Mm-hmm. Sounds sexy." Juju smirks. "That man is incapable of *not* being hot."

She has a point, but we are not here to argue the level of Milo Lombardi's hotness.

"He said I was being distant…back to *frosty Goldie*." I shake my head and scowl. "When he's the one who couldn't get out of my room fast enough the night before."

"Wait, you made out in your room? With Papa Everett nearby?" Erin says, laughing. "Get it, girl."

"No, it was outside against the house. It was amazing." I sigh.

"And then you moved it inside?" Juju asks, pressing her lips together in excitement.

"No, he just wanted to make sure I got in okay, I think."

"Aww," they both croon.

"No, *not* aw," I hiss. "I was willing to…you know…and he wasn't…he didn't…so he left and I felt stupid."

"I don't know how, but I think I followed that," Erin says. "You were hurt that he didn't want to have sex?"

I nod, my face flaming. "It was a big deal for me to get that far after the whole…lying thing…"

"Yeah," Juju says softly. "But I think he was probably scared to tell you after getting so close to you…and he probably didn't want to have sex with your dad in the house," Juju says.

"Or maybe he wanted you both sober for it," Erin adds.

"He did mention that he wanted to sink inside me and never leave, but wanted me fully sober for it." I cover my face with my hands and peek through them.

"Hot damn," Erin says. "He might be the only man who could make me want peen." She holds up her hand. "For your sake, of course."

"Oh, he wants you. He wants you *bad*." Juju clasps her hands together. "You *have* to take the Scarlett Landmark lingerie! Both sets. And listen to the latest Archer book on audio. That guy's voice gives me chills. You will be primed and ready."

They both laugh and I look at them in mortification.

"This is not happening. We work together. It was bad enough that we made out and had a fight the next day. You think we could have sex and recover?" I whisper-shout the words because the bar is loud tonight.

"As long as he's good with aftercare and you take a warm bath somewhere between railings, I think you'll recover just fine," Erin says.

I throw my napkin at her.

I don't see Milo until Friday afternoon.

That good ole denial comes into play and I put the trip out of my mind.

I almost forget we even planned this weekend. Okay, that's a lie. But I *try* to forget, if that counts for anything.

I bury myself in picking chairs and tables for the restaurant and lodge, spending time with Dad, and working on a painting in the other spare moments. Friday morning, I panic when Dad asks me if I'm still planning on going.

"What? Why am I just now hearing about this?" Grandma Nancy swoops in, her hands clasped and eyes hopeful.

"Because I didn't want you guys to get any ideas," I say, glaring at Dad.

He just grins.

"I hope you'll be nicer to that boy. He is so handsome. And so polite!" Grandma Donna says.

"Mmm. He's certainly got you fooled." And then I concede, "He can be nice when he wants to be."

They both beam at me, and again, I stare at my dad.

Sorry, he mouths.

"Take something pretty to wear!" Grandma Donna calls after me as I leave the room. "Do you need that pretty pink sweater I knitted for you?"

"Too hot, I think," I yell back, so very grateful that it's not winter and I don't have to wear that sweater today to make my grandma happy.

"And let us know as soon as you're back so we can hear all about it!" Grandma Nancy calls.

"Will do," I yell.

I rush to my room to shave all my bits and put a few things in a bag, tossing the lingerie in at the last second… while also telling myself that I will absolutely *not* be wearing it. A few minutes later, I hear Milo talking to Dad downstairs, and I glance out the window to see his black SUV idling. No more denying it, I'm going on a little trip with Milo.

I already feel overheated and weird. I glance at myself in the mirror. I look okay, calmer than I feel. And all right, maybe I spent extra time getting ready, so I'd look better than okay…possibly even my very best self. But I pace for another thirty seconds before I go downstairs.

"Hey," he says when I walk into the room.

"Hey."

"You ready?" He smiles carefully, like he might be nervous too, and it reassures me the slightest bit.

"Yeah," I manage, grabbing my bag. "Let's go before I change my mind."

He laughs softly. "Come on, Whitman. It'll be fun, I promise."

I kiss Dad's cheek. "Call me if you need anything. I can come back early—"

"Don't you dare. Besides, I'll be busy here. There's no peace with Mom and Grandma Donna hovering over me all the time," he grumbles.

I'd laugh, but he seems more on edge. He's actually not been himself lately. I don't know if it's all of us fussing over him or what. My grandmas are all moved in and are staying indefinitely. Our house smells like banana bread and blueberry muffins every day now.

"Are you sure you're okay, Dad?"

He looks at me apologetically. "I'm sorry, buttercup. I'm okay. Just a lot on my mind."

"Okay. Anything you need, just tell me."

He swallows and nods. "Noah and Grayson are coming for the weekend."

"Hug Grayson extra for me."

"I will. Have a good time." He gives me a direct look and I nod. "Love you, buttercup."

"Love you too."

He looks at Milo. "You're not too bad either," he says, pounding him on the back.

Milo laughs. "Right back atcha."

We get on the road and it's awkwardly polite for the first few minutes. And then I start paying attention to his playlist. It's all over the place—old Motown classics, indie bands I haven't heard of, punk-pop, top 40, and the obscure.

"I'm having a hard time distinguishing your musical identity," I say when FINNEAS fades into Otis Redding and that fades into Paramore.

"I'm a man of many layers," he says with mock gravity.

It leads into a conversation about songs I like and I play a few for him. Just like that, the tense drive I'd dreaded feels lighter.

We talk about random things. His old roommate, who still crashes at his place sometimes. My brothers and how ridiculous and great they are. We argue over the best kind of road trip snacks when we stop at a Kwik Trip—sour gummies and beef jerky for him, and Chex mix, Reese's Peanut Butter Cups, and Cherry Sours for me. We end up eating each other's snacks and agreeing that it's all delicious and gut-ache inducing.

"You don't talk about your life in Minneapolis much. Why is that?" I ask.

He glances at me and his eyes narrow. "Hmm. You're right. I think...maybe because your life seems so much more interesting."

I laugh. "Are you serious right now?"

"Yeah. I mean, there is nonstop entertainment with your family. Your brothers are hilarious. You have a dog named Kevin..." He lifts his hand like *what more is there?*

I smile. "I never expected the great Milo Lombardi to say something like that. Your life is so exciting. You've won awards, you've worked all over the world...you speak and people listen."

He clears his throat. "I didn't know how much I needed a break. I might be working in Windy Harbor, but it doesn't feel like it. When I'm there...I feel different. Life is simpler and I like it. More than I thought I would. It's like a different world. One I'm still taking in. I mean, Bosco could be a character study all on his own, and that's just one person."

That cracks me up. "Who else entertains you in Windy Harbor?"

"Besides your family? Juju and Erin are high up there." He laughs. "Miss Idella at The Rusty Trunk is also an interesting one. Did you know she has Earl Grey and a blueberry muffin every morning at exactly 6:10 on the dot? Fascinating."

I snort. "You are even weirder than I thought."

"I'm surprised you're just now realizing that." His eyes are still smiling when he looks over and he seems shy as he clears his throat. "I...thought maybe we could meet up with my friends Evan and Sara tomorrow. We don't have to if you're anxious to get back, but they're great and want to meet you."

"You've told your friends about me?"

"Yeah?" he says it like it's a given.

"I'd really like to meet them."

He nods and we're quiet for a few minutes before launching into a discussion about the garden Camden wants to plant for the restaurant.

We're about an hour from Lake Minnetonka when he glances over at me, his expression serious.

"Goldie?"

He clears his throat and my heart thumps faster. I look at him in question.

"You know I *can't* shut it on and off, right?" He swallows and looks straight ahead, his fingers gripping the steering wheel. "It's not just a sometime chemistry for me."

I gulp and stare at his profile. "It's not?"

He snorts and looks at me for a brief second before his eyes shift back to the road. "No."

"What is it?"

"It's an all-consuming, really *inconvenient* attraction that never lets up for a second, whether you're around or not. And it's more than chemistry or attraction…I like you, Goldie."

My face heats and I blink fast. I swallow hard again, nervous but unable to look away from him.

"I hate what your shitty ex did to you. I want to run into him just so I can punch him in the face."

My eyes widen and I bite my lip, fighting back a nervous laugh.

"And then I want to dip you back and kiss you until you're breathless right in front of him so he sees what he's missing, because trust me, he might be with someone else, but he misses kissing you."

I put my hands on my hot cheeks and take a deep breath. "Wow."

"I don't say anything to pressure you into anything you don't want or feel. I just thought you should know."

He turns up the song—"DYWTYLM" by Sleep Token. As the words, *Do you wish that you loved me?* play through the speakers, I think, *It's too late for wishing.*

I nearly say something, but I feel so overwhelmed by what he's said and what I'm feeling that I don't. I bask in the feelings, in having him by my side, that we have a whole weekend together, and I just enjoy the ride.

When we pull up to his parents' house, I'm almost relaxed.

Almost.

Because when we drive down his driveway, the nerves rush back.

The house is beautiful—a sprawling home with a lake backdrop. Milo glances over at me as he parks, his smile soft and tentative. "Are you ready?"

"Ready," I murmur, my heart hammering.

He grins and hops out, coming around to open my door, which just charms me more.

"Milo?" I say.

He pauses on his way to the trunk and looks back.

"Thank you…for what you said earlier and…for bringing me here. I…" I take a deep breath. "I like you too."

He's in front of me the next second. His hand comes up to cup my cheek and he leans in so very slowly and presses the softest kiss to my lips. My heart stutters in my chest and I gasp. He swallows it up with his kiss, and even though it's gentle and sweet, my knees threaten to buckle. I sway into him, and when we break apart, he smiles when I blink up at him, both of us breathless.

His arms circle my waist and his head falls back as he yells, "Woohoo! Goldie Whitman likes me!"

I crack up and shove his chest. He just laughs and pulls me back in, kissing me again.

"I like you too. So much," he whispers against my lips.

"You already said that. You must be obsessed."

He laughs. "I am. You don't even know." He kisses me again and then groans. "We should get inside before my mom comes out and hauls us in." He tugs my hand and we walk toward the house. "I'll come back to get our things."

I think he's right about his mom potentially coming out because we've barely stepped onto the front porch before the door opens wide. His parents are both there and rush toward us. I was braced for polite-but-distant, but no. His mom, Kathleen, wraps me in a hug within seconds of seeing me, and his dad, Anthony, beams at me like I'm an old friend.

"We're so glad you're here!" Anthony says. "Come in, mio figliolo." He kisses Milo on each cheek and then does the same to me.

"You've had a long drive. How are you feeling?" Kathleen asks. "Do you need to rest before dinner?"

I glance at Milo, who's smiling over at me. "Milo drove the whole way, so he might want to, but I'm good."

"I just got a burst of energy," Milo says, his eyes gleaming, "right before we came in."

My face heats and I try to hold back my smile but fail.

This man is going to wreck me and I can't even care right now when this feels so good.

CHAPTER TWENTY-TWO

A LONG WAY

MILO

I can't stop smiling.

Goldie's laughing with my mom over dessert, the two of them leaning close like they've known each other forever. My dad keeps cutting me amused looks across the table, obviously as charmed by Goldie as my mother is. As I am.

I wasn't sure how tonight would go. I knew everyone would like each other if they gave one another a chance, but I was concerned the Granger elephant in the room might derail things. But watching them fall for her, hearing her make them laugh, seeing my mom's face light up when Goldie complimented her garden and decorating, my dad asking about Goldie's art and how touched she is by that—it's all more than I could have imagined.

I catch her eye for a second and her lips tug into a smile— one meant just for me. My chest tightens. Yeah, I'm gone.

Completely gone over this woman. Suddenly, I can't wait to take her home. I want her to myself even if it's just to stare at her for as long as I want.

When the fuck did I get so hopeless?

Despite my inner clinginess, we stay for another hour and a half, thoroughly enjoying our visit. When my mom hugs me goodbye, she whispers in my ear, "She is spectacular, Milo. Don't let her go. The two of you are perfect together."

I kiss her cheek, grateful that she's willing to put aside any residual family prejudice against a Whitman for my sake. Something tells me it'd take a lot more to get Bruce on board with our relationship, but he's not someone I base any life decisions on.

We make our way to my SUV and I thread my fingers through hers. She looks up at me and smiles.

"You're quiet," she says as we drive away.

My hand finds hers again. This need to keep finding ways to touch her is new for me.

"I'm just…happy. They loved you. I knew they would."

"I loved them too. They made me feel right at home." She takes a deep breath. "You don't think they have any reservations about me being a Whitman?"

"They did at first. I told them about you a long time ago and they were concerned. But when I called my mom earlier this week…the morning after we…kissed..." I smile when she bites her lip. I know that if it wasn't dark out, I'd see pink cheeks. "She could tell that I was serious about you."

"You're serious about me?" Her voice is quiet.

I lift her hand to my lips and kiss her knuckles. "I am. Are you okay with that?"

"I…I think so." She laughs softly.

"Does it scare you?"

"Yes," she answers with no hesitation.

"Me too. Why does it scare you?"

"I don't want to wreck our working relationship."

"I think we're both too professional to let that happen."

She nods. "You're right."

"What really scares you?"

"That you won't mean any of it. Maybe you're still hung up on Roshana. Maybe none of it is true."

That slams into my gut. "Goldie. I was into you the night we met at the Walker, months ago. I've been invested in every argument, every joke, trivia night, your vision for art and your family resort, and every twist and quirk of these goddamn lips. You have invaded every thought and turned my life upside down. I couldn't stop thinking about you if I tried, and I don't want to. Yes, I'm scared. I'm scared you don't feel the same. I'm scared you'll let your fears about relationships frighten you away from me. I'm scared you'll change your mind. I'm scared you'll never fully let me in." I exhale and when we stop at a red light, I put the SUV in park and turn to face her. "Roshana fucking who? I'm scared because I've never felt this way about anyone, not even close to it, and it's fucking overwhelming."

Her eyes are glassy, but she smiles.

The car behind us lets out a loud honk, and she jumps, laughing.

I get back in gear and drive ahead, cursing. "I can't get you home soon enough."

"I've never felt this way about anyone either, Milo." She squeezes my hand.

"Not even Wes?"

"My best day with him was not even close to how good my worst day is with you," she says.

"Dammit, woman. I need to kiss you." I speed through the streets and she laughs.

When we pull up to my building, she whistles under her breath. "I've always wanted to see the inside of this building."

I grin as I park and lead her to the elevator, my hand resting low on her back. "Perfect. Your wish is my command."

"You sure are a lot more accommodating than you were in the beginning." She smirks at me and then her eyes widen when we step out on the penthouse level.

"It was hard to be accommodating when you were busting my balls every chance you got." I lean around her to unlock my door.

She giggles. "I don't plan to stop, so…" She lifts her shoulder and glances back at me, grinning.

I groan and have to adjust myself when she turns to stare at my place. She shuffles in slowly and I close the door behind us.

"Milo, this is insane."

I chuckle and toss my keys on the side table.

She lets out a breathy, "Wow."

I watch her wander through the room, trailing her hand over the back of my couch and walking to the windows. Two walls are entirely floor-to-ceiling windows, but the view has never been so spectacular. She stands there looking out at the skyline.

"These windows. This view," she says, turning around to face me. "Milo, this is gorgeous."

"We need all the light we can get in the winter, right?"

"So true. I'm impressed. I love the choices you've made. This lamp. That rug." She points to them as we walk to the kitchen. "*Beautiful*."

"Thank you." I can't hide how pleased I am. "That means a lot coming from you."

She grins. "Again. Not what I would've expected to hear from you the night we met."

"Ditto. You called my work a travesty, so I think we've come a long way."

She puts her face in her hands and shakes her head. "Me and my mouth."

"I'm crazy about that mouth."

She presses her lips together, her cheeks flaming. I love it when they do that. She glances away shyly and I stalk toward her just as she squeals.

"Is that chocolate-covered strawberries on your counter? Milo! Who even are you?"

"I had Jenny leave them for us. She cleans the place and leaves meals for me when I'm in town."

I put my hands on her waist and she wraps her arms around my neck, playing with my hair.

"That's so billionaire of you."

I groan. "Not something I love to be called these days, but I guess it's fitting. I remembered you saying you had a thing for strawberries…especially the ones covered in chocolate."

"I can't believe you remember that." She leans up and kisses my cheek. "That's really sweet, Mildie. And also, I know you're trying to distract me right now." Her eyes are bright with that mischievous gleam that makes me nervous yet on my toes. "I read that you have donated millions to charities…is that true?"

I shift, uncomfortable with this topic. "Also, not something I love being broadcast. A journalist got to one of my former accountants, who quit because she didn't want to return after maternity leave. She was chatty and said more than she should've."

She grins, and because I'm so tall and don't want her neck to hurt looking up at me, I lift her onto my countertop. I also happen to *really* like her on countertops.

"Back to the chocolate-covered strawberries, Golo," I say, kissing her neck.

Her breath catches and her head falls back, giving me full access.

"I'm not able to eat them sexily," she says, her voice breathy.

I laugh against her skin. This woman cracks me up.

"Everything you do is sexy." I kiss my way up to her mouth and pick up one of the strawberries next to her. "And now I have to see."

"You've been warned," she says, when I lift it to her mouth.

She takes a bite and half of the chocolate falls and strawberry juice runs down her chin. We both laugh. I lean in and catch the juice with my tongue and trail up to her mouth.

"Still sexy," I say against her lips.

I lean back and give her the rest of the strawberry, grinning as I hold my hand under her chin this time. Her eyes are playful as she takes the last bite. She's so damn cute and sexy and beautiful and funny, I live in a constant state of stomach flips and desire. It's insanity. I'm losing my fucking mind. And I'm hard ninety percent of the day.

I lift my thumb before the juice can drip this time and she wraps her mouth around my finger, sucking it clean.

I groan.

The next moment, my mouth is on hers. I scoot her toward the edge of the counter and she whimpers when she feels how hard I am. Months of tension, of skirting around this, come crashing down, and it's like we both combust. My hands slide into her hair, hers pull at my shirt, and our tongues tangle like they're made for each other.

I come up for air because I need to slow down, savor this, and I also want to check in.

"Do you want this?" I ask.

"More than anything," she says, tugging my mouth back to hers.

"God, I want you," I say, against her lips.

"You've got me." She sounds breathless.

I groan again and she smiles. I lift her off the counter and her legs wrap around my waist. I carry her upstairs, and between the kitchen and the bedroom, a few clothes are left behind. She unbuttons my shirt and tosses it aside and I lift hers over her head. I set her in front of my bed and she starts undoing my pants as I lower the zipper on the back of her skirt. She tugs her skirt off and I look down for a moment to step out of my pants. When I look up again, she's standing in this blue one-piece lacy thing that is God's gift to mankind.

"Fuck. *Me*. You're a masterpiece."

"Thank you," she says softly.

"Turn around."

She does and I curse again. There's lace at the top and then barely any over her ass, which is framed perfectly. I take my briefs off and my dick has never been happier. I stare at her and groan.

"Another work of art. I don't know which I love more," I tell her.

She looks over her shoulder, her smile seductive now. She knows the power her body holds over me already, I can tell. I want her to. Her eyes widen and she gasps when she looks down, which makes me swell even bigger.

"*Milo*." She keeps staring at my cock and when her eyes finally meet mine, I'm smirking because fuck, it's a good one.

I reach out and cup her ass, stepping closer until my chest is against her back. She's still wearing heels, so my dick fits between her cheeks. Her head falls back when my hands move to her tits, running my fingers over her peaked nipples. I bend down and nuzzle her neck.

"You're all I've thought about since we met. There's been no one else," I say gruffly.

"There's no one else for me either, Milo," she says.

"Those are the best words I've ever heard."

She turns in my arms and runs her thumb over my tip, and I swear, I almost lose it.

"This is beautiful, but how do I get it off?" I ask, my fingers skimming under the lace.

She smiles and undoes the two ties on the sides and one at her neck, and the whole thing drops to the ground.

My mouth waters when I see her.

We take a moment to look at each other, really look at each other, and I love every single inch I see.

"Speechless," I say.

She nods. "Me too." Her eyes scan over me again from head to toe and she swallows hard. "You are *something*," she finally says. "Something I don't think I can stop staring at."

"Good, because I don't want either of us to wear clothes all night long."

She laughs and her mouth quirks to the side when she looks at me. Like she's trying to hold back a huge smile. I know the feeling.

"I've never seen a body so perfect," she says.

"Take a look in the mirror and you will. Come here."

I tug her closer. Her hands span across my chest and lower until they're squeezing my cheeks. She looks up at me and grins.

"*Wow*," she says.

I slide my hand between her legs, smiling when I feel how wet she is, and I dip a finger inside for a second before bringing it out, only to glide over her sweet spot and dip inside again. I do that until she's squirming and I add another finger, my thumb doing tiny circles where she wants. I take my time, watching every reaction, and loving every second. I can feel it when she's close and I don't stop.

"Take it, Goldie. Take all you want."

Her head falls back and she cries out, her eyes squeezing shut as she comes. It's a sight to behold. When I slowly pull my fingers out of her, she lowers her head to my chest and takes a deep breath.

"Who knew you'd be such a giver?" she says.

I lift her and toss her on the bed and she's still laughing when I crawl over her.

"I need more of your sassy strawberry mouth," I say, kissing her.

I kiss her until she's greedy for me, her hands roaming all over me. I feel drunk on her. I grab a condom and roll it on as she watches, her chest rising and falling fast. When I lower my body onto hers, we both gasp. I look at her and her hands cradle my face, her thumbs stroking my jaw.

"Hi," she whispers.

I rest my forehead against hers. "Hi."

My first dip inside is slow, but there is an immediate spark.

"*Oh*," she says.

"I want to kiss you and I don't want to stop looking at you," I tell her.

"Let's do this all night. Please." She bites her lip when I go deeper.

"Is this okay? We can go slow."

She nods. "We're just beginning and I never want to stop."

My dick jerks at those words and I go a little deeper.

"Breathe," I say.

She does and relaxes a little more around me, allowing me deeper.

I lean down and kiss her, getting lost in her kisses, in how good this feels, until I'm all the way inside. We both moan when I get there.

"I'm so full," she says. "And it's so, so good."

She arches into me, and we begin to move. It's a torturous, slow pace, our eyes locked on each other. When I start to slide out slowly and then fill her up, I feel her clench around me each time. It's too good. I won't be able to last as long as I want to. The pace builds. I kiss her cheek, the corner of her mouth, her neck. Her nails scrape my back in a way that makes me curse as I bury my face into her neck. And then when I don't think I can take it another second, I lift up so I can watch her as I start a relentless rhythm. Her mouth falls open and her tits bounce as I thrust and thrust, again and again.

She whispers my name and then says it louder. "Don't stop," she cries.

I thrust deeper, loving the way her body responds to mine, like every part of us is in tune with each other. When she comes again, pulsing around me, I groan her name and follow, feeling like I might pass out with how hard I come.

For a moment, neither of us moves. Our breathing is synced as we stare at each other. I lean down to my forearms and smooth her hair away, and then I kiss her, soft and sweet. When I shift onto my side, I take her with me and we lie there, facing each other. Her fingers trace over my chest, and I play with her hair.

"Was that as amazing for you as it was for me?" I finally ask.

"I don't know. Was it a completely euphoric experience, unlike any other you've ever had?"

A smile breaks across my face. "That describes it perfectly."

CHAPTER TWENTY-THREE

COCKY SASS

GOLDIE

Did that just happen? Earth-shattering. I'm a bit shaken by it. The way his eyes worship me, his hands know exactly where to go, the way his body feels pressed against mine, his mouth finding mine like he wants every part of us connected.

Every inch of his body is fine-tuned. His chest is a wall, not too hard that he's all edges, but toned with precision. The ripples his abs made when he was over me…the vee, oh, the vee that leads to heaven…

His whole body is my weakness.

I blow out a long breath and stretch against his sheets, while he goes into the bathroom.

I smile when he walks back into the bedroom with a warm washcloth and carefully cleans me up. Erin would be proud.

But he makes it feel a little too good and I tug him back

down for a kiss, which leads to him flipping me so I'm on top.

"Best view I've ever seen," he says, his voice raspy.

His hands cup my breasts and the way he stares up at me makes me feel both sexy and powerful. He's so beautiful it hurts. I roll my hips, slowly at first, teasing, and we both groan. He hands me a condom and I slide it on. Things escalate in a hurry. I throw my head back, my hair falling against him, my palms flat on his chest. His abs tense under my fingers.

"Goldie…" His lids are heavy as he watches me.

I move faster, feeling him hit deep. We take a shuddering breath together. His hands move down my stomach and between my legs, where he rubs tiny circles over my bundle of nerves. I've never been with a man who finds it so fast.

My body aches for him, even as he's inside me, this need to consume him. I move faster and so does he, his eyes intent on mine. The city lights coming through his window cast a glow over his face, and he looks like sin that I want to partake in all night long. Desire pounds in my blood as I rock over him faster. His fingers don't stop and when I start coming, he drives up into me harder, faster. My eyes roll back and he makes a desperate sound as he comes with me.

When we finally slow, I lean forward, and our mouths meet again, kissing like we can't get enough. When we do break apart, we're breathless and slick with sweat. He takes care of the condom and shifts, that smirk tugging at his mouth.

"How about a bath?" he asks. "I never use it, but it sounds nice right now."

"I love that idea."

He sits up and sweeps me into his arms as he stands. I kiss his throat and neck as he carries me into the bathroom.

He sets me gently on the countertop and starts the water. The room fills with steam and he comes back to set me in the water. I sink into the water and sigh, already soothed in the raw places. I've never felt ravaged before, and by someone as big as him, and good God, it's intoxicating.

We face each other, the hot water lapping around us. His fingers find mine under the water, our fingers lacing together. We sit there, looking at each other, our smiles soft.

"So, the night we met, did you see us ending up here?" I ask.

He lifts my hand and kisses my knuckles. "It's what I wanted, yes. Wasn't sure I'd ever get you here, though, since everything I do seems to piss you off."

I lift an eyebrow. "Not everything."

He grins and puts his hands on my backside, scooting me closer. "I know that now."

"Was it how you imagined?"

"You're too far." He lifts me until I'm straddling him, and water sloshes over the sides.

His hands grip my hips and he's already hard.

"Better than I imagined," he says. "The sounds you make when you're close…I'm going to replay that over and over again."

I lean my forehead against his and slide my hands in his hair.

"The way you ride me like you were *made* for it," he whispers.

I grind against him and our breath hitches.

"The way you hit every spot I need you to and some I didn't even know about," I say, giving him a soft kiss.

"Yeah?" He brushes my hair back and kisses down my neck.

His mouth latches onto my breast and he tugs my nipple between his teeth.

My hips roll over him and I gasp with how good he feels.

"How do I already want you again?" I tug his hair and he looks up at me, his eyes glazed. "I'm on birth control…"

"Sink onto me," he says.

I lift, and he positions himself just right. I slide down slowly.

"*Fuck*," he whispers.

It's even better like this. I'm already pulsing around him. We both groan.

"Is this okay?" His hands come up to my cheeks and he lowers his head slightly to meet my eyes.

I exhale shakily. "I don't…I haven't…done this."

"Me either," he says.

"I'm a fan," I whisper, eyes wide.

He leans closer and smiles against my lips. "Me too. Big, *big* fan."

His eyes squeeze shut when I clench around him again. I feel him swell inside and I whimper. His hands move to my hips, and when he opens his eyes, they're hungry.

"Goldie…you are torturing me…in the best way," he rasps.

I lift up and then slowly sink back onto him, and the need for more builds with every pass. We start a merciless rhythm, his hands slamming me down faster and faster. It's hitting all the right places, and I begin to shake.

"That's it. God, you're so beautiful." His movements get erratic, but he doesn't stop until we're both flying, time standing still as we crest into oblivion.

All night long, we wake each other up wanting more.

I wake up with his mouth between my legs, and I eventually pull him up, desperate to have him. We're hurried and frantic, and it's so hot I can't believe this is even happening to me. Later, when he's hard against my backside, I think he wakes up when I arch against him. He slides inside, his hands cupping my breasts and roaming down my body, and it's slow and sleepy and so sweet. Our bodies keep finding each other in the dark, hungry for another taste, another touch.

We barely sleep, a tangle of limbs and sheets, even though we get up to change them once during the night.

The morning light shines through the windows when I open my eyes again. Milo is looking at me.

"I've never had a night like that," he says quietly.

"Me either."

He traces a finger over my chest and trails it up to my lips, where I kiss it.

"I think I've discovered something very interesting," he says, his mouth quirking up.

"What?"

"Well, I'm not certain it's true, but at least for the night… I *think* I fucked the sass right out of you."

I roll to my back and cackle, then take my pillow and wallop him over the head with it. He laughs and his hands are grabby.

"Come here, let me test it," he says.

"Don't get your hopes up, buddy. The sass is still intact. And it seems I did *not* fuck the cocky out of you."

He pretends to pout, but we're both still laughing too hard for that to stick. I let him pull me on top of him and burrow my face into his neck.

He squeezes my backside and whispers in my ear, "I love all your sass, Goldie Whitman. And I don't think you can ever fuck the cocky out of me. It enjoys being inside you way too much."

He rubs me against him to prove his point.

"See what I mean?"

"*Cocky*, not cock."

"Same difference," he says.

"I beg to differ."

CHAPTER TWENTY-FOUR

WARMER, WARMER, HOT

MILO

"Do we have to leave this bed?" I loop my arm around her waist and kiss her ass when she gets up.

She laughs and swats my chest. "You told them we'd be there in an hour and it takes at least twenty minutes to get there!"

"Fine." I pretend to be exasperated, but she doesn't buy it for a second. "I regret making plans today."

"You didn't foresee last night happening?" She grins, her hands winding through my hair.

I put my feet on the ground and pull her between my legs, looking up at her. "No. I wished, but no, I didn't see it happening at all. Did you?"

"*No.*"

I kiss her stomach and then pause. "So you always have that going on underneath your clothes?" I tap my forehead against her softly, as if I'm banging my head against the wall. "Had I known…"

"I didn't say that." She laughs. "Erin and Juju convinced me I needed to bring the lingerie, and I decided to wear it to feel pretty. I did *not* think you'd see it last night." She tugs my hair until I'm looking up at her again.

"Your friends know about us…" My hands find her ass and I squeeze two handfuls.

All I want to do is touch her, kiss her, bury myself in her, and never come up for air.

"Well…they know a little bit. I was nervous. I thought we might still be mad at each other."

"Yet you still agreed to come?"

She bites her lip and nods.

"Thank you," I tell her.

She bends down and kisses me, but it's not as long as I want.

"How would you feel about staying another night?" I ask.

Her lips quirk up. "Because you didn't get enough of me?"

I snort. "Not even close."

She taps her top lip. "I think I could pull that off. I brought an extra pair of clothes for backup. I'll just call Dad and maybe Grandma Nancy to see how things are going there."

"Do whatever you need to do. If you're tired, we can stay in and order takeout."

"No, I want to meet Evan and Sara. And I love the food at CōV. Okay, okay, I'm getting ready." She skirts out of my hold and laughs when I smack her backside.

I shower in the guest bathroom because we'll never leave if I get in with her.

I'm already shocking myself with the level of these feelings. I knew we would be good together because kissing her is out of this world, but I couldn't have known how intense it would be.

Goldie comes out in a sleeveless, short green dress that hits the middle of her thighs. Her hair is pulled back and she looks stunning.

"Wow," I say, walking toward her.

I hold my hand out and she takes it. I twirl her around, taking in the view before I kiss her cheek.

"You look beautiful." I slide her strap slightly to the side and groan when I see pale pink lace underneath.

"Uh-uh-uh," she says, swatting my hand away playfully.

"Now that I know what treasures lie beneath…" I tap my temple. "It's all right here, but the pleasure of unwrapping your package..."

"If you're sweet, maybe I'll let you unwrap me later," she teases.

"I can be sweet," I promise. "I can be so sweet."

"That's what I'm finding out…" She smirks at me as I hold the door open and we walk out.

She's antsy on the drive to CōV in Wayzata.

I reach over and thread my fingers through hers. "You okay?"

She makes a face. "Nervous."

"Of Evan and Sara? Don't be. They're going to love you. How was your dad?"

"He's good, and Grandma Nancy told me to stay as long as I wanted. She said Kevin is getting spoiled rotten." She grins over at me and looks a little more relaxed.

It's the perfect day—72 degrees and sunny, low humidity, and it's the time of year when everything is in bloom and the trees and grass are so green, it doesn't seem real. In the winter, it seems impossible that it'll look like this again, and in the summer, it's hard to imagine all of these trees bare or snowy.

We have a table overlooking the lake. The patio buzzes with chatter and clinking glasses. Evan and Sara jump up and wave when they see us, all smiles. I make the introductions and we all sit down.

"We ordered a lobster guac and halibut ceviche for the table—" Evan starts.

"And then were like, oh no, I hope Goldie likes seafood!" Sara says, making a face. "We can get another appetizer too."

Goldie laughs. "I love seafood! That sounds perfect. I haven't been here yet, but I've heard great things."

Our server comes with the appetizers and gets our drink orders. Sara and Evan ask Goldie a few questions and my hand rests on the back of her chair. My fingers brush the nape of her neck and I watch her respond to my friends with such poise. She's radiant and I can tell she's relaxing more by the second.

She takes a chip and dips it, her eyes closing with her bite. "This lobster guac is unreal."

"Isn't it great?" Sara says and they launch into a conversation about their favorite restaurants in town.

"My brother is my favorite chef," Goldie says. "You'll have to come visit the restaurant when it opens!"

Evan's eyes meet mine and he gives me a smug grin as he watches my hand. Goldie excuses herself to go to the restroom before the rest of our food comes. The moment she's gone, Evan and Sara pounce.

"Who *are* you?" Sara demands, leaning in. "I've *never* seen you like this, Milo."

Evan smirks. "Man, you didn't tell us you were cooked." He looks at Sara. "Did you see the—"

"I know, with the hair and the—" Sara does googly eyes to Evan and they both laugh.

They've been together since freshman year of college and usually manage to not be too annoying despite finishing each other's sentences. *Usually.*

"I do not look like that," I grumble.

Sara squeals. "You like her so much! I can't take it. The cuteness and the—"

Evan picks up. "Steam. I swear it was like about to go—"

"Rated *R* for nudity and adult themes," Sara finishes in a movie trailer voice.

"Don't make me regret introducing her to you clowns," I say.

Goldie walks to the table, the sun catching on her hair, and my chest tightens. I stand halfway, pulling her chair out for her without thinking.

Sara beams at me across the table and Evan lifts his brows. I roll my eyes.

"What did I miss?" Goldie asks, smiling around the table.

I shake my head. "You missed these two weirdos finishing each other's sentences. They've been like this since they met in college. It's so annoying."

"You love us." Sara laughs.

"We were just talking about how happy Milo seems," Evan says.

I laugh under my breath.

Sara turns to Goldie conspiratorially. "Goldie, I don't know what kind of spell you've put on him, but keep up the good work. This is the most pleasant he's been since—"

"We met him," Evan finishes.

I look at Goldie and shake my head. "This was clearly a bad idea."

Goldie laughs. "No, I'm having the best time. Tell me more."

"Even in college, Milo was like an eighty-year-old in that fine physique," Evan says, laughing.

"I was focused." I pretend to scowl and they all laugh.

"Focused and a bit…serious," Sara adds.

Evan leans in. "Tell her about the girl you stopped seeing because—"

"She used too many exclamation points in her texts," Sara finishes and they all crack up.

Goldie gasps, holding her stomach. "You did not."

I hold up my hand. "In my defense—"

"There is no defense," Sara cuts in. "She was sweet! But he got the ick and peaced out."

"I can't believe you two," I groan.

"This is so helpful," Goldie says. "More ways to push his buttons…bring in the exclamation points!"

I scoot her chair closer to me and lean into her ear. "You already know how to push my buttons."

Sara fans her face. "Good Lord, the two of you are Frank's RedHot. Evan and I have been talking about having a baby, and I don't think it's gonna take much effort when we get home."

"Check, please." Evan pretends to look for our server.

I laugh, pressing my fingers into my eyes. "You guys are too much."

"This is the best lunch I've ever had," Goldie says, clinking everyone's glass. Her eyes are still laughing when she looks at me. "You didn't tell me your friends were so hilarious."

I hold my hand out. "Nothing could have prepared me for this. They are…in rare form today."

"So are you, my friend," Evan says. *"So are you."*

After we say goodbye to Evan and Sara, we walk down the boardwalk, just enjoying the day. As we head back toward my place, we're not hungry enough for dinner, so I park in my parking garage and turn to look at her.

"Do you feel like a walk?" I ask. "It's a beautiful night."

"Sure!"

"Will you be okay in those shoes?" I look at her heels skeptically and she waves me off.

"Oh, these are wedges. I'll be fine."

"If you're sure. They look pretty high to me. The second your feet start hurting, we can get an Uber, okay?"

"Okay." She grins.

It's a pretty night, so we take our time walking to Flora Room. She's never been there, but I think she'll like the vibe. All day, the need for her has been building. She's been playful and flirty and I am like butter in her hands. I would've been happy to take her home, but I don't want her to think I only care about getting her in bed. I want to show her a good time, let her know she's special.

She loves the place. It's moody and romantic and we have to lean close to hear each other.

"So…do you have a lot of…" She looks up at me and her mouth shifts to the side.

Our hands are tangled together and if it's possible for hands to have sex with each other, ours are. Each trail she does with her fingers up my palm makes me harder.

"What? Say it," I say when she still hesitates.

"Do you have a lot of women on your roster?"

"On my *roster*?" I laugh. "No. I mean, I'm thirty, so I've gone out with my fair share of women, yes. I told you about Roshana. She wanted to get married and I just didn't feel…" I glance down at her and she's listening intently. "Something was just missing, you know?"

She nods. "And you said you didn't live together?"

"No. That's how I knew I wasn't ready. I had no desire to live with her. I wanted to feel more…I just *didn't*."

"How did it end?"

"She got upset that I was traveling more for work. I was gone for a weekend and I didn't call her. I think she thought I was cheating on her or something, but there was a big time difference and I was so busy. When I got out of a meeting, I checked my phone and there were at least twenty missed calls from her, each message getting worse. The last one was her sobbing and I—"

"You peaced out?"

I make a face. "Yeah, I peaced out. I broke up with her as soon as I got home. It didn't end well. She threw a vase at me."

She winces. "Oof."

"Enough about that. Do you like your drink?"

She ordered a Tuco Tuco and took a picture of it because it's so pretty.

"I *love* it. How's the Palo?"

"Here, try it." I hold it to her lips and she takes a sip, her pink tongue grabbing a drop from her lip.

I groan and she gives me a flirty smile but then makes a little face when the taste hits.

"I like mine better," she says.

She shivers slightly and I glance down to rub her arms and notice her nipples pebbled against her dress.

My dick protests the restraint.

"Are you chilly?" I ask, my voice husky.

She takes a long swig of her drink, finishing it. I smile and she leans in, moving toward my ear.

"I need you to take me home and warm me up," she whispers.

I stand up, throwing money on the table and then pulling up the app to arrange a ride.

"We're not walking?" she asks, biting the inside of her cheek.

We hurry outside.

"No, ma'am. I'm getting you home."

She glances down at the huge tent in my pants and smirks.

"Such a gentleman."

"Mm-hmm. Keep telling yourself that. I'm getting you home and fucking you so hard you'll never be cold again."

An older couple is walking by and the woman gasps.

"Mercy me!" she says, glaring at me.

"Oh, to be young again," the man says.

When we ride the elevator to my penthouse, I brace my arms on either side of her head and kiss her the way I've wanted to all day long.

"Milo," she whimpers. "I'm so ready."

The elevator dings while I'm sliding my hand up her dress. She kisses me while I'm unlocking the door and as soon as the door is shut behind us, I'm undoing her dress as fast as I can.

"Holy fuck," I whisper in awe when I see tonight's lace.

There's barely anything to it, but the way it highlights all her assets is fucking glorious.

"I can't believe you've been hiding that from me all day."

She giggles and does a turn for me. I growl.

"Go face the window," I tell her. "Hands on the glass."

Her mouth parts and she does what I asked. She looks like a dream and I hope to God that we'll never wake up from this. I want her. I want her more than I've ever wanted anyone or anything. I undo my pants and slide my briefs down along with them. I give my dick a tug as I stalk toward her. She gasps when she feels me against her back and arches into my dick.

"Do you like that people might see you like this?" I whisper.

"Yes," she says, breathless.

I trace from her ear down her neck, one hand twisting her nipple and the other sliding down between her legs. My fingers move under the lace and I rub her wetness over her before dipping inside.

"So wet for me…"

I get on my knees behind her and only have to wonder how to get her bare for a second when I feel the hook-and-eye closures. They're undone in seconds and she slams her hand on the glass when I do the first long swipe of my tongue across the length of her.

I don't go slow tonight. The foreplay has been simmering between us all day. I unleash my tongue on her, plunging it inside her, and she bucks against my mouth like she's starving for me. It doesn't take long for her to come.

"I need you inside me," she cries, still shuddering around my tongue.

I stand and she does quick work of taking the lingerie off the rest of the way. She looks at me over her shoulder, her eyes dazed, and I impale her. She lets out a long, hungry moan and it feeds me. I slide in and out and she meets every thrust. The sounds of us fill my penthouse and I've never heard anything better. I guide her hips over me, faster and faster. Our bodies are slippery with sweat and I grit my teeth, watching where I drive inside of her.

"Are you warm enough now?" I ask.

Her head drops forward and she twitches inside, strangling my cock as she comes again. I bow over her back, yelling as I empty inside her. I think I see heaven.

"Burning up," she says after a few minutes.

She looks back and I kiss her as she sags into me.

CHAPTER TWENTY-FIVE

MATCHY-MATCHY

GOLDIE

DAD

Your grandmothers are driving me crazy. Noah and Grayson left earlier and with Goldie out of town, they are next-level hovering! I need pics to pretend like I'm busy! They won't believe that I'm warm enough—it's SUMMER. <Pic of him in a purple and gold knitted hat, afghan to his chin. Kevin is on his lap with a matching hat.>

TULLY

Grandma Donna sent me that same hat and afghan. Let me go find it.

NOAH

Oh, same here! <Pic of him and Grayson in their purple and gold knitted hats, posing behind the afghan>

TULLY

<Pic of the matching hat and blanket tucked way back in his closet>

CAMDEN

<Pic of the hat and blanket hanging on a hook at work>

DYLAN

Does it count if you're not wearing the hat and the afghan? I think not. <Pic of him in his swimsuit at the surf shop, blanket around his neck, and the hat on his head. Bill is on the counter next to him, staring at him with wide eyes>

I'm cracking up while reading and showing Milo the pictures.

"Where's yours?" he asks, laughing.

"I haven't unpacked them yet."

"Mm-hmm. It's a nice hat."

"Would you like to wear it?"

"For *you*. Nice hat for you," he adds.

I text everyone back.

> Mine are at home and I'm not, but the pics made my day.

TULLY

Oh yeah. When were you gonna tell me you were in Minneapolis this weekend and didn't come see me?!

"Eek. Tully wants to know why I didn't see him this weekend."

Milo makes a face. "Shit, I was so preoccupied, I didn't think of it. I'd love to hang out with him…go to one of his games when the season starts. Sorry, we were kind of all about my family and friends this weekend, weren't we?"

"I loved getting to know them. You've been around my family a ton. I did wonder about seeing him at one point, but you distracted me…and it was worth it."

He grins. "I'm not sure I'll be able to get undistracted."

I'm grinning when I respond to Tully.

> Sorry about that, Tulls. It was a full weekend for sure, but it won't happen again, I promise. XO

CAMDEN

> What's this I hear about a trip to meet Milo's family?

I bite my lip and tuck my phone in my bag, uncertain how to answer that.

The ride back to Windy Harbor Sunday afternoon is much different than when we left on Friday. Milo's hand is either on my thigh or his fingers are threaded through mine. We keep looking at each other and smiling. The atmosphere is relaxed, if we're not taking the high level of lust into consideration.

"If you need me to drive, let me know," I tell him when we're halfway. "You must be so tired."

"You would know. You kept me up all night." His smirk sparks little flames throughout my body.

"I didn't hear you complaining."

"Not for a fucking second. Except to say *why are you climbing off of me?*"

We laugh and my stomach dips as his eyes drift over me, his smile lingering.

"So…how do you foresee things going now?" he asks, his gaze dipping to my mouth.

"What do you mean?"

"Are we keeping this between us?" he asks. "Loud and

proud with your family?" His jaw ticks as he turns back to the road. "Or are we going back to you hating me?"

"What do you want?"

He sighs. "Well, obviously I don't want to go back to you hating me."

"I never hated you…"

He shoots me a look. "Hmm. What shall we call it? Extreme dislike?"

I press my lips together. "Low trust of the male race?"

He snorts.

"And a Granger at that. You weren't exactly my number one fan either," I point out.

Another amused look from him that somehow feels like a caress.

"I hate *nothing* about you," he says.

That makes me laugh.

His hand slides up my thigh and he squeezes. "You knew I liked you—I kissed you the night we met!"

My mouth drops. "I'm not so sure. You said I kissed like I had something to prove!"

He groans. "That wasn't a bad thing."

"You just like riling me up?"

He chuckles. "Well, yeah…I do love riling you up. But I wasn't trying to upset you when I said that—I had no idea you'd take it the way you did. That kiss was the best of my fucking life…until this weekend. *Damn.* You have knocked me sideways with your mouth the past two nights."

My face flushes and heat floods through my body. He grins when I shift in my seat.

"I'll respect your decision," he says. "But I have no reason to hide this."

My heart stutters and something inside of me uncoils. "You don't?"

"I don't. Windy Harbor is small. People will eventually find out…if they don't suspect already."

I let out a nervous laugh. "You're right. Erin and Juju will know as soon as they see me."

He grins. "That freshly fucked look?"

I give him the side-eye. "Depends on whether we ever sleep together again." I lift my shoulder nonchalantly.

He stares at me in alarm, and when I eventually start grinning, he rubs his chest.

"That hurt," he says.

I laugh and he shakes his head.

"Who likes to rile who?" he says.

My laugh dies down and I trace circles over the top of his hand.

"Seriously, though…you don't worry about the project? Our families?" I ask.

"I don't know what will happen between our families, but you're not something I want to hide from them or anyone else. As far as the project…we've managed to make things work there. We're adult enough to continue with that, no matter what happens between us. But you should know, Goldie—you're not just a weekend fling for me. I've wanted this and I still do. How about you?"

His thumb is rubbing across my thigh and my insides feel like warm liquid with the things he's saying and the way he's touching me.

"I want this too," I admit quietly. "But I'd be lying if I said I wasn't scared."

"What can I do to ease your fears?"

I look down, thinking about it. "I don't know," I finally say. "What happened with Wes was so unexpected. I was so blindsided. I guess just be honest with me. About everything. That's really all I ask."

He lifts my hand to his lips and kisses my knuckles. "That I can do."

When we've pulled into the lake house driveway, Milo puts his SUV in park and turns to face me.

"I'll help you get your things inside, but…come here." He leans closer and puts his hands on my cheeks, his lips meeting mine.

It's slow and sweet. I sigh against his mouth, and he deepens the kiss, pulling me closer. My hands tug his hair—I've learned this weekend that sinking my fingers into his hair is one of my favorite things to do. I want to climb into his lap and get lost in him, but I end the kiss, my eyes dazed as I look at him.

"Thank you for coming home with me." His thumb caresses my lower lip.

"I had the best time," I tell him.

He leans his forehead against mine. "Me too. Best weekend I can remember, Golo."

"Me too, Mildie." I sigh.

He gives me one more kiss and groans. "I don't want to leave your mouth."

I smile against his lips. "Our lips are *really* good together."

I hear something outside the SUV and turn to look. Grandma Donna and Grandma Nancy are standing there grinning in what I can only describe as pure glee.

"Oh my God," I whisper.

Milo laughs. "They are the funniest, cutest ladies I've ever seen…well, my grandmas are right up there. But they could totally compete for who meddles most."

I give them a pointed look, which sends them in titters, and I turn back to Milo in horror.

"Forgive them for their lack of kissing etiquette."

"Not quite like giving the city of Minneapolis a show from the windows, is it?" He laughs when I smack his chest. "Should we kiss again and really make your grandmas happy?"

"No, we shouldn't." I get out of the SUV to the sound of him laughing and my grandmas swarming to hug me.

"Sorry, we interrupted. We came to help you get your things inside and then, imagine our surprise when things were heating up out here!" Grandma Donna says, patting my arm.

I fan my face. "No words," I say, glancing at Milo as he walks to my side.

"Evening, ladies," he says.

"It's a fine evening, isn't it?" Grandma Nancy beams at him. "Looks like you two got up to some fun this weekend."

"We sure did," Milo says, completely unfazed. "Your granddaughter is amazing, as you know. My parents fell for her, my friends fell for her…"

"And it sounds like you fell for Marigold too." Grandma Nancy's eyes are all lit up.

I press my lips together and shake my head, avoiding eye contact with Milo.

He surprises me by taking my hand and kissing it, and I swear, my grandmas both swoon in unison. His eyes are intense as he tips my chin up to look at him.

"I did. Though I think I fell for Marigold the night we met." His smile is sweet and sinful.

Grandma Donna puts her hand on her chest. "That is beautiful. Just beautiful."

I give him an apologetic look, but he just grins.

"You're enjoying this, aren't you?" I say under my breath.

"More than you know," he says, trying to hold back a laugh. "But it's the truth, too…" He tugs my back against his chest, his arms wrapping around me. "I'm pretty sure I'm yours," he says against my skin.

"Did he just say what I think he said?" Grandma Donna whisper-shouts.

Milo and I burst out laughing.

"Okay, Granny Whisperer. Let's get my things," I tell him.

"I've got it," he says, still laughing as he walks to the trunk.

"You should come in for some dessert. I made a lemon bundt cake," Grandma Nancy says.

"I've never had that," Milo says, walking between my grandmas.

He turns back to look at me as if asking if I want him to stay.

"It's delicious," I tell him. "You should try some."

He gives me a flirty grin. "Okay, sounds like a date, ladies."

They both giggle and I roll my eyes, laughing as I follow them inside.

Kevin is thrilled to see me. He twirls until he must be dizzy. He's wearing his purple and gold knitted beanie. Damn those Vikings for not having better colors.

"Oh my God. You are so cute, yes, you are!" I pick him up and he wiggles in my arms, so happy.

"How did he do?" I ask as I hug my dad. "And how did you do?"

"I am so glad to see you. Maybe it'll give them someone else to focus on," he whispers.

"Oh yeah, I think I've got you covered there." I pat his knee.

"You're not gonna believe what we just saw outside, Everett," Grandma Donna announces. "These two were smooching until the windows were foggy."

I put my hand on my forehead, groaning, as my dad looks between me and Milo with interest.

"Is that so?" he asks, chuckling.

"I hope it's okay with you that I'm all about your daughter, Everett," Milo says, and his unabashed declaration is the sexiest thing I've heard.

"I kinda figured, since you took her home to meet your family," Dad says.

Milo reaches out and takes my hand. "She was a huge hit."

"Well, you're a huge hit around here. Look at their faces." I point at the grandmas, who are gazing at him in adoration.

Grandma Donna fans her face. "He's such a looker!"

CHAPTER TWENTY-SIX

GOOOOD MORNING

MILO

After cake, which is one of the best I've had, we go through a long Minnesota goodbye. I didn't think anyone could linger at the door longer than my parents, but the Whitmans are right up there. Goldie follows me out, apologizing for her family's total disregard of boundaries and then gives me a kiss that nearly brings me to my knees. I feel intoxicated as I stumble away with my dick completely pissed at me for leaving her. I'm at my place just long enough to set my bag down before I call Goldie.

She picks up after the second ring. "Hello?"

"Want to come over?"

She laughs. "Miss me already?"

"*Yes*."

"I miss you too."

"Perfect, then come over. I'll watch for you and walk you

up…or I could come back to pick you up if you don't want to leave your car parked outside the cafe."

"You're serious."

"Absolutely."

She laughs again. God, I love her laugh. She gives it her all, the way she does everything, and in person, it's like the sun coming out on a cloudy day—everything around her brightens.

"I want to, but I should probably stay here to help Dad in the morning. As crazy as he is about the grandmas, I think he needs a buffer after the weekend. He's a little edgier than usual right now."

"Okay, I understand." I'm smiling like a smitten fool as I add, "I could also take you back before everyone wakes up in the morning."

"How about Friday night?"

I try not to sag with disappointment. *Smitten fool.* "Friday night it is…unless I can talk you into sooner between now and then."

She giggles.

"Give it your best shot," she says in a flirty voice.

"Prepare to be wowed."

"Your work is cut out for you. '*Would you like to come over*,'" she says in my deep voice, which makes me laugh, "while sweet, is not wow-worthy."

"Goldie, two nights with you were not enough. Falling asleep and waking up next to you was something I didn't even know I could miss, but now that I've experienced it, I don't want to miss another day."

It's quiet for a beat.

"Wow," she says softly. "That was really good."

"It's true."

"We hardly slept though...so...I don't see how it could *really* be true."

My laugh is husky and I move to my bed, leaning back against the headboard. I love the way this woman doesn't let me get away with shit.

"Okay, Marigold, my literal dove. True confession. Both nights you fell asleep before me and both mornings you woke up *after* me, and you know what?"

"What?" she whispers.

"I loved every second."

I hear her quick intake of breath and smile.

"Good night, Golo. Sweet dreams," I say, and hang up.

I work on sketches until I can't see straight, a surprise I've been thinking about for Goldie taking shape.

The next morning, I'm sitting by the cafe window when I see her pull up. She gets out of her car, the wind twisting her hair around her face. The sunlight makes her hair look as if it's spun from gold. I sit up straighter, my body on full alert. She's wearing a short summer dress today instead of her usual work attire of a tank top or sweatshirt with jeans. She looks beautiful in everything she wears, and especially with nothing at all, but *today*...fuck me. The wind picks up and her dress whips around, giving me a glimpse of her thighs as she tries to hold it down. I adjust in my seat.

She walks in and goes straight to the counter, picking up the iced coffee and scone that's waiting for her. Juju is speaking to a customer and stops in mid-sentence when she sees Goldie. A smile grows until she's beaming and she points at Goldie.

Goldie holds up a hand. "Don't say it." She laughs.

"I can tell you had a good weekend is all I was going to say," Juju says, as Goldie is going "Bup-bup-bup" over her, trying to silence her.

I laugh, enjoying the show from my seat.

Goldie turns and pauses when she sees me, but then she moves forward and comes to a stop at the table.

"You caught all of that, didn't you, you smug little thing." She crosses her arms and I lean back in my seat, taking her in.

"Oh, Goldie, you know nothing about me is small."

She hears the women at the table next to us snickering, and her head whips around.

"Because you're so *tall*," she says loudly, her face flaming. "So, so tall. Morning, Beverly." Her head dips. "Carol."

"Morning, Goldie," Beverly says, winking at me.

Carol waves at both of us, still laughing behind her other hand.

Goldie pulls out the chair across from me and sits, hissing, "And doing it all from *my* table, I might add, Milo Lombardi!"

I lean in until we're only a couple of inches apart. "There's a kissing tax to sit at this table."

Her eyes drop to my mouth. "You think you're getting a kiss after what you just pulled?"

"Yes, I insist."

We stare at each other for a long moment and she starts drifting closer, when a voice behind her says, "Just the person I wanted to see."

Goldie and I look up to see Ava standing there.

Goldie freezes and she and Ava stare at each other.

"Ava, did you want to see me about something?" I ask.

She looks at me, a tiny frown forming. "No, not you… her." She tilts her head toward Goldie. She takes a step forward and leans closer to me. "Although I have to say, it's disappointing to see you looking so cozy with a Whitman." She smiles. "I'll try not to hold it against you though, cuz. There's time to change your mind."

I'm so taken aback, I just stare at her in shock. As I'm about to set her straight, she turns her attention to Goldie. She places a flyer in front of her and points at it. I try to see it, but Goldie picks it up before I can.

"What is this?" Goldie asks.

"I'm giving you a warning. This is what we'll be bringing to the town meeting next week. There's time to stop your plans before it gets ugly."

"Save the Otters?" Goldie reads. "And what exactly do you mean, you're bringing this to the town meeting? We love the otters. We see them every time we're in town for the winter. In fact, one comes back to visit every year…Orion."

"Which is precisely why you must be stopped," Ava says.

"We're not damaging the otters' home. The renovations and buildouts will be where they are now, and we intend to maintain the integrity of the waterfront," Goldie says.

"We'll see what everyone thinks at the meeting." Ava shrugs.

I can't stand it, I have to speak up. "Ava, what is this about? I assure you, we've already taken all of this into consideration. Are you really so caught up in Bruce's fight that you're going to follow suit without even getting to know Goldie and her family?"

"I know enough about Goldie and her family," she says, her eyes flashing.

"I don't see how," I argue. "You've done nothing but try to stir up trouble for them since you got here."

Her jaw is clenched as she shifts on her feet.

"Seems like your mind's made up," Goldie says quietly. "I guess we'll see you at the meeting."

Ava nods and turns to leave. Before she reaches the door, she looks back at me and says, "Dad will be back in Windy

Harbor for the weekend. He said he invited you to dinner on Sunday, but you haven't responded yet."

"I'm not sure I'll be able to make it," I say.

She stares at me for a long moment then nods. "So, this is the way we're playing this...okay, got it."

She turns and leaves.

Goldie is visibly shaken after she's gone, and the whole cafe shoots curious looks our way.

I take Goldie's hand and thread our fingers together. "I'm really sorry about that."

"What did she mean about the way you're playing this?"

"I have no idea." I frown.

"You haven't been talking to her?"

"Only when Bruce introduced us."

She still looks troubled.

"Hey, don't worry. This town loves you. I might go Sunday just to see if I can change their minds."

"Don't bother," she says. "Unless you want to go..."

"I'd much rather stay buried in you, but if I must, I'll go and do the Lord's work."

Her cheeks turn bright red and she turns to see if Beverly and Carol are still listening to our conversation.

Beverly is in mid-sentence. "...and she said we all sound just like *Fargo*, which is absolutely ridiculous..."

Goldie gives me a pointed look. "You better be glad that *Fargo* once again offended a Minnesotan."

I smirk. "Well, you know we don't sound like that."

"I know that's what we all like to say, but I dare you to tell Grandma Donna that little tidbit with a straight face. She sounds just like Marge."

"Nonsense." I laugh and lean in. "Back to what's important...I'd love to know what you'd have done as punishment if they had been listening."

She leans even closer. "Wouldn't you like to know…"

"I have a better idea. Why don't we go upstairs and you can show me?"

She picks up her phone and tries to pretend my words don't affect her. She sounds breathless when she says, "Unfortunately, I have to get back to the house. I'm meeting with Noah."

"Interesting. I'm meeting with Noah too…in forty-five minutes."

She bites her bottom lip and my eyes are drawn to it.

"Are you teasing me, Golo?"

"What do you think?"

I get as close as I can to her ear, my voice low and raspy. "I think you're asking to be fucked this morning, Goldie Whitman. Is your love language: *try to get under Milo Lombardi's skin*?"

She lifts a shoulder. "Do you often speak of yourself in third person?"

I rub my hand over my face and let out a long exhale. "My door is unlocked. Go upstairs and get naked. I need to force my dick to cooperate long enough for me to walk out of here without giving the good folks of Windy Harbor a show."

"Aw, come on." She pouts. "They need some entertainment around here."

"You're not helping," I growl.

She grins and it's the she devil out in full form. Definitely not helping my situation.

She stands and puts her hand on my shoulder, bending down to whisper in my ear, "Distract them."

While she walks to the door that leads upstairs, I call out, "Juju, did I hear you made a new drink this morning?"

Everyone turns and looks at her and she nods.

"Put it on my tab, please, Juju. Round's on me for the whole house."

A cheer goes up and Goldie slips upstairs. After I get pounded on the back a few times by the customers, I slip out the door myself.

When I open my door, Goldie's standing by my couch.

I shake my head. "Goldie, Goldie, Goldie," I tsk. "What am I gonna do with you? You didn't do as I asked." I look her over and move toward her. I put my hand on her neck, my thumb tracing over her lip. "This is not naked at all," I say in her ear.

She turns and bends over the back of the couch and her dress lifts just enough for me to get a peek of her cheeks. I hum my approval and slide my hands up her dress, finding her completely bare. She looks at me over her shoulder and gives me a sassy look. I smack her backside and she grins. It turns into a moan when my fingers wander between her legs, finding her slit ready for me.

"Mmm. So wet." I work my fingers in and out of her, doing a swipe over her clit with each pass. When I press inside her again, deeper this time, she thrusts into my hand.

"You, Milo," she pants. "I need you."

I ignore her until she's close, her walls clamping around me, her whimpers fueling me. When she's about to fall over the edge, I slowly slide my fingers out and undo my pants just enough to pull my dick out of my briefs and slam into her. She lets out a long guttural moan and I'm right there with her. It feels too good.

"I missed you last night," I tell her, thrusting faster and faster.

My chest bows over her back and my hands are everywhere, one moving over her tits and waist and ass, and the other hyperfocused on her clit.

"I missed you—ah, I'm so close," she cries. "You feel so good."

"I'll let you come if you stay here tonight," I tell her.

"Fri…day," she moans.

I withdraw my fingers and she tries to grab my hand.

"Nuh-uh-uh," I say.

She swivels her hips and I squeeze my eyes shut. This little minx will get her way no matter what.

"Fine," I mutter, putting my fingers back where they belong. "But I'm not happy about it."

She looks at me over her shoulder and grins, her eyelids heavy. "You sure *feel* happy about it."

"Because you've bewitched me with your pussy," I grumble.

It doesn't carry any bite because in the next second, we're both coming harder than ever, gasps and moans and stars and mind-numbing bliss.

CHAPTER TWENTY-SEVEN

SOLIDARITY

GOLDIE

I smile the whole way home.

That smile drops when I see Ava Piper walking out of my house.

What the *hell* is she doing at my house?

She's opening her car door as I park and jump out of mine.

"Tell me you're not bothering my dad with your nonsense." I slam my door and stalk toward her.

She turns and leans against her car, folding her arms across her chest. "Your dad can fight his own battles, Goldie."

I get in her face and she straightens until we're standing eye to eye. *"Leave him out of this.* You want a fight on your hands? Bring it. You and I can go at it all day, but he is off-limits." I tap my chest and she scoffs.

"I've been dealing with girls like you my entire life," she

says. "You think you're better than everyone else…handed everything on a gold platter and expect the little people to bow to you." She takes a step closer and I smell her citrusy body wash.

She smells terrific, dammit.

"I don't know how you *think* you know me, but I assure you, I'm not the jerkface you're painting me out to be. Privileged? Yes. Better than everyone else? Not even close. You wanna come after my artwork? Fine. But trying to turn the town against my family is going too far. Do you even know the man you're siding with? From what I've heard, you haven't known Bruce for very long and this fight that he tries to keep stirred up all the time goes back to our *grandfathers*." I shake my head. "Why do we have to continue this? It doesn't have to be this way."

"It *didn't* end with our grandfathers," she says. Her voice is shaky when she adds, "And I may not know Bruce well, but at least he's claimed me. He's proud of me and wants to know me—that's all the reason I need to stand by him."

She turns and gets in her car, screeching out of my driveway. I stand there confused, staring after her.

What was *that*?

I go inside and look for my dad, but I can't find him. When I knock on his door, I hear a muffled hello and a little yip from Kevin.

"Dad, are you okay?"

He clears his throat. "Yes."

"Are you sure?"

"I'm gonna rest for a while, okay?"

"Oh, okay. Of course. Sorry. I'll let you rest." I pause. "Would you like me to take Kevin?"

"No, he's good. He's cuddled up here next to me."

That makes me smile. "Aw, okay, you two. Get some sleep."

The morning visits to Milo's apartment continue throughout the week. My dad has another chemo treatment and my quick morning trip to the cafe before he wakes up is the only reprieve I allow myself. I draw ideas on my sketchpad next to Dad's bed while he's napping. This time has been worse. He's had a rough week. We haven't even talked about Ava being here—he's either been sick or sleeping. Milo stops by to visit and to work on the property, but I don't spend the night at his place, even on Friday night.

He understands that I want to be with my dad and doesn't push it. Instead, he sneaks candy in for my dad, brings him word finder books and puzzles, and watches movies with us. On Saturday, my brothers come into town and when they walk in, they catch me crying in Dad's bathroom. Dad's sitting in a chair in front of the mirror and I've shaved one side.

His beautiful wavy white hair has fallen out in chunks this week and this morning, he asked me to take it all off.

Tully is the first one to find us, and then the rest of them file in.

There's a big hugfest, more tears, and then I get to work. When I'm done with Dad's head, Tully motions for him to get up and sits in the chair himself.

"All off, please," he says.

I'm a blubbering mess.

"I do mine too!" Grayson says.

"Oh, let's keep yours," Dad says. "You've got the best hair!"

Grayson feels Dad's head and sticks out his lip. "I want to see my head."

When Tully's done, Camden sits down and gets his shaved. Noah is next.

"I do mine too!" Grayson says again.

"But your hair is so, so good," I tell him.

"I like their heads." He points at Tully and Camden and gasps when I do the first swipe over his dad's head.

I gulp back tears and Grayson pats my leg.

"It's okay, Auntie. Dad says hair grows back."

"You're right." I sniffle.

Dylan hands me tissues and I blow my nose.

"You guys don't need to do this," Dad says.

His lip trembles and then he straightens his shoulders and his eyes brighten the way they do when he's about to tease us.

"I don't need to impress anyone," he says. "*You* guys still need to find the ladies."

Camden and Tully smirk, smoothing their hands over their heads.

"With these faces, I think we'll be okay," Tully says, studying himself in the mirror. He pats Dad's cheek. "And you're still a stud, Dad. You could get any lady you wanted to."

"No way," Dad says, laughing.

Camden takes a selfie of the three of them.

"Everybody okay?" Milo calls.

"I'll go get him. We have to keep this on the down-low until we're done or the grandmas will protest," Noah says.

"You're not wrong," Dylan says. "They're gonna lose their shit when they see all of us."

"Let me touch, Daddy," Grayson says.

Noah leans over and Grayson cackles.

"I do mine too," he says. "Please, Auntie."

"If your dad says it's okay, I'll do it."

Noah sighs. "It'll be a while before it grows back. Are you sure you're okay with that?"

Grayson nods excitedly and when Noah stands up, Grayson takes his place.

"Can I do a little mohawk?" I show him where I'd leave a little hair and he shakes his head.

"Like Dad and Papa and the uncles!" he says.

"Okay!"

He makes us all laugh with the way he squeals and cracks up with each swipe I do over his scalp.

"Hold still!" I say, giggling.

More selfies are taken when he's done. My face is one big red splotch in the photos, but I'm smiling so big at Grayson, it doesn't matter.

Dylan is the last one to sit down.

Kevin winds through everyone's legs and rolls around in the hair.

"Oh my goodness, Kevin, you're gonna be a mess!" I fuss at him.

Dad points at me as I'm shaving Dylan's head and Milo walks in to hear him say, "Don't you dare shave yours off, buttercup. That would break my heart."

I open my mouth to protest and he shakes his head. I've always wanted to do whatever my brothers are doing and this time is no different.

"But, we're in this together—" I start.

"Absolutely not," Dad cuts me off. "Please, baby girl. The thought of you cutting this off kills me." He runs his hand over my hair and shakes his head.

Milo's eyes are wide when his eyes meet mine in the mirror. He leans over and kisses my cheek, wiping the tears off my face.

"Looks like I've missed quite a party," he says.

My face crumbles and Dylan yelps. "Hey, watch the head. I don't want nicks."

I sniffle and laugh and get through the haircut. Dylan had the longest hair of all my brothers and is the most vain about it, but he's grinning when he stands up.

"I kinda like it. No one's gonna recognize me, but I still look badass," he says.

"Hasn't humbled you at all," I mutter.

Everyone moves into action to start the clean-up. I step to the sink, wash my hands, and move to get the vacuum when someone clears their throat.

I turn around and Milo is sitting in the chair. I put my hand to my mouth.

"No," Dad says, shaking his head. "Don't do it. I've caught my daughter playing with your hair all week."

Tears stream down my cheeks.

"If he's a real man, he'll do it," Tully teases.

"Tulls!" I yelp.

"Does he have it in him?" Noah adds, nudging Camden.

"I think he does." Camden nods.

"Nah. And anyway, bet you can't look this good," Dylan says, rubbing his head.

"You guys are the worst," I say.

Milo just laughs and nods. "I'm not scared. Say bye to this goodness, Golo," he says to me in the mirror.

"Aw, he's pulling out a nickname and everything," Tully says. "I think he's really into you, Golds."

"I'm going to kill you guys," I mutter under my breath. But the tears keep falling even as I'm laughing.

Milo looks back at me. "Do you need to sink your hands in it one more time before it goes?"

My brothers all shudder.

I move in front of Milo and put my fingers in his hair—because I want to, and to gross my brothers out. I lean down and take my time kissing him, despite the protests.

He kisses me back, not deterred in the slightest by my dad and brothers.

"This just got you so many points," I whisper in his ear.

"Ew, no whispering," Dylan says.

I smack Dylan's shoulder and move into place behind Milo, letting out a ragged exhale. I do one long buzz, Milo's beautiful dark hair falling to the ground in one large clump. A tear drips down my cheek and Milo's eyes caress me from the mirror.

This is the moment I realize I'm in love with him.

"We were just kidding, dude. You didn't have to shave your head," Tully says, earning a glare from me.

"It wasn't for you," Milo says, his eyes never leaving mine.

Dad squeezes his shoulder and Milo puts his hand on top of Dad's, patting it twice.

"Don't listen to these guys, Milo." Dad's eyes well up and he shakes his head. "You're all too much, but I sure do love ya. Every single one of ya. That includes you, Milo. Dammit, you've all got my waterworks going."

"Love you, Dad. And you're all right, Milo," Noah says.

Coming from Noah about a man I'm seeing, that is high praise.

One by one, my brothers thank Milo for this gesture.

He waves it off like it's the least he can do.

I finish shaving him and lean down to kiss his shiny head.

"I don't think you could possibly know how much this means to me," I tell him softly.

He puts his hand on my cheek. "It hurts seeing you cry."

He stands up, dusting his shoulders. He turns and looks at me.

"What do you think?" he asks.

"Your head is an odd shape, but I still like it."

He frowns and turns quickly to look in the mirror.

I step on my tiptoes and stare over his shoulder. "I'm just kidding. You're still ridiculously beautiful."

He turns and tickles my sides before wrapping me in a hug.

"And you've totally won my heart with this one, Mildie," I add.

"Is that right?" he asks, grinning.

A screech makes me jump.

"What is going on in here?" Grandma Donna cries. "Oh, fer crying out loud. Your *hair*." She goes to each guy and wrings her hands as she stares at them. She makes a face when she sees Noah and Camden. "You need the hair, honey."

She pats their shoulders and they just laugh.

"Nancy!" she yells. "You won't believe what these hooligans were doing while we were makin' peanut brittle!"

She tuts as she looks at her grandsons and lets out a little whimper when she sees Grayson.

"All your beautiful hair," she says, sighing.

When she gets to Dad, she takes his hand.

"You still look handsome as ever, Everett. Stella would still swoon over you." She pats his cheek.

"I'm not so sure about that, but thank you," Dad says.

"What about me, Grandma?" Dylan asks.

"It could be worse," she says. "You could've done this in January and then you'd freeze your patooties off."

CHAPTER TWENTY-EIGHT

ONE CONDITION

MILO

When we walk into the town meeting on Monday night, we make quite an entrance. The small courthouse is full and noisy…until they see us.

Goldie is on my right side, her fingers threaded through mine, and her dad and brothers flank us on either side, a full-blown posse. Goldie looks hot as hell in a short, fitted black skirt and a white blouse, dressier than her normal vibe, but she said it's a power move. The guys and I are in suits, which wasn't planned, but with our freshly shaved heads, it all looks intentional. Like we're the small-town mafia who's coming to set everyone straight.

There's nothing so sinister going on here, but I can tell we paint an intimidating picture.

Goldie says she's still caught off guard seeing all of us without hair, and it's a little jarring when I look in the mirror too, but I'm getting used to it. She also says I'm pulling off the look *extremely* well, but when I offered to keep it like this, she said *hell no…*

The grandmas are already sitting near the front. Everett tried to talk them out of coming in case it got heated, but they insisted. Miss Idella and Emmy are sitting next to them, chatting away, and Beverly and Carol are right behind them. Bosco waves at Goldie and she grins, waving back, before taking a seat.

A few news teams are here that I'm sure came at my uncle's bidding.

The meeting is called to order not long after we arrive, and eventually, the mayor, Meredith Strong, gets up to say a few words. I've only talked with her a couple of times, but Everett speaks highly of her. She's indicated that she's completely behind the resort. She's nice and seems like a smart lady. One morning last week, she was in Kitty-Corner Cafe and came over to say hi to Goldie and me. She mentioned how much she loved Goldie's mom, Stella —how they'd had a few lunches in Windy Harbor when Stella was there for the summer and a fun memory of running into her in Minneapolis when they were new moms. It was sweet and I could tell it meant a lot to Goldie.

Later, Goldie said, "Often people avoid talking about someone who's passed because they don't want to cause sadness, but there's already sadness. What makes me the saddest is to think that my mom would be forgotten."

When she says things like that, I say another prayer that Everett will survive this cancer prognosis. She's too young to lose both parents.

Everett gets up and talks in depth about the plans for the resort. A few people whisper when he gets up—the bald heads are creating some attention. He gets a few pitying looks, but mostly everyone is all smiles at how animated he is as he's speaking.

And then Bruce gets up and talks about how the Whitmans are destroying the waterfront and the peace of Windy Harbor. Ava talks about what this will mean for the otters. The way she talks about them, I doubt she's ever even seen one in real life. A few of the townspeople get up to speak about their feelings about the project, both positive and negative. When Juju gets up, Camden stiffens next to me. I shoot him a look, but he stares at Juju with a blank expression. He's the nicest guy, but for some reason, he seems to avoid Juju. When I asked him why he rarely comes to Kitty-Corner when he's in town, he said his best friend's pesky little sister is a brat. I was shocked that he was talking about Juju.

Erin gets up, and so does her dad, Jason. They talk about how nice it would be for Windy Harbor's economy to have a beautiful resort.

"We had it for years and miss what having that business up and running did for this community," Jason says. "And this will be even better than that, more jobs, more possibilities. I think we need it to keep the town flourishing."

The few who speak out against it say that the Whitmans aren't full-time residents of the town, so they don't know the impact of what this change will bring. But these comments are few and far between, compared to all who are for the project. I look around and spot Ava and she looks angrier as the night goes on.

Meredith gets up at the end. "Thank you for your input. Since permits for everything have already been issued, the Whitmans are within their legal rights to keep moving forward, but we can take a final vote to put the matter to rest."

Everyone votes and while the votes are being tallied, there's a low hum of chatter around the room.

It's not long before Meredith walks back to the podium. "We have the results!" she says, smiling widely. "There is resounding support for the Whitmans to continue their work —*99%* voted YES to the Windhaven Resort!"

A cheer goes up and Goldie squeezes my hand, looking at me in relief.

"Congratulations, now no one can get in the way," I tell her.

Afterwards, people come up to wish us well and I'm surprised to be included in that. Bruce and Ava stand on the other side of the room with their small group of people. When I make eye contact with Ava, she glares at me.

"I just don't understand why she's so angry," Goldie says, her voice low. "I know she wants to make an impression on her dad, but it's kind of crazy that she's jumped right into this argument."

"I agree," I say quietly. "I'm not sure what she hopes to gain. It doesn't seem worth it to me."

Before we leave, Everett thanks us for being there.

"That went about as well as it could possibly go," he says. "And as Meredith put it at the end, we've already gotten the permits for everything, so let's forge ahead. Noah, I know you need to get back home tonight to relieve the sitter, but would you mind stopping by the house before you leave tomorrow? I need to talk to you kids about something."

Noah agrees.

Before Everett gets in the car with Camden, Dylan, and Tully, he hugs Goldie.

"I'm good for the night," I hear him say. "Why don't you take a little break from mothering me? I've got two at home who've got it covered." He winks at me and Goldie's face is bright red when she looks at me.

"Love you, Dad. Maybe I will…hang out with Milo for a little while."

"Sounds good, buttercup. Good night."

"This night is certainly looking up," I say, opening the door of my SUV for her.

"I can't believe I finally have you here again. It's taken long enough," I tease.

I tug her closer, undoing one button at a time before the door to my place is even closed all the way. When her blouse hangs open and I see the lacy cream bra she's wearing, I let out a ragged breath. She leans against the door and I put my arms on either side of her, my face inches from hers.

"You're right where I want you," I tell her.

"What do you plan to do with me now that I'm here?" She looks up at me.

She runs her hand over my head and I groan.

"I still can't believe you shaved your head," she whispers.

I lean into her hand. "That feels *nice*. It's like all my nerve endings are on alert without the hair there. Not that I didn't enjoy the hair tugs, because, believe me, I did. But this is a whole other kind of nice."

She grins. "You're like a cat. Wanting all the pets."

I smile back. "You're not wrong. Whatever I have to do to get you to touch me, I'll do it. I'm not too proud, Goldie Whitman."

"Come here then," she says, putting her hands on either side of my face and kissing me.

I've been with her all week, but it still feels like forever since we've done this.

Our kiss is urgent, desperate. We can't get our clothes off fast enough as we hurriedly undress. My fingers slide down her body.

"You always know right where I want you," she says, gasping into our kiss.

I make long, torturous strokes against her, dipping my finger inside and out and over her clit and back inside again. Until her legs start to buckle. I move to my knees and she protests.

"I want you inside me…"

"I will be," I say against her thigh. "But first, I need to do this."

My tongue does a long swipe down her center and she gasps, already shaking.

"Oh," she shudders. "So good."

"You taste so good."

"I do?" she pants.

"Oh, yes. Fuck. You do," I tell her.

I lick her until she's chanting my name. Her hands hold onto my head as I feast on her, her head falling back when she cries out. When her aftershocks let up, I kiss my way up her body.

She giggles. "You look so proud of yourself."

I smirk as I pick her up and carry her to bed. I lean over and then surprise her by flipping her so she's on top. And she doesn't waste time.

"Mmm, I finally have you where I want you," she says, sinking onto me.

We both groan.

"You look so beautiful," I say, leaning up to suck her nipple.

My hands guide her ass, making sure she's getting the perfect amount of friction.

"How long can I get you to stay?" I ask.

"Can you take me back early in the morning?"

"You know I will."

"Okay," she says, her hips undulating over me.

"I'm afraid you won't get much sleep tonight."

She laughs and I feel it everywhere.

"All right. We can sleep when we're dead," she says, leaning forward to kiss me.

And then we don't speak for a long time.

We just let our bodies worship each other.

Later, when I'm buried deep inside her again, I look at her in awe.

"Is it working?" I ask.

"Is what working?"

"I'm trying to fuck you until you never want another man inside you again."

"Oh, that." She laughs between gasps.

Our bodies are slick with sweat and I just want to inhale her. Even when I'm as close as I can possibly get, I want to be closer.

"It's working," she says. "On one condition…"

I put my fingers between us and rub tiny, fast circles on her as I drag in and out of her. I watch where I enter her and it's the best fucking thing.

"What's that?" I ask.

I pull almost all the way out and slam into her. We both groan.

She's breathless when she says, "Leave Spoonbridge and Cherry alone."

"Done," I say.

She laughs and I do too as I kiss her.

She doesn't know that I gave up those plans a long time ago.

CHAPTER TWENTY-NINE

LUTHERAN SALAD

GOLDIE

DAD

Dinner tonight at home, just the fam? 5:30 work for everyone?

> I'm supposed to meet Erin and Juju this afternoon, but I can make it back by 5:30. Do you need me to reschedule, so I can help with dinner?

DAD

No, don't change your plans. Grandma Nancy has a roast in the Crock-Pot and she and Grandma Donna are having a dessert cook-off, I think. So far, there are seven-layer bars and an apple pie…

DYLAN

It's been too long since I've had Grandma's roast. I am in.

CAMDEN

Me too!

NOAH

Sounds good.

TULLY

I'll be there. You guys need to eat extra dessert so the grandmas won't hound me for skipping it.

NOAH

You're on your own there. I'm still on Grandma Nancy's shit list for not having seconds of her Lutheran Jell-O last Sunday.

DYLAN

I just threw up a little. Was it the lime and cottage cheese one?

NOAH

Yep. Grandma Donna puts a dollop of mayo on top. 🤢

DAD

🤤 Come on! That's the food of my childhood! Often served with SPAM.

CAMDEN

Okay, now you're just trying to be hurtful.

> Just to clarify…you haven't seen any signs of Lutheran Jell-O prep going on over there, have you, Dad? If you could encourage the red Jell-O and mandarin orange one, that would be great.

> **DAD**
> I'll do my best, but the grandmas are equal opportunists with the Jell-O flavors.

> **TULLY**
> Speaking of over THERE, why aren't you HERE this morning, Golds?

> **DYLAN**
> I'm hurt. I came all this way...

> **CAMDEN**
> It is very quiet over HERE.

> I'm at Kitty-Corner Cafe!

> **NOAH**
> I was just there...didn't see you...

> UGH.

> **DAD**
> Give your sister a break. She's subjected to the grandmas almost every hour of every day.

I fan my face.

"What's going on?" Milo's eyes narrow. "Who's making you so red?"

"No one to be jealous of." I snort. "My brothers are calling me out for not being home this morning."

He grins and comes up behind me, hugging my back to his chest. "I'm sorry we overslept. It's all my fault."

"It *is* all your fault."

"It is. You didn't want me keeping you up all night long. When you were screaming my name, you meant, 'Stop making me feel so good, dammit!'"

I laugh and he turns me around in his arms, leaning his forehead against mine.

"Seriously, I'm sorry. I told you I'd get you back before they all woke up and I didn't. I'll do better next time."

"*If* there's a next time," I tease.

"Oh, there'll be a next time. I'm the only man for you… remember? You said that last night."

I groan, leaning my head on his chest. "You are *insufferable*."

Whenever the brothers are all in town, we get a lot done. I show them the sample boards I have of nearly every inch of the project and let them vote on the final decisions for everything from furniture and wood choices to paint and lighting. It's a painless process since I've already narrowed it down to my favorites and have a good idea of what they each like.

Noah has called in every favor around the state, and because he and my dad have a great reputation with everyone they've ever worked with in construction and real estate, they've all been happy to help. We're also paying them well, but at least twelve guys have said they would have done it for nothing. I'm happy that Dad's seeing how loved he is, not just in this community, but from all over. All the extra hands are making everything go faster than usual, which is exciting. Most of the exterior work is done and anything we can finish before winter will be amazing. All the indoor work will get done during the cold months. The restaurant is almost complete, besides decorating it, and Camden thinks he can be here full-time in September, which is just a month away. He's conducted online interviews and will finalize the hires once he's met them in person next month. The restaurant's grand opening will be in early October.

When I originally made a plan to take Kevin to visit Sabrina, I didn't realize my brothers would all be in town, so I'm torn about leaving them. However, both Erin and Juju got off work early to make this happen, and after my brothers teased me so much all morning about Milo, I gladly bail right after lunch. We're all at Erin's place, a cute little house on Wildbriar Lane. The puppies are adorable together, rolling around on the floor. We're sitting on the floor too, so we can pet them and be close if they get too rough.

"Can you believe how big they are now?" Erin says, her lips poking out in a pout.

"I know. It's gone so fast." I lean against the couch.

"They make me want a puppy, but I don't think I could pull it off. Too underfoot at the bakery," Juju says wistfully.

"Oh hey, before I forget, I wondered if we could do a Paint and Sip night at Cox," Erin says.

"That sounds fun!" Juju says, laughing when Sabrina rolls into her leg.

They both look at me.

"Yeah, of course, I'm in. When are you thinking?"

"Whenever you'd agree to be our instructor," Erin says, giving me the side-eye.

I laugh. "*Oh*, I see how it is now."

"I'd open it up to everyone…they'd have to pay for supplies, of course, but I'm thinking something a little more exciting…"

"Like what?"

"Like those acrylic pour paintings you've done before. I'm dying to try one of those," Erin says.

"Sure." I nod. "Should we do a practice night first? We'll need to do it in your back room, so we don't ruin anything.

Or maybe The Cozy Palette? Hey—I can't believe I haven't asked before now. I haven't seen Percy around since I moved here. Is The Cozy Palette even still up and running? Are they still in town?"

Erin lifts an eyebrow. "Percy took a sabbatical and hasn't been in Windy Harbor since last summer. Maybe I could call them and see if we could use the space."

Juju and I study Erin and she frowns.

"What?"

"You have Percy's number?" I ask.

"Yeah," she says, like it's nothing. "What's wrong with that?"

"Nothing's wrong. It's just…we tried to talk you into getting their number for years! I didn't know you'd finally gotten it," Juju says.

"It's no big deal. I mean, maybe it is since they've basically disappeared, but it's worth a try." Erin shrugs.

Juju and I exchange a look. Erin has had a crush on Percy Oliver for years and now she's just nonchalant about their number?

"Highly sus," Juju mouths when Erin isn't looking.

I nod, wide-eyed, and try to school my expression when Erin faces me again.

"Well, let us know," I say. "I'll make time for it."

"Like you're *making time* for Milo Lombardi?" Juju says, poking me in the side.

I squeak and laugh. "I don't know what you're talking about."

"I'm talking about the way he sneaks you out of the cafe every morning when you think I'm not looking," she says.

"Gasp!" Erin says, and they both cackle.

"This is the day that it's coming from all sides," I say, sighing. "First, my brothers and now my best friends…if

Addy calls this afternoon, I'll know the universe is conspiring against me!"

"How is Addy?" Erin asks.

"Don't change the subject!" Juju glares at Erin and then softens it when Erin shoots her an apologetic look.

"Addy is great!" I jump in, happy to divert.

"Uh-uh. Spill! What is going on with you guys? I mean, it's been obvious for a long time that you're into each other, but…is it official? Are you guys exclusive?" Juju turns to face me, her eyes all lit up.

"Well…" I start flushing immediately, which just makes them laugh harder.

I hold up my hand and they try to contain themselves. And fail.

"Okay. Okay!" I gripe.

They school their expressions.

"He *has* said he wants to fuck me until I never want another man inside me again, so…I think that means something, right?" I give them an innocent look.

They're stunned speechless for all of three seconds and then they're both speaking at once.

Erin: *"What the fuck? I don't think any man has ever made me horny, but—is his schlong worthy? It's gotta be!"*

Juju: *"Oh my God, oh my God, oh my God, he is* all *about you! I'd say it's* definitely *official!"*

I cover my face and Kevin comes over to see if I'm okay. I focus on him while my temperature regulates and laugh when I look up to see them still staring at me.

"This is the best news EVER!" Juju cries. "I'm even happier than I was when Camden's shirt caught on fire at The Hungry Walleye that one summer!"

Erin and I pause our laughter and stare at Juju.

"Juliana!" Erin says, covering her mouth. "I don't think

I've ever heard you say anything rude in your life, but that… that was *rude*. Really, really rude." She leans over and squeezes Juju's hand. "I'm so proud of you."

Juju makes a face when she looks at me. "Sorry. That wasn't nice at all. But he wasn't hurt…bad…so it's okay to say that, right? I mean, Jackson doused him with the fire extinguisher, so…" She lifts her shoulder.

I snort. "Maybe once Camden is here full-time, you guys can make some sort of peace with one another."

Juju bites the inside of her lip. "Doubtful. He stopped by the cafe when he came into town this time and had the audacity to say he preferred Caribou's coffee."

Erin and I both gasp.

"That is…he *couldn't* have meant that," I say, horrified.

"That's what he said." She sighs. "I know we're supposed to be loyal to Caribou since it originated in Minnesota, and it's fine, but—"

"You originated in Minnesota too and your coffee is *way* better than Caribou," Erin says.

I nod. "It's true. Before I moved here, I always missed Kitty-Korner when I went back home. I can't believe Camden said that. I'm so sorry."

"Thanks, guys. And you don't need to be sorry for him. I handled it. I told him he could take his Cross Fox espresso and shove it up his snobby, uptight ass."

I can't help it, that cracks me up. I've never heard her talk to anyone like that, not even Camden, and he's the only one she clashes with.

She looks at us, a huge crease between her brows. "I didn't mean it," she says earnestly. "I love Caribou. Cross Fox is my favorite from there—in the Honey Lavender Espresso Shaker. I was just…so…mad."

"We need to unpack this," Erin says, just as my phone buzzes.

"Sorry. I leave my sound on all the time now in case my dad needs me."

"Don't apologize. We understand," Erin says.

I frown at the phone and pick up Kevin.

"Everything okay?" Juju asks.

"Tully texted that I need to get over there right away." I'm already on my feet and they get up too, helping me with my shoes and purse.

"Let us know if we can do anything to help," Erin says.

"And just…that you're all right." Juju scrunches her nose. "At least I hope everything is all right."

I hug them quickly and rush home.

CHAPTER THIRTY

DAYS OF OUR LIVES

MILO

I'm working on the east side of the pavilion when I hear something. I walk around and see Ava holding a gas can, her arm swinging back like she's winding up to pour it against the pavilion. And then to my horror, she does.

"What the hell are you doing?" I roar.

She startles and drops the match I didn't see her holding and a flame flickers. I jump into action, running to the nearest hose and dragging it over. I douse the flames, but they've multiplied in the time it's taken me to get back, the smell of smoke sharp and bitter in my throat. My shirt sticks to my back as I shout for Siri to call 911.

I give the address to the dispatcher and she says help is on the way.

Smoke billows around me, but in a few minutes, I manage to put out the fire. I'm nervous that it'd take very little to start another fire though, with all the gasoline she poured.

"I can't believe you started a fire. What the fuck were you thinking?"

"Don't start with me, Milo," she snaps, her dark hair whipping across her face. "The Whitmans aren't who you think they are."

I blink, chest still heaving. "So you set fire to their property?"

"They don't deserve all this."

"Well, why don't you enlighten me? Who does?"

She takes a step forward, too calm for someone who just committed arson.

Then she says the last thing I expected.

"*Me.* I'm your girlfriend's sister."

I stare at her, the words not computing.

"What? No. You're mistaken. Goldie doesn't have a sister. And you just tried to burn down her property? It doesn't add up."

Her jaw clenches. "It's complicated."

"Arson is not complicated."

"I'm telling you, I'm their sister. I have just as much right to this property as Goldie and her brothers," she says. "One big happy family, right?" She laughs, but tears are running down her cheeks.

"Hey!" A voice cuts through the haze.

I whip around to see Tully charging toward us.

"What did you just say?" he asks Ava.

"You heard me. This land is as much mine as it is yours. I'm your *sister*," she yells.

He looks frozen as they stare at each other. And then his eyes shoot to the scorched corner of the pavilion, the gas can, then to me and Ava, like he's trying to puzzle it all out.

"I don't understand," he says.

He takes out his phone and texts someone, his fingers shaky.

"I managed to get the fire out, but the fire department is still on the way…" I tell him.

Ava tries to back away and Tully blocks her path.

"You're not going anywhere. Who started the fire?" he asks.

Oh shit. Does he think I have something to do with this?

"She did. She lit it up like it was a damn bonfire," I say, glaring at her.

Sirens wail in the distance. The sheriff arrives first and then the firetruck rumbles to a stop, red lights spinning across the clearing. Firefighters leap out and rush toward us, coming to a stop when they don't see a fire.

I point to the scorched corner. "The fire was there and a lot of gasoline was poured all along there." I point to the side of the pavilion.

They nod and douse every side of the pavilion and the surrounding brush for any stray embers. One of them sends word to the other firefighters that it's under control.

The sheriff asks a few questions and then goes to talk to the firefighters.

My pulse is still thudding when I hear tires screech, and a few minutes later I see Goldie, her long legs eating the distance between us as she takes in the chaos.

Her eyes land on Ava.

"What's going on?" she asks.

Behind her, the rest of the brothers arrive. Camden, Dylan, and Noah spill out of Noah's truck. Ava doesn't flinch under their stares. If anything, she seems steadier now. But then Everett appears, walking slowly toward us. His face is pale and he looks like he ages ten years in ten seconds.

"Dad—" Goldie says, rushing to help him the rest of the way.

But Tully stares at Everett and it's the most anger I've ever seen from him, even off the ice.

"Dad, Ava is saying some outrageous things," he says.

Ava's voice shakes and she tilts her head toward Everett. "Tell them the truth. Tell them how you kept the truth from them all these years."

Goldie turns to her dad, confused. "Dad, what is she talking about?"

He looks at her and then at each of his sons. He looks heavy. Like he's been carrying this weight so long, he's not sure how to unload it without shattering everyone.

"I was going to tell you tonight. I wanted to tell you as soon as I suspected, but I wanted to be sure. Once it was confirmed, I wanted all of you together when I did..." He takes a deep breath. "Ava is your sister."

No one breathes.

Goldie's eyes fill with tears. "You...had another child?"

"No, Ava is...your mother's daughter."

"Dad, what are you saying?" Noah asks, stepping closer to his dad. "Mom had an affair?" There's disbelief and hurt in his voice.

Everett exhales, his shoulders sinking. "No, your mother would've never done that."

Ava scoffs and my jaw clenches as I will her to shut up with my stare.

"Your mom went out with Bruce Granger briefly in high school. She was sixteen and she got pregnant. When she told Bruce about it, he said they were too young, his parents would disown him, and he gave her money for an abortion."

"That's...not what he told me," Ava says.

Everett continues, "Instead of getting an abortion, she

went to a house for young girls in Rhode Island, and as soon as she had the baby, she was given up for adoption. Your mom never even got to hold you…which broke her heart, up until the day she died." He looks at Ava when he says those last words and I can tell they hit her hard.

She looks confused and she's shaking. If I weren't so upset with her, I'd feel sorry for her.

Everett moves closer to Ava and bends slightly so she'll look at him.

"It was the one thing your mom never got over. She wrote you letters," he tells her. "After you came to the house the other day, I started looking for them. I think they're at the Summit house, but I'll find them and give them to you."

Ava swallows hard.

"So you knew about this all these years?" Noah asks.

Everett turns toward Noah and nods, his eyes glassy. "Before your mom and I got engaged, she told me everything. She carried so much grief and guilt about it and she wasn't sure I'd want to be with her anymore if I knew the truth. It didn't change anything for me. I wanted to look for her child, but since she had agreed to a closed adoption with no contact, she knew she wouldn't be able to find her daughter. But then all these DNA websites came about…and she really wanted to try."

"How did you find out?" Camden asks Ava.

"23andMe," she says, wiping the tears from her cheeks.

Goldie stares at Ava and then her eyes find mine like she's just realizing I'm here. The color bleeds from her face.

"And you've known all this time," she says softly.

She backs away like she's been hit.

"Goldie!" I move toward her, but she takes off running.

I want to follow her, but the sheriff moves next to me, his thumbs in his pockets.

"I'd like to bring you each in for questioning, starting with Ms. Piper and Mr. Lombardi here."

"We'll be happy to cooperate, Sheriff Daniels," Dad says. "We won't be pressing any charges. This is just a big family misunderstanding and a mistake."

Ava looks at him in surprise and then she bursts into tears. "I'm sorry," she says. "I don't know what I was thinking. I was just so angry. I'm still so angry. And I don't know what the truth is anymore."

CHAPTER THIRTY-ONE
EVERYTHING HAS CHANGED

GOLDIE

I feel like my life just got tossed into the air like confetti, and now I'm trying to find each small piece, hoping that somehow, it will make sense.

It doesn't.

I don't think it ever will again.

I know we can't possibly know everything there is to know about our parents, but this is *big*.

My mom was everything to me. My anchor, my solace, the one who gave me the freedom to be who I am, the person I thought was the most honest in the whole wide world…and yet, there was this secret she carried our whole lives. *Our whole lives.*

And my dad carried it with her.

My stomach roils. I'm dizzy with how fast my life just changed.

The fire.

Ava.

I have a sister.

And then the second hit nearly takes me out.

Milo knew.

I go to my room and collapse on the bed, numb. My grandmas putter around the house, oblivious about this upheaval. Did Grandma Donna know all along? Did she encourage Mom to have an adoption? Did Mom feel like she had to do it?

My heart breaks for my mom and the pain she must have endured to go through that alone.

It's a while before Tully knocks on my door and then sticks his head in.

"You okay?" he asks.

"I don't know. No."

The second he crosses the room and sits next to me on the bed, I start sobbing. He wraps his arm around my shoulders and pulls me to him. I bury my face in his chest like we're five again and we're hiding in a scary basement during a thunderstorm.

"Yeah. It's hard to believe," he says. "How was she able to keep that secret for so long?"

"And Dad too!"

"I know. I think I'm in shock."

"And it's Ava freaking Piper," I groan.

"She had a meltdown apologizing after you left. Said she was so sorry. She's always wanted a family and was angry that she'd always be on the outside."

"Was that for the benefit of the sheriff or for real?"

"Who knows? It seemed sincere, but I don't know her." He sighs. "We have another sister and don't know her at all."

"And what I do know, I haven't liked," I say sadly.

I don't want to say it. But it claws its way out anyway.

"I think I'm falling in love with him." Tears drip down my cheeks. "And he knew. It's another lie."

"You're definitely in love with him. And this is all very messy."

"You think I'm stupid and I just attract liars?"

"You're not stupid at all." He pauses. "Hear him out. He's in love with you too."

"How do you know?"

"He's spending his own money to surprise you with something. Not just a little money either, *moneybags* money." He looks at me with his eyebrows raised. "A man doesn't just do that over a little crush."

I sigh. "I don't know what to do."

"Then don't do anything right now. Breathe. Be mad. Be hurt. But don't make any big decisions tonight."

I lean into him again and he rests his chin on my head.

We're quiet for a few minutes and then he pulls away.

"Need some snacks?" he asks.

"Chocolate and something salty."

He nods and leaves. I tuck my knees to my chest and there's a quiet knock on the door.

I don't answer.

The door creaks open anyway.

Milo steps into the room, looking haggard. His shirt is dirty and there are soot smudges on his jeans. His head has dark stubble where his hair is already growing out, and his eyes are wrecked.

"I had to answer questions at the sheriff's office or I would've been here sooner," he says. "They let me go after my statement."

I don't say anything.

He shifts, his expression pained.

"I'm so sorry that you found out like that."

I let out a jagged laugh.

He flinches.

"You knew, Milo."

"I found out today," he says quickly, stepping forward. "Right before you did. Just as Ava was about to—"

"Torch the pavilion?" I snap. "Yeah, I was there. I saw what she tried to do. And you were right there with her. Was this the plan all along? Gain our trust and then bring us down together? The perfect revenge for you as a Granger and the perfect revenge for her as our unclaimed sister?"

He moves closer, hands out like he's approaching a wild animal. "No, Goldie."

"I actually let myself believe you might be a man who wouldn't lie to me again."

His face caves. "I didn't, Goldie. I wouldn't…*I won't.*"

"I opened up to you. I let you in."

"I know." His voice is desperate now. "And I don't take that lightly. Listen to me, please. I had nothing to do with the Granger vendetta, and I had no idea who Ava was until today. I swear. I was just as stunned as you."

Tully steps in with our snacks and looks at me. "Are you okay?"

"You should go, Milo," I say. "I need time to process all of this."

He clears his throat and nods. "I understand. Take your time. You know where to find me. And I'm willing to talk things out whenever you're ready, day or night."

I swallow and nod.

He looks at me one more time before leaving the room.

Tully brings the big container of sea salt chocolate caramels and holds it out like a present.

I gasp. "I didn't know we had those!"

He grins and opens the container, holding it out for me to

take. I put my hand inside and grab two, humming with my first bite.

"I brought them with me," Tully says. "Thought you might be missing them in your life."

"So much," I say around a mouthful. "You're the best brother who ever lived."

He grins. "What have I been telling you? How did it go with Milo?"

"He says he didn't know. Not until right before we all showed up."

"Do you believe him?"

"I don't know. Maybe? I think so?" I groan. "Ugh. It just feels really far-fetched that he wouldn't know. Bruce loves to one-up Dad and shame him. It's hard to believe that once he knew about Ava, he wouldn't at least try to rub it in Dad's face that he'd had a baby with Mom."

"Well, if it went down the way Dad alluded it did, Bruce probably wasn't in any hurry for Ava to learn that he was an asshole. My guess is he saw someone eager to get back at us and capitalized on that."

I sigh. And then jump when Camden, Dylan, and Noah all cram into my room. Kevin trots in and jumps on the bed.

"You guys okay?" Noah asks.

"Just trying to process this," I say. "You?"

"Same," Camden says.

"Where's Dad?" Tully asks.

"Right here," Dad says, coming into the room. "I'm so sorry, guys. I let you down. I wanted you to hear all of this from me."

"How were you guys able to keep this a secret all this time?" Tully asks.

Dad shakes his head. "It wasn't easy. Your mom nearly told you every year around Valentine's Day…that's when Ava was born. It weighed heavily on her. When she heard about these new DNA tests, she wanted to see if she could find her daughter, but she died before she was able to."

"I think maybe I know where she kept the letters," Dylan says. "That little chest she kept locked. I always wanted to know what was in there."

"Me too!" I say.

Dad nods. "I bet that's it. The letters are definitely not here. I've searched everywhere. You're probably right—I bet they're in that chest."

"Do you know where the key is?" Noah asks.

Dad chuckles and shakes his head. "No clue."

"Did Grandma Donna know about the baby?" Camden asks.

"Yes, but Grandpa Otis didn't, and they went to great lengths to keep it that way. Grandma Donna thought he'd be too upset to forgive your mom."

"That's so sad," I swallow the lump in my throat. "Does Grandma Donna know that Ava is her granddaughter?"

"Not yet. I was going to tell her after I told you. I'll talk with her tonight." He looks around at each of us. "I know Ava's made it difficult for herself, but I hope you'll give her a chance. I think she's had a hard life and maybe started out wanting to know you, but then got resentful along the way about what great lives you've had."

"Is this why Bruce hates you so much?" I ask. "Because you got Mom?"

"It didn't help, let's put it that way. He already hated me because of our family history, but he *really* hated me when I started dating your mom during our senior year. He tried to get her back and she wanted nothing to do with him." He pauses. "I didn't say all of this to Ava because I hope she can have a relationship with her father, but he was awful to your mother. After he told her he wanted nothing to do with a baby or her, he bullied her at school. I saw him berate her multiple times in front of everyone. And then she left and was gone for six or seven months. I didn't think she'd ever be back. I was so happy when I saw her at school again. And I finally convinced her to go out with me. Once she finally agreed to a date, we were inseparable." He grins. "And then Bruce suddenly wanted her back." He shakes his head. "She'd seen who he was by that time and there was no turning back. And I was glad about it because I'd always wanted her to be mine."

"Look at you, Dad, swooping in to save the day," Dylan says, grinning.

"She would've given anything to know Ava," Dad says. "That's why I hope you'll give Ava a chance. For your mom."

CHAPTER THIRTY-TWO

PINK BIRDS

MILO

It's been a few days since I've seen Goldie.

I've tried to see her.

I've called, I've texted, I've knocked on her door.

She's texted back a couple times, so she's not completely avoiding me.

But, yes, she's totally avoiding me because I haven't *seen* her.

And then today, Everett lets me know that Goldie is in Minneapolis this week.

"She went to pick up what is left at MIA from her installation…and to get something for me. I told her to take her time getting back. She's had a lot to deal with and I think she could use the time away."

"Everett, I want you to know—I had no idea Ava was Stella's daughter. I should've asked who her mother was when Bruce told me, but I wasn't thinking about that. She didn't offer the information, and I was just so surprised that I was meeting a cousin that I didn't look any further."

"Okay…good. I believe you," he says. "And I appreciate you letting me know."

"How long will Goldie be in Minneapolis?"

"Another few days, I think."

I nod, deep in thought.

"I'm struggling to know what to do, Everett. She's upset with me. Maybe she still believes that I didn't know about Ava—I'm not sure. But regardless, she's withdrawn and I'm not sure how to pull her out."

He gives me a sympathetic look.

"She's processing all of this about Ava. She'll come around. But there was a boy who did a number on her," he says. "Really made her question her judgment and affected the way she trusts people…or *doesn't* trust people."

"Wes, right?"

"She told you about him?" His eyes widen and then he smiles and pats my back. "She trusts you more than you think."

"I hope so. I know some things are stacked against me—that I'm a Granger being high on the con list and especially that I didn't own up to it right away—but I care about her, Everett. I care about her a lot."

"I know you do. She'll come around. Don't give up on her. She cares about you too. I can tell by the way she looks at you."

"Yeah?" I say, smiling.

"And I can tell you're in love with her…"

"I *am*," I say in wonder.

"Was there any doubt?"

"Well, no. I-I can't really say I've been in love before, but yes…I love *her*. I really do."

"I mean, you shaved your head for her!"

"That was to support you!" I argue, but I'm laughing.

"Mm-hmm. And bluebirds are pink."

I snort and he squeezes my shoulder.

"You haven't been to your office lately. Are you sure you don't need to make a visit home to see what's going on there?"

"I take it you think I should?"

"Absolutely." He leans closer. "Goldie's not so much a roses kind of girl. She appreciates quality time. When she was little, she'd start acting out sometimes if she didn't get some one-on-one time with me or her mom. It didn't take much—maybe a walk, just the two of us, or a trip to Taco Bell, and then she'd be back, right as rain."

"You, my friend, are brilliant. Thank you." I hug him and head to the door.

"What did I do?" he calls.

"Just gave me a great idea on how to win your daughter back."

"I'll text you the Summit house address." He winks.

As soon as I wrap up a few things at Windhaven, I drive to Minneapolis. Once I'm in my penthouse, I make a few calls, and last but not least, I text Goldie.

> Do me a favor?

GOLDIE
Depends on what it is.

> Meet me at the Walker tomorrow night at 7.

It takes a few minutes for her to respond, and then it comes and I grin. It sounds like my girl is back.

GOLDIE

What are you up to, Lombardi?

Hopefully something that will show you how much I love you.

> I hope you'll come tomorrow night and find out.

And then I turn on some music and get to work.

The next night I stand alone in the dim gallery, shifting from foot to foot like an awkward teenager waiting for his prom date to walk down the stairs. I'm sweating. It feels like it's been months since I've seen Goldie, and even longer since I had her in my bed.

The Walker is quiet. Just the low hum of the lights and my pulse thudding in my ears. I had music ready! Damn, I almost forgot. I hurriedly pull up my playlist and Bluetooth it so the sound goes over the speakers throughout the gallery. I keep checking the entrance, wondering if she's going to come.

Right at seven, she walks through the door.

She looks hesitant and beautiful. She's wearing the emerald green dress she was wearing the night I met her and it makes me smile. I want to kiss that bare shoulder and slide my hands over her curves, sink my face in her hair and inhale. I look down and there are the Dr. Martens.

"I can't believe I never asked," I say.

"Asked what?"

"What you meant when I asked if you make it a habit of wearing Doc Martens with your evening gowns and you said you do now…I wondered what you meant that night, but I never asked. What did that mean?"

She takes a minute to answer. "They're my mom's boots. She stopped wearing heels because they hurt her feet and I wear these every chance I get because they remind me of her."

"I like that."

I hold my arm out and she loops her hand through it. We wind our way through the gallery.

"I've missed you," I tell her.

"I've missed you too." Her lips lift slightly and she gives me a tentative look.

"You look beautiful." I reach out and smooth a strand of her blonde hair around my finger.

"How is your hair already half an inch long?"

I smirk, rubbing my hand over the stubble. "My dad would say it's my Italian heritage, and my mom would say it's my French heritage. Who can really say?"

"It's growing faster than my brothers'. Maybe both of your parents are right and you're blessed with doubly-good hair genes."

"My parents would be very pleased with your diplomatic reasoning."

Her lips lift slightly. "Where are you taking me, Milo?"

"We're almost there." I stop where we first met, only so much has changed since then. "Remember this spot?" I smile as she looks around and her eyes narrow when she sees the architectural model.

I move to block her view before she gets a better look at it.

"I wanted to tell you how much I care about you…well, it's more than that…I love you, Goldie Whitman."

Her mouth parts and she blinks up at me.

"I love you," I say, stronger this time. "When you smile at me, when you're mad at me, when you won't let me get away with anything…I love how you look at me, spar with me, how you kiss me, how you make me feel alive every second we're together." I take a deep breath and a tear slips down her cheek. I catch it with my thumb. "I know it'll take time to earn your trust, but I'm not going anywhere. I promise to be honest with you, and part of that honesty means telling you how I feel." My voice is raspy and I clear my throat. "Maybe this will say it better than I am."

I move out of the way and turn to the model.

"You're saying it pretty great." She smiles then turns to look at the model and gasps. "*Milo*. This is…this is Windhaven…outside the pavilion."

"Since my other work was a travesty, I thought I'd make it right for you—"

She laughs and glances up at me apologetically, which makes me laugh too.

"—And in a place where you can enjoy it. If anything isn't just right, we can change it when it comes to the real thing."

She leans over so she can get a better look at each sculpture. There's a brick path winding around the pavilion and flowers on either side, wild and beautiful, just like her. And the sculptures accentuate the beauty of the landscape with their simplicity, which is all Goldie.

"Is that a marigold?" she asks, her finger pausing on the metal flower that turns like a windmill.

I nod.

"It's *beautiful*."

"And…is that…" She giggles and turns to look up at me, her eyes twinkling. "Did you create a *Cherry*bridge and Spoon?"

"I did. And I think I might even prefer it to the original. What do you think?"

"Well, of course you do. Your ego knows no bounds."

I laugh. "You're not wrong."

She leans in and whispers, "But I have to agree. This is superior. Very clever."

The cherry is huge with the stem angled as the bridge and the little spoon is nestled on top of the cherry, the opposite of the real thing.

We're under no pretense that my mini sculpture is truly better than Claes Oldenburg's work, but it makes Goldie smile and that is worth everything.

"And this...I love this." She leans closer to look at the golden metal sun. She flips it over and the other side is the moon. "I like their faces, especially the moon's. He reminds me of you."

I flip it back to the sun. "And this reminds me of you."

"It's perfect, Milo. I love it, everything about it. And I love *you*." She takes a deep breath. "I've had some time to think. I'm so sorry I went quiet on you this week. I've been trying to make peace with the fact that my mom had a daughter I never knew about and it happens to be Ava Piper...your cousin. Doubting whether I should believe you didn't know or not. I've been in a bad cycle for a long time, not letting these walls down. But we'd moved past that. I shouldn't have shut you out again. I'm sorry that I did. We should've worked through this together. I won't keep letting my distrust get in the way of us. I want to do better—I *will* do better, I promise. I...I know that you weren't keeping it a secret from me."

"You love me?" I turn her to face me and she puts her hands on my chest and then winds them around the back of my head.

She rubs my head and I turn into it, groaning. "That's what you heard out of all I said?"

I smile. "I heard it all and I'm happy about all of it…but especially that you love me."

She laughs. "I love you so much. You have no idea."

"You really do?"

"I really do."

"I have some idea then."

CHAPTER THIRTY-THREE

RELIEF

GOLDIE

I float out of the Walker, still flying high. The city's colors seem brighter, the sounds crisper, yet the atmosphere is a bit overwhelming after the quiet of Windy Harbor.

"Do we get to take that model with us?" I ask, stopping at my car.

Milo looms over me. I love how tall he is.

"Yeah." He grins. "I'll be back to pick it up before heading back to Windy Harbor. I wasn't sure you'd come tonight, so I arranged for it to be here through Sunday." He runs his hand over his head sheepishly.

"I'm really sorry I disappeared on you." The evening air is cool, but I'm still warm all over.

Milo Lombardi loves me.

He leans down, his lips close to mine. "You can make it up to me."

My breath hitches at the look he gives me. "Oh? How?"

His shrug is casual, but the heat in his eyes is anything but. "I have a few ideas."

I bite my lip. "Do you want to come over? You haven't been to the Summit house yet."

His smile is lethal. "I'd love to come over."

I give him a flirty smile over my shoulder and get in the SUV.

"Is this yours?" he asks, looking perplexed.

I run my hand over the leather interior of this fancy Porsche.

"It's one of Tully's. I rode back with him and he let me borrow it while I've been here." I grin. "He was gonna take me back when I was ready, but maybe I could catch a ride back with you?"

"It's a date." He grins and shuts my car door.

I glance at him every other second in the rearview mirror as he follows me to the house in his Range Rover. The anticipation of a night with Milo gives me all the butterflies. Hell, this whole night has been butterfly central.

We barely make it through the door before our mouths crash together, all hands and heat. I slip out of my shoes, the leather soft from years of wear, and toe off my socks without breaking the kiss. My mom's voice telling us kids to take off our shoes when we're in the house is deeply ingrained in me even now.

He laughs when he realizes what I've done and does the same, just as gracefully as I did. His mom must've had the same rule.

I pull him up the stairs and down the hall to my old room, breathless as he nuzzles my neck and then turns me around to face him. His eyes drink me in.

I was so nervous about what he wanted to see me about tonight that I've been hot and cold and hot again.

And then the love declaration caused a full-out sweat. I could use a shower.

I take a step backwards, and then another, and another… and he follows. When we reach my bathroom, he raises his eyebrows.

"Nice."

"The clawfoot tub or the oversized shower for…twelve?"

He smirks. "All of it, but for tonight, I'm leaning toward the shower." His eyes darken and he leans against the cabinet. "I think you should undress first…since you didn't talk to me for days."

"Oh, is this part of how I can make it up to you?"

He crosses his arms and nods, eyes gleaming.

Since there's not much to take off, I lower the one strap of my dress and slowly undo the back, letting it drop to the floor. His breath hitches when he sees what I'm wearing underneath.

"*What* is that?" he asks reverently.

"A torsolette."

It's black and has lace panels along the sides. I turn my back to him and bend over farther than I need to, to step out of my dress, grinning when he curses. The black lace cheeky panties are a hit, noted.

I look at him over my shoulder. "Should I take it all off then?"

"Hardest choice of my life." He adjusts himself, his dress pants doing nothing to conceal his massive bulge. And then he straightens and his expression is wicked.

"Leave it on for now, and get on your knees." He points to the space in front of him.

I swallow hard, my mouth already watering. I do as he asks, getting on my knees and sitting on my feet. I stare up at him. His chest rises and falls like it's taking all his willpower not to touch me.

I undo his pants and slide them down, all while eyeing his black boxer briefs with lust. When I take them off of him and feel his hot, smooth skin, hard like velvety steel, we both sigh. I wrap my fists around him and then slide one hand over the tip.

"No man should have to carry this massive weight alone," I say.

He grips the counter and moans my name. "You are so right."

I grin, biting my bottom lip.

"It's a burden I'd like to help you shoulder." Another slide over his tip.

"Help me," he rasps.

"What can I do to help?" I ask, my tongue slowly gliding up his length from root to tip.

He curses. "You can choke on my cock."

I gasp and stare up at him as he fists my hair.

"Too much?" he asks.

I shake my head. "I've never been more turned on in my life."

He grins and looks like a beautiful devil. "Then open wide."

I lift higher to my knees, and my mouth pops open. I take him in halfway before withdrawing. My tongue swirls over him before I take him in deeper. I stare up at him for as long as I can and he stares at me, his head falling back when he bottoms out. My legs press together and I withdraw again, taking my time with him. He gets close and I slow things down again. And again. His movements get wilder and he tugs my head closer, greedy for more. I put my hands on his ass and inhale him. He thrusts into me and my eyes water.

The next thrust, tears run down my face, but I want more. I hum and my cheeks hollow out, taking him deeper.

"You look...so...fucking...beautiful," he pants. "I'm close, Goldie. So close."

I feel him swell in my mouth and this time I don't let up, holding on harder as he fucks my mouth. He lets out a sharp groan and comes hard, filling me up. I swallow, but it still drips out of my mouth. He stares down at me like he's drugged then smears what dripped out over my top lip.

I drain him dry and my mouth comes off of him with a pop. He comes out of his stupor and lifts me up. His fingers deftly undo the long row of hook-and-eye closures and when it's on the ground along with my panties, he picks me up. He starts the shower and sets me down carefully.

"You shouldered my massive burden with the skill of a champion," he says, smiling as he leans in to kiss me. He pauses and pulls back. "I just need to check something." His fingers move between my legs, and he smiles when he lifts them and they're soaked. He puts his fingers in his mouth and licks them clean. "So good," he hums. "We'll need to take care of that right away."

And he gets on his knees.

We make up for lost time all night long. Or maybe this is just what we do when we have a night together. As the sun starts to peek through the windows, we give in to sleep.

When we wake up, his hand is splayed over my stomach, claiming me, and I smile before my eyes ever open. He leans over and kisses my stomach, my breasts, my neck, my chin...

"What are you smiling about?" he asks.

"You love me."

"I do." I hear the smile in his voice. "You love me too."

"I do."

"Are we staying in this bed all day? I vote yes."

"Well…actually…" I make a face. "I was going to meet Tully at Minnehaha Falls at eleven."

"Perfect." He starts to get out of bed and then pauses, looking back at me. "Wait…am I invited?"

I laugh and he reaches out and swipes his thumb over my bottom lip, grinning. "Yes, you're invited!"

"Your lips are red and puffy…and so is your chin."

"I can feel everywhere you've been," I tell him, stretching out.

He winces. "Are you sore?"

"In the best kind of way."

We get ready and head to the park. Minnehaha Falls roars in the background, powerful after a good season of rain. Tourists take selfies nearby, and we take one of our own as we wait for Tully to arrive. I didn't tell Tully I was bringing Milo and he grins when he sees him, giving him a bro-hug after he hugs me.

"Good to see you guys," he says.

"Sorry to intrude on your time together," Milo says.

"Are you kidding? This is great." Tully grins.

I get the Crab-Stuffed Avocado for myself and clam fries to share. We're early enough for the daily specials to still be available, which makes Milo and Tully happy. Milo gets the Sexy Ahi Burger, and Tully gets the Panko-Crusted Walleye. They get beer and I sip wine from my plastic cup, unable to stop smiling. Milo's hand rests on my thigh beneath the table and when we're done eating, his fingers trace little shapes across my skin.

"Here, let's take a picture to send to Dad." Tully holds up his phone and takes the shot, grinning when he looks it over afterward. "Yeah?" He shows us the photo and Milo and I nod happily.

"Looks good," Milo says.

"How is Dad?" Tully asks. "Has everything calmed down around Windy Harbor, Milo?" He leans his elbows on the table and his voice drops. "With our sister?"

"I think Ava retreated. I've called her, but she hasn't responded…like someone else I know." He looks at me pointedly and I give him doe eyes.

I've apologized and made it up to him in the sexiest, dirtiest, most earth-shattering ways.

"And I haven't seen her around town at all. Everett said he hasn't either," he adds.

He does a double take when he sees how flushed I am.

I swallow and avoid looking at him when he starts smiling. The man gives me countless orgasms and thinks he can read my mind now.

"Yeah, I've FaceTimed him while I've been here and he wants to try to get together with her when we're all in Windy Harbor again," I say. "Grandma Donna wants to meet her…"

I bite the inside of my jaw, trying to calm the anxious feeling that rises in my chest every time I think about seeing Ava again.

Tully puts his hand on my arm. "You okay?"

"Yeah. Just not looking forward to another interaction with her. But I think I'm going to have to get over that."

Tully nods. "I've talked to Dad too and he definitely wants us to give her a chance. I guess we owe Mom that."

I look down at the table. "You're right." I sigh. "We do."

"Have you found the letters yet?" he asks.

I make a face. "I will. I may have been avoiding looking very hard. I know Dad wants me to bring them back, but…it's hard knowing there are words from Mom that I won't get to read."

Milo puts his arm around me and I lean into him.

"I can come help you look," Tully says.

"No, this is the first day all week that you've had off of practice. I'll do it, I promise."

After a long goodbye with Tully, we drive across town to Milo's parents' house. They greet us at the door with open arms. We walk to the back patio, turning down offers of food.

"We just had a big meal," Milo says as we sit down.

"How are you doing, honey?" Kathleen asks. "I heard about everything that happened with Ava last week."

I scrunch up my nose. "I think I'm still processing it."

I look at Milo and he squeezes my leg.

"That must have been quite the shock," Kathleen says. "I know it was for me. I'd forgotten all about Bruce seeing Stella for a while. I remember that he liked her a lot, but I always thought she was too good for him." She doesn't say it with malice, just honesty.

Milo laughs under his breath.

"We still haven't met her. Can you believe that?" Kathleen looks at the three of us like we can help her understand it. "The whole thing is very odd. I've asked Bruce to bring her over, but he still hasn't."

"Very odd," Anthony agrees.

"I think Bruce has been too busy trying to bring the Whitmans down," Milo says, looking over at me. He shakes his head. "Hopefully, after the recent town meeting, he'll stop this madness."

"Has Ava been apologetic about the fire? Or any of her behavior?" Kathleen asks.

"She apologized the day it happened," Milo says. "Not enough, in my opinion, but maybe a start?"

He looks at me again like he's not sure of what to say.

"She seemed a little shocked by some of the details my dad told her. Didn't you get that impression?" I ask Milo. "My dad said later that he'd tried to say the things about Bruce as carefully as he could, but he thought it was important that Ava heard how much my mom wanted her."

"She was so young," Kathleen says, her eyes sympathetic. "And Bruce was two years older than her. Even though it was legal here, he should've known better."

My eyes fill with tears. "Growing up, I would've loved to have a sister. I still can't believe I have one! It's…well…I need to get used to the idea of it. I think I'd feel a lot differently about it if I hadn't had such a rocky start with Ava."

"Oh, honey," Kathleen says, reaching out to squeeze my hand. "Her behavior has been inexcusable."

I wipe my face and groan. "Ugh, sorry. I'll work through my feelings about it…another day." I laugh awkwardly.

"How about we talk about something lighter?" Milo says, leaning over to kiss my temple.

"Oh look, there's a Ruddy Duck!" Anthony points at the water. "That duck stamp artist I follow on TikTok drew that one this year for the competition." He grins. "So damn good. Her channel has educated me on all the ducks around here. And she's a local too."

He is *adorable.*

"Oh, I love that artist too!" I say, leaning to the right to see the duck better. "Is that a Common Merganser next to it?"

"Sure is." He looks at me, impressed.

"I learned everything from them as well," I say, laughing. "Kira Sabin, right?"

"Yes! You know her?"

"Not personally, but I'd like to."

We talk until it's dark and the air grows cool. I feel more relaxed than I have in a long time. And then Milo takes me home, and we take a bath together. With our fingers threaded together, his chest to my back, we talk until the water cools. After craving him all day, it's a relief when he takes me to bed and sinks inside of me. Afterward, we lay side by side, catching our breath. He takes my hand and kisses my knuckles.

"When we get back…I don't want to sleep without you," he says, pulling me into his side.

"Noah wants me and my brothers to start talking about how we want our houses to be. We each have a few acres set aside for that. None of us has given that much thought yet… too focused on everything else, but I've been dreaming about what I'd like."

"Yeah? And do you see me in that house?"

He leans over me and brushes my hair away from my eyes.

My mouth parts and I stare up at him. This man could afford to live anywhere, have multiple houses if he wanted…

"What are you asking?" I whisper.

"I'm asking for you to please envision me wherever you are...because that's where I want to be."

I tug his head down and kiss him until I'm dizzy.

"Yes, I see you in that house," I tell him.

He drags me on top of him and we get lost in each other again.

CHAPTER THIRTY-FOUR

BRIGHT LIGHTS

MILO

Mom calls early the next day and I get out of bed to answer it, walking into the other room so I don't wake up Goldie.

"Hey, Mom."

"Hi, love. I hope I didn't wake you."

I try to fight back a yawn, but it comes out anyway. "No worries."

"Aw, I'm sorry. Call me back when you're awake."

"No, it's okay, Mom. I'm awake now." I chuckle.

"Ugh." She laughs. "I've been awake for hours and didn't even check the time. Listen..." She clears her throat. "Would it be helpful if I invited Ava here...without Bruce...so we could all talk? The more I think about it, the more certain I am that he's avoiding bringing her here." She exhales and groans. "He knows I've always been able to see right through him, and knowing *him,* I'm afraid he's using Ava as a pawn to get to Everett, and I don't like it *one bit*. Maybe I could be a safe space for both Ava and Goldie."

"I absolutely think you should reach out to Ava and try to get to know her. Please do it in a neutral place like a restaurant, instead of the house. But we should let the Whitmans work through their relationship with her as they see fit." I bring the phone closer and lower my voice. "Mom, if I hadn't stopped her, she might've burned the whole place down. That certainly seemed to be her intention. She did show remorse afterward, but she was also cornered. The bottom line is…we don't know her. She's family and I want to get to know her, but the truth is, she's off to a shaky start."

"Goodness, she sounds really troubled. Do you know what her upbringing was?"

My mom is a bleeding heart and I can tell by the empathy in her voice that this situation is already eating away at her.

"No, I don't know much about her at all. I never could've imagined her being Goldie's half-sister, and yeah, it wouldn't surprise me if Bruce is using this situation to his advantage."

"I hope he'll do right by her." She exhales, but there's still worry in her voice. "Okay, I'll let you go. Just wanted to run that by you. And I'm glad I did." She laughs. "You know me—I would've been attempting a mimosa brunch here with Ava and Goldie to try to bring peace to them."

"I know, Mom, and I love you for it."

"I love you too, my boy. *Hey*," her voice perks up. "You and Goldie sure were cozy last night. Things seemed…*really good*."

I scrub my hand over my face, laughing under my breath. "Things are really good."

"Well, you won't hear me complaining about that. We're not getting any younger, either one of us, and I'd like to be young enough to chase my grandkids around, thank you very much."

I groan. "Let's not rush things."

She giggles and I'm glad that she sounds lighter than when she called.

"I love you, Mom. Keep me posted on how things go with Ava. You got the number I texted last night, right?"

"I love you too. And yes, I got it. I'll reach out today."

We hang up and I go to the bathroom I've been using when I'm not doing a water sport with Goldie in her bathroom. I get my toothbrush out of my shaving kit and brush my teeth before I shower. I'm shaving with a towel around my waist when Goldie leans against the doorway, her long hair wet. She's wearing jean shorts and a baggy sweatshirt.

I set my razor down and tug her toward me. "Why do you always look so fuckable?"

"Dear dirty sir, I think *you* have a one-track mind."

"When it comes to you...yes." I laugh.

She grins and picks up my razor, carefully shaving the last strip of foam on my cheek. When she's satisfied, she moves and turns the water on for me. I rinse and turn back to her. She runs her hand over my skin and lifts to her tiptoes. I lift her, setting her on the counter in front of me. She nuzzles her face against mine.

"Mmm," she sighs. "Nice."

"Did I wake you up?" My mouth brushes hers and I kiss her lightly, my hands wandering to her backside.

"I'm not sure, but I needed to get up anyway."

"What are your plans for today?"

"I need to get serious about finding those letters and get back to Dad...preferably by tonight." She pauses. "I can get Tully to take me back if you're not ready."

I lean my forehead against hers. "I came to win you back."

She runs her hands over my head. I think maybe she likes my stubble as much as she liked my hair. "I'm sorry I made you feel like you'd lost me. I was just lost, period. It was selfish of me to leave town without telling you. I didn't think about how it came across."

"I thought you didn't believe me and that you might be done with me."

"I can't quit you, baby," she sings.

I laugh, kissing my way down her neck.

"I didn't take you for a Led Zeppelin fan."

She holds up her finger. "Little known fact: that song was written by Willie Dixon and originally sung by Otis Rush."

I straighten, grinning at her. "You're right, I did not know that."

"Grandpa Otis made sure everyone knew it. He appreciated his name," she laughs, "and it bugged him that most people thought it originated with Led Zeppelin."

"Well, I'm glad I learned the truth."

"You would've made it up to him by having Otis Redding on your playlist. He was a big fan of him too, of course." She sighs. "I need coffee. Someone kept me up the past two nights."

"Someone kept me up too." I smirk and she reaches out and slides her hand up and down my dick.

"So I see." She scoots off the counter and I think she's about to drag me back to her bedroom, but she takes off, calling, "Sex will be our reward…later. Otherwise, we won't leave the bed!"

I groan, adjusting myself, and get dressed before I go downstairs. When I walk into the kitchen, the coffee is brewing and she's already pouring scrambled eggs into a pan.

"That was fast," I say. "What can I do to help?"

"Get your coffee. There's orange juice and fruit in the fridge, if you could grab that, please. Then have a seat."

I grab everything, including the silverware and napkins she's set on the countertop, and take it to the table.

"Thanks. This looks good," I tell her when she brings the plates of scrambled eggs.

She makes a face. "I don't have bread, sorry."

"Don't apologize. I'm getting a home-cooked meal."

She laughs. "If you think this is a home-cooked meal, you're hurting."

I shake my head. "Not hurting. This is just nice. I like this house too. I've always loved this street."

She nods. "Me too. Frank Lloyd Wright wasn't a fan, but I appreciate the European influences."

"And I appreciate your wealth of little-known facts."

"You *must've* known that one though," she says.

I grin. "I did. Now, tell me about this house of yours. What is your dream house?"

"Well, my plot is the one that has the smaller dock. I'd want to extend that dock so it feels like the house is right on the water without actually *being* right on the water." Her eyes are bright as she talks about it. "I'd like a wraparound porch that goes all the way around the house and endless windows. I love weathered wood, so I'd like a great room overlooking the water with floor-to-ceiling windows and weathered wood on the ceiling." She stands and grabs a piece of paper and a pen out of a nearby drawer and takes a few minutes to draw it out. "Basically an A-frame with Victorian elements. Wouldn't that be pretty?"

"Beautiful. I love the shape of these windows and the beams."

"And endless water right out there." She taps at the page.

"Do you miss being in the city? Your penthouse is beautiful, but do you ever wish you had more space surrounding you? More nature instead of buildings and bright lights?"

"I haven't missed the city like I thought I would. Being in Windy Harbor has been better for me than I expected. I've looked for every opportunity to be there more and when I come into the office to work here, I can't wait to get back."

She loops her foot around mine.

"It helps that you're in Windy Harbor," I tell her.

She holds her coffee cup in mid-air and gives me a sweet smile. "I thought I would miss the city more too, but I haven't at all. I miss not painting as much. That's been set aside a little since I've been there. I've painted some, but not even close to what I did here. But that'll change, I'm sure, when things calm down. I've loved working on Windhaven, but I need a big space to paint where I can make messes and not worry about it. Like a *mini* pavilion that would be all mine."

"You should absolutely have that. Would you like me to draw some plans up?"

Her eyes light up. "I would love that."

As we eat, she gives me more details. I make a few notes in my phone. After we eat, we wash the dishes and when we're done, she slumps against the counter.

"Okay, I've put it off long enough," she says. "I'm going to the attic."

"Do you want company?"

"I would love company."

She leads me to the attic, a fully finished space with an open area, a bedroom, and a bathroom. At one end of the open area, there's a door that leads to a room filled with boxes and old furniture.

"A lot of my mom's things are in here. We each took something of hers. I have her jewelry and a few clothes of hers that remind me of her…her boots." She lifts her shoulder. "But I left some things that I loved here too. It didn't feel right to take all of it. I guess I like knowing her treasures are still up here."

She points to a pretty box. It's brown wood with colorful metal flowers on top.

"That's where I think the letters are. My brothers and I were talking and we remember seeing a key in her desk that she'd never let us play with, and we always wanted to. It was one of those pretty skeleton keys." She leaves the box and walks to the far end of the room, where a sliver of light comes through the small window.

She pauses before she opens a drawer.

"This is one of my favorite pieces. I'd like it in my house one day. None of us could take seeing it all the time after she was gone because she loved this desk and worked here a lot. But I think I'm ready."

She opens one of the drawers and pulls out a tiny box, slowly lifting the lid. Inside is a skeleton key.

She looks up at me, her expression tentative.

"Are you nervous?" I ask.

"Yes. I don't know why, but I am."

She takes a deep breath and moves to the larger decorative box. She smooths her hand over it lovingly, then slips the key inside, her breath hitching when it opens. She looks at what's inside and I look at her.

When she blinks, tears fall down her cheeks. I put my hand on her back, rubbing gently. She picks up a stack of letters and then sets it aside, pulling out a tiny hospital bracelet and two doll-sized pink socks. She puts her hand to her mouth and picks up the smallest pink knitted hat. A sob breaks from her throat and she turns and buries her head in my chest.

"She must have been so afraid and so devastated. She was so young. I can't stand thinking about how sad she must have been all those years, thinking about her little girl out there."

"She'd be glad to know she's okay," I tell her.

"I hope she *is* okay." She looks up at me and I wipe her tears away. "I think I have to make sure she is…for Mom."

CHAPTER THIRTY-FIVE

NEGOTIATIONS

GOLDIE

We get back to Windy Harbor that night and I feel like I can breathe easier already. It's been an emotional day, an emotional week. We catch up with Dad and my grandmas, eating Grandma Nancy's Snickerdoodle bars. Before everyone goes to bed, I give my dad the letters.

"Thanks, buttercup. I'm glad you're back," he says. He waves the letters. "I'll reach out to Ava tomorrow."

"Okay. I'd like to be there when you see her," I say.

"All right," he says, squeezing my shoulder. "Night, Milo."

"Good night." Milo smiles at him from across the room.

I kiss Dad's cheek and he pads down the hall. Kevin looks back at me like he's torn between my dad and me, but then he follows my dad.

I can't even be disappointed because they're so cute together.

My phone buzzes with an incoming FaceTime. I glance at the screen and grin.

"Addy," I say.

"Ignore me. You should take the call. I'm happy to see you smiling like that," Milo says. "I can head out."

"No, stay." I hold onto his hand. "You haven't met Addy yet and she wants to meet you."

"Okay," he says, smirking.

I swipe to accept.

Addy's face fills the screen, looking gorgeous, as always. "There you are! I thought I might miss you again."

Her eyes narrow, and she leans in closer to the camera. "Is that…Milo Lombardi?"

He lifts a hand, offering a polite smile. "Hello."

"Hello." She beams. "So…you're Milo."

"I am." He puts his arm around my shoulder. "And you must be the infamous best friend who's married to my favorite running back."

"Aw, thanks, man," Penn says in the background.

Addy grins and turns it so Penn's in view. "His ears are always fine-tuned to praise."

We laugh.

Addy turns the phone back to herself. "So…Goldie… remember when you grilled Penn like a CIA operative? It's time for payback."

I stiffen and pretend to look at a watch that doesn't exist on my wrist. "Look at the time, chasing our guests away."

Addy's eyes are gleaming with excitement. "Nope, we're just getting started. Okay, Milo. First question. Have you ever made Goldie cry?"

He blinks and stares at me.

I wince. "I *did* give Penn the third degree when I met him…"

"True story," Penn yells.

"Uh, I've never made her cry on purpose," Milo says.

She squints. "That's good...I think. Do you believe in soulmates?"

"I probably can't pass, can I?" He smirks.

"Absolutely not." She crosses her arms over her chest and I fight back a laugh.

Addy is *not* a ballbuster, so this is hilarious.

Milo looks amused. "My parents are soulmates. I believe some people fit you so well, there's no other explanation but that you're meant to be together."

Addy glances at me and lifts her eyebrows. She approves of that answer, and so do I.

"How would you describe Goldie in three words?"

Milo doesn't hesitate. "Inspiring. Brilliant. Beautiful."

My chest tightens. Addy goes quiet for a beat.

"Well, damn," she whispers. "Golds, I like this one."

Milo chuckles and kisses my temple. "I like this one too," he says.

"Oh, you guys are so cute together," she says. "Okay, rapid-fire segment. No pauses, just the first thing out of your mouth. Ready?"

"Do I have a choice?"

"No," Addy and I both say.

He laughs.

"They appear so sweet, but they're ruthless when they want to be," Penn says, dipping in just long enough to show the side of his face and then he's back out.

"Oh, I know this one is," Milo says, giving me a look that sends fire licking down my spine.

I shiver and he smiles, like he knows perfectly well what he's doing.

"Fire away," he says.

"What's your biggest flaw?"

"According to Goldie, I'm infuriating."

I snort and Addy's eyes dance between the two of us.

"Favorite childhood memory?"

He pauses slightly. "Drawing buildings on the back of receipts from my mom's purse."

"That is adorable," Addy coos. "Golds!" She gives me wide eyes. "I thought you said the two of you can spar like two hellions."

"No, no. Don't let this gooey center side fool you. He can be lippy as all hell," I say.

Milo laughs. "I'm sure I don't need to tell you about the sass on this one." He tilts his thumb in my direction.

"Oh, no," Addy says, cackling. "My girl has the sass for days when she needs to pull it out. Do you remember what Goldie was wearing the first time you realized you were into her?"

"An emerald green dress that is sleeveless on one shoulder and goes up like this on the other." He drags his hand over my shoulder, smiling over at me.

I'm caught giving him googly eyes.

"That's what I was wearing the night we met," I whisper.

"I know. And I loved that you wore it again for me the other night." His voice is husky.

"It is getting steamy all up in here," Addy says, fanning her face. "Okay, a serious one. What are your intentions with my girl?"

"That's easy. To appreciate the way she shines in every situation. To never forget how lucky I am for every minute we have together. And to love her so well, she'll never doubt how I feel."

I feel Addy's eyes on us, but I'm too busy staring at Milo.

His lips tilt up, caught in my gaze. He finally glances at Addy.

"So we're talking love. Okay. Good, very good," she says softly.

"What else?" he asks.

"How do you feel about kids?"

"Addy!" I gasp.

"Payback," she sings.

"I do not think my questions were this invasive," I argue.

Milo chuckles. "I'm pro kids."

Nice. I file that away.

"And naked cats?" Addy asks.

"Hey!" Penn grumbles.

"What?" Milo gives me a confused look and I shake my head, slicing a hand in front of my neck for him to not say anything else.

"You haven't been showing him my daily photos, Golds?" Addy frowns.

"Heh heh, he's always…out when you send them." I only ever lie to Addy when it's about her Sphynx cats.

"Just say you like 'em," Penn calls.

"Okay…I like them?" Milo says.

Addy clasps her hands together.

"Amazing. Okay, that's all I've got. You answered everything to my satisfaction," she says. Her eyes widen at me and she mouths, *Oh my God!*

He chuckles and rubs his hand down his face. "You weren't messing around."

"You passed with flying colors, man!" Penn says in the background. "Well done."

Addy points the phone to him and Penn is petting Jezebel.

"*Ahh!*" Milo jolts and lets out what is not exactly a yell, but it's not *not* a yell either.

"Jezebel, our Sphynx," Addy says primly.

"Got it," Milo says weakly.

"I was going to say if you hurt Goldie, I'll come out there and slash your tires with a crochet needle, but I don't think it's even necessary!" Addy says.

We all laugh.

"You thrive very well under pressure," she adds.

He smirks and the temperature in the room heats. "Thank you." He looks at me. "What do I get for passing the test?"

I point at his face and look at Addy. "See that right there? That cocky attitude is when I have to bring the sass out and set him straight."

Milo's laugh is raspy. "You love every cocky part about me." He jerks to the side when I poke him and hit a ticklish spot. He laughs and gets up, leaning back down so he's in the camera. "It was really great to meet you, Addy. And you too, Penn. I'll let you two have some privacy so I can keep staying on the good side of this one right here."

He kisses my cheek and his eyes are full of promise when he backs away.

Addy presses her lips together and she fans her face. *Wow*, she mouths.

My cheeks are on fire.

Out loud, Addy says, "Well, this has been so fun and so enlightening. I will let you two get back to your night. Call me tomorrow and fill me in on the latest going on around there." She leans in closer and whispers, "And go give that man his reward."

"Okay, I will," I say, laughing. "Love you."

"I love you too. And I think I might love Milo a little bit after this conversation."

"Hey!" Penn calls.

"Slow your roll. For her. I love him for *her*," she says, rolling her eyes.

She blows me a kiss and we hang up.

Milo leans against the doorjamb, arms folded. His posture screams nonchalance, but his eyes tell me he's ready to pounce.

"Are we in your bed or mine tonight?" He lifts off the doorjamb and stalks toward me, bending down to hover near my mouth.

"We…you…" I squeak. "You want—"

"Remember how I said when we got back, I didn't want to sleep without you?"

I gawk. "I thought you were just being sweet…" I laugh when he nuzzles my neck and nips at my earlobe.

"I'm rarely sweet, Golo."

"I think you're very sweet." I put my hands on either side of his face. "We don't actually sleep when we're in bed together," I whisper.

"Let's get an early start." He looks at his phone. "It's almost ten." His smile is wicked when he looks up. "I'll give you two orgasms in the next twenty minutes and you can be asleep by ten thirty."

"Let's stay here then, so we don't waste any time."

"Done."

"And you get a pass to wake me up once in the night." I lift a shoulder. "You know…if we need more orgasms."

He tugs me up so I'm standing and lines my body up to his. I gasp when I feel how hard he is, and I'm instantly ready to start our twenty minutes.

"Now I understand what my parents meant when they said a happy couple is one who learns how to negotiate."

I laugh.

"Just so we're clear though. You can wake me up as many times as you want," he says.

CHAPTER THIRTY-SIX

OLD WOUNDS, NEW TRUTHS

MILO

I don't know why I'm nervous. I'm not the one seeing my half-sister. Or the one coming into the home of the people I committed arson against. But the unease in the room is thick before Ava even walks through the door.

Everett asked me to be here. I thought it was probably for Ava's sake, but the way he keeps checking on Goldie lets me know it was for her. Goldie and Ava have had a horrible start. I wouldn't blame the Whitmans if they didn't want anything to do with Ava, but it's just a testament to how gracious they are. After all, they've accepted me as a Granger.

I'm beginning to think that the whole family feud thing is one-sided at this point.

I walk into the kitchen to get a glass of water and it's impossible to avoid hearing Grandma Nancy and Grandma Donna arguing in the den.

"I don't know why Everett's doing this. It's crazy! I've

tried to talk him out of this little…get-together or whatever we're calling it…until I'm blue in the face, but he's not listening to me. Ho-no. Not listening to a word from his mother," Grandma Nancy says. "She is Bruce *Granger's* daughter, not his."

"Nancy," Grandma Donna sighs, "she's Stella's *daughter*. How would you feel if a child of Everett's showed up? You'd want to meet them, no matter what."

"Well, there won't be any children of Everett's showing up," Grandma Nancy huffs.

"That's not the point and you know it."

"She tried to set flames to our property! If that isn't enough to prove she's taken after her father, I don't know what is!"

"Oh, fer cryin' out loud! Maybe you better sit this one out, Nancy!" Grandma Donna says, sounding fed up.

"There's no way I'm leaving my family to fend for themselves around that girl."

"That *girl* is in her thirties."

"Like you said, that's not the point and you know it."

Grandma Donna huffs and when she walks into the kitchen, I try to act like I wasn't just eavesdropping.

I guess the Granger/Whitman feud *isn't* so one-sided.

The doorbell rings, and Grandma Donna and I walk into the living room. Goldie looks anxious and I take her hand.

"You okay?" I whisper.

She bites her lip. "I'm crazy nervous."

"It's going to be okay," I tell her.

She exhales and nods.

Everett walks to the door and opens it wide. "Hello, Ava. Come in!"

She walks in. She looks different. Softer. Hesitant. Dark circles around her eyes.

"Hi," she says, looking around the room.

Grandma Donna steps forward and holds out her hand. Ava takes it and Grandma Donna smiles, encircling Ava's hand with her other one.

"Hello, dear. I'm Donna, Stella's mother. Everyone around here calls me Grandma Donna and I hope you will too." She tilts her head back, getting a better look at Ava's face. "Beautiful. I believe I would've recognized you anywhere. You look so much like my sister Darlene; it's uncanny." She leans in closer and whispers, "She was the pretty one."

Ava's eyes are glassy, but she smiles at that. "Thank you. It's nice to meet you."

"Lovely to meet you, dear." Grandma Donna takes a step back. "Can I get you anything to drink? Water? Pop? Whiskey?"

That pulls a laugh out of her. "Whiskey sounds about right, but no, thank you."

Everett gestures to the chair across from Goldie and me. "Thank you for coming. Have a seat."

Grandma Nancy stands by Everett's chair and when he sits down, she crosses her arms and stares at Ava.

Everett glances back. "Have a seat, Ma."

Grandma Nancy doesn't look happy about it, but she sits down.

"I believe the only one you haven't met yet is my mom, Nancy," he says, waving his hand toward his mom.

"Hello," Ava says.

Nancy says nothing.

"My sons wanted to be here today, but it's probably a little less intimidating with just the six of us here," Everett says.

Ava swallows hard and looks around, her gaze pausing on

Goldie and then back to Everett. "I want to say again how sorry I am for…the fire. I wasn't thinking clearly." She clears her throat and her voice gets stronger. "I'm grateful you didn't press charges. I deserve a lot worse."

"Everyone deserves another chance," Everett says.

"I'm not used to…this level of kindness," she says, looking down. "My family is not so forgiving. The one I grew up in, not…" Her voice trails off.

"Are you close to your family?" Goldie asks.

Ava shakes her head. "It was just my parents and me, and we're…nothing alike. I didn't know I was adopted until I was twenty-five, and things sort of made more sense once I knew."

Everett picks up the brown box sitting next to him and carries it to Ava. He places the small box on top. "Goldie found your letters this week—"

"I didn't read them," Goldie interjects.

"No," Everett smiles, "no one has read them. I knew she was writing to you when she'd get that box out. The key is in the little box. She told me once that she had to lock away this part of her just to be able to withstand it. But she never stopped thinking about you, Ava. Never."

"It's true. She never stopped," Grandma Donna says. "I have a lot of regrets, that I kept it a secret, that I didn't keep you myself. My husband Otis was a good man, but he was old school. He never would've forgiven Stella if he knew… and he probably would've taken a shotgun to Bruce." She wipes her nose with a tissue.

"I was surprised when I found out how young she was," Ava says.

Her hand trembles as she takes the key and unlocks the box. She gasps much the same way Goldie did when she saw the tiny items inside, next to the letters. A tear drips down her cheek.

"Thank you," she says.

She touches the letters reverently.

"I've been so angry." Her voice is barely a whisper. "So bitter. We didn't have much growing up, so this beautiful house and all the land...it just felt so unfair. You all seem so close and I didn't have that either. My parents mean well. But they've never been affectionate. They don't understand me. When my mom told me I was adopted, she said their financial situation had changed after they got me, and...I think they regretted me."

Goldie flinches and wipes the tears that have fallen down her face.

Ava notices and her cheeks flush. "I only say that to try to explain some of my behavior." She holds back a sob. "I know it's not a good excuse. I can never fully explain it, but...I don't think I'm a bad person. At least I don't want to be."

She puts her hand over her face and Goldie gets up to give her a tissue. She almost comes back to sit down, but then turns toward Ava and puts her hand on her shoulder. Ava looks up, and the expression on her face is desolate. I don't think even the most hard-hearted person could look at her and not have compassion right now.

"I don't know if you want a relationship with us," Goldie says. "We're a lot. Noisy. *Trite*..."

Ava cringes and looks surprised when Goldie laughs.

"Sorry, I couldn't help myself," Goldie says. "We also like to tease each other. And honestly, you weren't wrong—I am trite."

Ava's mouth parts like she's about to argue, but Goldie continues.

"What I'm trying to say is, we're not perfect, but we love

each other. We'd like a chance to get to know you, if you're willing. We'll all have some trust issues to work through, but…" Goldie inhales and the only tell that she's nervous is from how she's twisting the hem of her shirt. "I, for one, have really been trying to work through my trust issues, so…I'm not going to be hard on you. We loved our mom so much. Meeting you and getting to know about another chapter of our mom's life, despite how hard it was for both of you and what a shock it's been, feels like a gift." She drops her hand and grabs a tissue for herself. "You don't have to decide today, obviously, but think about it."

She comes and sits down. I can tell she feels vulnerable and I reach out and take her hand, squeezing it. She looks at me gratefully.

"I'd like a chance to get to know you," Ava says.

"If I spot you around here with a gasoline can, I'm throwing you off the property, no questions asked," Grandma Nancy says.

Her tone is a lot less indignant than it was before this conversation.

Ava smiles. "Understood." She holds up her hand. "Don't worry. I won't be going near any gasoline cans again."

Goldie looks wrung out. And she's not the only one. Everett sits down hard when Ava leaves, scrubbing both hands over his face.

"That went better than I thought it would," he finally says.

"I thought so too," Goldie says.

She tucks a piece of hair behind her ear, and her fingers tremble.

I nudge her gently. "You need food."

"I'm not sure I could eat."

"How about we try?" I stand and stretch. "Dinner's on me. All of us. The Hungry Walleye. What do you say?"

"I wouldn't mind some fried fish," Grandma Nancy says.

"Excellent."

We pile into my Range Rover, the mood somber. Once we're at the restaurant, we perk up a little, and the noise in the place keeps us from being forced into conversation. I think everyone needs to mentally decompress and the distraction of the noisy restaurant seems to help.

"Thank you, Milo. That was delicious," Grandma Nancy says.

"You're welcome. I'm glad you enjoyed it."

The air is cool when we step outside. It's a beautiful night—until we hear raised voices.

Bruce and Ava stand under the streetlight.

"I'm not the bad guy here," Bruce snaps. "I'm your *father*. Why would you believe them over me?"

"Why do I have to choose?" Ava argues, her voice shaky. "Why can't everyone get along?"

Bruce scoffs. "You're naive to think they want anything to do with you."

"You haven't even introduced me to the rest of your family! I've asked to meet Dahlia for months! Does she even know about me yet? And even Milo's mom! I'd love to get to know the rest of my family." Ava holds her hand up and takes a deep breath.

"I wanted to give Dahlia…and everyone…time to adjust." He shakes his head. "But you just couldn't wait to jump in the Whitmans' camp. I'm so disappointed in you."

Everett mutters something under his breath.

Goldie walks toward Bruce and Ava and I follow, not

wanting her to do this alone. Bruce turns. His jaw clenches when he sees all of us.

"You should be ashamed of yourself." Goldie's voice is sharp, yet calm.

"Excuse me?" Bruce snaps.

"How dare you talk to her that way! You're disappointed in her? *Please.* She's your daughter and you've treated her like leverage in your ridiculous obsession with getting back at my family."

Bruce straightens, huffing a bitter laugh. "Don't you dare come over here and—"

I step between him and Goldie. "I'd watch the way you speak to my girlfriend if I were you."

"Oh, this is rich," Bruce says. "This is none of your business. It's between Ava and me."

Goldie moves next to me, fearless. "It became our business when you tried to turn her against us instead of taking the time to get to know her. You should want her to have all the love possible, not hide her away and pull her out like an accessory!"

Bruce shakes his head and looks at Ava. "One positive conversation with them and you've turned against me, is that it?"

"I'm not trying to turn against you," Ava says firmly. "I'm trying to figure out who I am. I'm trying to get to know my whole family, not take sides. You made me believe they were horrible people and they're not!"

"You know nothing!" Bruce yells.

Everett steps beside Goldie now, tall and steady. He looks healthier than he has in months. "Have some dignity, Bruce. Let this ridiculous battle go."

Bruce's gaze flickers between all of us, settling on Ava and then me. "I won't forget this," he says.

He turns and walks to his car, slamming the door hard. After he drives off, we stand in silence for a beat.

Goldie moves toward Ava and she jumps. Goldie pauses, holding her hands up.

"Sorry," she says. "I didn't mean to startle you."

Ava takes a shaky breath. "No, it's okay."

"It's been a good day," Goldie says. "Please don't let him ruin that. His words aren't your truth."

Ava's face crumbles and Goldie holds her arms out. Ava walks into them and they hug for a long time.

CHAPTER THIRTY-SEVEN

LET YOUR HAIR DOWN

GOLDIE

After an emotionally fraught week, it's nice to have a fairly low-key one.

Tonight, I'm on my way to The Cozy Palette. Erin was able to get in touch with Percy and they were okay with us using the building tonight. I'm lugging a few canvases to share since I don't know what is available at the shop anymore. When I walk inside, Juju and Erin are already there. I follow the sound of laughter and find them by the big workstation in the back.

Erin is wearing a helmet and holding up a blowtorch.

"Oh my God, what are we doing tonight? I thought we were doing wine and acrylic pours on a canvas. This looks hardcore!" I set the canvases on the island and tug off my zipped hoodie

"Oh, don't act like you don't know hardcore," Erin says,

grinning. "And oops, I forgot that's what I wanted to do." She makes a face. "I blame ADHD and a dream I had."

"I'm a little intimidated in the art department with you two," Juju says, "but I'm willing to try...whatever we're doing."

"You guys can paint on a canvas if you want. Or you can make something out of this." Erin lifts a big chunk of metal and points at the various metals laid out on the table.

"Ooo," I say, rummaging through the bucket with everything from buttons to knobs.

"I'm gonna try to turn this into a warrior with armor and everything," Erin says. "My very own Joan of Arc. I want it in my bedroom. It'd be fun to have a jump-scare every time I get up in the middle of the night, and then be like, 'Oh, hey, Joanie. Thanks for watching out for me.'"

Juju and I stare at her for a beat.

"How do you think of these things?" I say.

"I'm just blessed that way." She lifts a shoulder.

"Your mind is a fascinating place," I tell her.

"It is." Juju giggles. "Maybe you're the most well-rounded of all of us. A little scary, a little hilarious, and everything in between."

Erin slaps her backside. "Why, thank you. I prefer being told I'm shaped like a peach, but well-rounded works too."

Juju throws a sour gummy worm at her. "Okay, Ms. Peach. So, where is Percy?"

"Percy is in Montana," Erin says, "but it sounds like they might be coming back soon." She lifts an eyebrow over her shoulder and smirks at us.

"There's the smirk that was missing when we brought Percy up the last time. So you *haven't* lost your crush..."

"I tried." Erin sighs. "But then we talked on the phone and it was nice. So...no, never losing that crush, I'm afraid."

"Maybe because there's something there," Juju says.

"Ahh, I think that boat has sailed." Erin puts her hand on her hip as she tries to secure metal around a dress form. "I mean, there have been plenty of chances, and it's been a no-go."

"Well, I'm not giving up hope. And it was nice of them to let us use the space," I say. "I always loved coming in here as a kid. Percy's dad had the best art supplies. I got my favorite brush here and never looked back."

The Cozy Palette is bursting with color. Shelves of paint and brushes and canvases, along with scrapbooking and jewelry supplies cover every nook and cranny. Various artwork is displayed in every open space, and when I lean in to see who the artist is, I'm surprised more than once.

"Did you know Miss Idella and Emmy are quite the artists?" I point out their paintings.

"Nice." Juju nods. "I should see if they'd want to put anything in the cafe." She lifts her shoulder and scrunches up her face. "I'd rather have a G. Waters original, but…" She eyes me hopefully.

"I'd be happy to put something in the cafe. Whatever you want."

She shakes her shoulders in a little dance. "I bet we could sell a lot during the busier seasons. Oh!" She holds up her hand. "I've been shirking my wine duties! I'll get right on that." She pours a hefty glass of wine for each of us.

"To a girls' night and starting the first of many happy traditions," Erin says.

We clink our glasses and I set a large piece of plastic over the island.

"If you want to do an acrylic pour, I brought everything we'll need," I tell Juju.

"Yes, please," she says.

I hand her some disposable gloves and put on my own, then fill glasses with all different colors of paint, letting Juju pick the colors she wants. I pull out two of the smaller canvases and place smaller cups under them so they're not flat on the plastic. And then I show her how to layer her paint in one cup. She loves it when we flip the cup onto the canvas and then just leave it there while we combine dish soap and water.

"This is so satisfying," she says, when we lift the cup and let the paint fill the canvas.

I show her how to empty the cup on the edges and then let the paint drip off the edges. Juju loves flowers, so I show her the drip stick method and she is hooked.

Erin lifts her helmet off. "What is going on over there? Juju, you sound like you're in the throes of ecstasy."

"Yeah, right. I wish," Juju sighs. "But, look at this. It's amazing! I'm obsessed. This is so pretty!" The cells start to spread and look like flowers.

She's thrilled by all of it.

"We can add a little white in the center if you want to give each flower a pop," I tell her.

"Yes to the pop," she says.

Once we've done that, we sip our wine and admire the magic that takes place as the white expands.

"Have you seen Ava again?" Erin asks.

"No. I almost invited her tonight, but I lost my nerve."

"You should've. We could've made sure it didn't get hostile." Erin holds up her arm and pats her muscle.

"I don't *think* she'll get hostile again. She seemed devastated after her confrontation with Bruce. But baby steps. I did text her to see how she was doing this week and she said she was okay…but she didn't have much to say back, so I didn't press it. I don't think we're going to be close overnight or anything, but…" I take my gloves off and set them on the plastic. "I guess I don't know *what* to expect."

"She's probably so embarrassed by what she did and just lying low for a bit," Juju says. "It's a lot. I'm shocked you're handling it so well, finding out that *Ava Piper* is your sister."

"I'm *trying* to handle it well. I hate that Bruce is involved. Ava can't help it that he's her dad and Milo can't help it that he's related to him either, but I really can't stand the man. It's even harder to remain objective about him, hearing the way he treated my mom when she got pregnant. Grandma Donna said he stopped speaking to my mom as soon as he found out and then turned people against her at school." I shake my head. "*Anyway*…I have a sister and I'm not sure she wants to have anything to do with me."

"She said she wanted to get to know you," Erin says. "And I think she meant it. At least I'm hoping she does…so I don't have to show her the muscle."

We laugh and I'm glad that the mood lightens again.

Erin maneuvers the metal a little but doesn't get the results she wants. "I should've stuck to that." She points at our paintings.

"It's not too late." I hold up another canvas.

Erin moves to the paint and Juju sits propped on a stool, her chin leaning on her fist.

"How are things with Milo?" Juju asks.

"I feel like I'm getting asked all the hard-hitting questions tonight." I take another long swig of wine.

"Because you have the exciting life." Juju sighs.

She pours more wine into our glasses and opens another bottle.

"We have to deal with needy customers all day long…" she continues.

"You love the customers!" I elbow her. "Even the needy ones...like me."

She grins. "I know. I do." And then pouts. "But it'd be a lot more fun with a lover waiting to pounce on me the minute I got home."

We all laugh.

"True that." Erin holds up her glass and we all clink.

"It is pretty great," I admit.

"So is that nonstop smile you're wearing these days. After life-shaking news like a long-lost sister who bashed you in an art review, held Save the Otter shit over your head, and tried to set your property on fire...I've gotta say, you're looking mighty happy," Erin says, clinking our glasses again.

We crack up and empty our glasses.

"One more bottle?" Erin asks.

"Why not? It's girls' night," I say.

"We can walk home. Is someone picking you up?" Juju asks.

"Milo's waiting for me in his apartment."

"Ah! See?" Erin yells. "Your hottie is sa-tis-fy-ING!"

For some reason, that makes us laugh harder.

"So are you basically living above my cafe?" Juju asks.

"I spend some nights there, but Milo has been staying at the house too. He pretends like he's leaving and then comes in after everyone's gone to bed." I snort. "But this morning, when he pretended to 'arrive', my dad said, 'Milo, you were snoring so loud last night, I could hear you all the way from my room!' and Milo's mouth dropped and his face got red, and my dad pointed at him and said, 'Caught ya!' And then he told him he hadn't really heard him snoring but he *had* seen him sneaking in one night and to just make himself at home already."

We all laugh so hard we're wheezing.

"Stop making me laugh. I've gotta go." Juju runs, laughing all the way to the bathroom.

We start cleaning up. When Erin starts taking her stuff to the door so it's all ready to go, I text Milo.

> Iss been such a fin nighy. Missss yuu
>
> Yoo
>
> YOl
>
> Dammut

MILO
> 🐸 You on the happy juice, Golo?

> So haopy
>
> Cant waitto see yuu

MILO
> I can't wait to see you either

"We can leave our things here to dry. Percy said we can use the place as much as we want," Erin says.

So we leave our canvases on the plastic and gather the rest of our things. We hug each other and get tangled in Juju's wide-legged jeans. I trip and go flying and Erin catches me before I face-plant into the large turning rack of stickers. We're laughing so hard I can't breathe when we step outside, and I hear a low chuckle that sends a melty feeling in my gut.

I look up and see Milo leaning against a streetlight, his feet crossed. He looks like a tall, beautiful giant that I want to climb, and I must say it out loud because he grins and stands straighter. His fingers beckon me closer.

"Climb aboard," he says. "I'm rooting for you. It's time to branch out."

Erin puts her hand on her head. "I didn't think I was drunk, but I must be because you are punning all over the place."

"Sorry," Milo says under his breath. "It felt like the only time I could get away with it."

"No," Erin says, shaking her head. "Never a good time. But I'll forgive you because you're *so pretty.*"

"I can tell it's been a good night for all of you," Milo says, laughing.

"We had so much fun and I'm *so* happy to see you," I sing. "What are you *doing* here?"

He laughs again. "I thought you might be a while yet, but I wanted to be here to walk you home if you needed an arm to hang on to or…anything."

"He's so thoughtful too," Juju slurs. She flings her arms out. "Universe, I manifest a tall, beautiful giant…who is not Milo…to come walk with and provide an arm for me. No meanies with dark hair and blue eyes who think they are God's gift to women just because they can cook and because they have been written up in every cooking magazine. Only nice giants…preferably a giant who knows how to find my clit because I'm really tired of no man knowing where it is. Soon, please and thank you."

A deep laugh erupts out of Milo. Erin and I have already lost it and I have to hold onto Milo. Turns out I really needed his arm.

"I've never heard Juju say clit in my life." I whisper the c-word and that sends Juju and Erin into another cackle.

"I think I need to walk all of you home. Who's closest?" Milo asks.

"Juju," we all say at the same time.

"Lead the way," he says.

CHAPTER THIRTY-EIGHT

PAINT HER DREAMS

MILO

The last time we slept at my place was a few weeks ago, when Goldie got drunk at The Cozy Palette. I'm still laughing about how freaking funny and adorable she was.

Every night since, we've stayed at her place. It's a huge house, and once Everett let me know he wasn't oblivious to me sneaking in and out and that I was more than welcome to stay, I've done just that. I love being with her dad and grandmas. Camden's moved in now too, so it's the most people I've lived with. I love Goldie's family and enjoy being in the big, fat middle of them, but I'm starting to wish we had our own place.

I think about it all the way to Minneapolis.

That night, the bed is too big without her.

My penthouse has never been what I'd call cozy, but now it feels cold and sterile. The sheets don't smell like Goldie's shampoo, and she's not curled against my side, her leg draped over my thigh.

I glower at the ceiling, arm heavy over my forehead, and sigh.

Who knew one night apart could suck this bad?

I check the time on my phone. 10:40 p.m. I should've called her an hour ago, but my meetings went late. I do it anyway.

"Hey, Mildie," she answers, her voice like honey.

My chest loosens and I grin into my dark room. "Hey, Golo. You sound good. You in bed?"

"Yes, missing you."

"Same. Guilty."

Her voice is soft. "Are you still coming home tomorrow?"

I shift on the bed. "Yes, and it can't be soon enough. Without you here, everything feels both too loud and too empty. I'm missing my home…which is where you are."

"Milo," she says sweetly. "I know what you mean. It's been the longest day here without you." Her voice drifts.

I wait until her breathing evens out, and I lie there for a few minutes, listening to her breathe and thinking about how hard she works before I hang up.

Frankly, I'm shocked that she's not thrilled to have a night to herself. She's gotta be exhausted.

The pavilion is finally done. It is *stunning*. I'm proud of how it turned out, but I've gotten the most joy watching Goldie fall in love with it.

I'm happy that the pavilion will be more her baby. Because even after endless days of wrangling contractors, finalizing herb garden placements, and hanging mirrors *just so* in the restaurant bathrooms, or any other list of never-ending projects she has to do, she climbs into bed beside me like I'm the one she's been waiting for all day.

I can't wait to build her art studio, a mini replica of the pavilion, that can be all hers.

The restaurant opens next week. When Goldie's not racing around putting the final touches on the restaurant with Camden, she's working on the area surrounding the pavilion. Tully has worked alongside her, building a winding brick pathway, and she's planted an array of bushes, perennials, and bulbs that will be magnificent next spring. She has a bottomless well of energy that is addictive to watch, and it's impossible to not be inspired by her.

I get back to Windy Harbor the next evening around seven. The air is crisp today. Yesterday was eighty degrees and today it's fifty. You never know if you'll have summer or fall or even winter this time of year. All I want to do is find Goldie.

When I find her, she's crouched by the edge of the dock... talking to an otter.

I blink a few times, thinking sleep deprivation may have broken me, but nope.

It's still there.

Goldie's in frayed jeans and a thick orange sweater, her work boots damp. She carefully moves to sit, her feet dangling off the dock, as she chatters in a singsong voice to the sleek creature floating on its back.

I walk toward her quietly, hoping I don't scare the otter off, but he just blinks up at me like I'm interrupting their moment.

I know, buddy, I want her all to myself too.

She turns and beams when she sees me. "Yay! You're back! I would be hugging you so hard right now...I just don't want Orion to swim off without you meeting him."

"Orion?"

"Yes! Remember I told you about the otter who always

comes through? He's early this year." She makes space on the dock for me and I carefully sit down. "I usually don't see him until the winter, but he showed up this morning and we've been chatting for at least twenty minutes. Isn't he adorable?"

"I don't know why I didn't believe that he actually came to see you. I should've. Look at you. I'd want a sighting of you if I was an otter too."

She giggles. "I feel like it's a good sign that he came early. Like he's telling us it's all gonna be okay. It'll all work out."

"Yeah? Orion is prophetic?"

She nods. "I think so."

I stare at the creature. "What say you, great oracle? Is it all going to work out?"

Orion does a little flip onto his stomach and then returns to his back, his little paws tucked up.

Goldie gapes at me. "See what I mean?"

"I do! Let's ask him another question. Should Goldie be mine forever?"

Orion repeats his move and Goldie covers her mouth with her hands, barely covering her squeal. Her eyes are shining when she looks at me.

"Wow. I like this guy."

"Isn't he great? But you didn't need to waste that question on our little oracle here. Don't you know that I'm yours forever already?"

I grin. "I've hoped that you are. We talk about love a lot, but we haven't talked about forever as much."

"I'm yours forever."

"I'm yours forever too." I lean in and kiss her, and Orion lets out a long squeak.

We break apart laughing.

"Well, that wasn't very nice," I tell him. "You look like a wet slipper."

"He's majestic."

"Smug."

"Takes one to know one," she says.

I poke her side and she jerks, too ticklish to be still.

"I'd be careful if I were you. Don't judge. He remembers faces. Oh, and did you know otters hold hands when they sleep? I love that."

I look at her. Sunlight streaks through her golden hair and her cheeks are pink from the chill. Her eyes are full of wonder. I love her.

"I hold your hand when we sleep," I tell her.

"Hmm. Yeah, you do. I guess I *will* keep you forever."

Orion ducks under and disappears with a flick of his tail, and Goldie sighs.

"Come back soon," she calls.

And then she gets up and holds up her hand, ready to pull me up.

"Now I can hug you properly," she says.

"Will that be enough? It's hard to follow an otter."

She laughs. "Only if you kiss me too."

We kiss until she's melting into me, her hands tugging on the hair that's grown out a lot.

I hear a loud truck and break the kiss, excited for her to see my surprise. She doesn't know I commissioned artists to take my mini sculptures, the ones I made for her park model, and turned them into life-size pieces. They'll live here where I envisioned, a piece of both of us.

"I better talk to these guys," I tell her.

"What are they delivering? I didn't have any deliveries on the schedule."

"You'll see," I say, grinning.

Once I've directed the guys on where to take the sculptures, they get to work.

Goldie gasps when she sees what they're carrying. She sees the marigold first and then the sun.

"Wait…is that—?" Her whole face lights up.

I help the crew position them, checking with her to make sure they're where she wants them, and she just nods, blinking back tears.

They're beautiful. Even better than I hoped. Art tucked into nature, just like she wanted.

"Milo," she says, her voice cracking. "They're perfect."

I move toward her and pull her back against my chest.

"This is why you were in Minneapolis?"

I lean my chin lightly on her head. "I gave the final approval online last week and then went to see them in person yesterday."

She turns in my arms and buries her face in my chest. Her face is splotchy when she looks up and I brush a kiss against her pouty lips.

"You make me feel like all the parts of me that are too much or too weird are exactly right," she says.

"I'm glad because you *are* just right. You're exceptional."

"I feel like there needs to be a plaque in the middle of all the other plants I'm going to surround this place with…and maybe a bench. And the plaque will say something like: *Milo Lombardi Steals My Heart Every Day.* Or maybe *Milo Lombardi's Grand Gesture.*

I laugh. "I'd be proud of either one of those. I especially like the first one." I kiss her again. "I intend on stealing your heart every day…"

She takes my hand and we walk closer to the sculptures. Her fingers trail along the smooth steel like she's touching magic.

"If you want them shifted at all, we can move them. Any direction, any spot. They're yours. If you want them in your yard one day, we can move them there."

"They're perfect right here, where you envisioned them."

I slide my hand in hers and squeeze it. "I've got one more thing. If you've got time to take a quick drive."

She gives me a lopsided smile. "You're outdoing yourself, Mildie."

We walk to the SUV and take the quickest route to her lot. It's my favorite of all the lots and not just because it's hers. There isn't a bad choice on the property, but this one has gorgeous trees where I imagine the house going and a larger beach area closer to the water.

She squints at me curiously when we stop there.

I reach into the back seat and pull out a folder. And then I step outside and walk around, opening her door. She gets out, still dabbing her face from her earlier tears. I hand her the folder carefully, suddenly nervous.

She opens it slowly. And then her breath catches.

I watch her flip through the sketches—floor plans, elevations, little swatches of wood tones she's mentioned. Her kitchen, and her sunroom with a window seat. The screened porch with twinkle lights already drawn in.

"Right there," she says, pointing where the porch would go.

Her dream house. Down to the arched gate she showed me one time in a magazine and said, "That is totally my vibe."

Her fingers press over her lips and she doesn't say anything for a long time, just looks at every detail.

Finally, she chokes out, "Milo…" Her voice is barely a whisper. "This is exactly what I pictured. How did you do this? This is more than what we've talked about…"

"I've listened," I say. "You tell me in little ways the things you love all the time. What you dream about. I paid attention."

There's no stopping the tears now. She looks at me and the tears streak down her cheeks. "I can't believe you did all this."

"I talked to your dad and he agreed. Out of you and your brothers, yours should be the first house we build. He said it without hesitation."

He also agreed to my other question without hesitation, but I'll save that for another day. I want to give her a little more time to be sure this is what she really wants. That I'm who she really wants. There has been a lot of change in her life over the past six months.

She dries her face and inhales a shaky breath. "I want you to be there with me. When we build it. When we live in it. Every part. I want—" Her voice breaks. "I want us to do it together."

I pull her into my arms. She presses her face to my chest.

"I'm yours forever, remember?" I say into her hair.

"I love you, Milo. So much."

"My heart is yours, every part."

We kiss until we're breathless.

"Can we go to your place tonight? I don't want to be quiet." She smiles against my mouth.

"How soon can we go?"

She laughs and jogs to the Range Rover, hopping in and slamming the door.

I laugh and follow.

CHAPTER THIRTY-NINE

SPARKS IN THE DARK

GOLDIE

The sound of hammers and chain saws fills the air. I don't mind. Every bang means we're getting closer.

I'm on my knees arranging a fall display for outside the restaurant. I've made an arch out of branches and now I'm threading flowers and lights through it. Camden asked if I could make it look festive out here, but without the color orange. He has something against orange, which is really inconvenient when it comes to fall decor. I think I'm pulling it off by using every other earth tone—cream, brown, mustard, deep reds—and even pale pinks and peaches, with pampas grass and even a few dried hydrangeas that are the perfect sepia shade.

I hear the sound of tires behind me and turn, hoping it's Milo. I have a surprise that I've been waiting to give him and he's been in Minneapolis today. He left early this morning and it's probably too soon for him to be back, but that doesn't stop me from wishing. Kevin lets out a low growl and I pet him absentmindedly to calm him.

My stomach sinks when I see Bruce Granger walking toward me.

He glances at my work like he's smelling something rank, which isn't true. Me *and* these flowers smell fucking delicious and I know for a fact this arch is looking pretty damn fabulous too.

I dust my hands on my jeans and stand, looking at him suspiciously.

He doesn't make me wait long.

"I've heard from a couple of folks. People who've lived here long before you were born. They're worried."

"I've not heard from any of those folks, so I'm doubtful there really are any who are worried. If they are, we'll change their minds once they taste the food and see what we're creating here."

"You think you're doing something noble," he sneers, "but you're actually destroying what makes this place beautiful."

"This is a tired song, Bruce. And one I don't have time for. The restaurant's opening in five days and we passed our inspection. You're not at the center of this and that kills you."

His eyes flash. That hit.

"Why don't you admit this is over? You tried to put a stop to this and it didn't work and you're mad that Ava is seeing through your shit."

He looks around, his jaw set. In the distance, a few workers laugh. Sunlight filters through my arch and it practically glows.

"This isn't over," he growls. "I'll be watching and ready when everything starts falling apart. And you may have Ava fooled into believing in this fairy tale, but she's a Granger—she'll see through all of you."

My heart thumps faster, but I take a step closer to him.

"This place? It's not falling apart, it's just going to get better and better. And like it or not, Ava is one of us too."

He doesn't respond. He turns and stalks back to his car. When the engine growls to life and his tires squeal out, I let out a breath I didn't realize I was holding.

I hope my words come to pass and not his.

The sun glints off the lake, and for a moment, I let myself believe that everything hard is already behind us. That the tightness in my chest from seeing Bruce earlier has been carried off in the wind and drowned in the water.

However, I'm trying really hard to not live in denial these days. Sometimes life is hard. There's no avoiding that. Even when so much going on around me is good, there will still be hard things.

But that's for another day. Tonight we're celebrating my dad. He's finished his last round of chemo and we're going to rejoice in that.

The house is loud before I even reach the porch. Music is playing through the outdoor speakers, laughter rises and falls like the water against the rocks, my family is all here together…life is *wonderful*.

Kevin barrels ahead of me, little paws flying and his tail wagging so hard, his whole back half shakes. He makes a beeline for Tully, who's sitting in one of the Adirondack chairs. Kevin flops against his leg and looks back at Tully like *I'm here, why aren't you scratching my butt?*

"There he is." Tully laughs, ruffling the soft fur above Kevin's fountain tail. "The king of the land."

Kevin closes his eyes, blissed out.

"How did you manage to avoid a sweater tonight?" he whispers to Kevin.

"I got him out early before Grandma Donna could get one on him," I whisper back.

Tully laughs.

Grayson runs up and pets Kevin.

"Whoa, hold up. Where are my hugs?" I ask.

"Hi, Auntie," he says sweetly. "Where's Milo?"

"He'll be here soon," I promise.

I walk over to hug Dad and Kevin follows me. He loves scratches, but he loves to be wherever Dad and I am more.

Dad's eyes are bright when I pull back from our hug.

"You look good, Dad."

"Thanks, buttercup. I feel good. Hopeful."

"I'm so glad you're done with chemo. So, so glad."

"Me too, honey." He pats my cheek, his eyes filling with tears. "Sorry, I'm an emotional old man, but I'm just so grateful. Thanks for being with me through it every step of the way."

My lip wobbles. "Always. And you've earned the right to be emotional…even though you're not an old man yet."

He hugs me again and I sigh, beyond happy.

When Milo arrives a few minutes later, looking like a snack I want to inhale, my pulse picks up. This time in the best way. I feel like I haven't seen him in months instead of early this morning. I walk toward him, grinning, and his eyes are drinking me in too, like he can't ever get enough. Kevin gets to him first, twirling excitedly and then pressing his back end into Milo's shins.

"Hey, little guy." Milo crouches to give him a thorough scratch. "It's good to see you too."

Since Milo's been sleeping at the lake house, Kevin's gotten attached to him too. He still sleeps with my dad part of the time, but most times I wake up and Kevin is curled around Milo's legs.

Milo is a granny whisperer and a dog whisperer too.

All I need.

I walk the rest of the way and when I reach him, he straightens and pulls me in without a word. He kisses me like he's missed me too. It's quick, but it grounds me.

"You made it," I say when we break apart.

"Of course. There's no way I'd miss this."

He looks around, taking in the low buzz of my family spread out between the house and the water, and takes my hand in his.

Kevin herds us toward everyone and we let him lead.

By the time the sky turns a dusky lavender, we've lit a bonfire down by the shore. My dad wanted a fire and S'mores and he's getting whatever he wants. Grayson hands out the marshmallows to everyone, and the heat flickers across our faces as we hold our sticks above the flame.

I get lost looking at the colors of the fire.

"You okay, buttercup?" Dad asks next to me.

I think about brushing it off like I would've in the past. But this is my dad and I don't want to shove my feelings down anymore.

"I'm trying to just be hopeful about your health, but you know me, I still worry. And...Bruce came by this morning, trying to stir things up."

He huffs. "Did he threaten you?"

"Not me…more like…Windhaven."

"He can stir all he wants."

"You don't sound worried."

"I think we're building something worthwhile and it's rooted in love. Whatever he tries to bring our way, we still have each other. He'll always be empty and alone unless he learns to love."

A log pops, sending a swirl of sparks in the dark.

"Remember when we'd do these bonfires when you kids were little? It was always your mom's idea. My brain was full of work and she'd know how to draw me out of that, how to focus on what was important. I'm grateful she taught me that."

I blink fast, swallowing the lump rising in my throat. "I'm grateful she did too. She was such a good mom, and you're such a good dad too."

"Goldie, being your dad…you and your brothers'…it's been the greatest gift I've known."

I swallow back a sob and poke him in the side. "Now you're just trying to make me cry."

He chuckles and wipes his eyes too. "Nothing wrong with that."

"You're right," I say, leaning against him.

"Hey," I hear behind me.

I turn and it's Ava. She hesitates at the edge of the firelight.

"You came," I say, smiling. "Would you like a S'more?"

"No, thank you." She smiles tentatively and walks slowly toward me. "Thanks for inviting me. Congratulations, Everett. I hope you're feeling well."

"Getting better all the time," he says. "Thank you for coming."

Kevin sniffs her toes, tail wagging in cautious approval.

"Goldie, I don't want to take you from the party, but...I wanted to show you something," she says.

"Oh, okay."

I feel Milo's eyes on me and know he's trying to assess whether I'm okay or not. I smile and give a slight nod and his shoulders relax.

"Do you want to go inside for a few minutes?" I ask.

"That would probably be best. I'd like you to see this." She pulls out a letter and I recognize my mom's handwriting.

My breath hitches.

We go inside and sit at the kitchen table. It's hard to hold back my excitement. I'm greedy for new words of my mother's. I've been dying to read the letters she gave Ava, but I never would've asked to. She deserves to have that piece of our mom to herself.

She places the letter in front of me.

"The letters have been amazing. I feel like I've gotten an idea of what she was like from her letters." Her voice cracks. "It's been healing and painful...and so sad but joyful at the same time?" She lets out a nervous laugh. "It's been a lot, I guess, but I treasure every word I've been given." She puts her finger on the letter. "She talks about you in this one and I wanted you to read it."

My eyes are blurry, but I nod.

My hands are shaky as I open the letter.

"I love seeing her handwriting," I say softly.

"Me too."

My daughter,

I've told you a lot of my dreams for you already, but the one on my mind today is one I've been hesitant to bring up. I hope that you have such a full life that what I'm about to say won't hurt you. And maybe even if you have a full and happy life, it will still hurt you.

For that, I'm sorry.

I've said I have kids, but I haven't been specific.

I have four sons and another daughter. Their names are Noah, Camden, Tully, Goldie, and Dylan. Tully and Goldie are twins.

I can tell you about all of them sometime, but today I want to talk about Goldie.

She's eight years younger than you and is a twin, but from the time she could talk, she's wished she had a sister too. I don't know why I didn't tell my kids about you. It was never because I was ashamed of you in any way, but it just hurt too much.

I still hope that one day we can find each other, and that you can get to know your brothers and sister.

I wonder all the time what you're like. If you're like me. If Goldie is like you.

She's brave and stubborn and full of light. She's my gold thread. I took one look at her and knew it. It's why we call her Goldie. She loves hard and forgives easily and loves to paint.

I wonder what I would have named you. I thought maybe Iris, but I wanted to see you first to be sure. I wonder if you love to paint too or if you're into designing houses like me or if you have a whole set of skills that I don't have. I would love whatever makes you YOU. *I already do.*

If you meet Goldie, I hope you'll be good friends. Nothing brings me more joy than seeing my kids love each other.

Yours,
Mom (or Stella)

. . .

Tears are dripping down my cheeks and when I look up at Ava, she's been crying too.

There was a lot in there that got me, but her saying that I forgive easily hit home. Because I used to be that way… before Wes. I'd almost forgotten.

"She ends all her letters that way," Ava says, laughing quietly. "Mom (or Stella)."

"Mom was never pushy." I laugh and reach behind me for the tissues.

I hand her the box and we both blow our noses.

"Thank you for showing me that," I manage.

"I can show you the others sometime, if you want."

"If you're truly okay with showing me. They're personal, so you don't have to."

"I'd like to. I like hearing what you have to say about her. Like that she was never pushy. I could imagine that from the letters, but I wouldn't know for sure without your input."

"Then I'd love that."

She smiles, and for the first time, it feels like the space between us is closing.

CHAPTER FORTY

LEAD THE WAY

MILO

Goldie has no idea that yesterday I wasn't *just* going to work in Minneapolis. After I finished an early meeting, I went to my parents' house.

Grandma was there too and she was so sweet.

"I can't believe I haven't met this girl of yours yet," she said.

"I can't either, Grandma. We've gotta fix that. When can we come see you?"

"Well, I can make it easier on you by letting you know the next time I'm in town." She laughed and patted my face. *"I've got something for you."* She picked up the box from the side table and waved it in front of me. *"I had it cleaned up and it's so sparkly."*

"Thank you, Grandma."

I open the box and swallow hard. My grandma told me a

long time ago that when I found the woman I loved, I could have her ring.

"There was a lot of love surrounding this ring," she said. "It's a relic now." She laughed. "But it's still beautiful, I think."

"Oh, it's definitely beautiful. And it's the most unique ring I've ever seen."

With Goldie's love for sustainability and repurposing, I think she'd appreciate many different styles, but this one...I think she'll flip when she sees it.

"It was new in the '40s and quite outrageous." She chuckled. "White gold," she says, tapping the ring. "The center diamond is three carats and all these smaller diamonds add up to a carat. I think the way it's set gives the illusion of motion, almost like waves colliding."

"That's a perfect way to put it. I think you're right."

The sun is rising as I walk down to the water. I take in the beauty, still in awe of this beautiful place. We've had warm days and chilly nights for the past few weeks, so the leaves are spectacularly vibrant. There are still patches of green grass, but many orange, red, and yellow leaves are still hanging onto the trees for dear life, and the rest are quickly dropping to the ground. I miss the great restaurants and quick access to the office, but otherwise, I don't miss the city much. The sound of the water lapping against the shore and the blue stretching as far as I can see grounds me. I'm allowing myself this calm only for the time it takes me to drink my cup of coffee.

"Hey, Mildie," I hear behind me.

I look over my shoulder and see Goldie walking toward me in a pretty dress. I put the box back in my pocket and enjoy the view. My stomach falls out, seeing her smile, the way her curves fill all the right places, the deep V that peeks out at her neckline, and her perfect ass and long legs. Her delicate fingers, the mouth that I obsess over. Every inch of her is staggeringly gorgeous, sexy, and all woman.

She watches me check her out and her smile deepens.

"Hi," I say. "You look way too pretty this morning. But you're always beautiful."

"I was just thinking the same about you."

I tug her toward me and give her a lingering kiss. "How are you feeling? You ready for this day?"

"Now that I've had my coffee, I think so. How 'bout you?"

"I'm ready. I feel good about things. I might need another cup of coffee, but…" I grin.

Now that she's pulled back a little, I notice she's holding something.

"What's that?" I ask.

"I've got a little present for you." She smiles and lifts up a small box.

"What? A present?"

"I wanted to give you something…because I love you and because you've done so much for me and my family. You've picked up my brothers from the airport when Tully couldn't. You've driven to Minneapolis to get the cloth napkins when we found out they weren't going to be delivered in time. I saw the list you were working on last night and it's as long as mine." Her eyes glisten and she presses her lips together. "I just wanted to say I've noticed every sacrifice you've made, every way you've gone above and beyond what any architect would ever do…beyond any boyfriend I've ever seen too." A tear drips down her cheek and I catch it. "Goodness, all this buildup and the gift is just something simple, but I love you."

I press my lips to hers. "God, I love you. Thank you. I'd

do it all again to be with you. I love you and your family, and I'm proud to be around to witness what you're doing here."

"You're a part of this just as much as I am. I want you to know that."

I'm touched that she feels this way. I wanted to bring her vision and her dad and brothers' vision to life, and somewhere along the way, I became completely invested.

"Thank you," I say quietly. "Thank you for letting me be part of this."

"I couldn't have done any of it without you."

"You could've."

"Let's not go back to arguing," she says, sniffling.

I laugh and she hands me the box.

I open it and am stunned when I see an antique compass in perfect condition.

"Goldie," I breathe out. "It's beautiful."

"You are my true north," she says. "And no matter what we go through, I want you to always find your way back to me."

I lean down and kiss her. "I will. Always."

"I had it restored. The needle was re-magnetized, so it works!"

I lift it carefully out of the box and smile when the needle moves into position.

"This is such a thoughtful gift. I'm—" I shake my head, beyond moved. "Thank you. I love it."

"You're welcome," she says softly.

I place the compass back in the box and put it in my pocket, pulling the ring box out.

Her eyes go round when she sees it.

"I have something for you too," I tell her.

I get on one knee and she gapes. When I open the box, she gasps.

"I didn't know I could love anyone the way I love you, Goldie. You turn my heart inside out. You make me want to be a better man. You inspire me to dream big. You fill every missing part of me. I want to be by your side forever. Will you marry me?"

Her hand is over her mouth, shaking, and she nods. With a shaky voice, she says, "Yes. I want to marry you more than anything."

She puts her hands on my cheeks and kisses me hard, and then she kisses my cheeks and forehead and peppers my mouth with little kisses, saying, "Yes, yes, yes."

I bury my face in her stomach and hug her before standing up, and then I finally put the ring on her finger.

"Wow, this ring is stunning. I've never seen anything like it!"

"It was my grandma's and she is so happy for you to have it, but insists we work out a meeting soon."

"Absolutely. I hate that we haven't already met. I guess this whole thing has been pretty fast, hasn't it?"

I laugh. "Faster than I ever imagined. But when you know, you know."

We hear a loud squeak and turn, and in the distance, lolling around on his back, is Orion.

"Oh my God. See? Orion knows too. He came by to give his stamp of approval." She throws her head back and laughs.

I kiss her again because I can't help myself.

"Your dad gave his approval too," I tell her.

"You asked him?" Her smile gets lopsided and I think she might cry again.

"When we got back from our weekend in Minneapolis."

She leans her head against my chest. "I love that."

We start walking toward the house, the leaves crunching under our feet.

"Let me get another look at you," I say, lifting her hand and twirling her around. When she twirls into my chest, I grin and lift her.

"I'm so in love with you," I say, staring up at her.

She leans down and kisses me. "I'm so glad because it was really hard when I couldn't kiss your face off whenever I wanted. And hello, fiancé, now I can."

"Hell, yeah, you can."

CHAPTER FORTY-ONE

PHASE ONE

GOLDIE

The day of the restaurant's grand opening is gorgeous and *toasty*.

I get up early, unable to stop smiling. When I'm not staring at Milo, I'm staring at my ring. I love it so much.

I love him so much.

Milo looks like a fallen angel in bed, his lips extra pouty from how long we kissed last night. We barely slept, and I feel like I'll probably be walking funny today because we had sex like it was our last night on Earth. My heart gallops just thinking about it. His smile, the way his broad shoulders hovered over me, his perfect ass in my grip, his thick thighs, his forearms and his long, thick fingers. That V that I think about whether he's dressed or not. His exquisite cock. It's really not fair to the rest of mankind that it was all given to Milo Lombardi.

My fiancé.

I tiptoe out of the room to let him sleep a little longer because if I keep looking at him, I'm gonna have to climb on top of him.

And there's a lot to do today.

But first, at breakfast, once everyone is in the dining room, including Milo, I take the opportunity to lift my hand up for everyone to behold my ring's beauty.

"Milo and I have something to tell you," I sing.

I don't even know who shouts first or who hugs me first because there's a roar and Milo and I are bombarded with hugs. I laugh and cry because that seems to be my default lately, feeling all the things, all the time.

Mostly I feel so loved and so grateful.

Milo got ready before I did so I could have the bathroom to myself. He groans when he sees me in my dress. It's black with long sleeves and a low neckline…and hits me mid-thigh.

"You look hot as *fuck*," he says. "And elegant. And so unbelievably sexy." His hand goes to the back of his neck while he looks me up and down. "We have a few minutes before we have to go, right?"

I move toward him, and my five-inch heels put me closer to his height, but I still have to look up. He's in a black three-piece suit and looks absolutely delicious. I smooth his lapel and straighten his tie. And then I run the back of my hand over his smoothly shaven skin.

"Mmm, so soft. You look good enough to eat," I tell him.

He leans in to kiss me, and I put my finger on his lips.

"We don't have time now, but I'll make it up to you later, I promise."

"You're sure?" he asks.

His hands slide to my backside and I'm tempted, really tempted, to lift my dress and let him take me now, but sense prevails.

"I'm so sure," I say.

He pouts and lifts my hand to his lips, pressing a soft kiss to my knuckles.

"We might need to go to your place tonight, that's how sure I am."

His eyes light up at that because he knows we're as loud as we want to be when we're there.

"Let's do this," he says.

As we're about to leave, Kevin trots out. Grandma Donna had come to get him while I was getting ready and now I see why. He's wearing a little knitted sweater that looks like a tux. I have to say, it's one of her cutest creations.

"Look at you!" I go on over him and he dances around my feet.

Grandma Donna looks so proud when we walk out.

"His sweater tux is so cute, Grandma!"

"Aw, thank you, dear. You look gorgeous!"

"Yes, you do," Grandma Nancy adds.

"You both look lovely too!"

Milo kisses their cheeks and tells them how pretty they look and they preen under his attention. I swear, if they were younger, they'd be shooting their shot with my fiancé.

I probably think of the word fiancé every other second now.

Milo, Milo, Milo. Fiancé, fiancé, fiancé.

I haven't even thought about a wedding yet. I don't care what we do, I just want to be his wife.

We take his SUV since it's a little trek from the house and he lets me, my grandmas, and Kevin out before going to park. Kevin's just staying long enough for the fam to see him in his sweater tux and then Grandma Donna is driving him back to the house. I walk inside and glance around the room, so excited for everyone to experience Elm & Echo. The forty-foot windows are a showstopper in themselves, and the view will make it even better in the daytime. But it's still stunning in here at night.

One of my favorite projects is the tree I created out of combining all different kinds of branches, and then I covered them with tiny lights. It's standing in the back corner and is almost as tall as the ceiling. I had to put it together horizontally and then have five men help me stand it up. Hanging from the ceiling are thin branches with lights, and there's a massive glam chandelier too, but with the tables made out of distressed wood, it's the perfect juxtaposition of romantic, not too formal, and comfortable.

My grandmas gasp when they see everything. They've seen it at various stages but wanted to be surprised with the final look.

"You've outdone yourself," Grandma Donna says.

"Good gravy, this is gorgeous," Grandma Nancy adds.

"Thank you." I squeeze both of them. "It took a lot of hands on deck to make this happen."

I smile at all the new employees Camden has hired. Everyone is so nice and excited to be part of this new venture—I think he made great choices. I walk back to the kitchen and Tully is already here, standing next to Camden. I inhale the aroma of fresh herbs and garlic, meat and desserts competing with each other.

I'm barely in the door when Juju barrels past me, her heels clicking against the floor. She looks *livid*.

"I should've known better than to bring desserts for you!" she shouts over her shoulder. "You can find someone else to do your bidding, Camden Whitman!"

She nearly collides with me and stops just long enough to hiss, "You look really pretty. I'll let you deal with that a-hole."

Camden laughs. "May as well call a jackass a *jackass,* Juliana."

"Okay, *jackass,*" she mutters, going out the door.

"What did you do to her?" I ask, wide-eyed.

"She was later than I wanted with the pies and cheesecakes. And she made mousse cakes and bread pudding. I didn't ask for mousse cakes or bread pudding."

"You gave her a hard time for bringing extra desserts…" I stare at him, dumbfounded. "You *are* a jackass! I can't believe you. Why does she bring out the worst in you?"

"Did you hear the way she talked to me?"

"Like you deserved, it sounds like!"

He sighs. "Come on, don't pile on." He looks at me sheepishly.

"Okay, but stop being mean to my friend. Haven't you heard? You're the nicest brother."

"Hey!" Tully says. "Again, *I'm* the twin. He is not. Therefore, I am supposed to be your favorite everything."

"You're my favorite also," I tell him.

Tully grins and bumps me in the hip, until he hears the word *also*. I give him a side hug to make up for it.

"How are you doing besides being a temperamental jackass over getting extra desserts?" I ask Camden.

He wipes his hands on his apron and grumbles, "I *was* fine. Until she showed up."

Milo walks in and my dad, Dylan, Noah, and Grayson are with him. Everyone is dressed up in their best suits, hair to perfection, and the smell of aftershave is a little overwhelming in this space. Their hair has grown out more and they all look so handsome. Every single one of them, my dad included, could be models if they wanted to. They never would, but they *could.*

"I'm excited for this night. Amazed at how it all came together. Blown away by how many helped make it happen," Camden says. "Especially all of you."

Noah opens a bottle of champagne and fills a glass for each of us. For Grayson, he pulls his travel cup out of his bag. "Chocolate milk for you," he tells him.

Grayson beams up at him and then smiles around the room.

Noah raises his glass. "I'm proud of you, brother. To Camden. For creating something beautiful and inspiring."

We all click glasses.

"To Camden," we repeat.

"To family," Tully says, and we repeat.

"To food," Dylan says, sniffing the air dramatically.

"To Grayson," I grin at him, "for being the cutest one in the kitchen!"

Grayson laughs. "Cheers!" he yells, lifting his chocolate milk.

Camden exhales and grins. "Let's open this place up."

The restaurant is humming. Plates of roasted halibut and duck confit glide out of the kitchen. Every corner feels alive.

I've smiled until my face hurts. So many people from town have shown up to celebrate. Miss Idella and Emmy are still here, looking a little tipsy from their mulled wine. Bosco even showed up and is telling everyone at the bar about Francine. Friends from the Twin Cities even made the drive. Milo's parents are here, and his maternal grandma, and his paternal grandparents.

I'm kissed on both cheeks by both his grandmas.

"You are prettier than I could've imagined," Nana says.

"Absolutely stunning," his other grandma says.

"I'm thrilled to finally meet you both. Now I see where Milo and his parents got their beauty."

They both flush and hug me again.

I'm standing at the host stand with Milo when the door swings open, a wave of cool evening air rushing in, and a group comes in that turns every head.

I blink once. Twice.

"No way," I gasp.

Camden's just stepped out of the kitchen and he freezes. Then his mouth splits into a grin almost as big as mine.

"Addy? Penn?" I'm already moving toward them, arms open.

Addy barrels into me first and Penn goes for Camden.

"You didn't think we'd miss this, did you?" She holds out her hand to Milo. "Hello, Mr. Lombardi. I'm so happy to finally meet you in person."

"I'm happy to meet you too," he says, his smile warm.

Addy moves to hug Camden. "Look at you. Creating another gem."

Penn comes over to hug me and then introduces himself to Milo.

"Yep, he's a stud," Penn tells me.

Milo and I laugh.

"Yes, he is," I agree.

Rhodes and Elle walk in hand-in-hand, Weston and Sadie not far behind, followed by Henley and Tru, and then— Bowie and Poppy. My jaw actually drops.

"They all came," I whisper to Milo. "From Silver Hills."

Milo leans close, murmuring, "I didn't know Camden rolled with the entire Colorado Mustangs *team*."

"This group of players worshipped his kitchen in Denver." I grin.

Camden's laughing now, trying to keep it together as each one pulls him into a hug. I'm beside myself, seeing my brother so happy.

"Did you know they were coming?" Camden asks me, wide-eyed.

I shake my head, still stunned. "I didn't know anyone but Addy knew where Windy Harbor was!"

And then I hear Erin. "Oh my God! You people are gorgeous!"

She walks in like she owns the place—a cropped silver jacket with wide-legged black pants that shimmer when she walks. She has pinup hair and a red lip to die for.

"My girl, look at this place. It's *magic*," she says, hugging me.

Juju walks in behind her. She's changed since she was here before, and her blonde hair is down and glorious. It's usually pulled back when she's at the cafe, and she has the best hair. She's in a blue dress that skims over her body perfectly and she looks stunning.

"I'm here for you, not your brother," she whispers, hugging me.

"Thank you for coming. I'm sorry he was such a jerk," I tell her.

"Not your responsibility to apologize for him." She smiles at me and then shoots daggers at my brother.

Whew. Something's gotta give with those two.

The rest of the night goes without a hitch. The food, the flicker of candles, the laughter—it's all a dream. And it just feels like the beginning.

I press a hand to my heart, just for a second.

"What are you thinking?" Milo says, moving next to me.

I shift so I'm in front of him and put my arms around his neck.

"I don't think I've ever been this happy."

"Me either. And it's because of you," he says.

The last guests have gone. The lights are low. We won't do this all the time, but tonight Milo and my brothers and I pitched in and helped get the restaurant back in order.

It's been a long, perfect day.

And then Milo takes me to his place. I take my heels off and let them dangle from my hand. Milo's hands slide around my waist from behind. He pulls me flush against him and kisses my ear.

"You were unbelievable tonight," he says, his lips brushing against my neck. "Every time I looked at you, I couldn't believe that you're mine."

I turn in his arms. His sleeves are rolled up, his tie gone, and his collar open just enough for me to want more. His hair's messy, just the way I like it. And his eyes—warm and hungry.

My fingers trail just under his collar. "I felt you watching me."

He leans down. His kiss is slow. Mesmerizing.

"You are mine, right?" he whispers, his lips grazing mine. "Tell me."

I breathe against his mouth. "I'm yours. I've always been."

He groans, soft and low, before kissing me again, deeper this time.

"I'm yours too, Goldie," he says.

His hands tighten at my waist and mine slide beneath his

shirt. His kisses trail down my neck and he undoes the single side button at my waist. My dress parts enough to show the inside button on the other side of my waist. When he gets that undone, he slides my dress off my shoulders and drinks me in.

I give him a second to admire my black lacy number, another Scarlett Landmark original, before I stalk toward him. He catches me and lifts my legs around his waist.

"I want you," I whisper, my fingers tangling through his hair.

"I've wanted you all night."

I lean forward until our foreheads touch, noses brushing. "Then stop waiting."

He carries me to his bed, and for the rest of the night, it's just us.

Love unrestrained.

EPILOGUE
TWAS THE NIGHT BEFORE

GOLDIE

It's the night before Thanksgiving and we're at The Kitty-Corner Cafe after hours. The kitchen smells like cinnamon and sage and it's messier than Juju allows it during the cafe's business hours. I'm proud of her for not washing up behind us every two seconds.

Juju's got three timers going and keeps swatting Erin away from the pumpkin and apple pies. Erin is wearing a purple apron with glittery lettering that says *Stuff Me*, and she's singing Nicki Minaj songs into a whisk like it's a microphone.

Ava's standing near the counter with broccoli, rice, and the cans of cream of mushroom soup. Her sleeves are rolled up, and she's watching us like she's not certain how she ended up here.

I catch her eye and smile. "You good?"

She nods, grinning. "Yeah. There's a lot of…energy in here."

I laugh, tossing a peeled apple slice into my mouth. "You're not wrong."

Erin points at Ava. "I'm so excited you're making broccoli rice hotdish."

Ava's brow furrows. "I thought this would just be a casserole."

Erin waves her off. "Technically, yeah, but around here, you can just go with hotdish."

"Got it."

"You didn't have hotdish in Seattle?" Juju asks, eyes twinkling.

"No. Never heard of it until I came here," she says.

Erin puts her arm around Ava's shoulder. "You'll catch the lingo in no time."

Ava laughs and her shoulders relax a little.

We talk about recipes and favorite kitchen disasters.

"I once lit a ham on fire," I say.

"How?" Ava asks.

"Your house smelled for a while after that." Juju nods.

"There was rum involved," I say, wincing.

"Dylan tried to put it out with pop, which wasn't a great idea."

"Boys are useless in a crisis," Erin says.

Juju lifts her glass of wine. "To women and ventilated kitchens."

We clink glasses and burst into another round of laughter.

Erin and Juju launch into gossip about the love letters Miss Idella has been getting.

"Who are they from?" I ask.

"She doesn't know," Juju says. "She gets them and brings

them here, I think hoping someone will confess, but no one has."

"Miss Idella wants to get some," Erin sings into the whisk.

That cracks us up.

"Sorry," Ava says, laughing hard, "but I'm imagining that little old lady who owns The Rusty Trunk!"

"That's her!" I say.

"Oh, that makes it so much better," she says, wiping her eyes.

My chest warms at how comfortable it feels with her here. My sister, my best friends, all of us crowded in this messy, warm kitchen with flour on our clothes, and slugging back the wine. It's perfect.

The next morning, the house is still. The holiday chaos will be at the restaurant later. We've opened it for anyone who doesn't want to be alone or for those who just don't want to cook. But for now, it's just me and my grandmas. And Kevin. He snuck out of Dad's room to get some ear scratches when he heard the commotion in the kitchen. When I got back from the cafe last night, the boys were playing a game of cards that went late and they're still sleeping.

The coffee's hot, the cinnamon rolls are in the oven, and I'm curled up at the table in thick socks and one of Milo's flannels.

Grandma Donna's at the kitchen table next to me with her crossword. Grandma Nancy comes and sits on the other side of me, stirring creamer into her coffee.

"Happy Thanksgiving," I say.

"Happy Thanksgiving," they repeat back.

We sit quietly for a while and then Grandma Donna lowers her pencil and looks at me. "Goldie, can I ask you something?"

"Of course."

She leans in slightly. "That new bench Milo bought for you…out by the pavilion? Would it be all right if I used that bench?"

"Sure! You don't have to ask, Grandma."

"Well," she hesitates. "I saw something on the news and I can't stop thinking about it. I'd kind of like to have one here. A friendship bench. People come sit on it if they need to talk."

I blink. "A friendship bench?"

She nods. "I think I'd like to be the one who listens."

My heart catches.

"I'd be a little too inclined to offer my opinions," Grandma Nancy cuts in. "But you'd be perfect for it, Donna."

Donna chuckles. "Well, I do have plenty of opinions too. But sometimes people just need someone to hear their story. To be heard."

I put my hand over hers. "I love this idea, Grandma. And I think you're just the person to do it. That bench is yours. We'll have to spread the word around town."

Her eyes get a little glassy, and she gives my hand a squeeze. "Thank you, sweetheart. It's been on my heart lately. I'd like to give something back. I'm old, but I can sit and listen."

"You're invaluable and cherished is what you are," I tell her. "I think this is such a beautiful idea."

Outside the wind stirs, and the water crashes against the rocks. I picture my grandma sitting on that bench, a blanket across her knees, and a gentle smile for anyone who might need one. Her quiet generosity could be exactly what someone needs.

The day already feels special.

The outside of the resort is complete, and every time I see it, I'm blown away. Inside, there's still a lot to do, but so much progress has been made. It's hard to believe it'll all be finished in a few months. The pavilion has twinkle lights strung around it and the lights shimmer in the late afternoon light. It's cold enough for coats, but since we're only outside for a few minutes before walking into the restaurant, none of us are wearing them.

It's been a weird winter. We've barely gotten any snow. A foot the day before Halloween, which sucked royally for Grayson trick-or-treating, but it did not deter him in the slightest. It had thawed by the weekend and hasn't snowed since.

I wanted to decorate the restaurant for Christmas. Garland, wreaths, a massive tree, maybe even two…but Camden is a holiday purist.

"Not until the day after Thanksgiving," he insisted.

I don't know why he had to crush my Christmas dreams, but anyway.

He's lucky I adore him.

And I will have my way tomorrow. Free rein.

It's a motley crew of my family and friends, and a few new people in town that I don't know well but will after sharing Thanksgiving together. There's barely room to set down a napkin with all the food spread on the table. Everyone's talking over each other, reaching for the sweet potatoes, the clatter of forks, and laughter, a lot of laughter.

Kevin is sitting at attention near Grayson's feet, and I suspect he's getting a variety of everything Grayson doesn't want to eat.

"I've eaten three rolls and I'm still getting dessert!" Grayson announces.

Under the table, Milo's hand rests on my knee. His eyes find mine through all the noise and settle there.

"Happy Thanksgiving, Golo," he says, leaning in to kiss me.

"To you too, Mildie."

"I'm excited for what's ahead." He leans his forehead against mine. "A life with you. Our wedding—let's decide on a date, please."

I nod rapidly in agreement.

"A new house we're going to build together, and our fun, loving—"

Someone guffaws so loudly, we both jump.

"*Loud*," he continues, and we both laugh, "families."

"All the best things I can imagine," I tell him.

"You're the best thing," he says.

I kiss him, slow and sweet, and soak up this moment.

"Had I known when we met that we'd end up here, I would've kissed you so much sooner," I say.

He laughs. "Like when we first laid eyes on each other and you thought me and my work were a travesty?"

I grin. "Absolutely. Oh, wait. We kind of did kiss right away, didn't we?"

He laughs. "I'm just glad you kissed me again. Because the second I met you, you took my heart and turned it into mush."

"Infuriating mush, but that's beside the point."

"Bring that sassy mouth over here and let me kiss you."

I'm smiling as our lips touch, my heart more content than I thought possible.

Want more Milo and Goldie?
Get the bonus scene here!
https://dl.bookfunnel.com/c16n4iwuxl

Keep reading to get a sneak peek of what's coming next in *What it Takes*, book 2 of the *Windy Harbor* series! Camden Whitman and Juju Fair haven't always hated each other! But they do now, and it's *incredibly* inconvenient because he's her brother's best friend...

Pre Order What It Takes Here!
https://geni.us/WhatItTakes

COMING SOON
WHAT IT TAKES

Chapter 1
Grand Opening
CAMDEN

Present

It's a great day to be alive.

I'm completely stressed, running on fumes, and don't see sleep in my future for a long time, but it's the opening day of my new restaurant.

You only get that once.

My brain won't shut off. I went to bed at 2:30 and woke up at 4:30, my thoughts a whirlwind. I've gone over every possible worst-case scenario in my mind and am hopefully equipped for whatever goes wrong.

Because something will definitely go wrong.

I moved back home to Minnesota recently. I wasn't sure I'd ever live here again, not because I don't love it, but because I'd found my place in Colorado. I opened a restaurant there, and it's still thriving, but when I found out my dad had cancer and wanted my siblings and me to help him do a rehaul on the rundown resort next to our lake home, I got serious about making the move to be with my family. He's thinking about the legacy he wants to leave behind, and I'm thinking about being near him. I don't want to miss a single day with him.

Which is why, as soon as he texts his standard good morning to the family, I jump on it and pull up a separate thread with just the two of us.

> Are you up for coffee this morning? Get our day started out right before the craziness begins?

DAD

I'm always up for coffee with you, son.

> I'm at the restaurant already, but I can come back to the house. Or do you feel like getting out? I can have coffee ready at the restaurant in five minutes.

DAD

Choices, choices. Actually, I have a craving for one of Juju's scones. You up for going to the Kitty-Korner Cafe?

I groan internally. Juliana Fair, best friend to my sister Goldie, and the sister of *my* best friend Jackson, knows how to get under my skin. She owns the bakery in town and it's excellent. The girl has been a phenomenal baker since the day I met her as a kid and ate her homemade chocolate chip cookies.

As a chef, I'm particular about all things food, but Juju

has only gotten more skilled as the years have gone by. No one can bake like her.

We may butt heads, but I know an amazing scone when I taste one.

And I can't say no to my dad.

> I'll swing by to pick you up in twenty. Sound good?

DAD

Sounds perfect.

***

The Kitty-Corner Café is bustling when Dad and I walk in. The place is great, a charming overload. Juliana Fair stands behind the counter, looking all kinds of beautiful. Yes, as much as she can annoy me, I still think she's the most beautiful woman I've ever seen, which probably only serves to annoy me further. Long, blonde hair, vivid green eyes, and pink lips, all a deceptive disguise of the venom this girl can spew.

At least when it comes to me.

There have been times over the course of our twenty-one-year history—we met when I was seven and she was five—that we've had a peace treaty between the two of us. The first day was such an example. I saved the day by salvaging the cookies that had fallen, and she looked at me like I was her knight in shining armor.

It went downhill from there.

Today, she shoots me a withering glare and says, "I thought I wouldn't have to see you for a few more hours."

To which I say, "Today is your lucky day."

She rolls her eyes and continues helping Sandy, one of the locals, who looks back at my dad with interest.

"Everett, how are you?" she says. "How is that hotdish I sent over this week?"

My dad swallows hard and makes a point of not looking at me because he knows if he does, it's over. We won't be able to keep a straight face.

"Thanks again for that hotdish, Sandy. So thoughtful of you."

That hotdish is fucking awful. It's hard to make Tater Tot hotdish taste bad, but Sandy succeeds every time.

She beams at Dad and I quietly chuckle next to him. My dad, ever the diplomat. When it's our turn at the counter, Juju gives Dad her warmest smile. That's the thing about her. I know she's capable of being kind, friendly, and even sweet, but with me, ninety percent of the time, she pulls out the rotten.

We won't think about the other ten percent.

I think she enjoys keeping me on a never-ending roller coaster.

"You're looking great this morning, Everett," she says. "What can I get for you?"

"And you're looking lovely this morning, Miss Juliana," he says. "I woke up thinking about your scones. And I'll have your light roast as well."

"Coming right up," she says.

"Uh, I didn't order yet," I say when she walks off to get my dad's order ready.

"Haven't you asked enough of me today?" she snaps.

I shake my head. "Really, Juju? Are we really gonna do this?"

She slams the plate down and the scone almost falls off as she moves to pour my dad a cup of coffee.

"I don't know, Camden. I'm surprised you want any of

my baked goods for your perfect restaurant when it wasn't that long ago that you said Caribou's coffee is better."

I groan. "This again? Your specialty is baked goods. You don't have to have coffee down too."

She slides the coffee toward my dad and crosses her arms as she stares at me.

"My coffee is freaking delicious," she says, "and you know it."

"Well, I would prefer to deal with your bear claws, since that's all you seem to show me anyway."

She sputters and I think maybe she growls too. I grin. I'd forgotten how fun she is to turn sideways.

She puts a bear claw on a plate and slams it in front of me.

"And a cup of your light roast too, please."

If fumes could come out of her head, I think they would be right now.

"Unbelievable," she snaps.

My dad is chuckling when we sit at the corner table.

"Why do you have to pick on that girl?" he says. "She's like family to us and she has idolized you since the day you met."

I frown. "*Juju.* You're talking about Juliana? You're mistaken. We are like fire and ice. She hates me."

"Ah, son, for someone so smart, you sure can be dumb sometimes. Besides that, this little attitude you have when she's around, it's like you're a different person. As Goldie says, you're the nice one in the family."

I chuckle. "I don't know where Goldie gets that."

"She gets that because until she met Milo, she was also the sweet one, but he seemed to bring out the worst in her, the way Juju brings out the worst in you. I wonder what that's about. And look at where Goldie and Milo ended up." His grin widens.

"Don't start," I groan. "I haven't been in Windy Harbor a month and you're already matchmaking. You and Mom always had so much to say about me and Juju."

We both smile wistfully, thinking about my mom. I miss her every damn day.

I clear my throat. "Juju and I are not gonna happen. Did you see the way she flung that bear claw at me? She wished it was my balls on that plate."

I hear a gasp next to us and Beverly and Carol are staring at us with wide eyes.

"Pardon my language," I say apologetically.

Beverly titters, and my dad is trying not to laugh when I look at him again.

"See what I mean?" he says under his breath. "Tully and Dylan…and even Noah, wouldn't have apologized."

I laugh. "Just because they're assholes doesn't make me the nice one."

He just looks at me like *come on now* and I grin as I enjoy my bear claw.

It's a fucking spectacular bear claw.

Before we leave, I tap on the counter and Juju jumps. Her expression quickly turns from pleasant to volcanic.

"Please be on time with the desserts, Juliana. Today's a big day for me."

"I run my own business, Camden. I know how to be a professional."

I tilt my head and smile. "Great. Shouldn't be a problem then."

***

A few hours later, everything is in place. The tables are

set. The sauces are ready. Everything is primed, and the staff are all in place. There's a level of high anticipation in the air.

But I'm waiting on one thing.

Or rather, one person.

Juliana fucking Fair.

"She was supposed to be here half an hour ago," I mutter, stalking past the kitchen doors. "I should've known she'd try to sabotage this."

Bobby, my new sous chef, looks at me in surprise. "Sabotage? Like she'd want to bring you down?"

"No," I admit. "She wouldn't go that far. She just really likes to irritate me."

And I seem to fall for it every time. I revert to my teenage years, when Juju and I started this bickering that is our new normal.

That's easier to deal with than the soft Juju that feels like my friend, because almost always, she turns on me.

A couple of weeks ago, when I asked her if she could make desserts for the restaurant until I could hire a new pastry chef, her eyes softened.

"I'd be honored," she said. "You know that I'm really proud of you, Camden...right? I think what you've done with the restaurant in Colorado is epic, and I know this new restaurant will knock it out of the park too."

"Thanks, Juju," I said, surprised.

Her mouth parted slightly and I stepped toward her. I heard her breath hitch and could see the rise and fall of her chest..

"What is it?" I whispered.

"It's been a long time since you called me Juju," she whispered back.

"I always call you Juju in my head," I confessed.

We stared at each other for a long, weighty pause, and I could've sworn she wanted me to kiss her.

And then her brother walked in and we both took a step away from each other.

"My two favorite people. I'm shocked you're alone and not throwing dough at each other." Jackson laughed.

"Give it time and we'll be back at it," I teased, grinning at Juju.

Her jaw tightened and the warmth left her eyes.

I fucking hated to see it go.

But this was us, a seesaw that never balanced.

The door flings open and Juju rushes in.

Her hair is up, her cheeks flushed either from the cold or because she knows I'll be ticked. She's pushing a cart loaded down with desserts.

"You're late."

"I'm here," she sings. "And I brought the pies and cheesecakes you wanted…plus mousse cakes and bread pudding that I thought would fit nicely with your menu."

"I didn't ask for the mousse cakes or bread pudding. I asked you to be on time."

She stares at me indignantly. "I was doing something nice for you."

I exhale slowly. "I didn't ask you to be nice or to bring extra food that I may or may not be able to sell."

Her cheeks burn brighter. "You'll be glad you have them, you arrogant control freak."

"It's not about control, it's about not having waste, and doing what you say you'll do," I say between gritted teeth.

"Trust me, if you let the good people of Windy Harbor know that my mousse cake or bread pudding is a surprise dessert for this evening, they will sell faster than you can plate them."

"That's not how restaurants work, Juliana. I've already printed the menu."

"So tell them it's a special that isn't on the menu," she snaps. "Should I have brought store-bought cheesecakes instead?"

I take a step toward her. She does the same thing.

"Why are you always pushing?" I ask. "It's like you find a nerve and just poke, poke, poke."

"I can't help it that you're an uptight, bossy, overly sensitive, emotionally constipated man who—"

"I'm the uptight, bossy, overly sensitive, emotionally constipated one?" I yell back. "You don't want to go there with me, Juliana. If I remember correctly, you were the one who—"

"What is going on back here?" Goldie comes in, her eyes wide.

"I should've known better than to bring desserts for you!" Juju shouts as she walks toward the door. "You can find someone else to do your bidding, Camden Whitman!"

She says something to Goldie under her breath and I laugh.

"Call a spade a spade, *Juliana*, and a jackass a *jackass*."

"Okay, *jackass*," she mutters and leaves the kitchen.

Goldie rips me a new one when Juju leaves, but my sister never stays mad at me too long. One of the many things I love about her. And with this being opening night, she probably has more mercy on me than I deserve.

***

The night is a success.

Even more than I'd hoped it would be.

I had my family surrounding me, my best friend Jackson, and even my favorite players from the Colorado Mustangs team—Weston, Henley, Rhodes, Bowie, and Penn—along with their wives. I couldn't believe they all made the trip to Minnesota. My sister was thrilled to have her college roommate, Addy, who's married to Penn, by her side. And of course, Juju was there, looking like a bombshell in a blue dress.

Speaking of the bombshell, she's lingering after everyone leaves for the night. It's so late that I didn't expect anyone to be here still, but she's in the kitchen, gathering her pans when I walk in.

It's on the tip of my tongue to apologize for being a bastard earlier, when she says, "Are the rest of the desserts tucked away somewhere, or did you get rid of them all like I said you would?"

I growl, which delights her.

"You wouldn't be asking that question if you didn't already know the answer," I say.

"Oh, I know the answer. I knew the answer when I left them here. Too bad I won't be making any desserts for you again."

She carries her pans to the door and I call after her.

"Juju, wait. Let's not—"

She whirls around. "Let's not what? Be civil to one another? Have the common courtesy to say thank you?" Her voice cracks and I feel like the biggest jerk. "You've got it. Let's not…ever again."

She leaves and I slump against the island, every earlier feeling of victory squashed with her words.

Pre Order What It Takes Here!
https://geni.us/WhatItTakes

ACKNOWLEDGMENTS

All my thanks to...

Nate Sabin, my husband, the one who sees the good, the bad, the feral, and loves me anyway. I love you. Thank you for all you do to make everything work behind the scenes.

Greyley and Kira Sabin, first of all, I love you. Second of all, these covers are dreamy. Greyley, the special edition cover will make me smile every time I look at it. You have talent oozing out of your pores. Kira, the map is stellar, and so is the couple cover. I'm so honored and excited every time either one of you puts your touch on my projects. Thank you.

Indigo Sabin, my sonshine. You always have something positive to say, and it means a lot to me. From the first book to the last, you've been rooting for me, and I'm grateful. I love you.

Kess Fennell, I love everything about your artwork and you. :)

Christine Estevez, it's been so many years now that we've been doing this and I love you more than ever!

Natalie Burtner, thank you for making the formatting on allll the books spectacular, not to mention the eleventy billion other things you do for me. You have my heart.

Katie Friend, you're the special sauce to every project. Thank you for your time and the hilarity.

Georgie, dear Georgie Grinstead, I'm so glad I have an agent that I love so dearly. Thank you for everything!

To the VPR team, I couldn't do this without you! Thank

you, Nina, Kim, Charlie, Valentine, Kelley, Christine, Sarah, Jill, Jaime, Ratula, Josette, Meagan, Tiffany, Stephanie, Megan, Emma, Jessica, and Keriann!!!

To the Lyric team, Kim Gilmour and Katie Robinson, thank you for making this process easy and fun!

Andi Arndt and Christian Fox, I am so honored to have you on this project. You've been favorites of mine for a long time. Thank you so much!

Laura Pavlov, my soul sister, I love you so much. Catherine Cowles, there are no words big enough! I love you dearly. Love Chain forever!

Claribel Contreras, there will never be enough time to cover it all. I love you.

Tarryn Fisher, my bestie forever. Love you so.

My family and friends who are like family—thank you for the love. I'm so grateful for each of you!! Tosha Khoury & Courtney Nuness, you can't possibly know how much I love you both! Christine Bowden, the miles are vast, but we're always in sync. Love you. Kell Donaldson, I wish you didn't live across the world. Savita Naik, your love and prayers and support mean everything. Destini, I'm so glad you're in my life. Terrijo Montgomery, you are the best. I love you! Jesse Nava, till we're old and not gray, forever! ;) Troi & Phyllis Atkinson, thanks for cheering me on. I love you! Stefen Atkinson, cheesecakes, reels, and deep chats are so fun with you. Love you. Jared Atkinson, I love talking books and ideas with you. Love you! Winston, my writing partner through thick and thin, I love you.

Thank you for everything, Anthony Colletti!

Last, but not least, thanks to any of you who made it this far. I'm so grateful for you! Thank you for the beautiful graphics, the reviews, the sweet messages...it means so much to know you care about my books.

ALSO BY WILLOW ASTER

The Windy Harbor Series

Take This Heart

What It Takes

All for Love

Endless Summer Nights

Now and Forever

The Single Dad Playbook Series

Mad Love

Secret Love

Reckless Love

Wicked Love

Crazy Love

Landmark Mountain Series

Unforgettable

Someday

Irresistible

Falling

Stay

Standalones with Interconnected Characters

Summertime

Autumn Nights

Kingdoms of Sin Series

Downfall

Exposed

Ruin

Pride

Standalones

True Love Story

Fade to Red

In the Fields

Maybe Maby (also available on all retailer sites)

Lilith (also available on all retailer sites)

Miles Apart (also available on all retailer sites)

Falling in Eden

The G.D. Taylors Series with Laura Pavlov

Wanted Wed or Alive

The Bold and the Bullheaded

Another Motherfaker

Don't Cry Over Spilled MILF

Friends with Benefactors

The End of Men Series with Tarryn Fisher

Folsom

Jackal

FOLLOW ME

JOIN MY MASTER LIST…
https://bit.ly/3CMKz5y

Website willowaster.com
Facebook @willowasterauthor
Instagram @willowaster
Amazon @willowaster
Bookbub @willow-aster
Tiktok @willowaster1
Goodreads @Willow_Aster
Asters group @Astersgroup
Pinterest @WillowAster